The Sleeper

EMILY BARR

headline
review

The right of Emily Barr to be identified as the Author of
the Work has been asserted by her in accordance with the
Copyright, Designs and Patents Act 1988.

First published in 2013 by HEADLINE REVIEW
An imprint of HEADLINE PUBLISHING GROUP

1

Cataloguing in Publication Data is available from the British Library

ISBN 978 0 7553 8800 4

Typeset in Garamond ITC by Palimpsest Book Production Limited,
Falkirk, Stirlingshire

Printed and bound by CPI Group (UK) Ltd, Croydon, CR0 4YY

Headline's policy is to use papers that are natural, renewable and recyclable
products and made from wood grown in sustainable forests. The logging and
manufacturing processes are expected to conform to the environmental
regulations of the country of origin.

HEADLINE PUBLISHING GROUP
An Hachette UK Company
338 Euston Road
London NW1 3BH

www.headline.co.uk
www.hachette.co.uk

Emily Barr is the well-loved and bestselling author of *Backpack*, the original backpacking novel, and many other highly acclaimed novels. A former journalist, she has travelled around the world and written columns and travel pieces for the *Observer* and the *Guardian*. After living in France, Emily and her husband (whom she met backpacking) settled in Cornwall with their three children. To learn more about Emily and her novels, you can visit her website www.emilybarr.com.

Praise for Emily Barr's novels:

'A characteristically dark-hued tale, with unexpected twists'
Guardian

'Beautifully written with engaging, emotionally complex characters and a great plot. I couldn't put it down'   *Daily Mail*

'A real page-turner with a plot twist worthy of *Lost*' *Cosmopolitan*

'Toothsome twists . . . a Daphne du Maurier vibe haunts the hinterlands of this unconventional page-turner'   *Independent*

'Brilliantly written, tense and refreshing, you'll devour this fantastic read'
Closer

'This gripping novel will have you gasping in sympathy'
Company

'A great read from start to finish . . . believable characters that are variously biting, insightful and sympathetic'   *The Times*

'Barr has come up with the goods again: a buzzy, exciting work that refuses to bow to convention'   *Sunday Express*

'We can't praise Emily Barr's novels enough; they're fresh, original and hugely readable'
Glamour

'Compelling'
Heat

'Bright and breezy with a nasty little twist'
Mirror

By Emily Barr

Backpack
Baggage
Cuban Heels
Atlantic Shift
Plan B
Out of my Depth
The Sisterhood
The Life You Want
The Perfect Lie
The First Wife
Stranded
The Sleeper

For James, Gabe, Seb and Lottie, as always,
with lots of love.

acknowledgements

Huge thanks to an anonymous policeman (you know who you are) for invaluable help with police details, and to Amanda James for detailed advice on Lara's property development role. Both of you put in a huge amount of time helping me, and any mistakes are mine.

Vanessa Farnell, thank you for once again coming on the research trip with me, and selflessly helping me research Koh Lanta and Krabi. Thank you to Steve and Ali Brooks in Singapore for spectacular hospitality.

Thanks are due to the people who keep me sane on a daily basis: Kerys Deavin, Jayne Kirkham, Bess Revell and many others, and to my children for reminding me constantly that there is life outside the book.

My local bookshop, the Falmouth Bookseller, is a constant support: thanks to Ron Johns and all his colleagues.

I have had enormous support while writing *The Sleeper* from Sherise Hobbs and all the team at Headline, and from my wonderful agent, Jonny Geller, and everyone else at Curtis Brown. Thank you.

prologue

January

She should have been back two hours ago.

A person could not disappear from a train in the middle of the night, but apparently she had. She got on at Paddington (as far as we knew), but she did not get off at Truro.

'I'm sure she's fine,' I told him. My words hung in the air, improbable and trite. I cast around for an explanation. Once you discounted amnesia and sleepwalking, there were really only two, and neither of them would give her husband any comfort.

'I hope so.' His face was crumpled and his eyes seemed to have shrunk back under slightly hooded lids. Everything was sagging as, gradually, he stopped being able to pretend that she might be about to walk in through the door. His face was, somehow, at once both red and grey, patchy and uneven.

I had no idea what to do, and so, once again, I started to make coffee. He was looking at his phone, checking again for messages that might, somehow, have arrived by stealth, even though he had turned the volume right up and called it from the landline, just to see.

'Next train in seven minutes,' he reported. I set the coffee pot on the stove, lit the gas under it and left it. I opened a few cupboard doors, looking for something easy, something that he might eat without noticing it.

It was strange being in someone else's kitchen, flung into what I feared was the very early stage of the total breakdown of the life of a man I didn't even know. He was halfway off the cliff already, clinging on with his fingers to a flimsy clump of grass.

I put some custard creams on a plate.

The view from here was spectacular, but the only part of it either of us could focus on was the little station in the foreground. As a squeal of brakes announced the imminent arrival of the train, he was on his feet, hands pressed against the glass of the full-length window, staring. He would have forgiven her anything if she appeared now, walking around the end of the train, pulling a little case (I was sure she must have had a little pull-along case; people like her did). He would not have cared where she had been, what she had been doing, and with whom.

It had been cold and crisp this morning, but now the sky was filling with fast-moving clouds. They massed above us, waiting for their moment; the light suddenly changed and, though it was still morning, it was instantly as dark as dusk.

We both waited, suspended, for the seconds it took the two-carriage train to reach the end of the branch line and disgorge its few passengers. Most people had got off the train at Falmouth Town, the stop before this one.

In spite of myself, my heart thumped as four passengers emerged around the end of the platform. A grey-haired couple, all walking clothes, backpacks and hearty sticks, set off determinedly across the car park. They were heading, I was sure, for the coastal path. A young man with a skateboard under his arm sauntered after them, wrapped in heavy jacket, scarf and woolly hat. Finally, there was a woman.

She was about the right age, but she was small and hesitant. As we watched, she looked around and stood at the edge of the car park, waiting for something. She had a bag on her back. We both stared until a car pulled up in front of her, and suddenly she smiled and relaxed and opened the back door to lob her bag inside before sitting in the front.

It was not her. Of course it wasn't. I no longer expected it to be.

Rain started to splatter, half-sleety, against the window.

'We need to call the police,' I told him. He pretended not to have heard.

part one

Lara

chapter one

August

He stands next to me on the balcony and hands me the green mug his horrible mother gave me for Christmas. A train pulls into the station below us. It has two carriages, and thus is the biggest train that will fit alongside that platform.

'One cup of tea,' he says, with mock ceremony, and I try not to flinch. 'I hope it meets with madam's approval.'

It does not, but I cannot, of course, say so. I cradle it in both hands and try to arrange my features into the right expression. He knows which mugs I like, and he knows that this is emphatically not one of them. I cannot tell him that I care about such trivialities. He would pantomime wide-eyed, reasonable surprise.

'Thanks,' I say.

Our forearms touch as we lean on the rail, and we look out across the town. The sun is shining on the train in the station, the docks behind it, the town curved beyond them, hugging the harbour. Light glints off the water out there, and tiny dazzling spots of brightness come and go with the movement of the waves. On the other side of the estuary, the trees and fields and mansions of Flushing are glowing in the heat, unusual even for August. Seagulls stand in formation on the roof of one of the warehouses down at the docks. They are doing the bird equivalent of sunbathing. The almost uncomfortable heat on my skin, the salt in the air which I normally don't notice, the glimmer of the sun on the water all make me think, suddenly, of long-forgotten childhood holidays.

'It looks like a picture from a children's book, doesn't it?' I say. 'Station. Container ships. Warships. Sailing boats. Cars. Lorries. There should be words written underneath it.' I place them with my hand, under the station car park. '"How many different forms of transport can you see . . .?"'

He is staring at me, not at the things I am pointing at, so I turn my head to look at him.

'Yes,' he says. 'And those grabby things.' He gestures to the equipment at the docks. 'And the huge metal things that lift stuff. It's picture-book heaven.'

I reach out and touch his arm. The hairs on it are springy and blond. Even this exchange has taken us too close to the topic that I am trying to avoid, just because there is nothing more to be said about it. I change the subject, sipping my tea (which, as it so often is, is about half the strength I would make it myself), and gesture at the houses over to our left.

'And over there. How many different lives can we see? Thousands of homes. All those windows. All the things that go on behind them. I bet there's weirder stuff happening out there than you could possibly imagine.'

He squints at the houses. 'Than I could, or anyone?'

'Anyone,' I clarify, possibly too quickly.

Sam shifts his cup of tea into his other hand and puts

an arm around my shoulders. I lean into him. He is big like a bear, broad but not fat. I have always liked that about him. While I recoil from the idea of being the sort of woman who wants a big strong man to look after her, I do, nonetheless, enjoy his solidity.

'You remember that my friend's coming over this afternoon?' I say. 'The one I met on the ferry.'

'Oh yeah. You did say. What's her name again?'

'Iris.'

'Yes. Iris.'

He disapproves. He doesn't like anyone else being part of our life. We do not really have friends. I have invited Iris over precisely because I want to change that.

'But this feels like the first time in ages we've just hung out,' he says. He sounds nervous. 'You know. It's nice not to have the big conversations all the time. We made our plans and fate laughed in our face.' I brace myself for the bit about everything happening for a reason. 'Everything happens for a reason,' he continues. 'And I think all this has happened to bring us closer together, and because there's a child out there somewhere, in China maybe. Or the Himalayas, like you always say. A child who needs us. That's what's meant to be, I'm sure of it.'

'You just changed this into a big conversation.'

'Oh. Sorry.'

I breathe deeply. 'That's OK,' I say. He has made that little speech hundreds of times before, and maybe he is right. Perhaps infertility and everything else happened for some fuzzy, indefinable reason. Perhaps there is a child on a mountainside in Nepal who is destined to be ours. We don't have the option of getting on a plane to go and find out. Even Visa, lenders of money to all and sundry, are declining to fund our further adventures.

Sam is right: I always talk about the Himalayas. I always longed to go there, to rent a house on a mountainside and live for months and months in the crisp fresh air, to walk and look and exist. I would do it tomorrow; but even when we had more money than we knew what to do with, I never went because my husband never fancied it. He always diverted me to what he called 'a proper holiday'.

Perhaps my baby is, indeed, waiting for me out there, but I cannot get to her, or him. The thought is unsettling.

'I love you,' he says. 'We may be all out of money, and all out of options with no child to show for it, but I love you.'

'I love you too,' I assure him hastily.

'Lara.'

We lean into each other, feeling the sun on our bare arms and the tops of our heads, and stare out at the view and drink our tea. There is not much else to say.

I want to scream, and sometimes I do. On occasion, I scream as loudly as I can, but never when Sam is in the house. When he is anywhere nearby, I keep the angst repressed and internal. I cannot tell him anything close to the truth, and so, I suppose, our marriage is not what he thinks it is. He thinks we are solidly in love, battered but optimistic, ready to start on our new journey, one we did not foresee but whose destination is all the more wonderful for that. He thinks we will always be together, here in Cornwall, hundreds of miles from our two difficult families. He thinks we are a unit.

I would rather be single. I cannot possibly say that. I am secretly glad that we didn't manage to have that baby. He would be heartbroken to hear it. Nothing in particular has happened: neither of us has been unfaithful, and he has never been anything worse to me than incredibly, cringingly annoying. I married the wrong man, with an inkling at the time that that was what I was doing, and so it is my fault and I am stuck.

I wonder what he would say if he knew that I have always had an escape plan, always a bag packed and ready to go at a moment's notice. It is not because of him, but all the same, it is telling.

I convinced myself that the baby, if it arrived, would solve everything by giving me a new focus and something to love. I knew, really, that life does not work that way. It is lucky for the baby that he or she never made it.

Half an hour later I laugh out loud as I realise I look like the world's most submissive housewife: I am taking two halves of a cake out of the oven, using floral-patterned oven gloves and wearing a frilly apron, a cheap appropriation of the Cath Kidston effect. I feel like an interloper in someone else's life. I am a creature from science fiction, wearing an earth body to disguise my true self. Inside is someone Sam barely knows at all. The creature within is ugly and angry, cold and frustrated and mocking. I strive to keep it hidden because Sam does not deserve what would come with its unleashing.

The truth is, I do not love my husband. I do not love him at all. I like him, on a good day. I can see that he is a far better person than I am, and this makes me despise him all the more. It also, somehow, stops me leaving him. I hate the tea he makes: it is warm watery milk, coloured beige by the briefest of flirtations with a tea bag. When I drink it I wince in secret, but I knock it back because after five years of trying to get him to make it the way I like it, I have given up.

When he calls a crane a 'huge metal thing that lifts

stuff' with 'a grabby thing' on the end, I want to run, screaming, all the way back to London. I am married to a man who calls a phone charger 'the pluggy-in thing', and the remote control 'the buttony thing for the telly'. This, once almost an endearing habit, is now an affectation that drives me to the brink of homicide. I have to clench my teeth and force myself not to say anything, again and again and again.

For years I suggested a trekking holiday in Nepal, but even though he knew it was the thing I wanted more than anything else in the world, he repeatedly found reasons why it couldn't be done: a hypochondriacal 'bad knee', an aversion to altitude, not enough time off work to make it worthwhile. He always steered me towards beaches, to the Canaries or France; but we have beaches here, and anyway, beaches are boring. I want mountains.

The two halves of the cake are perfectly cooked. That is because when we moved to Cornwall from London we still had money, so we bought a top-of-the-range Smeg cooker. We had no idea that we were about to pour all our savings into three fruitless cycles of IVF. If we had, I would have made do with an oven that was thousands of pounds cheaper, and it would have been fine, though these particular cakes might have been a little less springy.

It never occurred to either of us that nature might not fall in with our plans. We were, in our own eyes, successful and fabulous super-people who made things happen. We were London professionals moving to a little house above Falmouth Docks, to start a family. Sam wanted us to have a girl, then a boy, and then a third child (no gender preference). They were going to be blond and wholesome, learning to sail in little dinghies and playing rounders on the beach.

I tip the two cakes on to the wire cooling rack, and put the tins in the sink to soak. I am good at this Earth stuff. No one watching me would ever suspect. It is lonely, being an evil alien in disguise.

Iris has a boyfriend she's ambivalent about, too. That was what drew me to her. We recognised it in each other; I am sure we did. That is why I have baked her these cakes.

I sometimes wish I loved him, but if I loved him I would not be myself. I would rather be myself, living a lie, trying to screw up the courage to do the right thing, than the simpering housewife he needs.

When the kitchen is tidy, and Sam, I see from the balcony, is in the garden below, cutting the grass, I rush to check my email. Once again, the only contact from the outside world comes from my trusted friend money-supermarket.com.

I sit down and start typing. My heart pumps so hard that I feel it throughout my whole body.

Leon, I write. *Any news? L x*

Then I send it, and delete it from the sent messages folder. Sam would never go through my email account, but I like to be safe.

The doorbell rings at exactly half past three, and when I open the door and see Iris, I grin, suddenly happy. If I do not talk properly to someone soon, I will probably murder my husband in his sleep.

She is wearing a floaty skirt with bare legs, and a bicycle helmet is swinging from her arm. Her hair is long and thick and tangled. It is dark brown, but blond at the ends.

'Did you cycle in that skirt?' I say, instead of hello.

'You know, I didn't even think about it. If anyone was at all interested in the view, good luck to them. I'm pretty sure, though, that they weren't.'

'Come in.'

I see women out in town, school-mum types, the sort of arty women who can manage to live here and scrape a professional living as a designer or a writer or an illustrator, and I think, often, that I would be immensely happier if I had a group of friends like that. We could sit in the Town House bar, just at the bottom of the hill, and drink cocktails and bottles of Pinot Grigio, and laugh about our annoying husbands. That is what people do.

Iris is my first step in that direction. She is, I think, around my age, or possibly a little older. I like her eccentricity. I know she has that boyfriend, the one she finds exasperating. I have not met him yet, but I would like to.

She is looking at me with a small smile, and I wonder what she sees. Does she see the perfect little blonde housewife, wearing her cotton dress and leggings, putting the kettle on and carrying an impeccable Victoria sponge to the table next to the window in the house with the view? Or does she glimpse the evil murderous alien? I want to ask.

'How are you?' I say, since I can't.

'Oh, fine,' she replies. 'Great, actually. The bike blows the cobwebs away.' She puts her fingers through her hair and tugs at a tangle.

'It's quite hilly, isn't it?'

She nods. 'That's the point. You kill yourself getting up some precipice, then have the joy of freewheeling down as fast as you dare, and you're halfway up the next one before you slow down. It takes nerves of steel in the traffic,

14

but it's worth it. I didn't cycle for years, because I was afraid, and then I thought, you know, sod it. Who cares? I just did it one day and it's been brilliant.'

I look around. Sam is still outside.

'Look, I've made a cake. All those years of university paid off. We could have a cup of tea, or would you prefer a glass of Prosecco?'

I know that she can tell what I want from my expression, and happily she obliges.

'Well, Prosecco would be lovely,' she says, 'if you're sure.'

'Oh, I am.'

'No one seems to mind if you're tipsy in charge of a bike. There's almost certainly a law against it, but the only person you're going to hurt is yourself, I suppose. The police, luckily, have better things to do.'

'Does your boyfriend cycle?'

She nods a little nod. 'Used to. Not so much these days. He's . . . well, he's a bit of a recluse now.'

I want to know more, but instead I open the bottle, which gives a pleasing 'pop', and we sit down. When Sam and I bought this house, our future family home, it had swirly carpets and a gorgeously dated seaside feel. We did the minimum of work, because I liked it the way it was. All the same, the carpets had to go, and varnished floorboards arrived. The Artex went, and plasterwork took its place. The horrible fireplace was wrenched out (slightly against my better judgement: it was so nearly horrible enough to be cool), and the inevitable wood burner now occupies its space. The house is lovely, as prisons go. It is nice to show it to someone.

When we had children we were going to extend, to make more bedrooms and a playroom and a tree house and all sorts of other things. Sam used to fantasise about sticky fingerprints on the windows; but the windows have remained pristine.

'This is glorious.' Iris is looking at the view.

'You never really get used to it, because it's different every day.'

'I bet. If I lived here I'd just stare out of the window all the time.'

'That's pretty much what I do.'

She laughs, but I am serious. I have nothing else to do. I haven't even been able to find an admin job. Every time I apply for anything, they come back with the same word: 'overqualified'. Yet there is nothing for which my qualifications would be any use. Every job in my field, in property development and architecture, is already taken. I have flirted with the idea of Asda, but Sam has stopped me.

'How's the proofreading going?' I am pleased that I remember that. Iris and I met on the ferry to St Mawes one afternoon. We got talking in an idle way, and discovered that both of us were going over there on a whim, just for the boat trip. When we got there we walked around in the harsh wind, and her hair blew all over her face and even mine started to escape from its grips and pins. Then we went and sat in a dark little pub up a side road and drank bottled lager. It was random, and transgressive, and I liked it.

'Oh, fine,' she says. 'I like working from home. Being able to set my own hours, take control of my work life.' Her face creases right up when she laughs, and this makes me think of a baby laughing. 'That sounds like I'm oper-ating sex lines, doesn't it? Or posing on the end of a webcam. I specialise in legal books. Rock and roll. But it's going fine, thanks. I should keep a diary. It would be the world's most boring document. Every day just precisely the same.'

'I used to keep a diary,' I tell her. 'Back when my life was interesting. You can't reread a diary, though, can you? Not without cringing mightily. But your work must be satisfying, in a way?'

'Yeah. Some days. You have to get in the right frame of mind. I have the radio on all the time, BBC 6, so there's music going constantly, but also – and this is a key thing for me – my boyfriend's around too. Laurie. He works from home as well, so there's just enough company. We both like the music. It's a cosy little world. You could say boring, but it suits me.'

I hand her a glass of Prosecco. 'Cheers,' I say.

'Cheers,' she responds.

I sip the drink, and in that instant I know that I could become dependent on alcohol too easily. It would be so logical, to slip into a habit of drinking every afternoon.

'So it's just the two of you?' I say. 'Like us. Sam and me.'

'Yes,' she says. 'You get pulled into your own little world, don't you?'

'Do you find it gets stifling?'

'I think I'm a hermit at heart, and Laurie is more so. Me and him and the cats. It's not for everyone, but it works for us. If I'd been born in a different era, I'd have been great as a nun in a closed order, or a wild woman living in a cave on a mountainside.'

'You live in your cave in Budock.'

'I do.'

'But not on your own.'

'No.'

'How many cats?'

'Just two.' She looks at me. 'Did you think I was going to say eighteen?'

'I wondered.'

'Happily things haven't got to that point. Desdemona and Ophelia. Our tragic heroines. They like a bit of drama. That's enough for me.'

Sam clumps into the room.

'Afternoon, ladies!' His plain white T-shirt is sticking sweatily to him. Only Sam would wear a plain white T-shirt. It worked on John Travolta back in the day, but on my husband it signals a lack of imagination.

'Sam.' I stand up and put a hand on his arm. I often, I realise with a flash of insight, put a hand on his arm. It is a way of showing willing, as far as contact is concerned, while keeping it as minimal as possible. 'Sam, this is Iris. Iris, my husband, Sam.'

He reaches out to shake her hand, but she stands up and kisses him on the cheek.

'You two met on the boat,' he tells her. 'Lara said. You're hitting the stuff with the bubbles, I see!'

Iris is making a polite reply of some sort when I hear my mobile ringing. Its old-fashioned ringtone cuts through the air, and I run towards it. My phone rarely rings.

I look at the name on the screen. Then I snatch it up and run outside on to the balcony. My heart is pumping.

'Leon.' I close the door firmly behind me. The air is cold but crisp. 'How are you?'

'Lara,' says my godfather, the man who knows me properly. 'Skip the small talk. Are you sure this is what you want?'

He has got it. I know it from his tone.

'Yes. Please, Leon. I have to. I can't carry on like this.'

I stare at Sam, watch him take a nervous sip from my

glass, cut himself an enormous slice of cake. He sits down and visibly racks his brains for questions to ask the strange woman at his dining table. I wish he wouldn't resent her presence quite so obviously.

'Then I've got something for you.'

'Tell me,' I say.

As I stare out at a purplish cloud advancing visibly up the estuary, he starts to speak, and a future begins to unfurl.

chapter two

I practise saying it, locked in the bathroom.

'I've got a job,' I tell my reflection. I like the feel of it in my mouth. I can barely conceive of the potential it holds. I hate the way Sam is going to react.

I need to tell him now. He knows I'm jumpy about something. He knew from the moment I finished speaking to Leon, went back to the table and drained my Prosecco in one gulp.

'What's up, Lara?' he keeps asking, and I say 'nothing', with one of my big shiny smiles.

'I've got a job.' I say it again, to my reflection. She looks sombre as she says the words, but her eyes are alight with the whole new world that is revealing itself before her. I make her practise saying it properly. Having a job is a good thing. I force myself to add the salient part: 'I've got a job, and it's in London.'

'Lara?'

I flush the loo, as cover, and pin up a couple of stray strands of hair. Iris has gone home. She went suddenly, when I whispered to her that I had to tell

Sam something. She probably thinks I'm pregnant: I will fix that later.

'Coming!' I call.

I have a job, and it's in London. The reality of that is astonishing.

I am a Londoner and I am craving it. I was born there, and I grew up there. Sam and I met there, and we lived there for three years, before deciding in a sudden flurry that the reason I was not getting pregnant was because we were spending hours every day on the Tube. It was, we reasoned, the environment, rather than us. It was all the other people, pushing and shoving and hurrying us along. It was the lipstick and the shopping and the pollution, the buses that chugged past our Battersea bedroom with all the people on the top deck at eye level looking in, the dashes into Sainsbury's Local to grab dinner on the way home, the fact that walking round the park was nice, but it was no substitute for getting out of town.

And there was, of course, the old cliché: as Londoners, we rarely went to the theatre, the galleries, the museums.

Now that we live in Cornwall, a trip to the capital would be a treat: we haven't been for a year and a half. It is intoxicating, full of possibilities. There are so many possibilities there for me, now. I am consumed with them.

The move was, naturally, his idea. One Sunday morning, he came downstairs, wearing pyjama bottoms and one of his many white T-shirts, and found me poring over a piece of work.

'What time did you get up?' he asked, moving blearily towards the coffee machine.

'I don't know.' I remember making an effort to focus

on him, to smile. 'Five-ish I think. I've done loads. I'm nearly finished.'

'Oh, Lara.'

I turned to look at him. He had his back to me as he poured himself a cup of lukewarm coffee. I loved working early in the mornings. He never understood that. I told him and told him but he always looked at me knowingly, and assumed I was putting on a brave face.

'What?' I made an effort and pushed my work away. He came and sat at the table with me. I picked up my coffee, even though it was cold, and cradled it for a vestige of comfort.

'Lara,' he said again. His face was crumpled with sleep. 'This is no good. You know? If we're going to start a family, if it's going to happen for us, and it is. It's only been a few months. We need to lead less stressful lives. We need to get out of London. There's a job advertised that I could go for.'

I sighed. Sam had always had a tendency to come up with grand schemes, and this, as far as I could see, was another.

'What's the job?' I was expecting it to be something dull, in Hampshire or Surrey.

He smiled.

'It's at a luxury yacht builders, in Falmouth. I've been reading up on Falmouth. It would be a great place to live. Absolutely perfect for a family.'

I laughed at that. 'Right. We'll go and live in Falmouth. Just like that. Where is Falmouth, anyway? Devon? What will I do?'

He got up and came to stand behind my chair. He leaned down and encircled me with his arms.

'Cornwall,' he said, into my hair. 'And you, my darling, will have a baby.'

'Sure,' I said lightly. 'You get the job, then. And we'll give it a go.'

I did not expect for one second that it would actually happen, as smoothly as if it had been preordained, or I would have been less flippant. Sam was offered the job, and we moved here. The shipbuilders wanted him to start as soon as possible, and within no time we sold our house (luckily for us, at the top of the market, though at the time it seemed as though prices were going to stay on the upward trajectory for ever), left our London jobs and drove west. When we reached the west, we drove west some more, and after that, we carried on driving west. Eventually, twenty or so miles short of the furthest possible westerly point, we parked outside our new house and started our new life.

I like life in Cornwall, in lots of ways. I love Falmouth. If I had a family and a job to keep my brain working, I could be content here. There are beaches and fields, woods and little shops. You can catch a train to bigger places, easily. I often quite like the feeling of being remote from most of the rest of the country. It is not Falmouth that's remote, it's everything else.

However, being here, just me and Sam, without a baby, without any close friends, without a job, is no good at all. Now we are closer to forty than we are to thirty, and I am not living like this indefinitely. Falmouth is fine. I am fine. Sam and I, wherever we were, would not, any longer, be fine.

He is upstairs, because our house is upside down, built on the side of a hill. I find him in the kitchen, washing up Prosecco glasses and cake plates.

'Hey,' he says. 'There you are.'

'We didn't finish that bottle.' I take it out of the fridge and hold it up to the light. 'Let's do it. Go on.'

His laugh is slightly nervous. 'It's not even five o'clock, Lara, and you've already had plenty. Seriously?'

'Yes. Come on. I'll dry those glasses. Here you go.'

'What's the matter?'

I was going to sit him down and tell him carefully, but in the event I just blurt it out.

'Leon phoned earlier,' I tell him. 'You know that. While Iris was here. Sam, I've been offered a job. In London, working with Sally's company. Doing exactly what I used to do. They've asked me to come on board for a development project in Southwark. Changing old warehouses into flats, retail, all the stuff I used to do. I'll be the development manager, and do my old job, essentially. All they've done is buy the site. The rest of it – team, designs, all the political stuff with making it happen – will be mine. Everything I'm good at. It'll be a six-month contract. Short-term.'

I stop, look at him, and wait.

'No way.'

I knew it. 'Think about it, Sam. The money is going to be amazing. Six months. It's not for ever.'

'But it's in London. I can't leave my job. So we can't go and live in London for half a year, can we?'

I gulp down a bubbly mouthful: it tastes thin and metallic.

'You can't leave your job,' I agree, sounding like the most reasonable woman in the world. 'But I can commute. I'll stay at Olivia's or with my parents. There's a train. A night train. I could catch it up there on a Sunday night and come home on a Friday night. We'll have a brilliant time at the weekends.'

'No.' His voice is flat. 'Lara, that's just not an option. We moved out of London to get away from all that. We're going to adopt. You're not going back to the rat race. Why on earth do they want you to turn your life upside down to do that, rather than use one of the thousands of qualified people in London who could do the job? You say that it's everything you're good at, but actually that stuff is what you *used to be* good at. We've moved on from those days, thank God.'

It is important, I feel, that he does not realise how this makes me feel.

'I want to do it.' I keep my voice flat calm. 'I miss using my brain, Sam. I failed at having a baby. This is something I know I can do. I *am* still good at my job. I can't get work down here. I want to work. And, the main thing is this: we can come out of that half-year with our debts paid off.'

I am going to take that job, even if I have to leave him. I am hot with guilt at this secret. I almost hope he says no. Then I will get to leave.

'Oh, Lara.' When he says that, my victory is tangible.

I knock my drink back. He does the same. He looks at me with mournful eyes. I have disappointed him, again. Outside, the sun glints off the water. Two pigeons land on the balcony railing. The crane swings around, carrying a huge square container bearing who knows what off the deck of a massive ship that has come from who knows where.

In the early hours of the morning, as the world outside is just starting to stir, I snap wide awake. Sam is turned towards me, snoring gently, his face pink and creased from the pillow.

I am going to London. My life will be busy. I will be on the move constantly. It will not, in any sense, be the easy option. I will have to work like I used to work, and after my years outside the workforce I'll need to prove myself. Going to London will mean throwing myself into being a professional woman again; it will mean looking immaculate, being poised and confident, working with plans and with people. My job will be to make things happen. All of this feels, from this distance, like diving into a refreshing pool on a hot day.

The birds outside are making such a racket that I cannot believe that he, and everyone else, is sleeping through it. The sun creeps around the edge of the blind and lights the room perfectly.

Our bedroom is small. You have to squeeze past the bed to get to the cupboard. We were going to extend the whole of the downstairs of this topsy-turvy house, when we had a family. This room would have become bigger, and there would have been paraphernalia. I know exactly what it would have involved, because we used to talk about it all the time. We read books and planned what was going to go where. There would have been a Moses basket, a changing table. The changing table would have had a shelf under it, and on the shelf would have been a little pile of folded Babygros and tiny cardigans.

Sam wanted a baby because he's a normal human being. I wanted a baby because it felt like the best chance I was going to get, now, of loving someone passionately and all-consumingly.

I stare at him asleep in the soft morning light. This is so intimate that I feel I shouldn't be doing it, but I prop myself on my elbow and carry on. He is vulnerable, unconscious, and I remind myself to think only kind thoughts since he is unaware of me.

He will be asleep in this bed on his own six nights a week for six months. After that, surely, we will know what to do.

If I left, I tell him silently, you would meet someone else in no time. You would meet the kind of woman you need. You might end up having a child with her, because there is nothing wrong with your sperm count. There is nothing wrong with any of my bits either, supposedly. It simply never happened.

You should never have married me. I send that fact into his head, using telepathy. You would have been happy with a wife who adored you, not someone who clung on to you like a life raft on a stormy sea and then wished she could cast you aside and move on when she reached land. By that point, it was too late. I should, as ever, have listened to Leon's advice. Leon warned me not to marry him.

'He's great for you right now,' he said, after his first meeting with Sam. 'But for Christ's sake, Lara. Don't marry him. He'll bore you senseless because he's too nice. Like that Olly bloke, but at least this one wouldn't do the dirty on you. You'd end up doing it on him.'

He was wrong about that part, at least.

More and more, I find myself imagining the woman he should be with. I try to picture his second wife. I looked at Iris today, wondering if she would do, but I knew she wouldn't. Iris has a boyfriend, but she also has secrets. She keeps huge parts of herself hidden. Sam needs a wife who has as few demons as he does.

The ideal Mrs Finch would have had a happy childhood, and she would not be professionally ambitious. She would be longing to dedicate herself to her family, and she would enjoy looking after the house. She would be organised and appreciative and she would think Sam was the sexiest, most fascinating person ever born.

She and I would not be friends.

I have, intermittently, attempted and pretended to be her. Nowadays I find myself seeking her out, like women in magazine articles who know they are going to die and start looking for their husband's next wife and their children's new mother before they go. It is weird when they do it, and it's even weirder of me, what with us being happily married and everything, and also because of the fact that the children never existed.

I wish I had a reason to leave. I wish I could accept that I have a handsome, caring, lovely husband who adores me, and settle down. I need one or other of those things to happen.

I will go to London. That way, things might shift and settle and be all right. Alternatively, we might drift apart and separate by mutual agreement, with no rancour or blame. This is the stuff my daydreams are made of.

I get out of bed as quietly as I can, and tiptoe upstairs to put the kettle on and watch the sunrise.

chapter three

September

Sam insists on driving me to Truro for my first Sunday-night train. He is so ostentatiously sad that I find myself, perversely, wanting to laugh. I would have preferred to go in on the branch line from the Docks station behind our house, but I could see that it meant a lot to him, and so I gave in quickly.

He is almost in tears when we say goodbye, at the ticket barrier at Truro.

'You take care,' he says. 'OK? Promise me you'll stay in touch all the time. I wish I could come with you.'

I smile and kiss him. 'Don't be silly,' I say, mock-stern. I can be as nice as anybody now. 'You work to pay the mortgage and the bills. I'll work to pay off the credit cards. I'll be back on Saturday morning. We'll have a wonderful weekend. Every weekend. Sam! No being gloomy, OK? I won't be here to cheer you up. Make sure you go out to the pub and all of that. See your friends. Go for a run. Keep busy, and I'll be back before you know it.'

He buries his face in my hair. 'Yes, miss,' he says, with

exaggerated meekness. 'I know. And start the processes for adopting from abroad.'

'Sure. Right. I'm going to go. There's no point us standing here being sad. Bye, honey.' He needs me to say that I love him. I know he does. He deserves to hear it. I cannot go without saying it. I draw in a deep breath. 'I love you, OK?'

I say it quietly, into his shoulder, but his relief is horribly obvious.

'Thank you, my darling,' he says, and I can hear his smile. 'Thank you.'

When the train draws in, I know he is still in the ticket hall, staring through the window. I find coach E, berth 23, its door open.

My little cabin is smaller than I expected, with just a bottom bunk (to my relief), a basin which I find under a lid, a mirror, a transparent bag containing toiletries, some bits of mesh stuck to the wall to put things in. There is a TV screen on the wall in the perfect position for lazy bed-bound viewing, and nothing else.

Everything about this tiny room is efficient and clean. The bed, made up with a surprisingly luxurious duvet with a crisp white cover, is narrow but pleasing. For a moment, I gaze around with nothing but the purest pleasure.

The blind is closed in preparation for the night. If I opened it, I would probably be able to see Sam through the window. He would be scanning the train, looking for me.

I close the door instead, and sit on the bed. With a little judder, the train starts to move.

It is ten o'clock. I have to be at work in the morning. I need to go straight to sleep.

There is a mirror on the wall, near the basin, and another on the back of the door. I look different, on the train. In Falmouth, I am a wife, not-a-mother, a nice woman who volunteers for things when she can drum up the energy and the requisite number of smiles. The moment I stepped on to this train, however, I became a commuter.

When someone knocks on the door, I am alarmed and annoyed. My first thought is that Sam has secretly booked himself on to the train to surprise me. I pray that he has not, and hate myself for it.

I open the door, because I can hardly pretend I'm not here. A woman with short curly hair and a ruddy complexion leans on the door frame, looking at her list.

'Hello, my love,' she says cheerfully. 'Miss Finch, isn't it? Yes? Can I just have a look at your ticket, darling? What would you like for breakfast, my love?'

I hand her the ticket and the reservation.

'I get breakfast?'

'Yes, of course you do.'

'You know my name?'

'On my list, darling.'

If I am on her list, nothing terrible will happen. I want to take her photograph and send it to Sam, to prove to him that I am in good hands. If I asked, she would probably let me.

Instead, I choose coffee and a croissant, knowing that they will be less appealing than they sound but certain, all the same, that they will do.

As soon as she leaves, I go down to the end of the carriage to the loo, squeezing past one person on the way, a tall man who is perhaps in his early forties. He has dark hair, and is tall and well built. He looks like a commuter too, and he gives me a warm smile as we pass, closer together than you would normally pass because the corridor is so narrow. Our bodies brush against each other in spite of my best efforts, and I hurry on, embarrassed.

I want to keep to myself on these journeys. Soon this will be a part of my routine, and I do not want to be having to stop and talk to people. This train could become a perfect decompression chamber between my two lives, two nights a week which involve neither work (nor, more specifically, staying at my sister's flat, which is looking less breezily casual a prospect than it once did, as I rattle towards London) nor home, with all its guilt and determined loveliness.

I lie awake in the narrow bed, feeling the train jolting over the rails as it takes me inexorably towards the city, and I grin, then laugh aloud in the near-darkness at the sudden change in my life. Six weeks ago I was aimless and bored: I was 'Sam's wife' and 'that woman in the waiting room'. I wandered around Falmouth and crossed to St Mawes on the ferry for no reason, even though I could barely afford the fare. Now I am myself again, dashing back into the city, turning my back on frustration and failure, and throwing myself into a job that I hope I am still good at. I pretend to myself that I am doing this solely for the money.

I do not think I will sleep, yet I do, quickly, and when I wake up, the train is still. I can hear sounds outside, sounds that, despite the docks, we do not hear in Falmouth. They are the noises of Paddington station in full flow. There are engines and squeaky wheels, a voice suddenly raised in warning, abrupt laughter. There is a muffled announcement, unmistakably about a train even though I cannot hear the words. My closed blind is a grey rectangle, the morning lurking beyond it.

As I reach for my phone, tucked into the mesh pocket beside my bed, there is a sharp rap on my door, and the friendly woman sings out: 'Morning! Breakfast!'

I reach across and unclick the door without leaving my bed, and she is in the room, putting down the tray table, making sure my tray is safely on it.

'You'll need to be off the train by seven,' she says, as she leaves. 'You can wait in the lounge at Paddington after that if you like. Do you know about the lounge on Platform One?'

'Thanks,' I tell her, 'but I'll go straight to work.'

The coffee is train coffee, and the croissant comes out of a plastic packet, but all the same, I savour them both. I take a photograph of the tray, with my breakfast half eaten, and text it to Sam. That seems like a nice thing to do.

At Paddington, I write. *They're feeding me. It's all fine. Off to work in a min. Will call you later. xxx*

Then I do my best to wash with the flannel the train people have given me, and apply a liberal amount of deodorant. I get dressed in the skirt, blouse and jacket I carefully hung up last night, and, since there is no chance of washing and drying my hair, I stand in front of the mirror and spend twenty minutes fastening it into a chignon type of affair, with the many hair grips I brought along for this purpose. I do my make-up the way I used to do it, when I was a Londoner. Finally I add the finishing touch: my work shoes. I have kept these for years, and they are probably officially 'vintage' by now. They are high, classic Mary Janes of the sort that a secretary from the fifties might have worn on a night out. They are dark red and I adore them. I step into them and into an abandoned, semi-familiar persona.

I smile at the mirror. I am the right Lara. There have

been many over the years, and this, I can now see, is the one I liked being the best. The busy one. The successful one. The polished one. The one who is fucking brilliant at what she does.

This is the selfish one: this is the single one.

It is seven o'clock. I step off the train directly behind a woman who is, I think, in her fifties. She, like me, is dressed for work, and she has dealt with the hair problem by putting on a wide hairband, the sort of thing people wear on the beach. It is pale green, the same colour as her outfit, and she makes it work.

'Morning,' she says with a grin, turning on the platform and waiting for me. I like her instantly. If this woman was in a colouring book, I would colour her in orange and red, with benign flames shooting happy things at the people around her.

'Good morning.' I feel a bit shy, but the sudden surge of camaraderie makes me smile.

'Straight to work?' she asks, eyeing my outfit. 'Or are you grabbing a coffee first? I always think the station ones are so much better than that shite they give you on the train that it would be criminal not to knock one back. Since they're free. Or not free. You've paid for it in the hefty cabin fare. It's already yours. You have to take it.'

'I was going to go straight to work.' I look at the old-fashioned clock on the wall in front of us. 'But it's my first day and I would only have found the nearest Costa and waited it out in there feeling nervous. So I might grab one, actually. If it's going to be a half-decent one, even better.'

I stop for a second to savour the London air. It is dirty here, and dusty with the mechanics of the station. I love it.

The woman flashes me a wide grin, and I follow her

through a door and past a uniformed man sitting at a table reading a paper, waving my ticket at him since she does. The room is filled with tables and chairs, a screen high on the wall playing silent, subtitled television. The woman heads straight to the coffee machine. We both take large white cups on saucers that remind me, with a jolt, of a cup Sam sometimes uses at home.

'First day?' she says, as we sit together at a table. There is food here, pastries and bananas and biscuits on big plates, but, like the woman, I do not take any. I sip the coffee. She is right. It is perfectly acceptable. 'What does that mean? Have you been on maternity leave or something?'

Again, everyone wants to talk about babies.

'Nope. It's a long story. Moved to Cornwall with my husband. I gave up work. He had a job down there.' I hesitate, reluctant to share our full story with a stranger. 'He still does. I was offered something like my old job back on a six-month contract, and we needed some funds, so here I am.'

'Weekly commuting for six months?'

'Yes. Is that what you do? Weekly commute?'

'Pretty much. Not all the time, but essentially you'll see me most Sunday and Friday nights. There's a few of us. We sometimes go for a drink in the lounge. Fridays are the best. I'm Ellen.'

'Lara.'

'Lara,' she says, looking at me with an assessing gaze. 'That's a very glamorous name. It suits you.'

'Um, thanks. I had no idea that commuting like this was a thing people do. I thought it was just me. What's your job?'

'Banking. You know. In London I'm one of the hated

bankers, but no one really hates us. In Cornwall I'm just a woman who works in London.'

'Why don't you live in London?'

She shrugs. 'I love Cornwall. I love my weekends there. It's glorious. I would far rather live like this, because you do get fond of that train ride, than have some stupid flat in Clapham like everyone else. My partner's in Cornwall. He's a farmer, so he can hardly do that in the big city. It can get knackering, but I do generally love it.' She smiles and looks around. 'There's nothing like the buzz. People hate Monday mornings. I don't.' She lifts a hand and waves to somebody. 'I relish them.'

'That's great to hear. Hey, this coffee isn't exactly amazing, is it?'

'Oh God, no. Not in comparison with actual coffee. It has caffeine in it, though, and it's relatively fresh. It's the caffeine that does the job for me.'

'Oh, me too.' I think of Sam, and the way he carefully gave up caffeine with me as part of our bid to conceive. We both operated under the solemn pretence that the absence of coffee-related products in our systems would suddenly propel sluggish sperm to recalcitrant egg and produce a child where there would otherwise not have been one. I knew all along that the subtle realignment of the universe to make it greyly decaffeinated was not, actually, going to tip the balance, but I went along with it anyway; just in case.

'Do you have children?' I did not mean to say that. I resent it greatly when strangers ask this of me, and here I am doing the same thing. 'I mean, I'm sorry, I don't mean to . . .'

Ellen chuckles. 'No, Lara, I don't. I never wanted them, actually. I was married for a while, but I held out against starting a family because it wouldn't have been right, and I knew that, really. Then when I met Jeff, that time had passed. I'm glad I never had them. I wouldn't be able to live this schizoid life if I did. I guess you don't either?'

I look at my coffee. The frothy milk has gone from the top of it now. This conversation, even with so friendly a stranger, is never easy. 'We tried for years. Me doing this job kind of marks the fact that we failed.' I look at her face and quickly add: 'It's fine, though. I mean, it really is. I was never that maternal or broody. It was Sam, more than me. I would have loved a baby, of course I would, but then it doesn't happen and the whole quest takes over your life, becomes this massive obsession, and every aspect of your life is suddenly governed by injections and cycles, and everyone asks you about it all the time – "So are you two going to be starting a family?", as if that's not the only thing the two of you ever talk about – and Sam could, actually, think and talk about nothing else, and by the time we did give up, I felt nothing but the most gigantic relief. I'm happy to be moving on.'

'Well, there you go.' She lifts her coffee. 'Cheers, Lara. Welcome to your new life. Joyous moving-on to you.'

We stand, gather our bags and set off together through Paddington station, at the beginning of the Monday-morning rush hour, towards the Tube, and work, and a London life.

chapter four

The working day is the easy part. I spend the first couple of hours meeting people, working out where things are and getting to grips with the project. It is going to be an interesting one, just behind Tate Modern: I will be turning industrial warehouses into flats and a restaurant. I start with the basics of the project, running over each step in my head. It's in an area with a high water table, a strong likelihood of archaeological complications, and a strong community watching our every move.

I am good at this, and I slip back into it easily and professionally. Despite my unexpectedly intimate conversation with Ellen this morning (which has left me feeling a little exposed, and which I regretted instantly), or perhaps because of it, I am determinedly friendly but distant with my new colleagues, many of whom are younger than me.

I leave the office at six thirty, pleased with myself.

Then I am cutting through Covent Garden, heading to my sister's flat. She lives in a street that is jarringly perfect, if you like to live in the middle of a city. It is early in the evening, the sun is shining, and the streets are busy with released workers and tourists and students, as well as assorted unplaceable people. I feel the buzz in the air, and although I love Falmouth and Cornwall, I know in my heart that I am a Londoner. I am a Londoner, and I have arrived home, and even the fact that I am about to have to negotiate Olivia cannot dent the upsurge of happiness.

For a second I picture myself in a book. It is a children's picture book, and its name is *Lara in London*. I am drawn in a stylised way, like a woman in a classy little fashion tome from the thirties, with a nipped-in waist and a chignon, and I am striding confidently through the city having adventures. There is no particular rhythm to these adventures, because *Lara in London* is a guide to the city's landmarks more than anything else. Right now, I am tapping, in my glorious shoes, around the edge of Covent Garden Market, past people determinedly shivering with beers at outside tables and a street entertainer juggling chairs on a red carpet, with a crowd gathered watching him. I wave to him as I pass, feeling so powerful in myself, all of a sudden, that I am sure I can make him wave back and ruin his act. He does not even see me, of course, but my mind instantly transforms him into his illustrated self, his stubble shaded in, his round cheeks exaggerated.

Marks and Spencer, opposite the Tube, is my first destination. As I buy wine and olives and clotted cream that I will not even attempt to pretend I brought all the way from Cornwall, I tell myself that it will be all right. I tell myself so firmly that I feel I can make it true. Olivia said I could stay with her, during the week, indefinitely. She would not have said that if she was not planning to be nice.

Unfortunately, she would have done exactly that, and I

know that perfectly well. I have not seen my sister for a year and a half, because we went to Sam's family last Christmas and by the time we got to my parents' on December 28th, she had gone somewhere, 'away with friends'.

I squash my dread with internal platitudes. Since we have had a break from one another, it will probably be fine. A break was exactly what our relationship needed. We were never friends as children, or teenagers, and as young adults we fell out catastrophically: all this is undeniably true. She has no idea about the big event of my life, but then neither does my husband. We have never been friends, not even in the most shallow of ways. She was born hating me; I suppose I must have done something from those earliest of days to provoke that, but I never meant to. Her hatred has been unwavering and true, and she has behaved in a way that has left me no choice but to hate her back.

I have always been sceptical of other people's much-vaunted sisterly closeness; in fact, I cannot help suspecting that it is all a sham, that underneath every pair of loved-up sisters is some variant of Olivia and me, constantly nursing grievances that started to pile up on the day the second child was conceived.

Now, however, we might be able to construct a new relationship. We are in our thirties, and we could make it work. There is a chance, I insist to myself as I put my debit card in the machine and ask for cashback, that this will happen. Perhaps I will soon be able to say the words 'my sister' without the stab of bitter distaste that accompanies them at the moment. This thought makes me dart off to grab a bunch of white roses from a display. I pay for them separately, with my cashback money. I look apologetically at the man behind me in the queue, wondering whether technically I should have rejoined it at the back before making a second purchase. He is a jumpy-looking man in his forties, and he nods and says 'nice flowers' in an Antipodean accent. I smile my thanks and try to shrug off the sudden feeling that I have met him before. This is London: of course I haven't.

Once in Olivia's life she said sorry to me. Soon afterwards we settled back into our habitual disdain for one another. She got over her misdeed conveniently quickly. It was the only time she did something concrete to me, something everyone knew about, something I could point to and say: 'You did that.' Yet if I were to mention it now, she would laugh at me.

Her street is different from the way it was last time I was here. It goes straight off Long Acre, and it is now achingly hip. There is an enormous vintage clothes emporium, a yoga centre, an entrance to a new courtyard full of upmarket shops. I walk down to the end and eye up the pub there. It looks friendly. The house next to it has millions of geraniums in window boxes, with creepers trailing down between them. A quick shot of vodka would give me courage.

I do not do it, of course, much as I would like to be that sort of woman. I walk back up to Olivia's mansion block, the clear evening sun suddenly cold on my cheeks. The outside of the building has been cleaned up since I was last here, and it is glowing, redbrick and classic. She bought this place shrewdly, when she got her first job, at a time when London was on the cusp of spectacular unaffordability.

Birds fly overhead with a sudden cry. A man is walking

towards me, and I look at him desperately, as if he might save me from having to press the buzzer. He walks past slowly on the other side of the road, talking into a phone.

'Yeah, sure we could,' he says, 'but you'll have to manage Goddard's reaction, mate. I'm taking no responsibility.'

I want to ask who Goddard is and what his reaction will be like, but I press the buzzer instead, and the door clicks open without a word from the intercom.

She waits for me on the landing. The carpet has been replaced since I was last here, but the walls are still grubby.

I take a deep breath.

'Olivia!' I gush, taking care not to notice the disdain in her flinty eyes. 'It's lovely to see you!' I walk towards her for a hug, then retract it when I feel the force of her frost. 'Thank you so much for having me. How are you? You look great. Here, I bought you some stuff. Flowers, and some contributions to the house.'

'Yeah,' she says. 'Of course you did. Thanks.'

She runs her fingers through her hair, which is bottle-black and shorter than I have seen it for a long time. It suits her short: she has had it cut in a gamine style that makes her look young and French, an unforgiving style that few could carry off.

Inside, this is a small dwelling but a beautiful one, with windows at the front that flood every part of the sitting room and main bedroom with light for much of the day. The kitchen, bathroom and small bedroom are gloomy in comparison, but I notice that she has now strung fairy lights everywhere to counter the darkness in characteristic aggressively kooky fashion.

She dumps the shopping bag in the murky kitchen

without looking at it, and I follow her into the sitting room and watch her throw herself down into the battered leather armchair that has been a part of this room for as long as she has lived here, though now it is covered in purple and silver cushions. I take my place on the cream sofa, and aim a fake and desperate smile in her direction.

'You're here,' she says, fiddling with one of her nails. 'So how was the first day back in the grand career?'

'It was fine,' I tell her, and inevitably, I start babbling. 'Actually it was great. Straight back into it. I spent the day checking the planning permission, which I always used to do. It was exactly like old times. But how about you, Olivia? How's work with you? And how's everything else?'

'Oh, you know. Not dramatic. Humdrum.'

I laugh. 'You have the least humdrum life. You know that.'

'That's not the way it feels from inside it. But anyway. The parents want to see you. They're coming up for dinner on Wednesday. Dad's booked Pizza Express. Obviously. As there is no other restaurant in London.'

'Oh. OK.'

I sit and smile a frantic smile. She pulls her feet up so she is curled in the chair like a cat. She is very skinny, I notice. I try to calculate how offended she will be if I go and fetch the wine I just bought, open it and pour both of us a large glass. She is ignoring it on purpose. She flashes a sarcastic smile back at me.

I am the older sibling. I am, as she has insisted for as long as I can remember, 'the golden child'. Golden children can take charge.

'Are you hungry?' I offer. 'I've got some bits of food. I can cook something, if you like.'

43

She will say no, but at least this gives me an opening to go into the kitchen and do it myself.

'I'm out tonight, actually.'

'Oh. Cool.'

'Cool? Yes, it is "cool", isn't it? Nice flat to yourself.'

'That isn't what I meant! I meant "cool" as in "totally fine". Where are you going?'

'Oh, just out.' She tries to twiddle a piece of hair around her finger, though her hair is not long enough for that, and chuckles privately.

I stand up.

'OK,' I say. It never takes long for this to happen, though I think this encounter marks a record. A big wooden carriage clock, the sort of thing I would pass over at a car boot sale because it looks naff, but which is somehow stylish in this setting, tells me that it is ten to eight. It is still light outside. 'I'll get myself some food then, if you don't mind. And some wine.' With a deep breath I force myself to be friendly again. 'Can I pour you a glass before you go out?'

'Sure.' She looks terminally bored.

My bedroom is the box room, which is also known as 'the study'. Over the years it has hosted various of Olivia's arch and unknowable friends, and in between tenants it becomes a dumping ground for anything she doesn't want to look at.

I push the door open and, because I want so much to be friends with Olivia, I am genuinely touched by the fact that she has cleared it, and cleaned it, for me. I three-quarters expected to find the floor covered with paperwork and boxes and things she was thinking about throwing out. Instead, the floorboards are perfectly clear, the single bed (this is a room that definitely could not host any other sort) is made with a duvet in an embroidered white cover, and two pillows. There is even a folded pale pink towel on the end of the bed. A clothes rail has hangers on it for my stuff, and there is a built-in cupboard for the rest of my things.

'Thanks for the room, Olivia,' I call. I wish I could call her Liv or Oli as her friends do. Some of them call her Libby or Libster or Ols, and the further the variation gets from her actual name, the more intimacy there is in it. I have never been able to attempt anything other than the full 'Olivia'.

It is not a dilemma that works in reverse. There is no obvious shortening for Lara. Only one person, in my whole life, has attempted one. Rachel used to call me Laz. I swallow, and push the memory away.

Even my mother has never gone off piste with so much as a 'La' (which would, admittedly, sound stupid). Nor has Sam. I am Lara, and people call me Lara, and that is that. I am not my sister, and unlike her, I cannot use my name as a weapon.

'You're welcome,' she calls back from somewhere, just as I open the cupboard to be hit by an avalanche of paperwork, discarded clothes, random items and what can only be described as 'assorted crap'.

I wonder whether to retract the thanks, but in the name of peacekeeping I just get down on my knees and shove the whole lot under the bed.

A rangy man with a beard and a tweed jacket appears at the door. He looks a bit like Jarvis Cocker, and I am pathetically grateful when he greets me warmly.

'Aha!' he says, pointing at me from the doorway. 'You are the famed sister! Loitering with wine! Cornish-woman come to work in the city, no?'

'That's right.' I don't want to know what she has been saying about me.

'Enchanted to meet you,' he says with a little bow. 'I'm Allan.'

'Hi, Allan.' He is looking expectantly at me. She clearly has never mentioned my name. 'Lara.'

He stretches out a long arm, and we shake hands with a strange formality.

'Lara.' He rolls the word around his mouth. 'Lara. Sorry to whisk your sister away on your first night, Lara. Would you care to join us, Lara?'

I am tempted to accept, just to see her face.

'No. Thank you, though. I've got lots to sort out. Have a good evening.'

'We most certainly plan to.'

Allan bids me a polite good night as they leave. Olivia pretends I am not there as she sweeps past me and out on to the new-yet-dirty landing carpet.

I speak to Sam for half an hour, amazed that I have not yet been away from home for twenty-four hours. As we talk, I pace around the flat, into and out of the sitting room that is bright even when dark closes in, illuminated by the street lights outside, into the tiny kitchen where I help myself to an olive, a piece of pitta bread dipped in hummus and then, on my third circuit of the flat, a refill of wine.

'What have you been doing, then?' I ask, hating my patronising tone. Sam does not seem to notice it.

'Oh, you know,' he says. 'Slept badly without you. Bed's too big. No one to complain when I wrap myself in the duvet. It's all no fun without you.'

'Oh, I know,' I tell him. 'Same here. Me too.'

'I'm rubbish on my own.' He starts speaking quickly, his pent-up frustration released in a torrent. 'I wish we weren't doing this, Lara. It's a mistake. I wish we'd laughed at it and called it a ridiculous idea. I wish we'd put ourselves, you and me, ahead of the money and everything else. I wish you were here, with me. This is all wrong.'

'I know.' I am not just saying this to make him feel better. Even though London has been exciting today, and being at work was stimulating and amazing, I suddenly wish I were in Falmouth, in our little house above the docks, with Sam. Sam makes me feel safe. He, and our home, suddenly look like a harbour in more ways than one. We could have struggled through without the money. 'I'll be back on Saturday,' I remind him.

'But it's only Monday!'

'It's the end of Monday. And I'll be back at the very start of Saturday. It'll go quickly. You'll get used to it. You can watch *Man v. Food* as much as you like! You can leave the loo seat up.' I stop because I know how pitiful this sounds.

'Yeah.' Neither of us speaks for several seconds. 'So,' he starts at exactly the same time that I say: 'And.' We pause, awkwardly, each waiting for the other to continue.

'Go on,' Sam says. We both laugh, and the tension is gone.

'I was just going to say, and at least you don't have to live with Olivia. At least you're in our home. Let's go out for lunch on Saturday. To one of the nice pubs.'

'Yes.' He is suddenly decisive. I like it when that happens. 'Yes, I'll book a table at the Pandora, or the Ferryboat.'

These are the two pubs we love near Falmouth, both situated on the water. The Pandora Inn is on the banks of the Restronguet Creek; it is a thatched pub that burned down then miraculously reopened almost exactly as it had been to start with. It has a jetty which, on a sunny day, has sailing boats moored to it while the sailors call in for lunch, where children catch crabs and throw them into plastic buckets.

The Ferryboat, meanwhile, is situated on the Helford Estuary, in Frenchman's Creek country, with a river beach, flat water, and boats moored for as far as you can see, while the eponymous ferryboat takes people back and forth across the water. Both of them are havens of tranquillity: they are places where nothing bad can happen. These are illusory, peaceful worlds, populated exclusively by people with money and security. Last time we went to the Ferryboat, I looked around at the families of upmarket beachgoers, at their healthy children expertly peeling prawns and drinking organic lemonade, and I tried to tell myself that everyone has sadnesses, that some of the adults would be hideously miserable in their marriages, that people would be having affairs and drinking too much and addicted to gambling, that lives would be on the verge of falling apart, families breaking up, businesses going bankrupt.

I convinced myself in the end, mainly by looking at Sam and me through the same eyes. To outsiders we must have looked perfect: a couple in their thirties having lunch together at a waterside pub. No one would have known, from the front we presented, that our third round of IVF had just failed, that we were trying to accept that we would never have a child of our own, that we were many thousands of pounds in debt, and that one of us was far more at peace with the idea of childlessness than the other.

Then, when I looked around, I caught the desperation

at the corners of people's eyes, their misery, the fake smiles they showed to one another. I saw people trying to text under the table, surreptitiously, but being foiled by the fact that there was no reception. It made me want to cry, and I wished I had kept the cynicism shut away.

'That would be lovely,' I say. 'Whichever you like. That's something to look forward to.'

'How's it been with Olivia?' he asks, and I love the fact that he is the only person in the world, apart, perhaps, from Leon, who genuinely cares about this. 'Is she giving you a hard time?'

I force a laugh. 'Oh, nothing I can't handle. We'll get through it by avoiding each other. Yeah. The sisterly reconciliation I was hoping for. That's not going to happen. She's gone out tonight with a nice stringy man who was kind to me. It's fine.'

'Don't take any of her crap, OK?'

'I know.'

'I love you, Lara. That's all that matters, really, isn't it? Everything else is detail.'

'Yes. It is.'

I put the phone down. Then I have a shower, because I know that if I went to lounge in the bath I would use too much water, and Olivia would come home and find me there and complain. I tip the rest of the glass of wine down the sink, wash up carefully, then shut myself in my tiny room and sleep fitfully, jumping awake as soon as my sister's key turns in the lock, listening to her crashing around the place. I smell the toast she makes and wish I could get up and join her.

She sobs, a sudden, ugly sound that she tries to stifle. I hear her ragged breathing. She is trying to keep it quiet. I check my clock: it is three in the morning. I don't want to listen. I want to go back to sleep, but I am transfixed. Olivia is crying, harder and harder. It is wrenching, heart-breaking.

She would hate it if I went to her, so I don't. I lie in bed, and I listen to her crying, and pretend to be asleep.

chapter five

October

Friday night at Paddington station is the only time I am genuinely and uncomplicatedly happy. I look forward to it all through the week, and when I step off the train at Truro I start looking forward to the journey back on Sunday. That truth makes me wince as I push through the crowds. It should not be this way, but it is.

The station is different on a Friday: the air is thick with expectation. People are going home from work and not coming back tomorrow; or they are heading away for the weekend, bags packed and ready for fun. I walk diagonally across the concourse, looking forward to seeing my friends.

Then I stop. For a second, I am convinced that someone is close behind me, so close they could reach out and touch me, wishing me harm. The malevolent presence is almost tangible: in fact, I think something did touch me, so gently it was barely there at all. I spin around, looking at the people in the crowd, scanning faces, but there is nothing. Nobody is even particularly close to me. Most people are walking in different directions, or standing still as I bustle past. Someone was there, though. Something was there.

It was not, I tell myself. Nobody was there. You are being ridiculous. This has happened several times. I feel something, eyes on me nearby, and I shiver, utterly convinced that someone is there and that something catastrophic is about to happen. I feel, at these moments, as if I am tightrope-walking like Philippe Petit between the towers, and wobbling.

I march straight to the first-class lounge, flash my ticket at a woman reading *Metro*, who smiles briefly at me, and go to join the rest of the waiting night-train passengers.

I am the first of my little gang, so I take a plastic bottle of fizzy water and a little packet of two biscuits, and sit down to wait. I am still shivering, despite the fact that nothing happened, and grab my phone to occupy myself.

I send Sam a text announcing my location, adding then deleting a rant about Olivia's latest rudeness (dumping the broken microwave in my bedroom), and look at the news headlines which are appearing in cack-handed subtitles across the bottom of a muted TV showing the BBC news channel.

'Lara,' says Ellen, sitting next to me, tapping on her iPhone, tucking her hair behind her ears and rearranging something in the pocket of her overnight bag, all in one go. 'Good evening. Happy Friday.'

'Hi,' I say, opening my biscuits, delighted to see her. 'Good week?'

'Fine. Yes thanks. You? How's that sister of yours?' She looks at me with narrowed eyes. As she has only had my word for it, she considers Olivia to be quite the witch. I constantly try to qualify my stories by adding things like

'I'm sure if you asked her she'd have a completely different perspective', but Ellen and Guy never care about that.

I look around quickly for Guy.

'Oh, you know,' I say.

'Get your own place! I'm going to keep saying that until you do, you know. You're a professional woman. You earn. You're allowed to rent yourself a studio. It doesn't have to be hideously expensive. You can take yourself out of that whole toxic relationship, you know.'

I sigh. Ellen, I have realised in the short time I have known her, says exactly what she thinks. She is right, I know it.

'If I tell her I'm moving out, she'll never let me forget it.'

She shrugs. 'And? You live in her box room. She snubs you at every turn. She makes you feel like shit. You don't have to be there. Rearrange your life.'

'I know. I'll think about it over the weekend.'

'Talk to Sam about it. Properly. You know he'll say the same as me.'

I look around, again, for the third member of the gang. Guy, Ellen and I are the only ones who do this every week, all the way from west Cornwall. He lives somewhere near Penzance, with a wife and teenage children. For the past two Friday nights the three of us have consumed too many gin and tonics in the lounge car on the way west.

'Is Guy coming back tonight?' I ask.

She nods. 'He said he was. Who knows? Maybe his family have come up for a London weekend or something. You see? That's another reason why you should totally leave Olivia's place. You could get Sam up for a weekend if you had a studio. Just a tiny place in north London or something would do it. It would barely cost you a thing.

Then he could come up and you could do the whole theatre-galleries-restaurant business.'

I decide against challenging Ellen's definition of 'barely costing a thing'.

'Do you do that? Does Jeff come to London?'

She waves a dismissive, and perfectly manicured, hand at the very idea.

'Oh Christ, no. Jeff hates London. And I don't want to do that shit anyway. Been there, done it. A weekend expedition for me is a walk to the pub at Zennor. Not fighting through Leicester Square. I'm talking about you, Lara. You get the buzz from the London thing. You guys lived here. From everything you've said about Sam, I think he'd enjoy a top-of-the-range London weekend with all the frills.'

'You know what? He would.' I think about it. Sam's birthday is at the end of July. That is too far away: perhaps I could do it for Christmas instead. I imagine us looking at the lights in Oxford Street, skating at Somerset House, sheltering from the biting cold in a cinema. We could stay in a lovely hotel. I resolve to sort it out, at once. 'Thanks, Ellen. Good idea. We could do it in December.'

A First Great Western woman strides into the waiting room and says, 'Just about ready for boarding, ladies and gents.' Ellen and I stand up and join the general shuffle for the door. We nod at a few familiar faces belonging to older men in suits, and I smile at a woman I have never seen before, a woman in her late thirties wearing a short skirt, a brightly patterned coat and a flower hairclip. She has to be a designer or a writer. Ellen says those are the people she likes to meet in the lounge car, the ones who keep the train interesting.

We get to board at 10.30, though the train does not leave until just before midnight. A train guard I have not met before, a young, earnest woman with a blond ponytail, shows us to our compartments, which are both in carriage F, five doors apart. I unpack just enough, putting my pyjamas on the end of the bed and the toiletries I cannot get from the pack of train freebies beside the flap that covers the sink, then take my handbag and head straight for the lounge car.

Ellen is, somehow, already there, sitting back in one of the luxuriously large chairs, flicking through the free newspaper. Two men in suits are at the next table, and more people are coming through.

'I took the liberty of ordering our usuals. They're not quite ready yet, but when they are, ours will be first off the block.'

I settle down opposite her. 'Lovely,' I say. 'Thanks, Ellen.'

'You're welcome. The first drink. The start of the weekend. I rarely drink in London. The train G and T is something special.'

'Isn't it? I drink most nights in London, now. I have to.' I think of Olivia, of the arch war of words and behaviour that we have drifted into. We are bristling against one another constantly. I try to smooth things over every single day, and that inflames her more than anything else I could possibly do. Perhaps next week I will try to smooth things over by being more confrontational.

'I know you do, darling.'

'Evening, ladies.'

My heart leaps, and I pretend it hasn't. Keeping my expression as neutral as possible, I shift up slightly as Guy sits next to me.

I passed Guy in the corridor on my first journey to London, the night before my first day back at work; I first spoke to him when Ellen introduced us in the waiting room at Paddington that Friday. He is handsome in an unmissable, Clooney-ish way: he is one of those men who settle beautifully into middle age. He is also excellent company.

'You're late, matey,' Ellen remarks. 'We thought you'd stood us up.'

'Sorry,' he says. 'Had to go to a work thing. Have you ordered? Bet you didn't get me one. It was a leaving do. Champagne and all that shit, in some stupid wine bar at London Bridge. I was glad of the excuse to get away.' He smiles at Ellen, then at me. 'I would have preferred water and packets of biscuits in the waiting room with you two to champagne in a wine bar with my colleagues. You know that.'

'I should hope you would.' Ellen gets up and goes to add a third drink to the order. While she is gone, Guy turns to me, and I try not to enjoy his attention. We are sitting so close together that our thighs are almost touching, and I am acutely aware of the small distance between us. His hair is thick and dark, flecked with grey, and his eyes crinkle at the corners.

'How's the week been?' he asks. 'Are you moving out of your sister's yet?'

'Thinking about it,' I tell him. 'Christ, that sounds pathetic, but it's a step closer, and that's as good as I can make it for today.'

It is the oddest thing, but I can be myself with Guy and Ellen, on the train, in a way I cannot with anyone else and in any other location. If I knew them in any other context my guard would be up. Here, on this train, it is down. I would, and do, tell them anything. I consider telling Guy about my weird shiver on the station, but decide better of it.

'Well, then it's progress,' he nods. He wriggles out of his suit jacket, slings it on the empty seat next to Ellen's and rolls his sleeves up.

'Barack Obama does that.' I nod at his forearms, which, I notice, are muscular and hairy in just the right amount. I look away quickly, smiling to myself. This is the most harmless type of crush possible, considering that we are both safely married.

'Barack Obama does what?' He sounds mystified, as well he might.

'He takes his jacket off and rolls his shirt sleeves up. It's a nice look, that's all. I like it when men do that.'

'Seriously?' He nods at his arms, leaning on the edge of the table. 'This works for the ladies?'

'For me it does.'

'Cheers, Lara. Good to know these things. Not that I'm in any position, or have any inclination, to act on it.'

Ellen comes back, followed by a lounge car attendant I recognise, who bears a tray carrying three gin and tonics.

'Thanks, Sarah,' says Guy, winking at her. 'You're a life saver.'

'Welcome,' says Sarah. 'Plenty more where those came from.'

'Good.' I take one and stir it with its little plastic stick.

'Cheers,' says Ellen. We clunk plastic glasses, and I relax. The week is frantic. This weekend is, I hope, going to be less difficult than the last one was. The pressure, when Sam has been looking forward to my return relentlessly all week, can make us bicker without stopping, and last weekend we were both in tears by Sunday afternoon, the uncompromising separation looming, raising the stakes, making everything a million times worse.

Three drinks later, Guy is leaning back in his seat yawning. His knee rests casually against mine.

'Do you find,' he says, looking first at Ellen and then,

for longer, at me, 'do you find that the weekends are almost as much hard work as the week sometimes? I mean, I get back Saturday morning, bloody fucking knackered, and then it's all "Dad, do this. Guy, do this. Be fun. Be nice. Fix this. Go and buy this. Help with homework. You have no idea what it's like being the one stuck at home all week, you've been in London, you can put the washing on for once . . ."'

'Nope,' Ellen says at once. 'Jeff's a farmer. You know that. Our day jobs couldn't be more different. The farm doesn't wind up for the whole weekend, though he makes that happen as much as he can because of our time together. I love the weekends. But then again, it's just the two of us, so I was never really going to have the pressure. If I was someone's mum, well, that would be an entirely different matter. Neither of us cares who does the laundry. It gets done, one way or another.'

They both turn to me.

'Mm.' The gin, followed by wine, has relaxed me. 'I find it hard,' I admit, making an effort to direct my words towards Ellen, because Guy is disconcerting me. 'It's early days for us, you both know that. But if I'm not sparkly and adoring and adorable, if we don't have a shiny precious weekend, then I feel hugely resented. Last weekend was hellish. You know that anyway because of how I was on the Sunday train. I can't blame Sam for it: as far as he's concerned, I'm in a high-pressure job, and negotiating my bloody sister the rest of the time, and then I'm on this train, and he has no idea how much fun this is, or that I sit up for most of the night drinking. So he thinks I'm toughing it out, which I am, and pining for our quiet life in Cornwall, which I'm afraid I'm generally not.'

'He probably lives for the moment you get back, Lara,'

says Guy. 'What's his job like? Does he go to the pub and have a life? Or is he sitting there all week looking at his watch and sighing and counting down the hours on his fingers?'

'Yes,' Ellen agrees. 'I'm intrigued by this Sam of yours. Will you get him to bring you to the station on Sunday so we can see him?'

This makes me laugh. 'But you two will've been on the train since Penzance. If he was waiting on the platform you'd be lucky to catch a glimpse out of the window.'

'No,' says Guy. 'We'd be at the door, waiting for Truro, and as soon as the train stopped we'd open it and jump down to help you with your bags. Both of us. A little chivalrous double act.'

'You'd freak him right out.'

Ellen nods. 'I thought so. Go on then. What's he like? How did you meet him?'

'He's lovely.' I say this in my firmest voice, as their amused curiosity about my husband makes me feel disloyal. I move my leg away from Guy's, and he does not attempt to reinstate contact. 'He really is. He's the most lovely man in the world, and if anything I've said makes you think otherwise, then that's my stupid fault. I met him when I was twenty-four. Twelve years ago. I'd been travelling in Asia for a bit. Things had . . .' The last thing I want to do is talk about my time in Thailand, so I bite my lip and jump away from what I was about to say. 'I got back and I'd got a load of stuff out of my system. I was ready to settle down, properly. In fact I was craving a stable, conventional life. I was qualified in property development. My godfather – my dad's best friend, Leon – he helped me get a job. Encouraged me not to sit around at my parents' house doing nothing. I started working, and

I worked hard. I rented a little studio flat, then bought a house. And I met Sam.'

'And you weren't close to your sister back then either?' Ellen interjects.

'Never,' I agree. 'She was in the same flat she's in now, even though she was in her first job, in PR. Olivia: the world's least likely PR woman, I always thought. The person who will go out of her way to let you know she doesn't like you. Turns out that's only with me. She's a brilliant schmoozing pro with everyone else. Anyway. Our dad encouraged me to buy a place as soon as I could, and I got a little terraced house in Battersea. Again, it seems impossible now, a decade later, but I did. I had the job, the mortgage, friends, and I just needed a boyfriend. I didn't need one, of course, but I desperately wanted one.'

'And you met him . . .?'

'And I met him. In a café, in Soho. It was like one of those meetings in a film. It was pissing down with rain, and I was sheltering with a drink, a coffee I think, on a Saturday afternoon, wishing I hadn't come into town, a few bags of shopping by my feet, considering going to watch whatever was on at the Curzon because it was at the end of the street and I wanted to sit somewhere warm and dry for a couple of hours without being bored. The café was packed, the windows all steamed up. I'm sitting by the window, and I'm so out of sorts that I'm drawing pictures in the condensation on the glass without even realising it.

'When someone politely asks if he can join me, I'm properly annoyed. I want to say no, but I know I have to say yes. And then I look at him. It's hard to explain, but probably not, for you guys, because you've both got long-term partners too. I just knew as soon as I saw him that he was the person I was looking for.'

'Love at first sight?' I glance at Guy, wondering if he is mocking me, but I do not think he is. His knee knocks against my leg, then retreats.

'Not love. Safety. Certainty. Conviction that this was the man I would spend my life with, the missing piece of the jigsaw, at first sight. And he was. He was tall, broad, and I like both those things. Blondish, stubbly. Beautiful eyes. And an air of . . . well, of rightness. He sat with me, laughed at what I'd drawn on the window.'

'Which was?' Ellen asks.

'Oh, a child's picture. A house, with four windows and a door and a tree next to it, and I think there was an outsized person, too, out of all proportion to the house.'

'That would have been the perspective,' Guy reassures me. 'The person must have been closer to the viewer.'

'Exactly. Thank you. So we looked at that, and I drank my espresso, and he spooned the froth off his cappuccino, and we went to the Curzon together and watched a gorgeous Almodovar film. Then we went for dinner. We were together. That was it.'

'Was he twenty-four too?'

'Twenty-eight. He'd had a girlfriend, obviously, and they'd split up about six months earlier. We were both in the right place. We got married a couple of years later.'

'Oh,' says Ellen. 'I'm too cynical for weddings, I really am. They get my hackles up like nothing else. All that horrific misogyny under the surface, the handing-over of the woman from one man to another. However, I have to break with my own tradition, Lara, and say that I bet you were the most stunning bride. Don't you think, Guy?'

Guy looks oddly awkward. 'Well,' he says, fiddling with his plastic cup. 'Given that Lara is one of those women who would look beautiful if she were wearing

61

a bin bag, then yes, I'm sure she was indeed a glorious bride.'

I move on quickly. 'It sounds like a happy-ever-after, but of course it wasn't. The baby never arrived. We moved to Cornwall, and now I'm doing this, and he's sitting at home waiting. He wants to adopt a child, and I don't. To answer your question of ages ago, no, he doesn't really go to the pub. He has friends at work, but not great friends. It's me he wants.'

'And no one else?' asks Ellen.

'Only one other person, or two or three, but they, it turned out, were never going to be born. He lives for the weekends. At least, I'm pretty sure he does. He could be cavorting around town with a different woman every night of the week, or going to lap-dancing clubs, or who knows what. But I really, seriously doubt it.'

'Yeah,' says Guy. 'I doubt it too. Well, I hope you have a good weekend, Lara. I hope it's not too pressured.'

'Hey, Mr Thomas,' Ellen says, turning to Guy. 'How's your job hunt going? Aren't you meant to be looking for something closer to home?'

He laughs. 'Yeah. Meant to be. On that note, I'm going to get another round in. Same again, ladies?'

'Why not?' I want to sit up all night, drinking with my new friends. I should be sleeping to make sure I am bright and energetic for Saturday. One more drink, however, will not hurt, and then I will have to buy another because it will be my round. After that, however, I will definitely sleep.

Before I stumble off to bed, at two in the morning, I kiss Ellen and Guy good night. Ellen hugs me tight and rubs my back and kisses my cheek. Guy brushes his lips quickly across mine, then holds me by the shoulders and looks into my eyes. I realise that my hands are on his waist, and I leave them there, liking the feel of him too much.

I look into his brown eyes. He looks back. Neither of us says anything. We could kiss properly at this point, but just as I think it might be about to happen, I pull away.

'Good night,' I say quickly.

He laughs quietly and steps back. 'Night, Lara. Sleep tight.'

It's chemicals, I tell myself as I lie on my back and feel the train bumping me westwards. It's pheromones and things like that. It's nothing else. I am married and so is he, and these things will happen from time to time. You just have to be aware of it and make sure everything is under control.

By the time I drift off to sleep, it's nearly time to wake up again and pretend that it never happened.

chapter six

It is one of those clear Cornish mornings, and as I step off the train on to the platform, a breeze stings my face and lifts up every strand of my hair. I had no energy to do anything but run my fingers through it this morning.

I look around, half expecting Sam to be here, even though I told him to stay at home and put the coffee on. My head is swimming with stale alcohol, and my morning world is disconcertingly blurry around the edges. I know I look terrible, with lank hair and no make-up, and yesterday's work clothes on because they were the nearest.

I nearly kissed Guy last night. I look back at the stationary train, wanting to see his face at a window, but there is no one. Other people are getting off here, most of them with work-style bags, a few with holiday suitcases. I want to ask every single one of them about their lives, to see who else is messing things up quite as badly as this.

The grey-black stone of the buildings at Truro station is lit up by the autumn sunlight, so much so that even they are verging on the dazzling. I smile at the tiny station, liking the fact that it is Cornwall's major transport hub at the same time as being a fraction the size of Paddington or any other London station. It is barely as big as a Tube station: it consists of two and a half platforms, two bridges, a small ticket hall, an inept barrier system and the inevitable branch of the Pumpkin café.

The Falmouth train is leaving at 7.14, in eight minutes' time. I turn and walk up to the small platform, Platform 1, concentrating on banishing my nausea, preparing myself to go home and be the wife Sam deserves. I should have put some proper clothes on. On the next train I will at least sort out my hair and try to apply some foundation.

The sleeper train pulls away, heading yet further west. I look again, but there is still no Guy.

Nothing happened between us. It was just a moment, or an evening of moments, that culminated in nothing. It is fine.

Falmouth Docks station, at the end of the line, is right below our house. I look up as my little train, carrying just me and, as far as I can see, two other people – a woman from the night train and a young man who got on at Penryn – approaches the station. Sam is not there. I wanted him to be in the conservatory, waving, with breakfast on the go.

As I step down, I gasp as he rushes up and clasps me tightly to him. I can hardly breathe, so I try to push him away, laughing.

'Hi, Sam,' I say, hoping I do not smell of train booze. He smells wholesome: he has clearly just showered and shaved. I make myself savour his familiarity and dependability. I am lucky to have this man here, waiting for me.

'Oh, Lara.' He nuzzles my hair. 'You're back, honey. Now we can live for a few days. The sun's shining for you.'

'Yes,' I agree, grinning up at him. 'I'm back. Come on.' I look up at the house, ugly and dependable, and I am happy to be back. I am. 'Is there some coffee with my name on it up there?' I ask.

'Yes! There is! There's coffee with the word "Lara" running through it like a stick of rock. You can't read it, because it's written in coffee, but it's there all right.'

'Wonderful! Let me at it.'

He looks almost imperceptibly disappointed in me already. 'Of course,' he says. 'Come on then. Let's get you coffeed up.'

We walk across the car park together, Sam wheeling my little bag.

'How was your week?' I ask, strangely formal. 'At work and stuff? And what did you do in the evenings?'

I have to ask this, even though we speak every day.

'It was fine,' he says, lifting my bag to carry it up the set of stairs that cuts through from the station car park to the front of our house. 'It was, in fact, phenomenally tedious. You absolutely can't do this job for more than your six-month contract, OK, sweetheart? I can't bear it without you. You know, the moment I see your train coming into the station, everything's all right. I'm so bored without you. We belong together. We always have done. I hate having the bed to myself. I hate sitting here playing Scrabble against myself on my phone.'

I laugh, without meaning to.

'Is that what you do? You play Scrabble against yourself on the phone?'

'I know! It's manly, isn't it?' He stops, turns to me and bites his lip. 'Do you want to know the worst thing about it? It's this: the reason I mess about on my phone is so that I have a legit reason to be holding it in my hand and staring at it, because all I'm really doing is waiting for you to call.'

'Sam! Tell me that's not true!'

'OK. It's not true.'

'It is, isn't it?' I want to shrink away from him. I must not.

'So how was the train? You look tired.'

He is unlocking our front door. I look at his back and imagine the hurt expression that would appear on his face if I told him the truth: I am tired because I was drinking gin and wine until two with my new great friends, and discussing him in some depth. And by the way, a handsome man pressed his knee against mine and I liked it. Then I nearly kissed him.

'I never sleep well on the train,' I say instead.

'I know. You poor thing. We could look at the flights sometime, if you wanted?'

'No, I enjoy it really. Honestly. A bit of coffee and I'll be perfectly all right. And breakfast. I couldn't stomach the railway croissant this morning. I'm starving.'

'Well, that's good news, because I'm going to make you the best breakfast you've ever had in your entire life,' he says, and I put my handbag down, and take off my coat, and go to the coffee machine and pour myself a cup. I am home.

That afternoon we go to one of the pubs in town. It is still sunny, but cold, with a wind blowing straight off the Atlantic. I am wearing my Cornwall uniform of skinny jeans, a blue and white striped top and a coat I bought in New York five years ago, before we spent all our money on useless fertility treatment. Sam looks every inch the Cornish shipyard worker in a massive cuddly fleece, jeans and clunky Timberland boots, again purchased years ago when we had cash.

'Cheers,' I say with a bright smile, holding up my vodka and Coke. Short of Red Bull, which would have raised an eyebrow, that seemed like the most stimulants I could cram into one glass. The alcohol makes me feel sick, coming as it does on top of an unshakeable secret hangover, but I press on, and soon I feel a million times better.

'Lara!'

I look round, grateful to whoever this might turn out to be, and see Iris. I have not seen her since I bustled her out the day she came for tea. I still feel bad about that.

'Hello!' I pat the wooden seat next to me. We are sitting at a huge round wooden table, and Sam and I are, naturally, right next to each other. There are acres of table free, kilometres of bench. 'Come and sit down. Sam, you remember Iris.'

'Yes,' says Sam, verging on the rude. 'How are you?'

'Oh, you know,' says Iris. She is looking more eccentric than ever, or perhaps she just seems that way to me, used as I am now to corporate London. She is wearing a pair of striped tights, a tiny velvet skirt that, I have to admit, she carries off magnificently, and a fluffy jumper. Her hair is still dark at the roots and blond at the ends, and it is loose down her back. 'Fine,' she adds. 'How are you? Aren't you working in London these days?'

'Yes, that's right.' I do not want to go into details. 'Back for the weekend. How about you? What are you up to?'

She smiles. 'Oh, nothing much. Working. Staying at home with my cats. Dancing round the kitchen. Nothing as interesting as you.'

I remember that she has a boyfriend whom she described as 'a recluse', and that the two of them rarely leave the house.

'How's your partner?' I ask.

'He's great, thanks. He's well. I miss London, actually. Occasionally.'

Sam snorts. 'Yeah, right! You live here, in the best place in the world.'

'I know. Easy to miss city life from a distance. Hey, Sam, it must be nice having Lara back?'

He nods. 'Certainly is.'

'I won't barge in any longer,' says Iris, getting up. 'I'll leave you two to it.'

'Are you sure?' I ask. 'Join us for a drink.'

Sam starts to stand up. 'What can I get you?' he asks, in a tone that clearly conveys that he wants her to insist on leaving.

She takes the hint and waves her hands theatrically. 'No, absolutely not. Thank you, though. I need to get going anyhow. Can't be drunk in charge of a bike again. Hey, have fun. Enjoy London. And if you're ever in Budock, look me up.'

'Thanks,' I say, and I watch her weaving her way through the crowds and disappearing. I wish she'd had her boyfriend with her: they could have sat with us and we could have had a drink together and the intensity of everything would have been diluted. We would have been like a normal couple, with friends.

'Enjoy London?' Sam looks confused. 'Weird thing to say.'

'Oh, she was just being nice. Hey, Sam, do you want to come to London one weekend?' Getting him a surprise trip for Christmas suddenly doesn't seem like a very good idea after all. 'We could drink cocktails and go to the Globe Theatre and things like that. Stay in a nice hotel. How about you do the reverse commute one weekend? Christmas shopping and stuff.'

'Hmm. Could do.'

He hates the idea.

'Don't worry. It was just a thought.'

He looks up. 'Oh, here we go again. Bloody hell. Adrian.'

A man in a pale blue V-neck jumper is standing between us.

'You two! Nice to see you out. Hey, Lara. Thanks for putting a smile on this one's face. He's been moping about since you left.'

'I didn't leave,' I tell him. I have never liked this man, one of Sam's colleagues. 'As you can see, I'm here.'

'Yes, yes, but he's quite the moper during the week. He misses his wife. Sweet. The rest of us would jump at the chance, you know what I mean, but not our Sam. You've got a good one here.'

'I know,' I say, turning away, forgetting to pretend to be polite.

'Yes,' says Adrian. 'Well. Have a happy weekend. Have lots of fun together. You know what I mean.'

As soon as he is out of earshot, I say: 'That man is such a twat.'

Sam looks hurt. 'He's all right, you know. Him and his wife keep inviting me to dinner.'

'You should go, then. Since you like him.'

I watch a seagull landing on the recently vacated table next to ours, and extracting crisps from a ripped-open packet that instantly blows away.

'No. You hate him.'

'I won't be there.'

'You want me to keep myself busy?'

I look at him. 'Of course I want you to keep busy, you idiot. I don't have a moment in London to pause. Then suddenly it's Friday. I want you to do the same. It makes it easier.'

Sam tries to swirl his pint around, but a bit slops over the edge of the glass and on to his hand. I watch him lick it off, relieved to find myself overwhelmed, at last, by tenderness.

'Shall we go to the cinema tonight?' I ask him, remembering the day we met.

'The cinema?' He thinks about it. 'Is there anything on?'

'There'll be something.'

'And we can afford it?'

'Yes. Nowadays, we can afford it.'

'You're sure? The last thing we need is for you to be doing this job and us to fritter the money away and end up back where we started.'

'Sam. We've been through this. We're not even going to go for dinner anywhere more expensive than Harbour Lights until the debts are paid off. What we *can* do is spend, what is it? Fifteen quid? Going to watch a film. Another few pounds on a drink to take in with us. It's fine.'

I shiver in my lightweight coat and think of the money I spend in London without even noticing it. Tuesday will be the first day of November. The past month has been tempestuously autumnal: sunny for five minutes, then suddenly hailing, then sunny again. When I have been in Falmouth, the sky has filled with rainbow after rainbow. They must happen in London, but I never notice a rainbow in London. There is always a building in the way, or something happening at eye level.

'Cold?' my husband asks, and I nod. 'Let's go home.'

'It's already been a month,' I remind him, as we cut through the marina, using the five-digit code to get through the heavy metal gates. We are not supposed to do this, but whenever they change the code, Sam finds out the new one from work, and we use it as a cut-through constantly. It saves us a few minutes, but more than that, it is always interesting: today, for instance, there are some dressed-down but clearly rich people down on the wooden jetty, fussing around next to a small yet magnificent yacht. They look up as the gate slams behind us, and raise their hands in an efficient wave of acknowledgement. If we have the code to the marina, we are in their circle and worthy of a wave. Our feet clang as we cross the metal bridge, and there is, as there always is, a puddle on the other side of it which requires nimble skirting.

When the second heavy gate has clanged shut behind us, Sam takes my hand. I like the way it feels. In spite of everything, we fit together in the same way we always have. We will be, I suddenly know, all right. He is pining away at home, not just for me, because that would be pathetic in a man who is approaching forty, but for the family life that should have been going on around him. We have never spoken of it, but I know that imaginary scenes from that life-that-never-was ambush him at every turn. I picture him at home in the evening, probably eating a bowl of cereal for pudding, with the television on. From the corner of his eye he catches a glimpse of a serious four-year-old, the child we would have had if it had worked out the way we blithely assumed it was going to, before it didn't. There is a baby asleep downstairs in the smallest bedroom, and the two- and four-year-olds share the bigger one.

Instead, he is all alone. We haven't spoken about adoption lately, but I know he is thinking about it. For the moment, I want to avoid the topic.

'Shall we order a pizza?' I am using my brightest voice to mask the fact that I am desperate for hangover food. Sam is standing in the conservatory, which juts out from the side of the house and, depending on my mood, makes me feel either that I am hanging over an abyss, or that I am suspended magically over the whole world. He is staring out over the docks and the water, to the mansions across the estuary, the curve of the town around the water of the mouth of the Fal.

He does not reply. I go to stand next to him. He puts an arm around my shoulders without looking round.

'We can't have Domino's,' he says, and as I watch he seems to pull himself together, to drag his focus back from wherever it was and on to me. 'This is your only evening. Earlier we were going to the cinema. Which do you want to do? I could cook for us. Or we could go back out and do something.'

We both look back at the view. It is raining in Penryn, down the river. The clouds that partially obscure it are the dark grey that signifies a downpour. In the foreground, the masts and the buildings that cluster round the harbour are lit by bright sunlight. The lighting makes it look like a dazzling Renaissance artwork. For a second I am in an Old Master painting, in the National Gallery, a figure in the foreground to make the background look more focused.

'Let's stay in and be dry,' I say, knowing that this is what he wants to hear.

He grins at that. 'Good call. I'll throw some food together. You can chat to me while I do it. Then we could have a game of Scrabble.'

I want to laugh at that. It sounds the epitome of dull, but I love Scrabble and always have.

'That sounds like a perfect evening,' I tell him, and now, at last, I mean it.

chapter seven

'Lara! Apparently you were phenomenally impressive.' Jeremy smiles at me. 'Thank you. You see? This is why we had to poach you back from deepest darkest Devon.'

'Cornwall,' I say quietly. He ignores me, shaking his head and smiling to himself.

'You know, Lara. There's no way we're going to let you go after six months.'

I leave work feeling happy. This, I think, is where I belong. This is what I'm good at. I love doing a job that stretches me. I stayed up for most of the night preparing for that, and it is appreciated. Jeremy is the one who agreed to have me back for this project, and the fact that he is so pleased with what I am doing makes me glow. The best thing is that I know he is right to be pleased. I went to a meeting to talk about our development and stood up in a room full of people who despise the concept of 'luxury flats' and talked them all around. We have now lost a significant degree of local opposition.

I even feel good about Olivia. I am going to tell her, I vow. Tonight we are going to be busy. Tomorrow I will tell her that I'm going to leave and find my own place to live.

I am heading straight to the restaurant. There is no need to change, but I nip into the work loos before I go, pull the hairpins out of my hair and shake it loose. It is shorter like this than people think it is, reaching only just below my shoulders. For a second, I try out a fringe, like a child experimenting. I pull a strand of hair above my forehead, and let its ends hang down. It looks horrible.

When my hair is brushed and shiny, I pin it back up. This chignon thing has become my default style. Anything else looks odd now. I started doing it when I started work, in my twenties, because it made me feel like a grown-up, and I never really stopped. Twisting my hair into place and sticking six pins in it is second nature. It got a lot more casual when I wasn't working; but now it is back in its full professional glory. It is crucial for me to look impeccable at work; and I enjoy that more than I could ever admit to anyone.

My work shoes are my best ones, red and high, and I am excellent at walking in them. The rest of my outfit is as boring as it usually is, but my shoes are always special. I have two red pairs now, plus a black pair and some yellow ones. People look twice at my feet, and I like that. I worked hard to learn how to walk on tiptoes, and it is a skill I treasure. Sam thinks it is ridiculous, and he is, doubtless, right. All the same, it pleases me.

I redo my eye make-up and put on lipstick, throwing the piece of tissue paper with smudged dark red kisses on it into the bin. As I'm on my own, I do a quick check of my purse: I always have cash, just in case, and my stash of it is safe and growing. I tell myself I will never need an emergency fund; but all the same, it makes me feel secure.

I never tell anyone about it, because I know it would sound crazy.

I have known for years that I am in danger. You don't get to do what I did and walk away unscathed. He is out of prison, and one day he will come to track me down; because I was the only one who got away.

I wish I could tell Sam, or Guy, or someone. It's too late to mention my past to Sam, and he would never believe it if I tried. I can't tell anyone else if I haven't told my husband. I am stuck.

When I am in London, I imagine eyes following me in a way I have never done in Cornwall. I tell myself, again, not to be paranoid. There are enough problems in my real life, without my adding imaginary ones.

Dad is taking us to Pizza Express, again. Of all the restaurants in London, that is his favourite. He has taken us to Pizza Express on every possible occasion, ever since we were small, and he did it on my first week in this job: I spent an evening being bright and cheerful while Olivia, I later discovered, live-tweeted the entire evening with variations on 'yawn' and 'zzz', hashtagged with the word #family.

We used to complain about dad's restaurant myopia, quietly, just Olivia and me. Moaning about having to go to Pizza Express all the time gave us some of our few moments of sibling bonding.

'Can't we go for a curry?' Olivia would mutter.

'But they don't do dough balls at the curry house!' I would whisper back, feeling wicked and transgressive.

'I know! And he'd never get his American Hot. He'd get . . . other hot food instead. More interesting hot food.'

'That would not do at all.'

It soon degenerated into sniping, but those conversations

give me some of my happiest childhood memories. I tried to do it again with Olivia this morning.

'Pizza Express, hey?' I said, looking at her speculatively. 'We haven't been there for several weeks.'

She shrugged. 'If he's paying, I'm there.'

The shutters were down. The shutters have not risen, even a chink, not once.

I get there first. The young waitress smiles, ticks our booking off on her chart and leads me to a table by the window. I sit and look out at Charlotte Street, wondering how much a little flat in this part of London, Fitzrovia, would set me back. More money than I could possibly afford, for certain. I try to imagine myself telling Sam that I'm spending (and I have to pluck the figure from thin air) fifteen hundred pounds a month, plus council tax and bills, on renting a studio in central London. That is not a conversation I would be able to initiate.

I love this street because it is almost entirely lined with restaurants. If it were up to me, we would be at the Indian vegetarian place up the road, but it is not, and that is fine. I check my phone. Sam has texted me good luck for this evening. I reply quickly, and then, as I press send, see my parents walking past the window and coming into the restaurant.

I stand up and plaster on a big smile. I wish I could kick back with my family, stop putting on a front, be myself. But I am far more myself when I am at work. I am most of all myself, I think suddenly, when I am drinking on the night train home. Guy is in my head again, and I push him away.

'There she is!' says Dad. As I look at him, I notice, as I always do, how old he is. In my head he remains about forty, and whenever I see him I have to fast-forward through time, twenty-five years, to the present day. He is tall, broad-shouldered, and slightly stooped now. His hair is grey and slightly longer than it should be in (I think) an attempt to preserve the fine head of hair of which he was always so proud. He is also morbidly obese, but we never mention that.

His eyes, though, are as piercing as ever. They strike fear into me still. I look at him and I crave approval.

'Hello, Dad,' I say, and kiss him on the cheek.

'Lara.' He smiles. 'You are looking extremely well. Your sister's not arrived yet, then?'

'Not yet. Hi, Mum.'

My mother is blonde and beautiful, but she is also opaque, unknowable, and the least maternal woman imaginable. I rarely give her a moment's thought. For my whole life she has done as she has been told by Dad. I have no idea what goes on in her head, or, behind closed doors, in their relationship. She is a woman who toes the line. I slightly despise her, while Olivia openly and rudely scorns her.

'Hello, dear,' she says, and we all sit down. Entirely predictably, Dad orders a bottle of Montepulciano d'Abruzzo, his standard Pizza Express tipple.

'You lookcd tall just thcn.' IIe leans around the table to look at my feet. 'I thought so! How on earth do you walk in those things?'

'I'm used to it. I like them.'

He shakes his head. 'Women! Your mother's never gone in for that sort of thing. The whole "ladies love shoes" gene passed her by entirely. You carry them off, though, darling, you really do.'

'Lara carries everything off,' Mum agrees, her tone as mild as it always is and always was.

'She does.' He smiles at me. 'So? Ready to chuck it in and run back to Cornwall? Or ready to drag Sam to the city?'

I pout as I ponder this. 'I'm enjoying work,' I tell him. 'Sam hates me being away. He wouldn't move up here, though. I'm happy as I am for now, but I know that's selfish because Sam's not happy at all. I'll do this and then settle back in Cornwall. Probably.'

'Hmm.' He is looking at me with his piercing eyes, but he does not pursue this any further. 'Leon's coming along later, by the way,' he adds, and this cheers me up.

'Sorry I'm late.' Olivia takes the empty seat at our round table. It is directly opposite me, between our parents. I look at her, then quickly away. She has done something to her hair, so it is spiked up a little bit on top. In her red and white striped Breton top and tight black jeans, she looks (as ever) like someone from a magazine. Her eyes are rimmed with kohl, her lips bright red.

'Olivia,' says Dad. He doesn't stand up, because she forestalled that by sitting down so quickly, but he leans across and plants an awkward kiss on her cheek. 'Good to see you. Have some wine.'

'Actually,' she says, 'I'll get a Peroni. If that's allowed.'

'Of course it's allowed.'

They say nothing, but their eye contact is challenging and exclusive. It never takes long.

Now that Olivia is here, conversation becomes stilted. Dad makes a point of looking at her shoes, and wordlessly comparing her tatty-yet-cool Converse with my shiny red heels. Olivia bristles. Mum drinks quickly and fiddles with the stem of the glass so much, in her anxiety, that she knocks it over and smashes it. Dad smoulders with fury and raises his voice at the waiter who comes to clear it away. I try to smooth things over, with him, with Mum, with the waiter. It is a perfect microcosm of the way our family life has always worked.

As a child, I lived in a constant state of heightened anxiety. I knew that, in Olivia's eyes, I was the chosen one, and she, by implication, had been discarded. I courted paternal approval, terrified that one day I might accidentally do something horribly wrong and that Olivia and I might change roles in his eyes.

Dad, though, has never wavered. He has always liked me, always approved of what I have done, appreciated my work, liked the way I have lived my life.

No one knows, not even Mum, that I single-handedly bailed out his business, years ago. We never talk about it. He never paid me back. And no one, not even my father, knows that if I had not bailed him out, I would not be uneasy and scared now, every time I imagine someone spying on me. He never asked where the money came from; I have always assumed his instincts informed him that he was better off not knowing.

It was always going to catch up with me, one day.

I look at Olivia across the table, at her petulant mouth and her sulky face, and I am fourteen again.

I got home from school that day as usual. I never dawdled, but walked sensibly with my sensible friends because, even though Dad was at work, that was the behaviour he expected. When I got home, I went around to the back of the house and let myself in at the back door as usual.

'I'm home,' I called, and put the kettle on; I was self-consciously making an effort to start to drink tea. I took out a mug and the tin of tea bags. 'Do you want a cup of tea?' I called.

'Yes please,' said Mum's voice from somewhere in the house. We lived in Bromley, in the house that is still the parents' home, an ugly Edwardian place. It looked like nothing from the outside, but inside it was strangely huge. I made us both tea, and took mine to the kitchen table, where I started my homework.

'Tea's in the kitchen!' I called. 'Shall I bring it to you?'

'No, darling. I'll be right down.'

Olivia is right. I must have been insufferable: I was so desperate for ongoing approval that I never, ever risked transgressing in any form at all.

Mum came down, smiled vaguely at me, and took her cup of tea.

'All right?' she said.

'Fine,' I assured her.

'Any sign of your sister?'

Both parents call Olivia *my sister* when they speak to me about her. They always have done. She said once that it is because they cannot bear the intimacy of speaking the very name they gave her. She might be right.

'No. I haven't seen her.'

I was two years above her at school. Our paths rarely crossed, and when they did, we carefully ignored one another. She was generally around the fringes of the school grounds, smoking with the cool crowd. I was more likely to be found in the library.

'As long as she's back by five. Your father's coming home early today. He called to say so.'

We both looked at the large clock that hung in the middle of the wall. It was quarter past four. Neither of us said anything.

Dad's key sounded in the front door at three minutes to five. I kept on with my homework, sitting up straight at the dining-room table like a good girl, but my heart was not in it. I was starting to worry, not only about his fury and its consequences, but about Olivia's safety.

He came in beaming. At this point he really was in his forties, and he was tall and strong, in his prime. He was only slightly fat.

He kissed the top of my head. 'Doing your homework? Good girl. What is it? Anything your old dad can help with?'

We discussed long division for a while, before he looked at the ceiling, signifying upstairs, and said: 'And where is that wayward sister of yours?'

Olivia was only twelve. She was banned from doing anything other than coming straight home from school.

'I'm not sure.' I did not dare to attempt to lie for her.

'She's not home?'

'Umm. Not sure. I don't think so.'

'Victoria!' Victoria is Mum's name. It suits her. She needs a formal, unabbreviated name. Like her namesake, she is rarely amused.

Once he had definitively established that she was not back from school, he went straight out to his car. Twenty minutes later he was back, a sulking twelve-year-old in tow.

'You can go to your room and stay there,' I heard him say to her, in an offhand way, as they walked through the door. 'But first, you need to come and see this.'

Then they were in the dining room with me. Olivia was staring at the floor, the epitome of sulkiness.

'I can't be bothered with your behaviour, young lady,' he told her. 'You can stay in your room until morning, but other than that, this is going to be its sole consequence.' He took out his wallet, opened it, and peeled out a stash of notes. 'This is your allowance for the rest of the year, Olivia. Twenty pounds a month, nine months to go. One hundred and eighty pounds. Why would I pay you when you behave like this? Should I give you an "allowance" for ignoring even the simplest of rules? Of course I won't be doing that. Lara, on the other hand, came straight home from school and started her homework. As she always does. Not only does Lara's allowance remain unchanged, I'm giving her this on top of it.'

He put the cash on the table next to me. I remember staring at it, knowing that things had never gone this far before. I did not dare to hand it back. I could not pick it up. It sat next to my maths books, red hot and impossible to ignore.

Olivia turned and stormed out of the room, visibly restraining herself from slamming the door. Dad put a hand on my head, ruffled my hair, and left the room himself. As I listened to Olivia's footsteps storming up the stairs, I knew she would hate me for ever, because of this.

And she does. Not just because of that, but partly.

'I'll have a Giardiniera, please.' I smile at the waitress. 'And could we have some tap water?'

'No way,' says Olivia. 'A Giardiniera? They probably have your photo in every branch of Pizza Express, with your order written next to it. "This woman has partaken of nothing but Giardiniera for the past twenty years. Do not bother to ask what she wants." Good to see you branching out, sis.'

She makes a point of ordering a new pizza, one that comes with a hole in the middle that is filled with salad, just to demonstrate to me how open-minded and impulsive she is.

'Evening all!'

I look up, delighted and relieved at the sound of my godfather's voice.

'Leon!' I get to my feet and hug him. He is standing right beside the table, having somehow slipped in without any of us noticing. I don't care about Olivia now. Leon is Dad's best friend from university, and, oddly, he is my best friend in the world. He always took a distant yet friendly godfatherly interest in me, until I really needed him. Then he came through for me like no one else ever has. Leon is the one person who knows everything.

'Lovely to see you,' he says quietly. 'You OK?'

'Better now you're here,' I tell him, sensing Olivia's mocking gaze, not caring. Leon is, like my father, in his mid sixties. Unlike my father, who is increasingly looking like a heart attack waiting to happen, Leon gets more stylish and better-looking as he ages. His grey hair is swept back and reaches almost down to his collar, while his bone structure is somehow enhanced by his ageing skin. His clothes help, too: he has always dressed impeccably, and these days he looks like the chic European man you would find in Paris or Milan. Though she has never said anything explicitly, I know from the smirks Olivia gives me every time his name is mentioned that she thinks we have had an affair, perhaps that we are still having one. She is wrong, though nothing I could say would ever convince her of that. Leon and I have a far stronger bond than that.

He turns to the rest of the family.

'Olivia,' he says, with a warm smile. 'You're looking spectacularly stylish this evening. As ever, yet somehow more so.'

She doesn't reply, but inclines her head towards him, one stylish person to another. I sit down as Leon kisses

Mum on each cheek, shakes Dad's hand and pulls up a chair between me and Mum, who looks at him with a small smile, then picks up a doughball and starts tearing it into tiny pieces. Dad refills everyone's glasses. The room echoes with the sound of other people's friendly chatter.

'So, how's the Wilberforce family?' Leon asks, looking around.

'Fine.' Olivia answers quickly, which is unusual. She has pushed her glass away, and in fact I notice that she has not drunk anything. 'Actually, there is some news.'

I close my eyes. Whatever this is, I can tell from her tone that I am not going to like it. In a second she is going to start telling everyone why I am such a terrible lodger. I will be forced to defend myself, and there will be carnage.

She notices.

'Lara, you've got your eyes closed. I'm not going to hit you.'

'I know. Look, I've opened them. Is that all right?'

'Jesus. Look. Everyone. It's not anything terrible. I've got used to the idea now and it's actually a positive thing.'

Someone drops something on the other side of the restaurant, and the whole room is suspended for a second as everyone listens to what must be several plates smashing on the floor. Then normality is resumed, with staff rushing around and conversations starting up again; except on our table, where we are all staring at Olivia with transparent dread.

She rolls her eyes. I realise what she is going to say just before she says it.

'I'm pregnant.'

I watch as all three of them turn their gazes to me. Everyone but Olivia is now checking my reaction.

'Congratulations.' I do not look at her. 'That's lovely.'

'Yeah. Cheers.'

'When's it due?'

'April. April the twenty-third.'

'Shakespeare's birthday. No pressure then.'

Of course she is pregnant. I make myself inhale. I have put all of that behind me, have determinedly moved on, but the years of monthly dashed hopes, followed by the injections and intrusive scans, the bills, the torment and the marital strains that changed our relationship fundamentally all come flashing through my mind before I shove them away.

Dad leans forward.

'Do you mind me asking one thing?' he says, his voice dangerously casual. 'Who's the father?'

She glares. 'Yes, I do mind. I mind you asking who the father is before saying congratulations or being pleased that you're getting a grandchild after all. Yes. I mind that, so I'm not going to tell you.'

'Oh, for fuck's sake, Olivia.'

I stiffen. I hate it when Dad swears. It always means danger.

'For fuck's sake yourself,' she retorts. 'You only want a grandchild if it comes from the sainted fucking Lara, don't you? You don't want my lesser genes passed on, do you? Well, Lara's not come up with the goods and it seems that, accidentally, I have and that's that. Get used to it. Things change.'

Oddly, it is Mum who rises to this. She does it while Dad is still drawing breath.

'Olivia,' she says, leaning forward, tucking a lock of hair behind her ear. She so infrequently steps into a row that I am transfixed. Her voice is soft, rarely used, so we all listen. 'That's not fair on Lara. You've taken us by surprise, that's all. Give us a few moments to get used to this, please.'

My sister laughs. 'Right! Of course. Because this is all about you guys.'

'No,' says Mum, and she is perfectly calm. No one has the faintest idea of what goes on beneath the surface with her, so this is all we can go on. 'It is, of course, about you, and even more than that, it's about the baby. And it will be lovely to have a baby in the family again.'

Everyone but Olivia, I realise, is still looking at me, while pretending they are not.

I look at my sister, and she holds my gaze with triumph in her eyes. Although I have heard her crying – and now I suppose I know why that is – and although I know very well that she did not plan for this, she has beaten me on something. She is revelling in this fact.

I wanted a baby. I did. However much I have determinedly moved on, everything but the baby is plan B and it always will be.

'You OK?' Leon says quietly.

'No,' I say. 'Come for a drink?'

He looks around the table.

'Of course.'

I make myself stay calm.

'Olivia,' I say. 'I'm happy for you. I really am. Congratulations. But right now I'm going to go and have a drink, away from here. I'll move out of the flat too. I've been meaning to for a while and you'll be needing the space.'

'OK.' She shrugs, as if the thing I have been steeling myself to do for so long is no particular deal. I look away. I will see her smirking, whether she is actually doing it or not.

'Lara, are you sure?' asks Dad. I am on my feet now, checking my bag is with me.

'Yes.'

'I'll go with her, Bernie.' Leon's hand is pressed to my shoulder, briefly.

'Thanks, Leon.' Dad nods.

Mum looks at me with a pale smile and sips her drink without a word.

We step out on to Charlotte Street, where people are hurrying around through the dusk. Everyone has a place to go, a coat pulled tight, a scarf. The balmy September of six weeks ago when I started my job has settled into uncompromising winter.

It is almost completely dark, and the street lamps are lit. Although it is not raining, water seems to hang in the air, dampening my face and hair as I walk.

'Here.' Leon steers me into a pub, a small one that is full but not too full. We find a little table in a corner and he makes me sit down, then goes to the bar without asking what I want.

He comes back with four drinks: two are small and two are tall and clear.

'This first.' It is an amber liquid. Whisky, I think, or perhaps brandy. I sip it and force a smile. It warms me all the way down.

'Drinks like this are great,' I tell him. 'Everyone should drink more of them. The ones that are so warm they burn you on the inside. Good for winter.'

'Drink it up.' I look at him and take another sip.

'Thanks for this.'

'I'm sorry we haven't seen you much since you've been up here. You've not been happy at your sister's. I know that. Where are you going to go? You're welcome to the spare room, but I'm sure you'd like more independence.'

'Thanks. There's a place near work, a corporate sort of hotel. I might get a room there for a bit and see what happens.'

'A hotel? Lara, that doesn't sound like the best way of getting your debts at home paid off.'

I shrug and put the glass down, empty.

'I want a bit of space. Just for a while. I'll sort out something more sensible in a week or two.'

'And how are things in Cornwall?'

I realise I have not given Sam a thought.

'Oh, they're OK.'

Our eyes meet. Leon told me years ago that I shouldn't marry Sam because I would end up bored. I attempt to acknowledge the fact that he was right with a look, and to signal that we are not going to talk about it.

I pick up the second drink and sip it.

'Vodka and slimline tonic,' he says.

'Thanks.'

'Your sister is poisonous, but even she will not have done this on purpose.'

'I know. I know she didn't. I've heard her crying at night, and having muffled phone conversations. I've got no idea who the father is because she wouldn't tell me if she had a boyfriend. It might be the tall, stringy guy. Allan. He seems nice. But I know it's not about me, it's about her. I can't ban everyone around me from getting pregnant. It's just . . .'

'I know. It's still raw for you.'

'You know what? It is. I didn't realise how much it is. I've just been telling myself that I'm half relieved, that Sam's the one who's upset and that I'm perfectly happy to move on.' I knock back half my second drink in one go. 'But it's not that straightforward. And I do think it's destroyed Sam and me. I asked you to get me this job because I was desperate to get away from him. Absolutely desperate. What does that say? Nothing good. We're finished. I know that, but I can't tell him because he has no idea.'

He raises an eyebrow, waiting for the rest.

'And,' I continue, because Leon is the only person I could possibly tell, 'I've kind of met someone else.'

I look at him.

'Mmm.' He nods. 'That's difficult, sweetheart, but I'm not surprised.'

'Oh God, Leon. I don't know what to do. I have to stay away from him.'

My godfather nods again.

'Things will be much less complicated if you stay away. Work out what you want. Do you want to tell me about him?'

I think about Guy, about his warm eyes, his thick hair, the muscles of his forearms. I think about the reality of him, and shake my head.

'No,' I tell him. 'It'd only encourage me.' Then I realise what it is that I really want to ask him. 'Leon,' I add. 'Look. You're the only one who knows about what I did.' I pause, wondering whether to say it, but I cannot let the words pass my lips. He knows. 'In Asia,' is all I can add as clarification. 'This sounds stupid, but sometimes I think it's catching up with me. I knew I wouldn't get away with it. I did bad things to scary people. It terrifies me.'

He narrows his eyes and fixes me with a serious stare. 'Has anything happened?'

I try to smile. 'No. I just . . . I don't feel safe. I think people are watching me. I don't know which is worse: if they really are, or if I'm cracking up and imagining it.' I look at Leon and feel instantly better, and a bit silly. 'Am I imagining it?'

He leans forward. 'I'd say so. You're under a lot of stress, Lara, but not because of the past. That's long been over and done with. Because of the present. The future. You don't want to adopt a child, and Sam does. That's a confrontation that's going to have to happen, and you know it. This new man, whoever he is, is a distraction. As are these thoughts of Thailand, though keep a proper eye out. If anything actually happens, you must act. But I think, to be honest, that you're trying to come up with other crises to avoid having to look at the real one.'

I sigh. 'You're right,' I tell him, and I force myself to think of the present, instead of the past. 'I know you are.'

I knock the rest of the drink back in one go, and try to think of a way of breaking Olivia's news to Sam.

chapter eight

On Friday night, all I want to do is drink and talk. The only people I want to talk to are Ellen and Guy. I get to the station early, but because they don't serve alcohol in the first-class lounge, I go up the escalators to the pub at the top of the station.

This smells like a generic pub. It feels like a generic pub. I'm vaguely surprised that it's possible to be in a station without feeling as if you're in a station. A man sits at a table reading a tabloid article about cancer; a couple with big suitcases sit opposite each other, a packet of crisps torn open on the table between them, him with a pint of lager in front of him, her with half a pint. No one looks up as I walk to the bar, sit on a bar stool and order a vodka and tonic from an implausibly young blond barman with acne scars.

I knock it back. I don't think or talk. Then I order another one and do the same.

I spent the night of Olivia's revelation, the night of the letter, in her box room, carefully avoiding her in the morning, and packing enough stuff to keep me going until

I can bear to go back and pick up the rest. Last night I slept at the hotel in St Paul's. It is a business hotel, perfectly tolerable though utterly impractical financially.

All the same, it beats going to the place my father insists on referring to as 'home', and commuting in from there, a grown woman living with my parents.

'Come on, Lara,' he said on the phone, that evening. 'It's your home. It always will be. Let us look after you.'

I shook my head. 'I can't, Dad,' I told him. I was as firm with him as I have ever dared to be. 'I live in London to avoid the commute. I need to be near work so I can give it everything I've got during the week. Honestly, I do. I need to stay late, go in early. Thank you, though. I'll find a little studio or something.'

'Your sister . . .' he mused, and I tensed, desperate to defuse him.

'She's all right,' I said quickly. 'It's not her fault. I'm pleased for her, I really am. I just need to be away from her for a while.'

'She is not all right,' he corrected me. 'She had no business being so cruel. Now, are you sure? It would cheer the place up no end having you around, and to be honest, I could do with your level-headed advice on some matters.'

I concentrated on sounding neutral while my heart contracted with dread.

'We can get together any time you want for something like that,' I said, hoping with all my being that we would not. 'I don't really get time for a lunch break, but we can meet up after work sometime. I need to be close to the office, though.'

To my enormous relief, he accepted it. I am now keeping as far from every member of my toxic family as I possibly can.

*

It is only when I am sitting on the train, a traditional Friday gin and tonic in my hand, Ellen next to me and Guy opposite, that I start to do anything close to relaxing. I sit back and listen to Ellen relating a story about a Skype conversation with Singapore, and I find myself exhaling and kicking my shoes off.

I laugh as the story ends.

'You all right, Lara?' Guy asks. When I look up, I see that he is watching me with some curiosity. I put up my barrier, trying to be distant with him.

'Oh, fine,' I tell him. 'Just a bit . . . tense.'

'Your sister?' asks Ellen.

'No. Well, yes. It is. Quite a week. Big family showdown. I don't want to talk about it.' I look at her expression and laugh. 'Not because I'm traumatised. But because I'm just so fucking bored of it.'

I hardly ever swear. I like the way it sounds. I take a sip of my drink.

'Let's talk about something else then,' Guy says at once. 'Do you want to hear my current issue?'

'Oh yes please.' I lean over slightly, towards him. 'What is your current issue?'

'Let me guess,' says Ellen, her voice dry. 'There's a job come up in the West Country.'

Guy laughs, and his eyes crinkle at the corners. I like that. 'You and I have been train buddies for too long,' he tells her, and she raises her glass to him. He turns to me. 'Yes indeed. You know I live outside Penzance with my family? Beyond Penzance, near Sennen – nearly as close to the edge as you can get?'

'You moved there to be close to your wife's family.'

'That's right. Diana's dad died very suddenly, three years ago. Long story, but we ended up moving down so that

Di could look after her mum, who's frail in one sense, but stronger than a team of oxen in another. The kids were in the early years of secondary school, so they made the world's biggest fuss about the move, and to be honest, I was silently cheering them on. Surrey to Cornwall is a big thing if you're thirteen. If you're any age. But we had to do it, I knew that really. Poor old Betty wasn't going to be able to look after herself, and she was definitely not in the market for moving to the Home Counties, so we had to go to her. Di always said it was payback for her happy childhood, and maybe it was. Actually Di was delighted at the chance to move back to where she's from.'

'But there aren't exactly many jobs down there.'

He nods. 'Precisely, Lara. There's nothing down there for me. I would literally have had to get a job in Tesco. McDonald's. Argos. So we agreed that I'd do this and keep an eye out for something closer to home. I like my life this way. I'd go crazy if I had to live in West Cornwall the whole time. In a house full of teenagers – I only have two, but they do fill the house – and with my mother-in-law rearranging everything the whole time. So I've settled into this way of doing things really rather happily. Just me, during the week, in a shabby B&B room, but I don't care. And now there's only a bloody job come up in Truro. I mean, Truro! Since when was there a good job in Truro?'

'What is it?' Ellen's voice is mild, and when I glance at her I see the amusement on her face. She sees me looking, and winks.

'Town solicitors, but a big practice. It would involve buying a stake and going in as a partner.'

'Oh, Guy. You would be the perfect man for the job.'

'I know! I'm going to have to make a token effort. Then make sure I fuck it up. More drinks, ladies?'

At one in the morning, Ellen stands up.

'Right,' she says. 'Charming as this is, it's my bedtime. We've got a busy weekend ahead. I'll see you on Sunday, guys.'

'Night, Ellen,' I say.

'Good night, Johnson,' says Guy. 'Won't be far behind you.'

'I should definitely go to bed in a minute,' I agree. 'We'll be in Truro in six hours.'

'Six hours! That's a surprisingly long time, actually,' Guy muses. 'I think we can stay up a little while longer. I know! I was going to show you how to use Twitter, wasn't I? What's your email address?'

I laugh at this pathetic excuse as Guy starts fiddling with his phone, and tell him. Soon he hands the phone to me.

'There you go. Your Twitter account. Go on, write something. Your password's lovelylara.'

'Oh, thanks. Classy password.'

'I know. If I were sober, you'd have had a better one.'

I stab at his phone until I have written 'Trying to work out how to use Twitter.' Then I pass it back.

'That's one thing to cross off the list, then,' I tell him. 'I've written my first, and definitely my last, tweet. Another thing my sister can do better than me, but at least I've tried. Now I'm going to go to bed.'

I think of Sam at home, desperately awaiting my return, pinning all his happiness on the expectation of a perfect weekend. If I got six hours' sleep, I would be in an acceptable state for that. I would fall in with whatever he has planned, and I would be able to do it properly.

I am about to stand up when I realise that my leg is pressing against Guy's under the table. I note that it has been for quite some time. I leave it there.

'OK.' My voice is quiet. The bar is open all night, but at the moment there is no one here, under its bright lights, but us. Everything has changed.

'Lara,' says Guy. He opens his mouth to say something more, thinks better of it, and stops.

'Yes.'

'This is . . .'

'I know.' I do not, of course, know. I have no idea whether he means 'this is dangerous', or 'this is suddenly different, compelling and wildly, all-encompassingly exciting'. This is good: that is bad.

The atmosphere between us is electric. He leans forward and takes my hand. His is warm, his skin dry. I look down at our two hands, entangled with one another. They should not be like that, but they look right together. We are holding each other's right hands, so wedding rings are not part of the tableau.

'Can I come over to your side of the table?' he asks.

I look into his dark eyes and see nothing but warmth.

'Yes,' I whisper, and I watch him slide out of his seat. Then he is beside me, and his hand is on my waist. I am turning towards him, in spite of myself, and tipping my face up to meet his.

It is an odd thing, kissing a man who is not your husband. There is only one person in the world I am allowed to kiss like this, and the fact that this is not that person makes me so intensely excited, so desperate to cram as much as I can into these moments before reality catches up, that I feel every nerve-ending in my body tingling.

Guy's mouth is new. His lips are soft, and his tongue gentle as it explores my mouth. I am doing something gloriously and utterly forbidden. It has been many years since I did something that I was absolutely not allowed to do. My long-dormant bad side comes joyously to the surface, and rejoices as Guy's hands move from my waist upwards. One of his hands is on my breast, then inside my top, finding its way inside my bra.

The sensible me wins out for a while, and I pull away. He withdraws his hand.

'Oh Christ,' he says. 'Lara. You are amazing. Apologies for overstepping.'

This is the moment. I recognise it even as it happens. This, I know, is the moment when I could draw back. I could call it a mistake, forget it ever happened, and avoid Guy for the next few weeks.

Or I could do what I actually do.

'You're not overstepping,' I say quietly. 'Or if you are, we both are.'

He grins, and his whole face is alight. He leans in close.

'You're sure? I mean, you must have seen me looking at you. I knew it the instant I saw you, which was quite possibly the first time you travelled on this train. I just . . . I mean, just because you're married, that doesn't mean you don't notice people. And then I got to know you. Oh God, listen to me. No one tells you you'll still be able to feel that way at forty-four. Is this a midlife crisis? It is, isn't it?'

'Guy? Shh. It's just two people meeting each other on a train.'

One of his arms is around my shoulders. I lean into him and feel him kiss the top of my head.

'I want to take you back to my compartment and undress you,' he says quietly. 'What do you think?'

I make an effort to control myself. 'Yes,' I tell him. 'Yes, but.'

'Yes. But . . .?'

'But it would feel like too much.' I should not say the next part, but I do. 'I would love to. You know I would. Every part of my body is screaming at me to go for it. But we can't, Guy. Because we're both married. A kiss is one thing: you know what would happen if we were in a little locked room together.'

'I do. I very much do. OK, you're right. Let's be a bit sensible.' I can hear the reluctance in his voice. The knowledge that I could be, right now, having sex on a train with a handsome man who is not my husband, and that it is my decision not to, gives me a surge of tremendous power.

I think of Sam. I think of Diana, at her home near Penzance, dealing with her elderly mother and her two teenagers, waiting for her husband to come back for the weekend. I imagine her desperately hoping that he gets the job in Truro and comes back to live with her again. I know he has no intention of getting that job: does she, I wonder, know that too?

'We really can't do this,' I say. 'I've been married for nine years, and I've never done anything like it. You have an effect on me, Guy. No one's ever done this to me before. Just one person, once, in the past. But I'm not going to fall into bed with you.'

'Right,' he says. 'And in the cold light of day, no doubt, I will appreciate your scruples.'

He leans back down towards me, and we are kissing again. I decide not to let him know how easily he could change my mind. I am exhilarated. I do not care, for these moments, about Olivia, about my parents, my marriage, my strange transitory life. Guy makes me forget it all. It is transgressive, but, briefly, the fact that he makes me happy cancels out everything else.

I do not sleep at all. I lie in my narrow bed, staring at the ceiling in the sickly glow of the light that never quite goes off, and I think of nothing but Guy. I try, in spite of myself, to work out the mechanics of the tiny sleeping compartment. There is no chance of two people sharing one of these beds. Sex in here would have to be a functional thing, not a comfortable one. I picture us standing up, picture myself straddling him on the little bed. I try to think of other things, sensible ones, but I cannot.

I step on to the platform at Truro aware that the spell is breaking. I am going to have to pull myself together, to let Sam have the weekend he deserves. I will drink as much coffee as I can, and I will not flag.

I stand on the Falmouth platform, and catch sight of Guy's face at one of the windows in a door as it flashes by. The glimpse of him is so brief that it is impossible to read his expression.

By the time I reach Falmouth Docks, I have realised that I was mad.

I can see Sam waving from the conservatory window, holding up a coffee cup, and I make myself smile and wave back. I kissed another man. I hate myself. Sam is entirely good and would never believe me capable of such an act. I have always been a good wife, and now I am a bad one, and nothing will ever be able to change that.

I walk slowly towards the end of the tiny platform. A crane swings around in the docks to my left, and there is a sudden siren, and a series of industrial beeps. In front of the station there is an oddly placed block of student housing, and I watch a girl walking towards it across the car park, clearly wearing last night's clothes fumbling with a set of keys.

I stop and draw in a deep breath. I must pretend that it never happened. Sam must never know: it would hurt him far too much. I close my eyes and tell myself to be nice.

'Darling!'

I jump, and gasp. Of course he has run down to the station. Of course he is here. He has been waiting for me to step off this train for five days. I have been lost in my own angst, and this flawless man has been sad solely because I was not with him. Meanwhile, he has been (I admit it to myself) very low down my list of priorities.

My stomach contracts with guilt. He is hugging me. I make a conscious effort to relax. I deliberately loosen my grip on all my muscles, only realising as I do so how entirely tense I was.

'Hello, darling,' I say into his shoulder. I will never do anything like that ever again. I love Sam. I would be nothing without him. 'Sorry,' I mutter. 'I was miles away then.'

'Were you?' He sounds amused, rather than worried. 'Where were you?'

'I was thinking how wonderful it is to be home.'

'Not as wonderful as it is for me to have you home. Your coffee's ready. And I'll do some poached eggs, shall I? Would you like that?' He takes my bag. 'How on earth do you walk in those shoes! Come on.'

I smile. 'My London shoes. I'll change into boots.'

'That's the way. How are you feeling? What would you like to do today?'

I try not to wince as I give the answer Sam deserves.

'I would like to do whatever you want to do. Shall we

go out somewhere?' I turn and look back at the view of Falmouth behind us. The sky is grey, but pale grey; the sun is trying to break through. 'It might be a nice day. We should go for a long walk or something.'

'Yes.' Sam is happy. 'We should. Really give you a blast of Cornwall. Do you fancy that? Really? How about Zennor?'

'Zennor would be gorgeous. I just need some coffee and I'll be fine.'

I force myself to walk on the cliff path. As we go, I decide I should tell him about Guy. If I admit it, confess everything and say how sorry I am, perhaps it will all go away. Sam is, after all, my best friend. My telling him, at this point, will stop me from ever doing it again. In future I can stay in my cabin and ignore Guy when I see him, and everything will be fine. I know that I need to tell him.

It twists inside me. I am having to concentrate, as I walk under slatey skies, because I could so easily stumble in my exhaustion. At some points it would only take a small misstep to send me tumbling off the cliff. There are not many places where that could happen, but where they exist they are terrifying and magnetic in equal measure.

'Sam,' I shout, on the wind, to his back. Seagulls are circling us, squawking.

'Yeah?'

His back is wide and reassuring. He is shorter than Guy, but broader, like a rugby player.

'Look,' I shout. 'There's something I need to tell you. It's . . .' I take a breath and force myself to keep speaking, but even as I say the words I know I cannot do this. I am not brave enough to tell him. I cannot bear to inflict the suffering on him, but mainly I don't have the courage. 'It's not going to be easy. Sam, Olivia's pregnant.'

I did not tell him this on the phone, worrying that he would be more upset by it even than I was, and he is. He slows his pace while I tell the story of the showdown in Pizza Express to his back, through the wind. He does not react as I yell: 'I don't think Dad has spoken to her since. And then that of course makes me feel sorry for her. I know she didn't do it deliberately.'

'Maybe she did. Maybe she didn't.'

He turns to wait for me, puts two heavy arms around my shoulders and pulls me towards him. When he kisses the top of my head, I lean into him, hating myself.

'Why didn't you tell me, Lara? Why didn't you tell me on the phone?'

'I didn't want to say it. I just moved most of my stuff out and spent a night in a hotel and came home.'

'Maybe you should stay home. Knock the London thing on the head.'

'I've got a contract. I can't walk out of work at this point, Sam. I really can't. But I'll find a more sensible place to live. Maybe I could even go to Mum and Dad's. It might not be the end of the world.'

I expect him to scoff at this, but oddly he doesn't. Sam has never got on with my parents, because in my father's eyes no man could ever have been good enough for me. The acceptable son-in-law does not exist.

We stare out at the sea. The waves are black, uncompromising. The water rises and falls like a creature breathing.

'Maybe you should,' he says. 'It wouldn't cost you anything. I'd like to know that people were looking after you.'

We carry on walking, barely talking, along the edge of the continent, over the cliffs, around boulders, down to coves and back up to clifftops.

The clouds become blacker, and then they cover the sun

entirely. An ominous wind blows off the sea, pulling strands of hair out of place and blowing them around my face.

Sam stops.

'It's going to rain,' he shouts. 'We should head back.'

I feel the exhaustion seeping through me, and with a huge effort I fend it off and turn round.

The first drops fall on us a couple of minutes later. It is impossible to hurry, because parts of the path are made so treacherous that one wrong step on mud could send you hurtling to certain death. I want to grab Sam's hand, but the path is not wide enough for us to walk side by side.

By the time we get to the cove, we are soaked. My hair is clinging to my face, and all my hairpins have been washed away. A couple are in my pocket, the rest left as unobtrusive litter on the cliffs. The climb down here was steep, and the climb up for the section of the path that will take us to the car is going to be horrible. We stop and stare out at the water. I wonder how long we have been walking. It feels like hours. I hope it was only twenty minutes or so.

The sea is heaving ominously, breaking with showers of white spray. The dark sky throws water on us. I reach for Sam's hand, and we run to the foot of the cliff at the edge of the beach, where an overhanging rock provides the smallest possible amount of shelter.

'This is interesting,' I shout through the storm.

Sam pulls me close to him. I lean into his familiar bulk.

'It's mad,' he shouts back. 'This was not meant to happen.'

He looks into my eyes, and I force a laugh, to go with his. We stand and stare at the sheets of rain pounding the sand, leaving pockmarks all over it. The water is wild. The wind blows a huge piece of driftwood across the beach. I hear thunder.

'We can't just stand here in the storm,' Sam decides. 'We can make it back to the car, if we're careful.'

I want to stay here and watch nature battering everything.

'OK,' I agree, and I follow him, running across the sodden sand and starting our nervous ascent to the clifftops.

Sam starts the car engine and moves the heating dial around to its hottest setting. I find one of his jumpers on the back seat, and use it to wipe my face and hair, then pass it to him.

'That was oddly fun,' I say, watching him clear his ears with a jumper-wrapped finger.

'In a way, yes it was,' he agrees. 'Now it's over. My jeans feel disgusting.'

'Mine too.'

He starts the engine. 'Let's get home, then. You look tired, darling. Get some sleep if you can.'

I nod, pathetically grateful. Despite my rain-drenched clothing, despite the caffeine and adrenaline cocktail that was meant to keep me awake all day, I feel my eyes closing the moment I lean my head against Sam's damp old jumper on the window. I doze all the way home, my sleep punctuated by disconcerting dreams in which Sam and Guy change places and become one composite person.

chapter nine

At seven o'clock on Monday morning, just as I think I have managed the journey competently and am setting out to immerse myself in London, Guy catches up with me. Paddington is alive with the focused bustle of early commuters, and I am trying to make my way to the Tube when I hear him call my name.

I consider running to the Underground station. The moment I am on a train, he will have lost me. Instead I turn around.

'Lara,' I cannot read his expression.

My reaction to the sight of him is a huge betrayal. Everything I have been telling myself all weekend is suddenly and horribly overshadowed by the most outrageous blast of physical desire.

'Hey, are you OK? I was hoping to see you last night.'

I pull myself together and hope that I am arranging my features into a sensible and cool expression. I must be dignified, must not allow him to see my longing.

'Sorry. I just . . . I couldn't see you, Guy.' The station is never as busy, early in the morning, as you would expect it to be, but all the same I am aware that people are walking past us, every one of them as purposeful as you have to be if you are on a major train station early on a Monday morning. We stand still, slightly too close together, and the world moves around us.

Everything about his face works. He reminds me of a man from long ago. Guy feels safe. I can say anything to him. I push away the knowledge that he is married and transparently eager to cheat on his wife.

'Look, I'm sorry,' he says. 'It shouldn't have happened – that goes without saying. Neither of us is in a position to get involved in this sort of thing . . . But we're friends, aren't we? Please don't avoid me, Lara. It will never happen again. All right? We can go back to the way things used to be. We'll never be together without Ellen. She can be our chaperone. That way we'll be sure to be safe.' He puts a hand on my arm, and without meaning to, I mirror his gesture and touch him back. Instantly I regret it, and I pull my hand away, then try to smile at how awkward that move must have been.

'Lara. I'm very fond of you, you know. I look forward to seeing you, every week. We both got carried away after too many drinks. Let's just continue being friends, yes?'

I nod. 'OK.'

'Good. Well, I'll let you get going, but I'll see you on Friday, OK? No worrying. No complications.'

'Thanks. Have a good week, Guy.'

'You too.'

We both hesitate. I wonder whether he, like me, is considering a goodbye kiss. I decide quickly that it would be too dangerous, so I turn, raise my hand and walk off, through the station, towards the Tube. I want to look back, but I force myself not to.

*

On Friday morning, I check out of the hotel and take my pull-along bag to work. All through the day, which I spend brightly on the phone to councillors, flattering them in advance of the planning permission decision, I try not to think about him. I am bad. I will not do it. My behaviour makes me feel sick. I do not want to be this sort of person. Years ago, I pulled myself away from being that sort of person.

The day passes slowly. The councillors wield their power, making me squirm.

I arrive at the station having convinced myself. The rainy walk I had with Sam last weekend was lovely, and I am pleased to be on my way back to Cornwall. He texts as I am going up the escalator on to the concourse at Paddington: *How about a trip to the Lizard this time? Kynance Cove? Come home soon and safely xxxxx.* I reply with as much warmth and enthusiasm as it is possible to cram into a text message, and head to the lounge, my stomach flipping treacherously.

Guy arrives in the lounge earlier than he usually does. Ellen comes in just after him, and I wonder whether he has somehow contrived to arrive with her as a chaperone, as he said. We drink fizzy water and eat biscuits, just because both of them are there, and free. We talk inconsequentially about our days, and compare notes about the upcoming weekend, and I am happy. I am doing well.

On the train we carry on, drinking our usual gin and tonics, eating the free crisps they unexpectedly give us, and being entirely proper. I manage to manipulate the seating so that Ellen is by the window, with me next to her and Guy opposite her. This puts us as far from each other as it is possible to be. Even after two drinks, I am successfully quelling my yearning, learning from my mistakes and being the sensible married woman I am.

The little voice that protests, that forces me to seek eye contact with Guy and then to look away, that persistently remembers sensations from this time last week, is irritating, but I override it. I am better than that.

'Right,' I tell them both, after two drinks. 'Sorry to quit so early, but I'm knackered. I'm going to bed. See you on Sunday.'

'We *will* see you on Sunday, won't we, Lara?' asks Ellen. 'Last week you didn't come out to play.'

'Sorry.' I avoid Guy's eyes. 'It was a tough weekend. I never really caught up with myself. I needed to crash out.'

She nods and pushes her curly hair back from her face. 'Fair enough. We've all had weekends like that. Well, sleep well and see you soon, sweetie.'

I do all the normal things. I am in my pyjamas, in my bed, staring at the ceiling and refusing to address the longing that is close to overriding everything. I am doing the right thing: I'm going back to Sam. To do anything else would be horrendous. It would be unthinkable.

It is not quite unthinkable, because if it were, I would not be thinking about it so hard.

The gentle knock on my door takes me by surprise; I have been longing for it and dreading it in equal measure.

I stand up, suddenly shaky, and open the door a fraction.

'Guy,' I say. He comes in, and I close the door behind him. Then I lock it. I look at him. His black hair is sticking up: it looks as though he has been running his fingers through it. I want to reach out and stroke it back into place, but I do not.

'I'm sorry,' he says, his voice quiet. 'I shouldn't be here.

I wasn't going to do this. Yet somehow I couldn't bear not to.'

'I was trying to do the right thing. I've been desperately hoping you'd turn up. How did you know where to find me? You didn't ask anyone, did you?'

He laughs. 'Of course not. Just looked at your reservation when we were in the waiting room.'

'The great detective!'

'Elementary deduction was required. Have you really been hoping I'd come? I wasn't going to. But I had to, even if it was just to talk, because I wanted to see you, Lara. I've been so on edge tonight. God knows what Ellen makes of it. I bet she has an idea.'

'She's not stupid.'

We stand and look into one another's eyes, and the atmosphere between us changes. My body betrays me with its response to him. It prepares itself with alacrity for what it hopes is coming. I feel myself soften, all the way through.

I am phenomenally physically attracted to Guy. Now, as I stand in front of him, touching him is the only thing that matters. I do not think about Sam. I am incapable of considering anything but the man before me, and how very desperately I want him. I want him obsessively, and all of a sudden I love that.

I step forward, put both my arms around his neck and draw him towards me. We are kissing, then pulling at each other's clothes. This cabin was not built for sex, but that does not matter. He sits on the narrow bed, and I am straddling him. I undo his belt. He slides a hand inside my knickers, and I stand up for long enough to take them off, then sit down on him. I kiss him again. We are fumbling like teenagers.

We realise at the same time, and pull away from each other.

'I, er, don't suppose,' Guy asks, his mouth twitching, 'that you brought a condom?'

I laugh. 'I wasn't planning on this. It wasn't even an outside possibility. I don't walk round with condoms in my pocket.'

'Neither do I. And despite the fact that I've turned up at your door like a cad, after you'd so graciously removed yourself from my company, I was not that well prepared.'

'Maybe we can work around it?' I say tentatively, and I kneel down on the floor in front of him. We cross so many lines that I soon forget all about my husband, and his wife, and everything apart from the movement of the train and the reality of Guy inside my mouth.

Later, much later, we squeeze together into the tiny train bed, both of us naked. I am on a high, and still so utterly in the moment that I do not feel even a momentary pang of guilt.

'We really shouldn't do this,' I say, nuzzling into his neck. 'I love the smell of you, by the way.'

'Why thank you. I adore the smell of you. It drives me wild.'

'Good.' I smile and run my fingers through his chest hair. 'What you did to me just then? It was . . .' I stop, suddenly shy. 'Well. You know what you're doing. That's all.'

'It's not me, Lara. It's you. It's us. Together we make it work like nothing else I've ever known.'

'You have known it, though, really. Be realistic. You just haven't had the excitement with someone new for a long time.' Suddenly, I realise I am probably wrong. 'What I mean is, *I* haven't. You know I haven't. You may well have done. I don't mean to assume anything – if I'm one of a long line of conquests, that's fair enough.'

'Oh, Lara!' He kisses the top of my head. 'You're not one of a long line. There's no reason for me not to be entirely honest with you, though. I haven't always been a great husband.'

'That's a euphemism for shagging around?'

'It is indeed a euphemism for shagging. Not around. I've had a couple of flings over the years. I'm a bastard. My wife is a saint.'

'Does she know, then?' I suddenly imagine him telling her that a woman on the train gave him a blow job, and that he reciprocated with panache. The thought chills me. I feel myself tensing up, pulling away from him. His wife could track me down, turn up on my doorstep. She could tell Sam.

'No, not really. We've never had a showdown. I've always felt she probably does know, but it's one of those things that if you don't talk about it then you don't have to deal with it. Which probably suits both of us.'

'Guy! That is so easy for you to say. Your poor wife.'

I can think about her objectively, and side with her, and sympathise. This is despite the fact that I am lying so close to her husband that our bodies are touching all the way down in every place, and both of us are naked. I could almost be swayed to gamble on the withdrawal method of contraception. I would not get pregnant anyway; but given Guy's history, that is not the main concern.

'You think?' he asks. 'You think I'm having my cake and eating it?'

'Yes! What if she was doing the same? What if right now, she's cuddled up with the milkman?'

He considers it. 'We don't have a milkman. Does anyone these days? Milkmen are almost obsolete. But I take your point. If she were the woman in this scenario right now, and some gorgeous hunk was the man, then obviously I'd be outraged. But if she's done it in the past – and who am I to say that she hasn't? She might have done. It's unlikely but odd things happen. If it turns out she's been unfaithful to me, then I accept that and I'd much, much rather not know about it, thanks very much.'

'Hmm. Which, funnily enough, is a moral position that comes close to giving you carte blanche to carry on exactly as you wish without breathing a word to her.'

'It does rather, doesn't it?' He kisses me. 'Sorry. I am a shit, I fully acknowledge and own that fact. At least you know I won't be telling Di, and she won't be coming to your house.'

'Oh, fucking hell. That's exactly what I was worrying about. So that's something, I suppose.'

'And you? I'm assuming you won't be stepping off the Falmouth train and breaking down and confessing all?'

'I can't even bear to think about the weekend, actually. I'm OK right here, right now. It's going to come crashing down around me, I imagine, as soon as you get out of my bed. No, I'm not going to tell. I couldn't do that to Sam. I spent all last weekend agonising. I've got a hell of a lot more to agonise over this time. I'm scheduling in some very heavy-duty agonising indeed.'

He puts his arm right around me, round my waist and on to the small of my back, pulling us even more tightly together. I love his fingers on my skin. No one touches the small of my back, not even Sam.

'Lara.' He sounds hesitant. 'Look. Tell me to fuck off if you like. But you know, maybe you don't need to give yourself such a hard time. People do it all the time. Half the people you know will be doing it in secret. Sam could be, stuck in Falmouth on his own all week. As I said before, Diana might be, though there are so many demands on her time that it would require an impressive level of planning. Maybe it's just the way people get through their lives. Perhaps this kind of thing is the secret to the long union.'

'Guy! Stop it. That doesn't work.'

'I know it doesn't. Sorry. I just wanted to hear how it sounded. It could have worked.'

'Didn't. But.' I don't want to say this, yet somehow I do anyway. 'But the thing is, you don't need to try to find ways to tie yourself up making me think it's OK. I can't bear to kick you out of my bed. I know it's wrong. I'm doing it anyway. I should have left Sam ages ago. This just proves it to me.'

chapter ten

Christmas Eve

Iris lives down a lane, near some woods, in a cottage that, from a distance, looks somewhere between tatty and bohemian. It is raining softly, the sort of rain that hangs suspended and allows you to walk through it, rather than bothering to fall on you. The lane is stony, with a line of scraggy grass down the middle; at its end the house, with bare flowerpots and a bike clustered outside it, looks like a down-at-heel distant cousin of the stately home with sweeping drive.

I walk down from the top of the lane, where I have parked, as she told me to, nervously, when I called.

'Don't come to the house,' she said immediately, offering to come to me or to meet me in a café, a pub, anywhere but here. I insisted, because I needed to. I feel bad about what I am planning to do here, but I will make it up to her one day.

'Please,' I begged her in the end. 'I need to get out. I'd love to see where you live. I won't stay long. I just want to be away from Falmouth. I'll bring cakes.'

She paused, then laughed. 'Well, if you're bringing cakes . . .'

I sensed that she does not invite anyone to her place, ever, and this has made me particularly intrigued.

As I get closer to the house, I see that it is in a worse state than you would think, from a distance. The wooden window frames are rotten. The white rendering is falling off in places. A cat stalks around from amongst a group of trees to my left and rubs itself on my legs. I stop to stroke it. It has long hair and the inevitable enigmatic air, and its black coat looks fluffy but is, in fact, wet.

I stand on the doorstep, the cat at my feet, and pull a chain which rings an old-fashioned genuine bell just on the other side of the door. It clangs back and forth, completely different from other people's doorbells. While I wait for Iris, I allow myself to savour the solitude.

I am being as nice to Sam as I possibly can. He senses this and clings to me ever tighter. He is at my side constantly, bringing me cups of tea, asking what I would like to do and looking hurt if it does not involve the two of us being exclusively, endlessly together, holding hands and smiling. I know that he deserves my full attention, and he has had it since I came back from work on Friday night. However, sometimes you just have to get out.

I am having an affair. The words go around my head so often, and they are so shocking and transgressive, that I worry I am going to say them in my sleep. I am constantly worried that I will call Sam by the wrong name, that I will blurt it out, get something wrong.

As it is Christmas, and Guy and I are with our families (or rather, Guy is with his family and I am with Sam), we have agreed not to contact one another until we go back to London after the new year. I am being determinedly and relentlessly nice to my husband. I am not texting Guy, not calling him, not showing up on his doorstep even though I know exactly where he lives, in a village near the edge of the world.

Sam and I have a Christmas tree, cards, a houseful of food. We will spend Christmas looking out at the mild drizzle, eating and drinking and watching television. Nobody is coming to visit us: Sam has insisted that his frail mother and his aggressive brother stay at their home in Sussex, producing our weekly separation as a trump card, effective at keeping all potential intrusion outside the fortress.

'We'll just have a quiet one this year,' I heard him say on the phone. I had no idea who he was talking to, and it didn't matter. 'Just Lara and me. That's the best present I could ever have.'

My thoughts are treacherous. The guilt makes me kind to him, and he is innocently happy.

Today, however, I have come out. I wanted to see Iris, mainly to escape the stifling togetherness but also for a second, equally reprehensible reason. As footsteps approach the door, I wonder whether her boyfriend stifles her or whether their relationship is darker than that. Instinctively, I think it is, and I find myself hoping that I am about to meet him.

'Lara! Hey. Good to see you.'

Iris is motioning to me to come in. She is dressed in skinny black jeans and a thick jumper that I have to reach out and stroke as I pass her because it is so obviously gorgeously soft.

'Is that cashmere?' I ask. She laughs.

'In my dreams. It's H and M faux-cashmere, ordered

from the internet. How are you? Tea? Coffee? Something stronger?'

Suddenly I wish I had cycled here, like she does.

'A coffee would be great. Thanks. If I didn't have the car, I'd have loved something stronger.' I hand her the Tupperware box of brownies.

'Yeah, that's why I offered to meet you in town. But that's fine. Coffee it is. And brownies? Thanks.'

I follow her into a kitchen that is homely and warm, and not at all as tatty as the house's exterior would imply. The floor, throughout, is battered wooden boards, and the kitchen is dated but lovely.

'I like your Aga,' I tell her. She pushes her hair back from her face.

'It's not a real one. It's electric – essentially it's an electric oven disguised as an Aga – but yes, it looks good. In fact, I've got some mince pies in it. I hope you like them.'

'Of course. Thanks. You can't not like mince pies. Is your boyfriend at home? Laurie?'

She pours hot water into a bizarre contraption made of two plastic cylinders, and starts pressing them together over a jug.

'He's miles away, I'm afraid. It's a shame – he's such a homebody normally, but he's had to go and do a duty family visit. You know. Christmas. His family are . . . complicated.'

'Tell me about it. It took me years to realise that everyone's family is complicated. I always thought it was just me. Then I realised that when you scratch the surface, there's no such thing as normal. Or at least, to be weird is to be normal.'

'That is definitely true. I'm just glad I managed to stay home while he's gone visiting. Me and the cats.'

'You're not alone for Christmas, though, are you? What about your family?'

'Oh, I don't really speak to them much. They live in Putney, but I haven't been for years, and they don't come here either. But no, Laurie's going to be back late tonight. I won't be on my own. I can't wait to hear the taxi at the top of the lane. It's only at this time of year that he ever goes anywhere, and that's just because it's inescapable.'

She takes an oven glove and crouches in front of the Aga, producing a tray of mince pies with a flourish that, I sense, ends the conversation. I want to ask about her family. I am intrigued by the fact that she never speaks to them, not least as I wonder whether Olivia and I are ever going to exchange a single word, ever again. I want to know what that will feel like.

Instead I say, 'Bloody hell, Iris! Home-made ones! That must have taken you hours.'

She smiles. 'I love it. I'm incredibly good at making pastry. Cold hands. If I ever feel the need to move to Paris or somewhere, I'd be able to get an apprenticeship in a bakery. Other people might be good at maths or brilliant at, you know, particle physics. But I'll generally be able to beat them at jam tarts.'

'And people will always want jam tarts.'

'That's true. Come the Apocalypse, I'll just have to assemble some flour, fat and fruit, and I'll be able to barter sweet pastries and get the essentials.'

She hands me a mug of coffee, and puts my brownies onto one plate, and her mince pies onto another. The mug is wide and chunky, with a design of roses on the side. She is using a matching one, though I notice that hers is chipped on the rim.

'That must be a relief,' I say, picking up the brownie

plate and following her along a dark passage to a sitting room with French windows that look out on a bare but well-tended back garden. The grass is short, the beds turned over and free from weeds. 'I mean, knowing what you can do when society collapses.'

She gestures me to a big comfy chair, and sits down on a sofa, moving a copy of last Saturday's *Guardian* magazine. A cat materialises from thin air and settles itself on her lap. 'You can stay, Desi,' she tells it maternally, 'but not if you try to lick my mince pie, OK? But you'll be all right too, Lara. You know how to build a house. You'll be the most popular woman in whatever remains of the world.'

'I'll build you a house in exchange for anything you've baked,' I offer. 'These mince pies are amazing.'

'Thanks.'

'I can't really build, though. I'd have to have a gang of workers to boss around.' I think about it. 'And no one'll even need planning permission, will they? There's a significant part of my skill set, redundant.'

'No – you'll be fine with the bossing around. You'll be the queen before you know it.'

'Does that mean I can instruct other people to reinvent electricity rather than attempting to do it myself? That's good.'

I look around. The room is pretty, and I can see all sorts of traces of Iris's and Laurie's lives in here. I can deduce that one of them reads thrillers and the other reads literary fiction. They buy the *Guardian*, but mainly on Saturdays. Judging by the matching dark rings on the coffee table, they both drink red wine. There is a little, real Christmas tree by the window, decorated mainly with silver baubles, and with an angel perched precariously on the top that looks as if it were made by an artistic community in Guatemala, but there are no presents under it. There are only two Christmas cards on the mantelpiece, and I bet if I looked at them I would see they were from Iris and Laurie to each other.

'This place is lovely,' I tell her. 'Don't you get bored?'

'No.' She curls her feet up under herself. 'I guess I'm boring. We're both incredibly happy like this.'

I feel the familiar yearning, the one I am intently ignoring every moment of every day. I shut it away, again, and focus on the reason for my visit. I am not just obsessed with Guy: I am deeply uneasy in a way I cannot speak of without sounding mad. I almost want to confide in Iris.

'You know what,' I say, hesitantly. 'This might sound weird, but can I have a little tour of your house?'

She looks at me. 'Really? It's not very interesting, but you can if you want. If you don't mind it being boring and messy. Why? You cannot possibly have any sort of professional interest in this place.'

I sigh. 'I can't help myself. I like looking at buildings. I'm converting an old warehouse right now. Into flats and a wine bar. I love making a place like this look different in a way no one could possibly imagine.'

She stands up. 'OK. Even though we rent it, tell me what you'd do if we owned it and had unlimited money. To make it into an amazing home.'

With our coffee mugs in hand, we walk around the house. There is, it turns out, very little to see. A door from the sitting room leads into a dining room with a heavy table and some books and paperwork piled on it.

'I work here,' Iris confirms. 'This is the scene of the dreaded proofreading.'

'It's a nice room. You could do a lot with it. Great natural light.'

She stands at the window. 'It is nice, isn't it? Cold in winter, since the wood burner's next door, but not as cold as it would be if this were a real winter.'

I walk to the window and stand next to her.

'Yes, the drizzly winter of the south-west. Wouldn't it be lovely if it was all blue skies and bright sun and snow out there? With icicles and cracked puddles. Like, I don't know. The Himalayas, or something.'

We both contemplate the drizzly scene.

'It's twelve degrees all year round,' she says. 'Still. At least it's green.'

I smile. 'That's something. Yes.'

Apart from a tiny bathroom, I have seen all the downstairs. Upstairs there is a bedroom that is clearly Iris and Laurie's, with the duvet pulled back and men's and women's clothes scattered around. The second, smaller bedroom is where I want to be.

'This one we just use as an office,' she says, standing on the threshold. 'All the paperwork's in here.'

'It looks very organised.'

There is a desk, the sort of thing you buy if you're getting the cheapest thing from somewhere that is like, but not, Ikea, since there is no Ikea anywhere near Cornwall. It has piles of paperwork on it, but tidy piles. The walls are lined with bookshelves which carry so many books that they are piled on top of one another, a whole extra layer lying down on top of the standing ones. Then there are the filing cabinets.

'Not really,' she says. 'All the bills and stuff get dumped in here.'

My phone is in my pocket. I feel terrible about doing

this, but it is the only plan I have been able to think of. I walk over to the window and look out at the front of the house, the stony track, my car waiting damply in the distance.

'This room could be good too. Is there an attic? You could get a skylight if not, really flood the place with light.'

There is a loud, old-fashioned ringing sound, as a phone somewhere in the house fills the place with a demand for attention. Iris looks confused.

'That's the landline,' she says. 'Weird. No one ever calls it. I suppose I'd better answer. It's too annoying to have it ringing.'

She disappears, and the moment she is out of the room I open the filing cabinet. I feel horrible, but it is the only answer I can think of. One day I will explain, or put it back. She probably won't even have noticed.

A minute later she is back in the room, shaking her head.

'Everything OK?' I ask, turning away from the window, walking right up to her.

'Yes,' she says. 'I think so, anyway. There was no one there. When I did 1471, there was no number.'

We walk across the little landing and back down the stairs.

'That happens to us all the time. It's spam calls. They just call every number there is.'

'Really? OK. It hasn't happened before. Anyway, who cares. Shall we have another coffee?'

'Yes,' I tell her. 'That would be wonderful.'

chapter eleven

January

Christmas, eventually, ends. Sam and I celebrate the new year by going for dinner and drinks in Falmouth, a watertight unit of two. We do not speak to anyone else, but meander home through the post-midnight crowds, cut off from all the revelry. On the first evening of the new year I embrace my husband and set off, heart treacherously light, pulse treacherously thumping, to catch the train. Guy is waiting for me in the lounge car. It is as if the break never happened.

The weeks pass like a blur. I am obsessed with Guy to the point of insanity. I have never known anything like it. All I want to do is to be with him, to touch him, to talk to him. Nothing else matters.

I know every inch of his body. He knows mine. I look around at strangers and colleagues and wonder if they have known this sexual obsession. Have other people's marriages started off with these fireworks? Is this why Leon advised me, when I met Sam, not to marry him? Could he see what I couldn't: that one day something like this would come along and snatch me up and carry me away?

I have been good for so long. Once upon a time I was bad, and now I am bad again; this time I am differently bad, and the stakes are lower. Perhaps that is how I manage to do it.

Even the guilt, the deception, the excitement on Sam's face when I get home on the first Saturday morning, his sadness when I leave on Sunday night, cannot stop me. I know that what I am doing is wrong. I know that my marriage is over. I want to end it instantly. Something always stops me: sometimes it is the expectation that the spell will break and I will rush back to Sam and beg his forgiveness, wondering what on earth I was playing at. Other times I open my mouth to confess, then find that I cannot do it. I want Guy, just Guy, all the time.

I am lovely to Sam when I am home, as I was over Christmas. I'm nicer than I have ever been. I'm considerate and thoughtful, interested in everything he says, and I summon the energy to go for walks and sit in pubs. Occasionally I have sex with him, imagining that he is my lover. I hate myself for doing it, hate myself for not doing it.

I see shadows and phantoms everywhere. I feel someone watching me, know that I am in danger, though whether it is real danger or my mind distilling all its unease and making it external, I cannot tell. I try to convince myself that I am imagining the malignant presence following me around corners, lurking outside doors. I half hope someone is photographing Guy and me out in London, because that would force a change. But I catch a train out to Hendon and spend an afternoon making my final preparation; and after that I carry my escape kit around with me constantly. That makes me feel a little bit better. I cannot tell anyone what I have done, because no one who wasn't genuinely terrified for their own safety would understand. I hope no one ever has to find out. I have always been ready to escape if need be; and this plan is my best one yet.

It is a slate-grey day, and I am standing in the rain on Waterloo Bridge. I have an umbrella, a huge one I found at work, that seemed to belong to no one. It is tartan-patterned and ridiculous, and I am constantly aware that I am potentially poking people in the eye with its spiky spokes, but it keeps me dry.

I spin around quickly, feeling eyes on me from the other side of the road, but there is no one there. This is my secret: I have not even mentioned it to Guy.

The rain is falling into the murky Thames, making concentric circles that touch each other and die. A tourist boat passes, almost empty, beneath me. The Houses of Parliament, the London Eye, the South Bank: I can do serious sightseeing just by standing here and waiting.

I see him coming when he is still far away, a single figure among the post-work crowds. It is almost dark, the street lamps on, the buses and taxis creating little waves of spray as they lumber past. Yet I know him instantly, and I stand perfectly still, holding my umbrella high to mini-mise the inconvenience to others, and watch.

I love him, completely and passionately. This is the secret I cannot share with anyone, least of all with Guy himself. If I told him, he might be scared and stop seeing me, and that would end my world. I wish we had met at a different time, when we were both single. I wish his children were my children. I wish we had a life together, a mortgage, council tax to pay. I wish we could spend weekends reading the papers and hoovering the house, getting grumpy with each other. I could do all of that, because our relationship would be founded on absolute love and lust.

'Wilberforce!' He has taken to calling me by my surname, my old one. I like that. Nobody calls me Lara Wilberforce any more; and she is the person who can behave this badly. Lara Finch would never do these heinous things. Besides, as Guy said: 'Wilberforce is a funny name. In a nice way. Wilber sounds a bit puny, and then the "force" jumps up and punches you in the face. It's a name that gives you a false sense of security. Like a kitten that scratches your eyes out.'

'Um, thanks,' I said, and since that day I have been Wilberforce to him, and him only.

'Guy.' I can only call him Guy.

I hold the umbrella aside, causing a passer-by to swear in annoyance, and let him sweep me off my feet. He picks me right up, as he so often does. I try to do it to him sometimes, but he is so big and so muscular that I cannot.

'Put me down!'

He puts me back on my feet and kisses me, full on the lips. We can do that, in central London in the rush hour.

'What would you like to do tonight?' he asks. Thursday nights have become our special night. We try to use them to sample the different things the capital can offer. I take his hand and we walk north, towards Aldwych.

'I found something that might be good,' I tell him, 'or that might be weird. We could try it later. It's in an old public loo. The gents'.'

'It sounds ravishing.' We walk to the Lyceum pub and step in, out of the rain, and find an upstairs table.

*

Much later, we are in the underground bar a few metres away. It is, indeed, in the old men's loos: according to the menu, these ones were frequented by the likes of Wilde, Orton and Gielgud, thanks to their West End location. Now they have been transformed into a cocktail and burlesque venue, and happily none of it is quite as tacky as it sounds.

The barman, who is blond and undiscriminatingly cheerful, greets us as if we were old friends, and says, 'Look, there's a table! Grab it quick. Gold dust!'

We sit at a tiny table, picking at free popcorn and drinking our way through the cocktail menu. The other customers are a random but presentable selection of travellers, couples and a group of women on what eavesdropping reveals to be a post-divorce celebration. The woman in question keeps bursting into tears, and then snogging her friends.

'Let's have one with absinthe,' I decide. 'I've never tried absinthe. Have you?'

'Not me. I skipped the wild youth. Hey, they have snuff, too. That sounds odd. Did you ever do anything like that? Not snuff, I mean. They're obviously selling it as the closest they can get to cocaine.'

'Oh God, no,' I tell him. 'I never did anything like that.'

'Me neither. Not really. Absinthe martini?'

'Just the one. Then we'll go.'

'Deal.'

A woman is setting up in the corner of the room, ready to sing. She is wearing a black corset and tiny skirt and has a huge mane of black hair and bright red lipstick, and she is laughing with the divorce party at the table closest to her.

'I wish we didn't have work tomorrow,' I remark.

He leans forward. 'Could we maybe find a way of staying up for a weekend one day? Have a proper Friday and Saturday night?'

We could do that. We could do it by leaving our spouses and making our London life legitimate. I cannot say it. You cannot ask someone to leave his children.

I take his hand across the table. It is warm and reassuring, as it always is. I belong with you, I think, suddenly. I love you. It takes all my willpower not to say it.

The woman starts singing 'Sex on Fire', in an almost unrecognisable acoustic version. It is oddly lovely. Guy mouths something at me. I think, for a second, that it was 'I love you'. Then I wonder if it might have been 'Where's the loo?' I laugh at myself, move our drinks out of the way and lean across the popcorn to kiss him.

Later we stroll down Fleet Street to the hotel, hand in hand. I am drunk but not outrageously so, and happier than I deserve to be. I have been behaving terribly for weeks now, and I am going to do the right thing. This is where it ends, for me. It is time for me to destroy Sam's world.

I rarely leave the building at lunchtime, unless it's for a meeting. Nobody does: the days of the professional lunch hour are gone, and I generally like that. Today, however, I stand up at half past twelve.

'I'm going to have to pop out for a second,' I say quietly to Jeremy. 'Got a dentist thing. Is that OK?'

He barely looks up. He is eating a pungent sandwich from a lunch box that he's brought from home, and tapping at his laptop.

'Sure,' he says. 'Whatever you need to do. As long as you'll be back for the architects later. You're right – get your teeth fixed up here, not down in Devon. Don't want yokel teeth.'

'Cornwall,' I say, and I slip away to meet Leon for the quickest of lunches, and to tell him I am going to leave Sam.

We sit in one of those little cafés with wobbly metal tables and a deli counter, and drink coffee and water as we eat, because neither of us has time for a post-lunch caffeine hit, but we both need one. Leon looks at me over the top of his sandwich.

'I can see that you need to do it, Lara,' he says. 'He'll be fine, you know. As will you.' I inhale deeply. This is the man who has bailed me out before, the only person I completely trust. 'I'm not entirely sure,' he adds, 'what's been holding you back.'

His voice is so familiar, so reassuring, that suddenly I feel ridiculous. I reach across the little table and take his hand, just for a second.

'Thanks,' I say quietly. Leon is a father figure in the most straightforward manner: he looks after me in a way my own parents never have. Since I've been an adult, there has been the finest thread of attraction there, never mentioned between us, and that adds an extra edge to it. It is the most subtle thing.

'I'll ruin his life,' I say, with a sigh. 'That's been holding me back.'

Leon waves a hand, dismissing this fear.

'Women love a man like Sam Finch. He'll be swept off his feet by rescuers.'

I think about it. It is true. 'But don't dash into anything with Guy,' Leon warns. 'Seriously. Be by yourself for a while. Give yourself a chance. If he leaves his wife and children for you, your relationship will change completely.

You'll need to put the brakes on a little if you want any kind of long-term thing. Don't you think?'

I shake my head. 'The trouble is, I'm so wildly in love with him, I'm not sure I could cool it off. But anyway. I'm not going to make him do anything. I could never do that. I'm just going to see what he says when I tell him I'm leaving Sam. Maybe he'll run for the hills.'

'Maybe,' Leon agrees, where I wanted him not to. 'And if he does, Lara, you'll be absolutely fine.'

I pretend to believe this.

After work on Friday, I walk quickly along Fleet Street to Covent Garden. The winter air is harsh and frozen on my cheeks, but the sun is shining, and everything is edged with ice. I adore London on a day like this. Cornwall is beautiful too, in its entirely other way, but I do not want to think about that yet.

Covent Garden is filled with people: they are in bars and restaurants and cafés, walking briskly down the street and ambling along looking at things and talking. The buzz is so strong you can almost feel it crackling in the air. This is what happens when the sun comes out, even in January. I try to smile, to look like a normal person.

Guy is already in the random bar he nominated for our pre-Paddington drink. It's a half-seedy little place offering jugs of watery cocktails and endless happy hours. I see him at a table near the window as I approach, and almost run the last bit.

He has bought a bottle of Corona for each of us.

'Hey, gorgeous,' he says, and I stand next to him while he puts his arms around my waist and presses his head into me. I stroke his hair, which is more flecked with grey from this angle than it normally appears.

'Hey.'

I sit opposite him.

'Do we just drink alcohol all the time?' I wonder. 'Should we be worried?'

'No. Well, yes. We drink alcohol all the time. But that's because we go to work all day and home all weekend. We only have the evenings. Before I met you I'd rarely drink on a week night. But we only get utterly rat-arsed on Thursdays.'

'That's true. And on the train sometimes.'

He nods, his eyes crinkling. 'And on the train sometimes. Yes. Now, next week I thought we could have a cinema week. You were saying how hard it is to get to the cinema in Cornwall. Well, it can be done, obviously, but one doesn't really bother. What's your schedule like? In my ideal world, we'd both be free in time to go to a screening at nine-ish, every night. Monday to Thursday. What do you think? We could see a bit of everything: a classic, an action film, a comedy, a romance.'

'That would be lovely. I'm not sure. I wasn't great at work today.' In fact I had to make a gargantuan effort to get through the day and to give the usual impression of efficiency and attention to detail. 'An absinthe hangover isn't fabulously conducive to getting things done, it turns out.'

'How about this: cinema without drinking? We take water and Coca-Cola and sweets in with us. Like kids. No boozing.'

I can barely focus on what he's saying. I am too busy scanning the faces of every single person who passes outside. Because it is already dark, they are all lit by the creepy street lighting and everyone looks half sinister. A man is loitering opposite, wearing a strange lederhosen ensemble that either makes him a hapless tourist or achingly hip: I have no idea which.

'Maybe,' I say. The lederhosen man is holding a red rose. He is not looking at me. I cannot take my eyes off him.

'Or we could hang out at the hotel every night.'

A woman walks up to him and he kisses her cheek and hands her the flower.

'Now that would be wonderful,' I say, as the two of them walk away hand in hand.

When someone does arrive, it turns out just to be my sister. I am almost glad to see her: her brand of trouble is so prosaic.

She is unmistakably pregnant now. As well as the bump, there is something different about her. The sharp contours of her face have softened.

'Lara,' she says, looking at me speculatively.

'Olivia,' I say. I try to smile. She looks from me to Guy and back again. She knows. 'How are you? You're looking great.'

'Yeah. Thanks.' She turns to Guy. 'Hi. I'm Olivia. Lara's sister.'

He is on his feet. 'Hello, Olivia. How lovely to meet you. Lara's talked about you. I'm Guy. A friend of Lara's.'

'Clearly. And I'm quite sure she's talked about me.'

She is looking at me with a small smile. I should not have been so complacent as to think I could come for a pre-train beer in her neighbourhood. She lives minutes from this bar. Of course she's here.

Silence hangs heavily for a while. I decide to do the right thing.

'Hey, I'm sorry, you know,' I tell her. 'Really. I didn't

mean to storm away that night. I should have been in touch before now. I really can't wait to meet the baby.'

'That's cool,' she says lightly. 'Give me a call, then. Right now I'm meeting a friend, but that would be nice. Ring me next week?'

'I will. Thanks.'

And before I can say anything else, she has gone.

Guy is smiling.

'Hey, I met your sister! She doesn't look at all how I expected. Not remotely the woman I had in my head.'

I am barely listening. 'Really? What did you expect? She's going to tell everyone she saw me with a man. She knew at once. Definitely.'

'Does it even matter?' Guy asks.

'Well, not really to me. Although I wouldn't have chosen it. Actually, Guy. I wasn't going to tell you this. But.' I stop, and decide to continue. 'I've decided to end things with Sam. I can't carry on like this.' I think of Leon's words. 'It's not fair on him, because he has no idea. If he was single, there'd be loads of women swooping in to look after him. He deserves that. I can't bear this secrecy and all the lying.'

'Now,' says Guy. 'It's strange you should say that, Wilberforce. Because, although my situation is more complicated, I've been having similar thoughts. How can I be this much of a shit? It's going to be difficult, but I'm going to tell Di. Our relationship can't last like this, yours and mine. I want to be with you, Wilberforce. That's it. Everything else can work itself out. It's monstrously selfish, but . . .'

'I know.'

I can hardly speak. A future with Guy and me together officially and forever is opening out. It's going to take some negotiating, but we will do it. We will make it work.

I want to tell someone, but there is nobody who will understand. Only Ellen and Leon know about us, and we will see Ellen on the train tonight. I take out my phone and type a quick text because I am desperate to share the news.

Leon. I can't tell anyone else, but Guy's just said he's going to leave his wife. From Monday we'll be together. Thank you for listening to me. This is going to be messy but it's going to be amazing. Just wanted to tell you. Dinner next week with Guy and me? L xx

I rehearse my speech to Sam. I will tell him in the morning, as soon as I get home. Then, from tomorrow, my new life will begin.

chapter twelve

The station concourse is busy, as it always is. Guy and I negotiate the crowds, walking close together, shoulder to shoulder. I love the fact that everyone here is moving, even the people who are just standing and waiting. Paddington station is a place of transience: you come here, you wait for your train, or you run for it, and then you are en route to your real destination. Alternatively, you arrive here by train and go straight to the Tube or the taxi. It is a place for passing through. It would, I think, be strange to work here, odd to be one of the fixed points in the hubbub.

He stops and puts a hand on my shoulder.

'Hey, Wilberforce. I have to pop in there. I'll see you in the lounge.'

Guy is nodding towards the card shop, the place that used to be Paperchase. I know this means he has a birthday in the family, and decide not to enquire further. It doesn't matter any more. I will meet his children at some point, try to build a relationship with them. Buy birthday cards.

'Sure,' I agree. He dodges off and I keep walking.

I should be used to Guy by now. We ought, by now, to

have scratched below the gilded surface and confronted sordid reality. We should have woken up to ourselves and rushed, horrified, back to our spouses, thanking the universe for letting us get away with it. Because we haven't done that, I think, knowing that it is simplistic, we belong together.

Our relationship has grown to fill all the space available for it. Guy has all but moved into my hotel room and we have both effectively been leading two lives. My relationship with him is the biggest, most amazing thing in my life.

I should never have married Sam. I did it because all I needed, back then, was security, a feeling that I was safe and that nothing devastating could ever happen to me again.

I have messed it all up. When I tried adventures, they went wrong. Now I have tried security, and that went wrong too. Both times I have ended up inflicting the horror on someone close to me. I need to leave Sam, for his sake and for mine.

I dream of next week. We will do what we have to do this weekend; and next week we will look at the future.

I wander along Platform 1, heading for the lounge.

I can free Sam to meet someone else: in my current position, that is the least nasty course of action. He would meet someone instantly. He would settle back down with a woman who appreciates him, and have babies this time. He would not spend all week waiting for me to come home, innocent of what I am really like.

The prospect is daunting. He will be devastated. I will only tell him about Guy if I have to.

I smile, while my stomach flips in terror and excitement. When Guy touches my shoulder, I turn, but he is not there. Nobody is there. A train has just arrived on the platform, and people are surging off it, swarming past me. No one is still, and no one is near me. Yet I know that I felt a hand on my shoulder. It was warm, with a deliberate pressure, and then it was gone.

A family pass me, pulling huge suitcases and looking lost. Three young women with huge backpacks stride past deep in conversation in what is, I think, a Scandinavian language. People who have come straight from the office, in their work clothes, walk purposefully towards the taxi rank. Nobody has stopped. Nobody is interested in me.

I decide it was just someone brushing past: an accident. I am haunted by everything I did years ago, and I vow that on Monday I will tell Guy the whole story. I will even dig out my old, hidden diary this weekend, and let him read it for himself. Then we will be able to start a relationship with no enormous all-consuming secret. The thought is amazing.

I speed up my pace and go into the first-class lounge. I take two bottles of fizzy water, a couple of packs of biscuits, and I throw myself into a chair.

An hour later, as we leave the lounge to get on the train, which is waiting right outside, in its usual place on Platform 1, I hear someone calling something from the far end of the platform, and when I look up, towards the place where the station ends and the tracks go out westwards, I see a figure.

For half a second, I freeze. My blood thumps in my ears. My legs tense up, ready either to crumple or to run. I feel my face flush red before the blood drains out of it.

It is nobody I know, no one I recognise. It is just a person standing on a station. The night-time station smells of engines and mechanical things. The temperature must already be below freezing. I shiver in my coat, and close my eyes.

We sit on the train, at our usual table, and Guy goes to the bar for drinks and crisps. Ellen has invited a woman along from the lounge; she is an illustrator called Kerry who lives in Bodmin. I try hard to be bright and engaging, and Kerry is impressed by life on the Friday-night train. She tells us about her life, juggling a young family with work.

'My parents have to come and stay when I need to go to London,' she says, her cheeks dimpling as she sips her drink. She is wearing a thick mustard jumper and white flowers in her hair, which looks incongruous but somehow pleasing. 'It needs ruthless organisation, but the moment I step on the train I'm a different person. I love it.'

'Yes,' I agree. I am staring at Guy, who is chatting to the barman. Kerry's phone beeps, and she looks at it, then stands up.

'I'm going to have to love you and leave you,' she says. I never really know why people say that. It is an odd phrase. 'I need to call home. I'll be back in a little bit, though, all being well. Save my drink.'

She walks off, pressing her phone then lifting it to her ear. She is being a good wife.

Guy is gathering up the drinks, talking to someone else at the bar. Ellen reaches across and puts a hand on my cheek.

'Hey,' she says. 'Lara. What's going on?'

I flinch, then look at her and decide that if I could trust anyone, it would be Ellen.

'What do you mean?'

'Oh, don't do that. You're not yourself. You're incredibly on edge. Come on, sweetie. What?'

I bite my lip and look at the darkness outside the window. Paddington station is still out there. It is only quarter to eleven: the train won't leave for another hour.

'I'm going to leave Sam,' I tell her, my heart thudding as I say the words. 'I can't do this any more. And Guy's going to leave Diana. This weekend. Tomorrow.'

Her eyebrows shoot up.

'Is he? Is he really?' She pauses, weighing up her words. 'Just don't be surprised if he comes back and says he couldn't do it. He'll have an excuse. The moment wasn't right. Et cetera. It's a big thing to do, to pull a family apart.'

I am ashamed of myself. 'I know. And of course he can take as long as he wants. I'm leaving Sam no matter what.'

'Will you move back to London? Will we lose you from the train?'

'I suppose.'

'We'll still see you in London. Well, Guy will, of course, but I hope that I will too.'

'Of course, Ellen. Always. And Ellen?'

'Yes?'

'There's something else . . .'

But I stop, because Guy is back, passing each of us a drink. Ellen has a little bottle of white wine, and Guy and I are both having gin and tonics. He puts Kerry's miniature wine bottle down on the table. I signal to Ellen with my eyes that I cannot tell the story in front of Guy, not now, though I am desperate to offload it.

'This is yours,' he says, carefully giving me the plastic cup with the black stirring stick in it.

'Why's it mine? What's different?'

'Oh, I took the liberty of getting you a double. Bloke at the bar said you looked as if you needed it, and when I looked over, you did. You really did. Dutch courage for the weekend.'

His voice is so kind, his concern so genuine that even though I remind myself that he is married and a father and on his way back to his unsuspecting family, I am overwhelmed with love for him. I want him desperately. I long to be with him legitimately.

'Thanks,' I say. 'I told Ellen about our plans. Sorry. I couldn't help it.'

'Cheers,' says Ellen, pouring her wine into her plastic glass.

We all raise our cups.

'To you, Lara,' Ellen says, just before I take a sip. 'This is you doing the right thing. And to you, Guy – and good luck with working out what the right thing is.'

I hear Guy say: 'Oh, tell me about it,' as I take a gulp from my drink, and then another.

I feel the alcohol coursing through me, and numbing me. I take one more sip. The periphery of my vision starts to go black. I am more tired than I realised.

I will just lean back, rest my head for a moment. Without meaning to, I let my head slump sideways and feel myself slipping down so I am resting on Guy's shoulder.

I vaguely hear their voices. 'Lara!' they both say. 'Lara, are you OK?' I hear the woman, Kerry, coming back, hear the concern in her tone without being able to make out the words.

'Yeah, fine,' I hear myself answering. I open my eyes a little. 'Fine. Just tired.'

'She's very stressed,' Ellen's voice says, and then she is taking charge. 'Come on. She knocked half that drink back very quickly. No wonder she's keeled over. Let's get her back to her compartment and tuck her in. You leave her alone tonight, matey. OK? Next week she'll be all yours, by the sound of it.'

'Oh,' he says. 'Right. Yes. All right. She'll be all right, won't she? Hey, Wilberforce?'

It takes an enormous effort to force my legs to walk, but I do my best, and with one of them on either side of me and Kerry somewhere nearby, we make our way slowly to my compartment, which is in the carriage next to the lounge car.

They put me on my bed. I hear their voices, though now they are so muffled that I cannot even distinguish individual words. Someone takes the shoes off my feet. They pull the bedding over me, and switch the light out, and then they are gone.

I feel the blackness breaking over me like a wave, and as the train clanks along the tracks, I succumb.

The chime of an incoming email pierces the darkness, and I am wide awake, as if the noise had activated my 'on' switch. I reach for my phone in the dark, but because I did not put myself to bed, it is not in its place in the mesh net beside my head. Normally I turn its volume off at night but leave it on. The blue light is bathing everything in the room in a woozy half-glow, but I have no idea where the phone could be.

The train is moving. I have no idea how long I have been asleep.

I feel horribly sick, and then I realise I need to move quickly. I stand up and lurch to the basin, fumbling with the lid and clicking it up just in time.

As I hunch over it, waiting for the eruption I know is

about to happen, I hear a second message arrive and register the fact that the phone is still in my bag, just as I am sick into the basin, hugely, urgently sick with a stream of acidic liquid. I hope the little sink is up to the job: the idea of its not draining is horrendous.

I wash it away, wipe my mouth on the First Great Western flannel, and shakily brush my teeth. Then I make my trembling legs take me back, to sit on the edge of the bed. I find the bag, locate the phone in its front inside pocket.

Then I laugh. I was woken by two junk emails, one from Pizza Express and the other from the dotcomgiftshop, from whom I bought a little light once and who now email me more regularly than any actual human being. There is, however, also a text from Guy, from what I realise was only an hour ago, when I was comatose. I have hardly been asleep for any time: it is only half past midnight.

Lovely Wilberforce, he has written. *I'm going to be worrying about you all night, but I know Ellen's right and I must leave you to sleep. If you wake and want to see me it's F21. I love you. Truly. We will make this happen. xxx*

I stand up, wobbly but surprisingly well recovered, and try to unlock my door, realising as I do so that it was not locked in the first place, because I had not been capable of doing it.

I stumble along happily, and his words run through my head again and again. He loves me. He has never said that before, and I have carefully not said it to him either. We will make it happen. He loves me. We will make it happen.

I walk down the narrow corridor, enclosed in my familiar world, with its institutional train smell, its reassuring constant movement. In the space between carriages, I pass a man in pyjama bottoms and flip-flops heading towards the loo. He gives me a 'we're in this together' smile, and I return it. I knock on Guy's door, and when he doesn't reply, I try the handle and push it open.

The scream rises in my throat. I grab the door frame to keep myself upright while I stare at the scene in front of me, a scene that makes no sense at all.

The train grinds to a halt, and everything is still.

part two

Iris

chapter thirteen

It was one of the sobbing mornings. They were happening more and more frequently, and I hated them. I was furious with myself for behaving so illogically. This kind of thing was not meant to happen.

I woke, in absolute darkness, crying, hiccuping, and feeling hopeless. For a second I thought Laurie was not beside me, that he had slipped away in the night, but then I saw that he was there, sleeping peacefully on his side, his mouth slightly open. I had not even disturbed him.

The only thing I could do was to get out. I took my bike and rode away into the blackness.

It was better at once. There was something invigorating about being out on a dry winter morning with my bike lights on (I put two on the front and two on the back as a nod to safety), my long hair squashed on top by my helmet, my furry coat covered by a huge reflective jacket. As soon as my feet crunched across the frozen grass, something lightened inside me. I was just a tiny part of a huge universe, and nothing really mattered. Every single thing was temporary, and one day all of us would be gone without trace. It was an intensely soothing thought.

I retrieved my bike from the place I left it when I remembered, hidden in the hedge. I appreciated the fact that the little noises of cycling – the heaves and squeaks of a bike setting off, the crunch of a stony lane under tyres – were the loudest thing in this tiny corner of the cosmos.

I knew it was past six o'clock, but it felt more like two in the morning. There were owls screeching as I set off down the lane, and invisible night creatures fled into undergrowth at my approach. I could hear the occasional distant car, and I liked the feeling of solidarity, and particularly the certain knowledge that whoever was in that car would never think to wonder if there was a woman on a bicycle somewhere nearby, listening.

I knew, as I cycled towards the main road, that one day I was going to have to stop running away. Things were not right between me and Laurie and I knew that, if I were braver, I would have been addressing that fact. One day he would leave. He would have to. It would be better if I were to take control and make it happen, rather than continuing to limp on like this.

Sometimes I came close to losing my poise completely. I could feel myself edging closer to yelling at him, swearing, demanding that he get out of my bed and my head. When he went away just before Christmas, relief had ambushed me. I had functioned fine. I even had a friend over to the house, like a normal person, and even though I had panicked when she insisted on coming to my house rather than meeting in town or at the beach, it had ended up being the most satisfying interaction with someone from the real world that I'd had for years.

That was what I would do, I decided as the light from the street lamps on the main road started to illuminate my surroundings. There was the church, the trees, the houses set back from the road. I would go and call in on her. That would calm me down. It would give me enough of a blast of reality to keep me functioning for a while.

I had spent the previous evening sitting by the wood burner, painting my toenails carefully lilac, and trying to pluck up the courage to ask him to go away again, to travel, to do something without me. I was his whole world, and he was mine, and that, I was finally suspecting, was not healthy. Other people did not live like this. We kept people away by being rude to them. It was not the way I was brought up, but it was quite enjoyable.

'I'm not going to leave you,' he kept protesting. 'Not ever again,' and I was so infuriated, and so annoyed with myself for being a tiny bit grateful for his insistence, that I'd burst into tears and stormed off to bed.

We lived on the outskirts of a village which itself was on the outskirts of Falmouth, which was, I suppose, a town on the outskirts of Great Britain. The two of us had hidden here for years, shutting out everyone, and it had suited us both, for a while. We lived with the cats, Ophelia and Desdemona, and I worked at home, proof-reading impenetrable legal books that arrived by special delivery every few weeks. Our life was small, but then one week I bought a lottery ticket with the Saturday paper on a whim, and now everything was surreally different.

I had not told Laurie that I had won the lottery. My plans were not going to include him.

I pulled on to the main road, which was pleasingly

empty of cars. I would, I thought, go into Falmouth and wander around for a while, have breakfast in a café now that I could do such a thing without counting the pennies, and then I would go to visit Lara. I liked the idea of our setting up a little routine of going to one another's houses, with neither Laurie nor her grumpy husband involved.

I did not know Lara well, at all. She lived in London for most of the week, making lovely old buildings into horrible identikit 'luxury apartments', and her husband, on the two occasions I had met him, had made no secret of the fact that he wished I had not been there. I had done my best to radiate his hostility right back at him. Nonetheless, getting to know Lara felt like a first tentative step back into the world. She was, unwittingly, my test friend. I made an effort, with her, not to shut her out, not to be brusque or sharp. It was hard at first, but I liked it after a while.

She had spoken enthusiastically about her commute on the night train, when I saw her on Christmas Eve. She loved that train. She would be getting off it that morning, transferring in the grey half-light to the Falmouth service. I would show up and see what happened. If they told me to go away, I would. If she was busy, I would cycle home. It was just an idea.

I chained my bike to a traffic sign outside Trago's as it started to get light. The street lights were still on as the sky turned pink, and I was warm on the inside from my bike ride, and cold on my cheeks. It would be a while until I was able to get breakfast, I thought, so I would find the coast path and stroll for a bit instead.

I walked for an hour along the clifftops, until the path descended to the beach at Maenporth. That stretch of coast path was crunchy, with glassed-over puddles and solid peaks and troughs of frozen mud. The sea was as perfectly still as a pond, and the bare branches of the trees around me did not move at all. I passed one runner, a skinny man with the muscular leanness and hollow cheeks of one who exercises too much, and one dog walker, a woman in her forties with wild insomniac eyes.

The sea air was painfully fresh and filled me with ideas and possibilities. I lost myself in daydreams of travel, and was surprised to reach my destination so quickly. I walked across the beach to the place where the high tide met the stones and deposited its seaweed, and stared out at the solitary tanker close to the horizon, I decided to turn around and walk straight back, all the way to Pendennis point and around it to Lara's house.

I knew I should go back to London, just for a visit. Laurie wouldn't mind that. I walked back quickly, tentatively planning. From London you could be in Paris in a fraction of the time it took to get anywhere from Falmouth. From Paris you could catch a train to anywhere in Europe; or you could go to an airport and pick a destination. This money, my secret money, could literally take me anywhere in the world. I did not have a clue where to find the courage to start.

During my walk back I played fantasy destinations. I tried to picture myself looking out of a train window in India, or learning to tango in Argentina, or bungee jumping in New Zealand. Sometimes I got close to thinking I might actually be able to do it. Then I remembered that I was the least adventurous person in the world and that my grand plans had always stayed in my head, and that my passport had been firmly in the filing cabinet for the past five years. I could not leave Laurie behind; not without telling him. If I left, I had no idea what would become of him.

Lara's house was an odd little modern one, bright white and unusual, somewhere between a Californian art deco place and a British seaside bungalow. There was a car in the drive, the same blue Renault she had driven when she came to visit me. Because the house was on a hill, the actual garden was at a lower level, and I leaned over a railing and found I was looking down on it from a storey up. It was a nice garden, grassy, with a clematis and a camellia briskly awaiting spring, and a brown-leaved palm tree towering high above everything.

I rang the doorbell, energised by the exercise and suddenly starving, because it occurred to me that I had forgotten the part of my plan that had involved breakfast. I would stop at the shops on the way home and fill my basket with food.

There were heavy footsteps inside and the door flew open.

Lara's husband was broad and blondish, with bits of grey that were barely noticeable in his light hair. He was wearing jeans and a baggy jumper and old man's slippers. I took all this in while noticing that the moment he saw me, his face dropped dramatically, from an already low starting point. It was verging on the crumpled.

'Oh,' he said. He was shorter than I remembered and his appearance was a million times more shambolic. He was even less welcoming than he had been last time. If he'd had an aura, it would have crackled and sparked with hostility. I tried to stop mine doing the same. Mentally, I smoothed myself down. I stood in the faint winter sunshine and forced a smile.

'Hi.' I tried to remember his name. 'Hi, I'm Iris. We met before. I'm a friend of Lara's . . .'

He interrupted. 'Yes. Lara. Where is she?'

I stared. 'Where is she?'

'Is she with you? Have you got a message? What's happened?' His voice was rising. 'Where is she? Tell me. Where is she? What has happened to my wife?'

chapter fourteen

'You're sure you haven't seen her?' he asked again. 'Or heard from her? When did you last hear from her? Why isn't she answering her phone? Why have you turned up if you didn't know something was wrong?'

I sat on the edge of the sofa. The sitting room was bright, even in this pale morning light. Other people's central heating always smelled odd, because our cottage was only heated by its wood burner. Radiators made houses feel nostalgically comforting.

'She's late getting home,' I told him. 'People often are.' I wondered if I could ask for a coffee, since he clearly wasn't going to be offering. Food was obviously not going to be an option.

Her train, according to her husband, had arrived at 7.38, right on time. But she wasn't on it. 'She's always on the train,' he told me. 'Well, once she wasn't because the sleeper was late, but she called me to say that and then she was on the next one. And now the next train's already come and she wasn't on that either.'

Sam. That was his name. I was almost sure of it.

'Right,' I said. 'I'm sure there'll be a reason. Maybe she's lost her phone. Perhaps the train's late and she's lost her phone or it's broken. My phone goes wrong a lot. I bet they've broken down outside Liskeard or something, where there isn't any reception.'

He was staring out of the window, at the Docks station behind the house. It was a good vantage point for examining people arriving: no one could get off the train here without Sam seeing them. I could feel him willing her to saunter off the next train with an excuse that, the moment she said it, would make perfect sense.

'She works so hard. Spends half her life on the sleeper. All to pay off our debts. It's taking longer than we planned: her life in London is expensive because her sister . . . Anyway, I need her. Where is she?'

He was on the verge of falling apart, and, much as I did not want to, I knew I had to take charge. I was afraid on Sam's behalf: not that she was not safe, but that she wasn't coming home to him. I kept staring at his phone, waiting, like him, for something to change.

'Sam,' I said, and when he did not react I knew I had his name right. 'Sam. We need to call the train company. First Great Western.'

'I looked on the website. It didn't say anything. In the stuff they have about broken-down trains and all that. There's some things but not that. Can you check it again?'

'Of course. And can I make some coffee? You look like you could do with it.'

I was pleased with this. Making it for him, supportively, while getting my own much-needed caffeine fix: this was a plan with no down side.

'In the machine. I always make it when she's due back. Chuck it away. It's been there too long.'

His face crumpled again, and I had to push him down

into a chair, then go to sort out the coffee. I was desperate for it. There were four croissants on a plate, but I knew it would be too crass were I to eat one. I could not be the woman who came to this house and scoffed a missing woman's croissant.

'I'll call the train people,' I told him. 'Websites don't always get updated, do they? Particularly not early on weekend mornings. So if she normally gets off the train at half past seven, she's not much more than an hour late yet. Honestly, Sam. She'll be fine.'

Their coffee machine was a stove-top percolator. I tipped out the old, cold stuff and looked for a pan so I could warm some milk to go with it.

Other people's kitchens were odd, I thought. There was a strange intimacy to finding your way around, to trying to imagine where they might keep the cups and whether the coffee would be in the fridge or somewhere else.

For a moment I pretended that I was Lara, and that this was a routine domestic chore. It hit me with a flash, and I jumped back, knowing at once that she was bored with Sam. He was boring. She was not. She had probably left him.

I loitered, spooning ground coffee into the right component of the machine. All I could hear was Sam's laboured breathing, and I became more certain that she would be in touch only to say she was not coming home. She had been jumpy on Christmas Eve. There were things she was not telling me.

According to the website, the train had left London on time, and had reached Truro on time before arriving, on time, at its end destination in Penzance. However, Penzance station, I noticed, was now closed, 'due to an incident'.

That generally meant someone jumping under a train, I thought. It would be hard to jump under a train at Penzance, the terminus: trains would surely be going too slowly to make it worthwhile. Still, people were inventive.

The train had come, but without her on it. She had decided not to return home today. I did not like to bring up this glaringly obvious potential scenario.

Sam sat at the table beside the window that looked out at the Docks train station, and called her mobile every few minutes.

'Where does she live in London?' I asked, cradling my coffee. 'Could you call her flat?' I wanted him to catch her out, to force her to admit to whatever she was doing.

'She doesn't have a flat.' He did not take his eyes off the train station. There were a few people waiting on the platform, and so I supposed that a train was due soon. 'She stayed at her sister's place for a while but that didn't work out. That's why we haven't paid half the bills yet. She's been at a hotel. Terrible idea financially, but it's made her happy. I think it has.'

'Well, call the hotel, then.'

I saw him think about that. 'Will you do it? Sorry. I don't even know you. Will you ring the hotel and see if she's left for the weekend?'

He was looking more wretched by the second.

It took me ages to get through to a human being, but eventually I was talking to a man who was brisk and efficient, with a slight eastern European accent.

'Lara Finch?' he said, and I could hear his fingers tapping away. 'Oh yes. She's always here on a Monday, and they always leave on a Friday morning. No change this week. She checked out yesterday. Is there a problem?'

'Yes,' I told him firmly. 'There is. She's missing.'

That startled him. 'Missing? Do the police know?'

'We're about to call them. Um.' I looked over at Sam. A train had pulled into the little station with a dramatic squeaking of brakes, and he was on his feet, his hands pressed to the window. I left the room and took the phone into the hallway, out, I hoped, of earshot. 'Is anyone else in her room? Could you go and have a look in there?'

'I'm sorry, madam. The room has been cleaned and it's now being occupied by other guests. We have a quite different clientele at weekends from during the week, you see. If Mrs Finch is missing, we will be more than happy to help out in any way we can. I do urge you to call the police. I will ask the cleaner if Mrs Finch left anything behind, of course.'

'Thanks,' I said. 'Can I give you a number, just in case?' I had no idea what Sam's mobile number was, so I gave him my own number and made a mental note to turn the phone on. Then I wandered into the kitchen and spotted a postcard pinned to the fridge: landline: 551299. I gave him that number too.

'I am sure she'll turn up safe and sound,' he said, talking to me in the same tone I had been using with Sam. 'We hope to see her on Monday.'

One look at Sam's face told me that, again, she had not stepped off the train.

'Sam,' I told him. 'You need to speak to the police.'

I sat next to him on the sofa and took his hand, which was squashy and hairless and completely different from Laurie's. Laurie's fingers were long and slender and beautiful.

'Can you put your hand on my arm?' he said. I looked at him.

'What?'

'It's what Lara does. When we're talking and things. She puts a hand on my arm, right here.' He pointed to the spot. 'And keeps it there while she talks. It's comforting. Silly, I suppose.'

I put a hand on his forearm, in the spot he had shown me. I had no idea how long I was supposed to leave it there.

I came here to visit my tentative friend Lara, on a whim, and now I was sitting on her sofa, self-consciously holding her husband's arm, waiting for the sound of her key in the door. This was why I never did impulsive things: you had no idea how they were going to turn out.

Sam was so close to me that our thighs were touching, and I wanted to move away but I couldn't. I did not want to be that close to him. I wanted her to come back. At the very least I wanted her to get in touch. It was horrible of her to leave him waiting like this, imagining unspeakable accidents.

I imagined it so hard, harder with every second that passed, that it seemed I really heard it. I heard the metallic fumble of a key being fitted into a space that precisely enclosed it. The twisting of the lock mechanism. The pushing of a large wooden flap so there was a gap in the wall. The rustles and footsteps of a person entering the building. A voice. 'Sam?'

There was a dead weight in my stomach. That was not real. It was not going to happen.

chapter fifteen

When somebody did come to the door, I got to my feet slowly. It was not going to be her, and yet there was the smallest of chances. Perhaps this would be the moment when she walked in with a breezy explanation and salvaged it all, and I got to go home. Maybe, I thought, she was ringing the bell rather than using her key as a gesture of sheepishness, because she knew she had done something bad by not letting Sam know what had happened to her.

Lara had always been full of life and energy. The air around her sparkled with bright white light. If she were there now she would be in a cloud of apologetic maroon. That would be fine.

Sam stayed on the sofa, conspicuously pretending to be casual. I made my steps stay measured as I strolled to the front door, past a formal photograph of the two of them at their wedding, past a framed film poster of Hitchcock's *Vertigo*. Neither of us alluded to the fact that this was the first approach of the outside world since she had gone. This was, in a way, much the closest she had been to coming back.

There were two police officers. I instantly felt that I was

162

guilty of some terrible crime. The outside world rushed in with an icy blast: it was colder out there than I remembered. I quelled my sudden urge to run down the hill and find my bike and ride home, puffing and frozen.

'Hi there,' said the woman, who was much shorter than me. She had hair cropped slightly shorter than her face could handle, and earrings that were studs in the shape of little hearts. She also wore the face of a person who would take no nonsense. 'We had a call about Mrs Lara Finch.'

The man nodded, looking into my face, assessing me. I looked back, at his Harry Potter glasses and his smooth face, so cleanly shaven that it was still pink, and reminded myself that I had nothing to hide. He was so much taller than she was that together they looked almost funny, but both of them bristled with brisk efficiency, and since they were police, I decided not to point out the comic disparity.

I thought of Laurie, and reminded myself not to say or do anything that would make these people turn up at my house.

'She's missing,' I said, wondering how many times you would have to say those two words before you stopped feeling as though you were parroting lines from a TV drama. If Lara had left Sam, then she was missing on her own terms.

'Come in.' I stepped aside like a gracious hostess, noticing the man giving my hand-knitted cardigan an amused once-over as he passed. Sam was on his feet, his hand outstretched before they even came in. He was transparently, pathetically grateful for the attention.

'I'm Iris,' I told the woman. 'A friend of Lara's. I actually just dropped by to see her. I had no idea . . .'

'DC Jessica Staines,' said the woman.

'Lovely view from here,' the man said. 'DC Alexander Zielowski.'

'DC Alexander Zielowski? That's like a cop's name from the telly.'

He nodded, apparently mildly amused, but not very.

'Yes,' he said. 'Though it will astonish you to discover that I'm not actually the hard-bitten New Yorker you might expect from my name.'

'Can I get you a coffee?' I said. He nodded.

'Yes please.' Jessica turned to me, taking charge. 'That would be great. Thanks. So, we understand that Mrs Finch was travelling on the sleeper train last night, and that she has failed to come home. Could you tell me all about the circumstances, please, Mr Finch?'

She was much more businesslike, less casual, than I would have expected, considering that we were talking about an adult who had simply not shown up at her own house. Very soon I came to suspect from the urgency of their questions that the police knew something we did not. I fumbled with the coffee, put it on the gas ring, and went straight back over to them.

'We had unsuccessful fertility treatment,' Sam was saying, 'and so we decided to look into adopting from abroad. Trouble was, we'd spent our savings. We needed some cash. Lara was offered a six-month contract working back in her old line of work in London. She's in property development – a project director, working on a development at the back of Tate Modern. She's brilliant. The money was literally three times what I earn at the shipyard, with some extra allowances towards travel and all that. So she went off to do it.' He sounded as if he were not expecting to be believed. 'She's doing it for us, so that we can start the adoption process. That's why.' His voice cracked and he started to cry.

'Now,' said Jessica, sitting on the sofa beside him. DC

Alexander took the single chair, and I hovered on my feet, close to the kitchen. 'So here's the thing. This is not going to be easy to hear, I'm afraid. When last night's sleeper train arrived at Penzance this morning, the First Great Western staff discovered a body in one of the cabins.'

Sam gasped. I reached for the wall to steady myself. The coffee whooshed and bubbled like a steam train. The words 'she's dead' filled my mind, repeating themselves on a loop.

'A *man*'s body,' DC Alex said quickly, raising his voice to be heard over the sound of the coffee. 'Not your wife's. I do apologise.' He looked at Jessica. 'We should have made that clear. Penzance station is closed until further notice, and the train is a crime scene. Every passenger is being questioned by our colleagues in Penzance, working for the MCIT.' He looked at our blank faces. 'Major Crime Investigation Team. In this context, obviously your report of Mrs Finch's disappearance is being taken extremely seriously. We were asked to come because Penzance had no spare manpower, but they are quite likely to want to talk to you soon, if Mrs Finch does not turn up safe and well. If she does, they will, of course, want to speak to her urgently.'

I went to pour the coffee. The percolator only made enough for two cups, so I gave them to the police. Sam did not look as if he would be able to swallow anything; and I knew I could not.

'Did this man die of natural causes?' I managed to ask, as I carried the cups shakily to the officers. An elderly man having a heart attack on the train would be almost palatable, verging on the ordinary. I imagined him lying on a train bed, whatever such a thing was like, and clutching his chest, his face contorting into the last grimace it would ever make. In my mind he was very old, so old that everyone would immediately be able to say that he'd had a good life and at least he was active right up to the end: 'He was amazing, wasn't he? The sleeper train at his age!'

That man's death would not have given rise to a crime scene, and I knew it.

'Early indications,' said Jessica blankly, 'are that this is not the case. It is being treated as a suspicious death. Thanks, this coffee's brilliant. Beyond that, we are waiting for more details. The body was discovered by staff shortly before arrival into Penzance; they go round the cabins ensuring everyone is awake. All the passengers were detained at the station, fingerprints taken, travel tickets seized and so on.' I saw Sam sit up, transparently hoping that this explained Lara's disappearance, but of course she continued: 'As Mrs Finch would have left the train at Truro, she was unlikely to be among them. We checked, of course, when we got your call, and indeed, she was not on the train at that point.'

She was very calm, though her fingers fiddled cease-lessly with a piece of lined paper she had folded into a fan shape. When she sipped her coffee, the cup trembled slightly. I wondered how often Falmouth police had to deal with something like this. I was sure that most of their time must have been spent issuing fines for dog shit and policing the students' exits from what nightclubs there were in the early weekend hours.

I decided to make coffee for Sam and me, partly because he would probably need it – I certainly did – but mainly to give me an excuse to walk away. I listened to them taking Sam through Lara's movements again, as method-ically as they could make him do it. I could not believe that I had stumbled into this.

'So you have no idea whether or not she got on the

train?' DC Alex asked. I clicked the gas on and watched the blue flames licking the side of the coffee pot once more. 'Did she normally let you know when she was at Paddington station, or leaving work? Would you speak on a Friday night?'

Sam sounded defensive.

'When she started the job, she'd call twice a day. Then, you know, she kind of settled into it and we didn't need to be on the phone all the time. We always speak at some point during every day, though. No matter what. There are people she talks to on the train every week,' he said quickly. 'They'd know if she was there. There's a woman who lives in Penzance. Ellen. Lara likes her a lot. And I think there was a man too, though she hasn't mentioned him for a while. But she used to go for a drink with them on the train. Loads of people would know if she caught it or missed it. Those same people you're talking to . . .' His voice tailed off.

'She checked out of her hotel as usual,' I called over. 'I rang the place where she stays, this morning. They said she left as normal.'

In fact, the man had said 'they' left as normal, but I was trying not to consider that as anything other than a harried hotel receptionist using the wrong word. I was certainly not going to be mentioning it to the police in front of Sam.

'The moment you hear from her,' said Alexander Zielowski as I poured the second lot of coffee into two stripy mugs, 'please let us know. Instantly. This is absolutely crucial. Tell her to contact us as a matter of the utmost urgency. Meanwhile our colleagues will be asking the other passengers for any information that could help us trace her movements.'

There was something gentle about Alex Zielowski, and I liked the way you could tell that he had depths. If I was colouring him in, I would use a gentle pale blue, my favourite colour. I was intrigued about what might be going on under his surface. I never met new people, ever, and this morning, under the most unsettling of circumstances, I had met several.

I was colouring in the police (Jessica was orange, with some more vulnerable yellow around the edges) in an attempt to stop thinking about Lara. Someone was dead, and she was nowhere. I fought hard not to picture her twisted body lying in a track-side ditch, flung from the train by a shadowy figure because she had seen too much.

Now Jessica took over the questions, wondering, in a far blunter way than Alexander had, whether Sam and Lara had argued last weekend, whether she was the sort of person who would sulk, whether there was any reason he could think of for her to have stayed away. Did she, Jessica wondered, ever mislay her phone and purse? Did she have any ongoing medical problems? It went on and on. In the light of the man's death, these looked like kind questions, questions that, if answered the right way, could bring Lara back with an apology for all the bother.

While she was mid-probe, and I was trying to busy myself clearing up the kitchen, Alexander took a phone call. As soon as I heard his tone, I stared at him and focused. He wandered towards me as he spoke, to take him away from Sam. Jessica was pretending to concentrate on Sam telling her that he and Lara never argued, ever, but I could see that she too was listening intently to her colleague.

'Ah,' he said. 'I see. I'm with her husband now, in fact . . . Yes, of course.'

When he hung up, the silence solidified. It was the only thing in the room. When he broke it, he had adopted a formal tone, as if he were at a press conference, distancing himself from the words he had to say.

'So,' he said, 'the passenger is confirmed as having been murdered. He has been identified as Guy Thomas, and several regular passengers and staff on the train have suggested that he was close to your wife, Mr Finch. Has she ever mentioned him?'

Sam closed his eyes.

'Close to my wife?' he said, trying out the phrase, testing its meaning. 'She might have mentioned him once or twice. There was someone called Guy. But he definitely wasn't close to her.'

After a flurry of phone calls and low-voiced consultations, Alexander left. Jessica stayed behind but announced that she would keep in the background. 'Pretend I'm not here,' she said, and stood by the window staring out at the view. She listed things we were not allowed to do, the main one of which was that Sam was not allowed anywhere near his computer.

He slumped on the sofa and leaned heavily on me. It was uncomfortable, but I bore it as long as I could. I wanted to put the news on and see what they were saying about dead Guy Thomas. I wanted to go online and find out everything.

'Sam,' I said, in the end. Mainly I wanted to be in front of my wood burner with my cats, telling all of this to Laurie. He no more knew where I was than Sam knew where Lara was. 'You need someone else with you, not me and Jessica. I'll call somebody. It's insane that no one but the two of us and the police, and maybe that hotel receptionist, I suppose, knows that Lara's missing. I'm sure it'll be on the news in a second, and then everyone's going to want to talk to you. You don't want your family, her family, to find it out that way. Give me numbers and I'll ring people. Who's your best friend in Falmouth?'

He looked at me, completely blank. His face was crumpled. I wanted, suddenly, to shout at him to pull himself together. This was not a moment for falling apart. Not yet.

'Stay here, Iris. You're Lara's friend. Stay with me. Please. Don't leave.'

'Sam. Do you have parents? Siblings?' I did not like to assume anything. 'There must be somebody.'

He put his head in his hands and groaned. It was a weird, animalistic noise.

'Oh fucking hell. Look, I know you have to call my mum. She'll kill me if she sees it on the news. She and Lara never really . . . But Iris. Will you hold off at least until they know whether she was on the train or not? Will you do that? I still think she might just rock up. I don't care what she's done. As long as she's safe.'

'I'm happy to stay as long as you want.' I wasn't, but I could hardly say so. 'But you'll feel better if it's not a stranger here making your coffee and answering your door. Really you will. I won't contact your mum yet if you don't want me to, but let me just get you a friend.'

Jessica wandered into the kitchen. 'Mind if I put the kettle on?' she asked. Sam said nothing.

'Go ahead,' I told her. 'Sam. Who shall I call?'

He was not having it. 'Please, Iris. Please. I have friends at work, I suppose, but not the sort you're talking about. Any of my colleagues, if they got a call from you asking them to come and babysit me, would be . . . taken aback, I suppose. They'd assume I had real friends for this sort of emergency. Lara and I. We've always been so close. There's never been any need for anyone else. We have each other.'

And she'd had, in one way or another, Guy Thomas. The words hung in the air, unsayable.

Sam's elbow knocked his phone off the arm of the sofa, and he leaned down and snatched it up from the floor, his face suddenly alive with the hope that a message might have arrived without his hearing it in the nanosecond for which it was away from him.

'Nothing,' he said. 'Iris. What the hell is going on? What was she doing? Where is she? She can't just . . . not be here.'

I sat next to him and touched his arm.

'We'll find out,' I told him. I had no desire at all to be grumpy with him any more. His situation was terrible, and it was going to get worse. 'At some point, we will. And I know what you mean about not needing anyone else. Not many people would get that, but I really, really do. If I were you I wouldn't have anyone to call either. I know how much you've missed her. It's funny, you know: the two of you gave the impression of being one of those couples with hundreds of friends. I thought you'd be going to people's houses for dinner every weekend. You know. Stuff like that.' I realised I had used the past tense instead of the present, and hoped he hadn't noticed.

'Not at all,' he said. 'We just want to be with each other. That's all we do.'

'I'm the same.' I glanced up at Jessica. She was fiddling with her phone next to a noisy kettle, and seemed not to be listening to us. 'Me and my boyfriend, Laurie. We're like that.'

'Who wants loads of "friends" texting all the time and trying to get you to do things you don't want to do?'

'Not me. I like having my music as loud as I like. And doing things the way I want to do them. And having Laurie to talk to, just Laurie. We've lived like that for years.'

I thought of my old life, when I had lived and worked in London. In those days I'd had lots of friends. I had been missing that, lately. I never thought it would happen. It was a hankering for something else that had led me to Sam's door that morning.

He looked at me with a sad little smile.

'You do understand,' he said. 'So imagine if your boyfriend vanished. And someone was dead. And it was all horrific and nonsensical, exactly like a nightmare but actually real. And if they told you that your boyfriend was "close" to the dead person. How you would feel.'

I refused to entertain that scenario. 'If Lara had been here as usual today,' I said instead, patting Sam's hand in what I wanted to be an affectionate and reassuring way. He immediately grabbed my hand and held it so tightly that it hurt. 'And I'd turned up on the doorstep, just dropping in to say hello, you'd have been pissed off, wouldn't you?'

He laughed, but without smiling. 'I would. But when she comes back, you can drop in whenever you like. In fact, please, please do. You get to be our friend. No one else. Just you.'

'Thank you.'

I joined him in the strenuous mental effort he was making to pretend that everything was going to be all right. It was becoming harder. A man was dead and she was missing. That implied so strongly that she was dead too that I had to turn away from the thought. It dazzled me, so bright, so obvious that I had to look in the opposite direction. I had to pretend she was about to arrive home, flustered, with a complicated story, but safe. The police-woman in the kitchen would smile and set off for her next engagement.

I paced around the house. As the upstairs was almost entirely open-plan, there was not much to discover, and I did not like to ask permission to go and poke around.

'Your bedroom's downstairs, then?' I asked.

'Yep.' He looked at me and produced an unexpected laugh. 'Go ahead. Have a look round the house if you like. Nothing to hide. I can see you want to. Lara would too.'

It could end up being a crime scene, but since she had not been home, and that was the whole point, I felt it was safe to give myself a little tour. She had, after all, done the same at my house.

I looked at Jessica Staines. She shrugged. 'OK, but don't touch anything.'

Sam ignored her.

'Unlock the back door down there,' he said to me, 'and go into the garden. You should explore properly.'

'You'll be OK? Yell if anything happens.'

'Of course.'

He looked a bit excited, as if a small change in the status quo might have been going to impel the phone to ring. I was secretly hoping the same.

I liked the fact that the house was, to conventional eyes, upside down. At the bottom of the stairs there was what should have been a landing, but as it was on the ground floor I didn't think it could be called that. Perhaps it was a hall, instead. I pushed the nearest door and found myself in what must have been the marital bedroom.

The duvet was pulled so straight on the king-size bed

that there was no crease in it at all, and the room smelled of cleaning materials. It was not the way you would expect the room of a man living alone most of the time to be. Not if you lazily assumed all men to be slobs.

I looked at the photographs, because they were all over every wall. It was, in the light of the circumstances, verging on the chilling. Before my eyes they were morphing into photographs that you see on the news, on the front of newspapers. There was Lara, beautiful and glowing, on her wedding day, standing with her hand on a younger, slimmer Sam's arm, smiling into the camera. I had no time for weddings in general, but I had to admit that the archaic white dress and the bouquet of rosebuds suited her. Sam was bursting with happiness at her side: I could tell that across the years and through the images.

More pictures showed them on holiday in New York, and on a beach somewhere, and in London. There were many posed photographs, and a few of Lara on her own, looking up and smiling as Sam snapped her while she was watering a geranium, reading a book, cooking in a wok. There were no reciprocal shots of him.

I imagined him sleeping here while she was away, surrounded by her image. The room was a shrine to her.

One of the bedrooms was a study, and that, too, was antiseptically tidy. A laptop computer was open, but switched off, on the desk, and I did not dare go anywhere near it. The bathroom was clean, and I suddenly realised that he had cleaned and tidied the whole place for her, and that he did that every Friday night. The place was poised for her return, immaculate, courting her approval.

It was odd, the futile wait for someone who was not coming, the lurking presence of a police officer a constant reminder that there was unlikely to be a happy outcome. Since there was nothing at all to do, it was both boring and tense, and Sam begged me not to leave.

'Call your boyfriend, if you like,' he offered, but I shook my head.

'He can fend for himself, for once,' I said, and I thought of Laurie dozing, barely awake enough to notice that I was gone, assuming, when he woke properly, that I was at the shops. He often slept all day because he had little else to do.

I sat on the armchair and flicked through last Saturday's paper, wondering what tomorrow's headlines would announce to the world. Sam was waiting for Lara; I was alert for Jessica receiving news. A train arrived at the little station. Both of us got up as soon as we heard the squeal of its brakes, and watched, in spite of ourselves, as Lara did not get off it. This happened every half-hour.

Eventually Sam let me call his brother, who was aggressively surprised.

'What? You're saying what? She's where? He needs us to drop everything, does he?'

Sighing at the inconvenience, he said he would talk to their mother. I heard him switching a television on, in the background.

When things happened, they came quickly. Two new police officers arrived, both of them men this time. Sam looked at them, transparently longing for an improbable piece of good news. Instead, they arrested him for Guy Thomas's murder.

'It's the most efficient way of getting him in for interview,' Jessica told me, as he was led off, blinking and baffled, his mind as yet unable to catch up with this latest turn of events. 'They'll get samples from him, take his computer, check his alibi. The most straightforward way of doing all that is while he's under arrest.'

I tried to imagine whether Sam might, in fact, be responsible for whatever had happened to his wife. I was pretty sure he was not that good an actor, but I did not know the man. He could have got in that blue car and driven to some point along the train's route. He might have intercepted it, jumped aboard at a stop, and dealt with his wife and this man, Guy Thomas. It was, I supposed, possible.

'Can Iris come too?' he asked, standing at the front door, pulling back, and both he and the two policemen looked at me.

'I have to go home, Sam.' I said it as firmly as I could, and took my bag. Jessica stayed in the house, and I said a guilty goodbye as Sam got into the back of the car. He looked exactly like what he was: someone who was being arrested. I could see how, on paper, he was the obvious suspect. He mouthed something at me through the window, and the police officer who wasn't driving glanced at me with interest.

I stood and watched the car go down the hill and around the corner before I set off in the same direction, heading towards my bike, trying to make myself believe that I had not betrayed Sam by abandoning him.

I cycled fast to get to Laurie with the fish and chips while they were still hot. I ate far too quickly and told him everything. He looked back at me, his eyes wide, and listened intently. The story sounded outlandish, yet he believed it. I wondered what I had ever worried about. My secret plans for solo travelling seemed ridiculous. So there was money in the bank: it was our money. I needed to tell him about it. For now, however, I shared my dreadful day. Now that I was away from Sam, I had the mental space to be horribly, grimly afraid for Lara. If she were alive, she could not be anywhere good. I could no longer convince myself that she was fine.

'So what do you think happened?' he asked, curling up on the cushions on the floor and eating chips with his fingers. 'Someone's killed that poor bloke? And she's maybe seen too much and run away? Or do you think her husband actually did it?'

I wiped my mouth with the square of kitchen roll I had put on the table for this purpose.

'I'm sure Sam wouldn't have had a clue where to start,' I said. 'It can't possibly have been him. Even the police don't really think it's him – I think they just arrested him because you have to eliminate the husband first, if Lara was having an affair with this Guy. I suppose she must have seen too much and . . . I don't know what. It's hard to make sense of it. I don't actually know her well. I like her, though.'

'You should have invited her over here. Introduced me.'

'She came when you were away, before Christmas.'

'She should have come when I was here. She would have got it. You and me. By the sound of it.'

'I can totally see her leaving her husband. There's still a chance that's what happened, isn't there? I mean, she might not even have made it on to the train. It could just be a coincidence, that this guy was killed and she'd decided to stay in London. But she would have told Sam if she wasn't coming. You should have seen him today. Lara wouldn't have done that to anyone, least of all someone she cared about. Her life partner.' I turned away so he wouldn't see my eyes brimming with tears. 'The man she'd wanted to have children with. She'd have told him to his face. At the very least she would have called him. Or written to him. She would have done something. She wouldn't have left without a word.'

'She'd have been a monster.'

'Maybe there's a letter lost in the post. A phone message he hasn't picked up.'

'You realise the chances of her being OK are negligible?'

'Don't say that!'

'You won't leave me, Iris? I wouldn't know what to do. I'd be nothing without you.'

I took a chip from his plate even though I still had plenty on my own, just to show how together we were.

'I'll never leave you,' I said. 'This is the life we've chosen. This is our life. It's all I want.'

I looked into his warm eyes, and he looked back at me, radiating love. I pushed my treacherous daydreams so deep inside myself that I knew he would not see them. I was stifled, but secure. This, I tried to tell myself, would do. Security was enough. Desdemona climbed on to my lap. I started to push her off and then let her stay.

'I'll clear up,' I said. 'I love you, by the way.'

'I love you more,' he retorted, and I wondered, not for the first time, whether he might be right.

chapter sixteen

February

Guy Thomas's house was in the wide-open countryside beyond Penzance. I had to take my bike on the train and then cycle up and down hills for half an hour before I reached it. Although I always felt that Falmouth was in the far west, I now remembered that it was not. There were miles and miles between where we lived and the real west Cornwall.

Here the land was rocky, and the light was different. It was almost ethereal. Here, I knew that I was on the very edge of a continent, on the rocks that stood up from the vast bed of the Atlantic. The air was fresh because there were no cities after Truro, which was many miles to the east. There was Penzance, and there were villages.

The Thomas residence was a solid stone farmhouse outside St Buryan, which itself was not far from Sennen and Land's End. It felt like the end of the world, in a transformative way filled with possibilities. Angels could have glided down from the sky and landed on the road in front of me. Bushes could have burst into flames.

The outside broadcast van parked in the entrance to a field was the first incongruous thing. Then there were cars, half in ditches, all the way up the narrow lane. The gate to what was clearly the Thomases' house was padlocked, and the crowd of journalists hung over it, chatting, callously casual. Their breath huffed out into the air, making little clouds, and they were stamping their feet and texting and looking both bored and surprisingly young. I had somehow imagined grizzled old Fleet Street hacks, but these rosy-cheeked teenagers looked as if they were on work experience.

I barged straight through them and climbed over the gate. Everyone rushed towards me, and they took photos, just in case, when I was halfway over and looking the most inelegant I could possibly have looked. I would have taken my photo if I had been them: I was, however you looked at it, an unlikely visitor to the grieving widow. They had no idea.

'Hello, are you a friend of the family?' said a nice-looking young man. 'How is Diana doing?'

'How are the children?' said someone else.

'Sorry.' I felt I had to say something. After that, though, I could not think of anything, so I walked up the drive, past two cars (one small and red, the other huge and black, a four-by-four kind of thing), and pretended I couldn't hear them.

Everything had changed with the police's confirmation that Lara had been on the train when it left London, and that she had undeniably been having an affair with Guy Thomas, to the extent that their relationship had spilled over into their London existence and they had both effectively been living double lives. Everybody on the sleeper train knew about them. The staff used to take them breakfast together in the mornings, knowing that, apparently, they would often have pulled down a top bunk so they could spend the night in the same cabin. According to the papers, the beds were not wide enough even for the most star-crossed of lovers actually to sleep together. And now Guy was dead, and Lara was still missing, and, as Sam had swiftly been eliminated as a suspect, everyone had made the grotesque leap to assuming that Lara had killed Guy Thomas (probably by accident, it was generally agreed, after a fight about whether or not he would leave his wife) and run away.

Guy Thomas's wife, Diana, had discovered first that her husband had been murdered, and then that he'd been wholeheartedly cheating on her. She had the press outside her house, focused on the next day's headlines. Her husband's sex life was all over the press and television: the world could not get enough of it. I could not begin to imagine what was happening inside her head.

I was intensely curious about her, and desperate to meet her, and when Sam asked me if I would go to visit her and convey his sorrow and confusion, since he could not bear to leave the house himself, I had leapt at the chance. I made my request through Alexander Zielowski of the Falmouth police, and Diana Thomas had agreed at once.

It might be masochistic, she had written in her email, *but I feel I would like to hear about Lara from someone who knew her, rather than from the press, which I am attempting, unsuccessfully, to avoid. Why not? Come along. Nothing else can go wrong.*

Lara's disappearance was as mysterious as it had ever been, but the shock faded and her vanishing was now stony

181

reality. A week had passed, it was Saturday again, and very little had changed. The investigation, which was now called Operation Aquarius, was being run from Penzance police station, under the direction of a Major Crime Investigation Team, which, according to Alex Zielowski, was a specialist detective team. Much as he wanted to be, DC Zielowski was not a part of the investigation.

Laurie and I discussed it endlessly, but we just went around in circles, and the theorising was becoming stale. According to the police and the excited press, Lara had gone to bed early after keeling over (this, speculation had it, was to give herself the alibi of being tucked up in bed). However, she was soon back on her feet: another passenger had seen her at around half past midnight, heading towards Guy's cabin. In the morning she was gone, and Guy was dead, killed by a small but sharp knife that had Lara's fingerprints on it. Passengers in the cabins on either side reported hearing voices, but not raised ones, and a scuffle, but nothing dramatic enough to make them feel, at the time, anything other than annoyed at being disturbed.

Every passenger in the sleeper part of the train had been traced. It was easy, because everyone who travelled in the sleeper carriages was listed and ticked off by the attendants, like on an old-fashioned train. There was, however, a second section, which sleeper passengers called 'cattle class', where people sat in a chair all night. I trusted Alex when he told me that he was almost completely sure that none of the sleeper passengers had been involved in the murder, so I was certain that the killer must have been travelling on the 'cattle' part of the train, and must have left it long before the train reached its terminus

Nobody else seemed to think that, at all. Once it was not Sam, the entire world had decided it was Lara.

The police were checking the ground along the train's route, but that covered many miles and I thought they were mainly looking for her body, working on the basis that she had flung herself from the train after accidentally stabbing her lover to death. The papers preferred more exciting storylines: she had melted away and could be anywhere. She could be right next to you now! their excitable chatter pointed out. As you're reading this! On the bus! Keep an eye out, everyone! It was like when a child was missing, except that instead of the innocent angel, the entire country was scanning the faces on every street searching for a beautiful yet depraved murderer. It was very exciting entertainment for people who didn't consider any actor in a drama like this to be a human being.

I had been back to see Sam once, and then only briefly. I could not bear to be near his pain. That, I knew, was bad of me. He told me about his hours in custody at a centre in Camborne, the forensic checking of his computer and his car and his home. 'That was the good bit, though,' he added. 'It didn't feel it at the time, but at least things were happening, then.'

His mother was frail yet formidable, his brother thick-necked and shouty, and Sam had all but clung to me as I extricated myself. I told myself that I owed him nothing; but I knew I should have stayed longer. He had no friends to speak of, and he had lost his wife twice over, and he was plainly hating the company of his family.

DC Alex showed up on my doorstep the day after she went missing. That had been unexpected and unsettling. It was Sunday lunchtime, and I was cooking. I was not expecting anyone, and when the bell jangled, Laurie sighed.

'I don't want to see anyone,' he said. 'Not unless it's Lara Finch herself. I'll be upstairs. Don't tell them I'm here.'

'Yes, your highness,' I muttered as he stormed off, but not loud enough for him to hear.

The policeman, tall, skinny and kind, looked at me apologetically as he stamped on the doorstep to keep warm.

'Sorry,' he said. 'I should have called, I know.'

'Um. That's OK.' He was being oddly informal, and I could tell from his face that there was no good news. 'Come in,' I said, because I had to. I trusted Laurie to stay shut away upstairs for as long as he had to. He would, I knew, go to any lengths to avoid the police.

'I just wanted to talk to you as a friend of Mrs Finch's,' he said, when we were inside. 'Oh, you're cooking. That smells amazing. I really am sorry to interrupt. Are you expecting people? Is it a bad time?'

'No,' I said. 'Really. Have a drink. My boyfriend's not here. I'm not expecting anyone else.' Suddenly I wanted a proper drink. Laurie and I did not often drink alcohol. 'I suppose I can't offer you a glass of wine? Is that banned if you're working?'

'I wish I could. A coffee or something would be lovely, though. Sorry, Iris. All you do is make me coffee.'

'Oh, this is only the second. I think that's OK.'

He stood in the kitchen while I made the coffee, and explained that he wanted to have an informal chat.

'This whole case is so bizarre,' he said. 'So enormously unusual. I can't get my head around it. Mrs Finch seems to have disappeared from the face of the earth.'

'Hey,' I said. 'That's surely where you come in?'

'I know, I know. Though I'm not even involved any

more. Going to visit Mr Finch was the extent of my involvement. I'm Falmouth, and, as you know, it's being run by the MCIT out of Penzance. But it's not often something this bizarre happens down here.' He pulled himself up on to the worktop. His legs were so long, his feet nearly reached the floor. 'I like your skirt, by the way. Is it vintage?'

That made me laugh out loud. My skirt was an ancient floral dress I'd bought from a charity shop. I'd had to wash it three times before it stopped smelling of musk and dead people.

'Charity-shop vintage, not couture vintage. Thanks, though. It's actually a dress.' I lifted my cardigan to prove it.

And then I was smiling at him, and he was looking back at me, and I was enormously confused.

'So. Lara,' I said quickly. 'Yes. I didn't know her that well, actually. I had no idea she was seeing Guy Thomas. Poor bloke. Because he's dead, I mean. Not because he was seeing Lara. Oh, you know what I mean.'

'I do.' He nodded solemnly. 'It seems it was only the regulars on the train who knew about the connection between Lara and Guy. And the hotel staff, if they cared. And her sister, actually, and her godfather in London says he had an idea but that he hadn't met Mr Thomas.'

'How are her family?'

'They're how you would expect. Look. I'm sorry to have to do this, but could you just tell me how it was that you were with Mr Finch yesterday morning? I mean, there's no suggestion that there was anything untoward. I know he's already been released without charge. It's just . . . if a woman's illicit lover is dead; you have to look to her husband. And when you go to visit the husband and find he's with another woman, well . . .'

'They teach you that in police school?'

'Fairly early on, yes.'

I told him exactly what had happened. I went through the day from the moment I woke up until the point at which Sam was taken away in the police car.

'And your partner?' he asked. 'Would he be happy to give a statement, if we needed him to? Just to tie everything up? Though I can't imagine it will be necessary unless anything changes.'

That gave me the confidence to say, 'I'm sure that would be fine.'

'Could I just take his name?'

I didn't have the presence of mind to lie to the police. I could not do anything except say it.

'Laurie Madaki.' I instantly wished I could retract, and carried on speaking, too quickly. 'Look, I'm having a glass of wine. Are you sure you don't want to join me? Just a small one?'

Alex grinned and jumped down from the worktop.

'I could be persuaded. I go off duty in twenty minutes. You're my last job of the shift. So no one would ever know. Thank you. That would be lovely.'

I tried not to think of Laurie, upstairs and seething, and told myself he could not possibly have heard me telling his full name to a police officer. Instead, I opened a bottle of velvety red wine and sat down with the oddly engaging policeman, feeling my betrayal with every nerve-ending in my body, yet callously revelling in it.

If I were single, I thought, I would be drawn to Alex Zielowski. I would be pulled into his orbit. I would want to know everything about him. If I were single.

And then he had coordinated my visit to Diana, as Sam's representative, and here I was because I was desperate to meet her. As I walked up to the Thomas family's front door, the journalists kept shouting. They should have gone away by now, moved on to the next big story. The trouble was, none of the proper news was anywhere near this salacious. This was about sex and death and railways; the economy, by contrast, was dull and depressing. Everyone wanted a scandal, and the entire country was going wild about Lara.

Guy had had a Twitter account, rarely used, which suddenly, posthumously, had nearly half a million followers in place of its previous twenty-seven. Everything he had ever written on it (which was not much) had been held up for inspection and found disappointing: almost all he had ever done was link to news articles from the *Guardian* and the BBC. It was generally agreed to be the most boring Twitter account ever, and despite the scrutiny, no coded messages between the lovers were found within it. Lara, meanwhile, had an essentially never-used Twitter account and a long-dormant Facebook account that was similarly and unsurprisingly unyielding. That morning I had seen a desperate article on a tabloid website headlined: 'Can a successful woman really have only 47 friends? "A psychotic need to exert control," says top psychologist.' The barrel was being scraped.

The door was varnished wood, with a brass knocker which bounced when I picked it up and released it. Diana Thomas opened the door instantly; she was far better-looking in real life than she was on the television or in the papers. She was taller than me, with wavy black hair cut in a straggly bob with grey threaded through it. She looked terrible, of course; everything she was going through was etched on to her face, but she tried to smile.

'You're Iris,' she said, with a glance at the excited press

pack who were leaping around behind the gate taking her photo. 'Come in, quick.'

'Thanks for seeing me. Thanks loads. It's really kind of you. I'm so sorry for everything you're going through.'

My words were trite, but I had no idea what else to say.

'You had to climb over that gate, didn't you? I saw from the window. We have to keep it padlocked. You understand?'

'Oh God, yes. Of course. I left my bike on their side.'

'It should be safe there.' She did an almost-laugh under her breath. 'I don't think there's much danger of one of them cycling off. I don't think it's really their style.'

'Thanks for seeing me.'

She sighed, blowing her breath out through pursed lips.

'In a perverse way I want to know more about that woman. From someone who knows her, not the rubbish the papers print. Sam Finch and I have never set eyes on each other, but it turns out we've been linked for all this time without having a clue. I can see why he wanted to make contact. When all these bastards have gone home, maybe we can actually meet.'

I followed her down a dark hallway, with the kind of worn-smooth tiles on the floor that denoted an old and cared-for house, and into a kitchen with French windows that led out into a grassy back garden. There was washing on the line outside, but it looked as though it had been there some time: it was stiff with frost.

One family photograph hung on a wall. I tried to look at it unobtrusively. It had been taken at some kind of party: Diana was wearing a turquoise dress that was a tiny bit too bright for her skin tone, and Guy was squinting into the camera, his pale pink tie loosened, his top button undone. He was a good-looking man. I could see where Lara's temptation had sprung from, though I was still amazed that she had been capable of so massive and prolonged a deception.

There seemed to be nobody else in the house. That was strange. I had expected it to be filled with friends and family, rallying round.

'Are you all alone?' I asked, as she filled an old-fashioned kettle with water and put it on the gas burner.

'I've tried to be, these last couple of days, but everyone wants to come and be comforting. The kids are upstairs with friends. That seems to be working for them better than anything else. My brother came and took my mum off for a bit. She lives with us, you know. We have a Family Liaison Officer from the police, and she's been utterly wonderful, a total rock in a way I would never have been able to imagine before any of this. But she only comes over once a day now. The rest of the well-wishers come and go. Sometimes I just can't bear it. Sitting there drinking tea with people who are so desperately sorry for me, and knowing that, while they try to say the right thing, they have no idea. To have your life ripped apart. Your husband dead. And then to discover all the rest of it and not even be able to be properly angry with him. I'm fucking furious with him, in fact, the bastard, and by getting himself murdered he's outmanoeuvred me so we can never have a conversation about it, and I don't even get to . . .' She bit her lip and took some deep breaths. 'Anyway. Let's have some tea, shall we? I'd rather be on the hard stuff, but I'm trying to resist because I know where it will lead. Tell me about her. Lara Finch. Did she kill my husband?'

'No,' I said. 'I'm absolutely sure she didn't.' I had slipped easily into the exaggerated version of our friendship. If

Lara did somehow show up, innocent, I was going to have some serious backtracking to do when it came to the strength and duration of our bond. Real friends of hers, and colleagues and acquaintances had popped up in the papers, baffled by her dramatic story, insisting that illicit sex was out of character for her, let alone murder. 'I was with Sam last Saturday, because I went over to see her and she wasn't there. But all we knew then was that she hadn't turned up from the train. I had no idea that she and Guy were . . . I'm so sorry. She never spoke about him at all, not to me. I mean, I'd never even heard his name.'

Diana turned her back and started fiddling with a teapot.

'Poor bastard,' she said. 'Sam Finch, I mean. He must be in pieces. Being arrested so dramatically on top of everything else. I knew. I didn't *know* – Guy obviously didn't tell me or anything like that. Why would he? But it wasn't exactly a first offence, and I can read him like a book. One minute he was mentioning this woman on the train all the time, and then suddenly he never spoke of her again. That was his pattern.'

'His pattern?'

She turned and looked me in the eye. Every line on her face spoke of a woman holding herself together by willpower.

'I've been married to Guy for over twenty years. Was married, I should say. We're forty-seven years old, both of us, and we know each other inside out. His affair with Lara Finch was, depressingly, absolutely in character for him, though everything that's been in the papers about them living together in London during the week and effectively having double lives makes him even more of a fucking bastard than I'd suspected.

'They're saying she killed him because he wouldn't leave me. That doesn't make sense to me, because to judge by everything the papers have unearthed, he probably was building up to leaving. I can hear the words he'd have said. "Di. There's something I need to talk to you about." He'd have hated every moment of the conversation. Sometimes I felt he was leading up to it. I'd see the look on his face and everything in me would contract with dread. And then he wouldn't say it. But who knows? Maybe he *was* refusing to leave. Maybe she wanted him to. It sounds that way, you know.

'That woman from the train, Ellen, who the kids and I met once by the way and who knew exactly what was going on, so that's nice. She seems very convinced that Lara was going to leave her poor husband and that Guy was offering to do the same. Happy ever after. Maybe he was losing his nerve. I don't know anything any more. It would only take a moment of madness. People do psychotic things.'

The kettle started screeching. I watched Diana turn the gas off and spoon tea leaves into the teapot.

'I use proper tea leaves too,' I told her. 'Hardly anyone else does. It's much nicer.'

She smiled at this, and her entire face changed for a fraction of a second.

'Isn't it? My mother insists on it, and because I was brought up that way, I do too. It's a different drink from tea-bag tea.'

'Like the difference between proper and instant coffee.'

'Yes! Very few people understand that. Everyone's snobby or apologetic about instant coffee, but tea bags are entirely socially acceptable. I'm glad you appreciate that.'

I watched as reality descended back on her like smog, crumpling and crinkling her face.

'I really don't think she did it,' I told her. 'Lara. I mean, who am I to say, obviously, but I cannot believe it of her for a single moment. I think something else went on.'

'Such as?'

'Well, yes. I don't know. Someone else. Maybe she witnessed it. Maybe she's dead too.'

'They'd have found her by now.'

'In a lake or something? Or maybe the killer forced her off the train with him? She could have been taken somewhere. I'm sure there's more to it than the things we know.'

Diana said nothing. She poured milk, then tea, into two matching mugs. They were proper farmhouse mugs: cream, with roses on the sides. A cat walked silently into the room and rubbed itself against my legs. Diana slumped down next to me on the sofa.

'Oh Christ. I have no idea. I'm not set on the idea that it was exactly the way it looks – how would I know? I'm just trying to get my head round reality. You know? You kind of have your life story in your head – you get married and have kids and come to live in Cornwall, and you think it goes "Guy wasn't the greatest of husbands and I was a bit of a doormat, but we got on all right, and the kids left home and my mother wasn't around for ever, and we got old together with some ups and downs but in a mainly happy and companionable way." That was how my future was going to be until last week. Now I keep having to remind myself that it goes "And when I was forty-seven my husband was murdered and I . . ." I have no idea how it goes after that. At first you just don't believe it, and wake up every morning expecting him to be there, or to come back on the train. And then you remember. And then, slowly, you realise that this is actually how it's going to be from now on. The grim, banal reality.'

'God, you poor thing.'

She forced a little smile. 'Yes. So, how is Sam Finch? They didn't have children. How's he coping?'

I sighed. 'I have no idea how he's going to get through this.'

'Yes.' She nodded and stared at something far away. 'The same as me, but different. His wife. My husband. Both gone. Fucking hell.' She tried to smile. 'I never swear, by the way. I'm not the type. So tell me about her. How do you know her? What was her life like before she decided to help herself to my husband? And did you genuinely not know? Because I won't hold it against you if you did, my dear. I honestly won't. I'm so far beyond. We've all supported girlfriends in unconscionable behaviour. God knows, I have.'

I shifted on my chair. 'I didn't know. But I did have an inkling that she wasn't completely happy with Sam. I met her on the ferry . . .'

We settled in for the afternoon, and I told Guy's widow everything I knew about the woman everyone thought was his killer.

chapter seventeen

The press pack ran after me when I left, but Diana had warned me they would. She said that all you had to do was to be firm and keep going. 'They'll tire of us soon enough,' she said. 'Here's hoping, anyway.'

'How's Di doing?' yelled a woman, right up close to me.

I ignored her and grabbed my bike, grateful that none of them had stolen it. Diana was right: despite their youth, they did not, on the whole, look like cyclists.

'How is she? How's Diana?' called others. I got on it and tried to leave. They were blocking me in, the whole intimidating crowd of them. I decided just to go and hope they got out of the way. If I were a car, after all, they would. I pulled my helmet down over my forehead, feeling it right across my eyebrows, and put my foot on the pedal. Then I set off, wobbling slowly at first. There was a man in front of me, quite a good-looking one. He was smirking in my face, blocking my path. I rode towards him and he declined to get out of the way.

It was the slowest of slow-motion crashes. I kept riding, though I was lurching a bit as I had had no time to get any speed up to balance myself. He was standing in my path. I could not go round him because people were in the way there too, so I just rode straight into him. He did not perform the necessary side-step. My tyre hit his leg, and I had to put my foot back on the ground.

He burst out laughing.

'She biked right into me!' He was addressing the crowd. He had the unmistakable accent of a local, and I wondered whether he was from one of the Cornish papers.

'You were supposed to get out of the way,' I told him. 'You would have done if I were a car.'

'True. I would. But you're on a fucking pushbike!'

'Am I meant to say sorry here? Because I'm not going to. All I'm trying to do is leave. Let you get on with your relentless harassment of a grieving widow.'

'Nah. I'm probably meant to say sorry to you, but I'm not going to either. All I'm trying to do is get you to talk to me.'

'Oh, shut up and let me go home.'

'Seriously, though.' His voice was lower, solemn. 'Off the record. How is she?'

'No you don't.'

His cheeks were red with the cold and he looked about twenty-five. That made him more than a decade younger than me.

'Oh bloody Christ,' he complained. 'Why do people have this thing about not being able to talk to the press? Like we're Hitler or something. I'm from the *Western Morning News*, not the freaking *Daily Star*. Though obviously some of these guys are from the tabs. All you have to do is say "She's . . . whatever" and we'll all be able to say "Friends said that Mrs Thomas was . . . whatever." Then we won't have to stand here, freezing, trying to get half a sentence to put in the paper.'

'But surely you just say "Friends said that Mrs Thomas was . . . whatever" anyway? You make it up.'

He sighed. 'It would be better if it bore some resemblance to the truth, don't you think?'

I got ready to pedal away, then paused.

'OK,' I told him, impulsively composing something in my head. The rest of them were gathered around, ready to pounce on whatever I said. 'She's a very strong woman, and she's doing as well as she could be, considering. Her children are her priority, and she'd appreciate it if you guys would leave her alone. She's not going to come out and cry for your cameras, so in fact you might as well bugger off.'

'Who are you?' yelled the crowd. 'What's your name?'

As I started to cycle off, the young man reached over and dropped something into the pocket of my duffel coat. I stopped at once.

'What was that?' I demanded.

'My card. Just in case you think of anything else you want to say.'

At that, the rest of them started surging forward with their cards too. I rode off as fast as I could, down the lane, past their little cars parked in the ditch, past the van and down the hill. All of a sudden the world opened out again, and I was able to look at the open spaces, the rocks, the slatey line of the distant Atlantic. The air was fresh, the winter sun occasionally emerging from behind a cloud. I freewheeled down hills, took blind corners faster than I should have done, pedalled frantically in a low gear until I felt my cheeks flush, warmed from the inside but still cold on the outside. My legs began to ache and I was free again.

There was something inside me, unfurling and demanding attention. Lara did not do this. Someone else had been on the train. Somebody had killed Guy and set Lara up. I could imagine her having the affair, I told myself once again, as I sped through a hamlet that was half bungalows, half stone cottages. Sam was intense and needy, though I only really knew him since his faithless wife had vanished without a trace, so that was not a fair assessment. All the same, he had devoted his life to waiting for her to come back from London, and I could see how stifling that would have been.

I could see her leaving him. He would have been devastated, yet, as Diana had said, it was not exactly an untrampled path. Marriages ended.

I wondered whether to call Laurie and say I would be back soon. He would not expect it. He was used to waiting for me. I wondered what he would think if I ventured further afield. He had not forgiven me for drinking wine with Alex. I was pushing the boundaries.

As I chained my bike up outside a Penzance pasty shop, I found that I could not stop looking at the people around me, just in case. There was the slimmest of chances that she was here, in the town at the end of the line. She could have got off the train at Penzance and slipped away.

She had not, of course. Penzance was not a place in which anyone could disappear. If she were in Penzance she would have been found days ago.

People walked past, their breath making clouds around them. The sky had lowered since I left Diana, and now it was only just overhead, black with the promise of imminent freezing rain.

The pasty shop was empty. I knew that I could have gone into any restaurant I wanted for lunch, but I wanted a pasty. The secret money in my bank account, the fact that I never needed to worry about my finances again, seemed so unlikely that I mainly lived as though it were not there. If I spent three pounds on a pasty and a can of Diet Coke, things were reassuringly normal.

At home I cooked the most lovely meals I could for the two of us, considering my small budget. I made soups with local vegetables, and baked bread. I ate well and exercised and was healthy and boring. I could not do anything extravagant at home, because I had not told him about the money. If I told him now, I would have to explain why I hadn't mentioned it before. It became increasingly impossible.

As I walked along the seafront, past the outdoor, seawater Jubilee Pool, feeling the first drops of rain on my face and licking flakes of pastry off my fingers, I scanned the faces I passed. It was instantly obvious as soon as a figure appeared in the distance that it was not Lara. Everybody was too old, or too young, or too fat or too tall; and anyway, if she were alive, she would be miles and miles away from here, the town in which Guy's body had been discovered.

The coastline stretched away in both directions, crinkled and craggy. The sea was wild, the wind getting up. I turned my back on Newlyn and changed direction, heading instead towards the castle of St Michael's Mount, cut off from land by the high tide, pushing my bike back to the station.

I fed the cats, made us both a cup of tea, and went online with Laurie, moody and suspicious, at my side. I looked up everything I could possibly find about Lara (there was nothing new, though a couple of newspaper sites were already bearing photographs of me clambering over that gate, and I hoped no one I had ever met would see them).

I called Penzance police, to the annoyance of the man who answered the phone.

'But,' I told him, 'I think there was someone else involved. You should be looking at all the passengers, tracking every one of them down. One of them did it, not Lara.'

He was almost polite.

'We are of course pursuing every angle and talking to every passenger,' he said. Then he made me get off the phone, quietly but ruthlessly, and I knew he saw me as a nuisance caller who was one of the hazards of answering the phone at the police station.

The press and the internet were interested in Lara and Guy for now, but soon the next story would come along. Lara's body would be found, or she would be caught, or she would never be found. Those were the only three possible outcomes.

'I want her to be all right,' I told Laurie.

'She's not, though.' His voice was flat. 'And you know it. Whether she did it or not.'

'I know. Shall I open some wine?'

He laughed. 'Oh! Drink with *me* for a change. That's good of you, my darling.'

'Look, Laurie. There's something I'm thinking about doing.'

'What?' The anxiety in his voice made me backtrack instantly, as I had known it would.

'Oh, it's nothing really. Look. Let's have a drink. There's some of that soup left over, too.'

He did not reply. I could not meet his gaze. There was only one bottle of wine in the house, and because I had drunk the nice one with Alex, it tasted rough. I could remember buying it: it had cost me £3.49, and it tasted cheaper than that.

All the same, cheap red wine was soothing in a way, and I sat on the floor in front of the wood burner, wearing my thick cardigan, jeans and chunky socks, and tried to work up the courage to share my plan. Ophelia came and rubbed herself against me, and Desdemona walked straight up to Laurie, who ignored her as he always did. He was ignoring me, too. I spoke to the cat instead, inside my head so he wouldn't hear.

'It's none of my business,' I told her. 'There's nothing I can do. All I can do is let it go.'

'You don't want to, though,' she countered silently. 'You want to know.'

'Well, yes. I do want to know. I want to know what really happened.'

'Well,' said Ophelia, clambering on to my lap so I had to lean right back on my hands, and trampling me down until I was a suitable seat. 'Why don't you go to London and see what it looks like at that end?'

'I could do that. Couldn't I? Who would look after you guys?'

She sat on me and started purring. Her contribution to the conversation was over.

'It would probably beat sitting around having conversations with a cat,' I said, but her eyes were closed. When a cat doesn't care, it doesn't care.

In the middle of the night, I jerked awake. Laurie stirred next to me.

'You're obsessed with that woman,' he said.

'Shh,' I told him, and he went back to sleep.

I was imagining someone cracking up. It had happened to me, years ago, and my cracks were showing now, more so every day. It was catching up. Perhaps that was what I had recognised in Lara, and what she had seen in me. Maybe that was why we had struck up a casual conversation, then spent the rest of the day together, drinking, talking intently.

I was amazed that the situation with Laurie, our odd set-up, had lasted as long as it had. Laurie never left the house. I could not live like that for ever.

I could suddenly empathise with a person running away on the spur of the moment, leaving everything behind and making herself invisible. It was, after all, possible that Lara might have done that. The papers had established the train's schedule, the places where it stopped in the night to prolong its journey so that it reached Cornwall at a time when people might want to be setting off into the world. There were many of them.

She could have stumbled on the real killer, and turned and run away. I could imagine her panicking, her pulse racing faster and faster until she suddenly knew that she had to get out, immediately. The train could have been pulled in at a siding somewhere. No one had been watching: whatever had happened, that had been established. She could have climbed out of a window and vanished, terrified and unable to think straight.

She could, just possibly, have melted away at Reading: they thought Guy was killed at around the time the train stopped there. There was no one who looked like her on the station's CCTV, but the cameras did not capture every passenger getting out at every door. The killer could have got on there, or got off there, or taken Lara off with him.

I slipped out of bed and crept into the study, and closed the door. When I switched the light on it dazzled me for a second, and made everything, all the boring paperwork of a modern life, look harsh and almost sinister.

She would not have stopped in London, if she had fled back there.

My passport was filed under P in the big metal filing cabinet. I pulled the drawer out so hard that it gained its own momentum and smashed into my leg, making me gasp.

There was nothing there. A few other things beginning with P were in there (contact details for a painter, an envelope of photos that I could not bear to look at), but there was no passport. I took everything else out and checked through it. Still no passport.

It had been there. I had not taken it out.

Laurie could have hidden it to stop me leaving. I would ask him, and I knew that I would be able to tell instantly from his face if he was lying. It would not have been his style. He would not hide my passport to keep me at home. He kept me at home with his presence.

If it was not him, however, there was no one else.

I thought about it. Nobody came upstairs in this house. No one was left alone in this room for the time it took to open a filing cabinet and retrieve a passport that was filed under P. Nobody at all. We had not been burgled. No one had even been to the house. Had they?

I sat on the floor and tried to work it out.

chapter eighteen

My bag was next to the door. I had almost nothing with me: everything I was taking fitted into a largish shoulder bag and a canvas handbag. The shoulder bag had been my father's, long ago when there was such a person in my life. It was black, plasticky faux-leather, with a sturdy strap, and it was the only suitable receptacle I owned. It held the very minimum of clothes and toiletries.

It was the end of the day, almost dark outside and an odd time to be setting off.

I stood in front of Laurie before I went, and tried, again, to explain it to him. He looked back at me without a word. I hated it when he did that. In the end I walked away. He and the cats would take care of each other. I had left the cats lots of food, and had filled the fridge and the cupboards with everything that any of them could possibly need.

If I ended up staying away longer than I expected, I would ask the neighbours to drop in with more supplies. I felt entitled to ask for that favour since for years I had fed their teenage boy's snake when they went on holiday. Whenever that happened, I half wanted to put one of the cats into the snake's tank and see what happened. My money would have been on the cat, but testing that out would have been unneighbourly, even though I would have been poised to step in the moment things became heated.

This was fine, I told myself. I had been in Cornwall for years, and going back to London was not a big deal. Everyone went to London. Lara had covered the ground I was about to cover twice a week.

It was only London. Laurie would still be here. I would come back.

The wood burner was blazing fiercely, to look after them for the first bit of my absence. I had announced myself unavailable for all work for the foreseeable future. My bike was propped in the hallway, safe and studenty. In my handbag were ticket, purse and phone, and a book to read. The sun had set hours ago, and normally I would be drinking tea in front of the fire, probably wearing pyjama bottoms and a jumper, and thinking about going to bed with a man, a book and a cat.

I tried to leave without saying goodbye, but I couldn't.

'I love you,' I said, back over my shoulder. 'I'll miss you. I'm sorry. I'll be back.'

'Sure,' he said. He was trying to be casual. 'That's fine. Have fun. Don't worry, Iris. I love you and I always will. Come back to me.'

I walked, in blackness, to the top of the lane to wait for the taxi, blinking hard. The night air breathed coldly on to my face: I should have had a single tear frozen to my cheek, but instead I had a snotty nose, which I wiped elegantly on my sleeve.

There was a sprinkling of stars between the clouds,

but the moon was hidden and all I could make out of my surroundings were the jagged edges of bare trees reaching up.

When the headlights came out of the night, I stepped back, wanting to shrink from the brightness. The cab stopped beside me in a crunching of gravel, and the driver got out to open the boot for my bag. It didn't need to go in the boot, but I let him do it.

'Didn't know anyone lived all the way down there,' he said.

'Yes,' I agreed. I was going to the city now: I was going to have to do small talk good-naturedly. 'It is quite remote.'

'That's right. Where you going, love? Truro, was it?'

'Yes. Truro station, thanks. I'm catching the train to London. The sleeper train.'

'Oh, the famous sleeper train. My daughter gets that sometimes. It's a good service. Still. You take care of yourself.'

'Yes.'

'Bad business. Make sure you keep that door locked.'

I smiled at him, forced myself not to snap or swear. 'I'll be fine,' I said. 'But thank you.'

As I stepped up from the shadowy platform on to the brightly lit train, I pictured Lara doing the same thing. Guy Thomas would already have been here, waiting for her. I wondered whether he had stood at the door to the carriage, extending a hand, helping her up, pulling her close, kissing before they even pulled away from Truro. Maybe they had waited until they were a distance from home turf, chugging through anonymous dark country-side.

There were about fifteen people, I thought, getting on

at Truro. I had booked this deliberately for Sunday night to retrace Lara's steps, so some of these people were, presumably, going to go straight to work at the other end of this journey, like Lara had. Nobody was in business-type clothes. A few people had huge bags and were obviously heading for an airport. Others were in jeans and big coats.

My sleeping compartment was tiny, but it looked comfortable enough. You would have to be extraordinarily committed to the idea of an extramarital affair to carry one out in here, but for one person alone it was fine. I would not have slept tonight no matter how luxuriously appointed it had been.

I could not imagine how two people had shared this bed, which was smaller than a standard single one. They must have slept on top of one another, or not at all. No wonder their affair had swiftly spilled over into their London lives.

I sat on the narrow bed and felt the train jerk as it started to move.

I wanted to call Laurie, but I knew he would not answer.

People from my old life were, I was sure, still living in London. When I first came to Cornwall they had emailed, for a while, concerned and regretful and all of that. I ignored all of it. We didn't need them, Laurie and me, and eventually they took the hint. I changed my mobile number, closed down my old email account and never sent a Christmas card.

If they saw me in the city, they would want to talk, to know what I had been doing for all this time. It was only the fact that it was London that made it safe. We could have been hiding in a corner of London for all those years and the chances of our running into anyone would have been slim. This trip was about Lara, not about me. It was not about Laurie.

And besides that, now that I had my unlikely funds, I was building up to doing all sorts of things. If I were to travel and see the world, I would need to be able to go to London first. This was a bit of a trial run; it was a test of my bravery. It was the first separation.

It was also a place to apply for a new passport. Mine had vanished without trace. I was uneasy about that. I had told no one, and I was certainly not going to tell Laurie. I was, however, considering mentioning it to Alex Zielowski.

A woman was standing in the open doorway, in train uniform. She was short, older than me, a comfortable maternal figure.

'Hello there,' she said. 'Now you'd be . . .' She checked the clipboard in her hand. 'Iris Roebuck. Yes? Could I have a look at your ticket, my love?'

People were having illicit sex in every corner of the compartment. They stood pressed up against the wall. She sat on the edge of the sink. He was on top of her on the bed, with no option of lying side by side. Then they were no longer Lara and Guy, but Laurie and me, then Guy and Diana, Sam and Lara, Guy and one of his other women, Sam and me, Laurie and Lara. Me and DC Alex Zielowski. I grabbed my handbag and set off in search of that gin and tonic, and Ellen Johnson.

The bar carriage was almost empty. Its luxurious seats waited expectantly, the free newspapers on each table tempting no one but two middle-aged men.

'Yes?' said the young barman. I felt sorry for him because those acne scars were going to be with him for ever, even when he was properly grown up.

'Gin and tonic, thanks,' I said, looking round again for

the mysterious woman who had been Lara and Guy's friend. She still wasn't there.

'Sure.' He started reaching for things. 'Ice and lemon?'

'Yes please. Do you always work on this train?'

He sighed, knowing what was coming. 'Yes, often.'

'So you knew . . .'

He leapt in before I could finish.

'I did. I should make a little sign saying that. "Yes, I knew them to serve a drink to. But I know no more about what happened than you do." *Everyone* wants to know. I wasn't working the night when . . . Well, you know.'

He picked up a sliver of lemon with a miniature pair of tongs and dropped it into my drink. It made the tiniest splash; like a fairy jumping into a swimming pool.

'I bet you see all sorts of things in this job.' This seemed the right thing to say.

'Oh, you wouldn't believe the things that go on. Terrible business, him getting killed. On the train! Right here! Those two'd been at it for ever. People think we're invisible or something. Or they just don't care.'

'I'm actually a friend of Lara Finch's,' I told him. He looked at me with narrowed eyes.

'Are you?' he asked. 'Really a friend, or someone pretending?'

'Really. I live near her in Cornwall.' I could see that I needed to parade some credentials, so I went on: 'I was with her husband when she was first missing. That's not something I ever want to see anyone go through again.'

He poured in the tonic without looking at me. 'Oh. I'm sorry. I hope I didn't . . .'

I waited to hear what he hoped he didn't do, but he was not planning on finishing the sentence.

'Not at all,' I assured him. 'I'm heading up to London to see her family, actually.'

'Are you? Fuck. Well, for what it's worth, we were all amazed when we heard. She always seemed a lovely woman, always so friendly, always with a nice thank you and a please, and the two of them couldn't keep their hands off each other. I reckon it was a lovers' tiff. I think he was maybe threatening her, and she was defending herself and it went too far. Maybe he had the knife and she grabbed it off him.'

I took the drink. 'Could be. I hadn't thought of that. So their friend, Ellen Johnson? Does she still use the train?'

'Oh, she does indeed,' he said, taking the five-pound note I was holding out. 'She's on this train now all right, but she sticks to her sleeping compartment at the moment. Hasn't been out here since it happened. Can't blame her. Doesn't want everyone looking at her. She'll be back out and about in a week or two, I reckon. Nice woman.'

'Is this the . . . well, you know. The actual same train?'

For some reason this had only just occurred to me. There was an outside chance that I could be sleeping in the very bed in which it happened.

'Nah. It was on the other one, and anyway they've taken the carriage off, apparently. Forensics. Won't be back in circulation for a while, I reckon.'

I doubted that was true. Would a train company really have a spare carriage lying around to substitute for the murder scene? Were they running shorter trains than before? I was grimly sure they would have cleaned it up and put it back into circulation.

When I took my first sip of gin and tonic, Lara's train drink and the first alcoholic drink you choose when you are young and trying to be grown up, it fizzed on my tongue. The sweetness of the tonic water hit the top of my mouth, and even though the lemon was limp and had been cut up many hours or days ago, I smiled at the forgotten pleasure. I had not had one of these for years.

There was a man sitting opposite me drinking a can of bitter and reading a book that he was holding so low I could not see its cover. If I stared for long enough he would probably look up. I tried it. Eventually, of course, it worked. People cannot help looking at you in the end, if you don't stop looking at them. They are not used to the attention; and this man certainly would not have been. He was grey-haired, with an enormous bald patch that was threatening to become his entire head, and he looked extraordinarily ordinary.

When he glanced up, his expression said: 'What do you think you're staring at, young lady?'

I directed an insincere grin his way. 'Do you often do this journey? It's my first time on this night train.'

'Oh. Yes, I do. Not all the time, like some people.' He gave the free copy of *The Times* a pointed look, even though Lara was on an inside page, not the cover. 'Just once or twice a month, when I have a meeting to get to.'

'Do you? Did you ever see them?'

'I don't believe so. I've given it plenty of thought, as you'd expect, but I can't drag out a single memory. I mean, life is full of middle-aged men. But I'm fairly sure the young lady would have stuck in one's mind.'

'Yes.'

He turned back to his book.

'What are you reading?'

He did not reply, just lifted it so I could see the cover.

'Harry Potter?'

He shrugged. 'Why not?'

The gin kept me awake for a while as the train chugged and clattered through the night, leaving my quiet and comfortable life further behind with every clunk of wheels on rails. I lay in the narrow bed, the duvet pulled up to my chin, trying not to think of a man stabbed to death in a bed like this.

Then suddenly someone was knocking on the door, and before I could even feel alarmed or confused, a female voice said: 'Breakfast!' and I realised we were not moving any more.

When I opened the door and took the tray, she answered my questions before I had even managed to formulate them in my head.

'Paddington. If you could get off before seven, that's all we ask, my lovely. Here you go. You're all right with the tray?'

'Thank you.'

There was no sign of Ellen Johnson when I got off the train. She was not in the lounge next to the platform, and I imagined she had plunged straight into London when the train stopped there, long before I woke up. I had failed to find a phone number for her, and my email to her Facebook account had gone predictably unanswered. When I went back home, I would find her at Paddington. I would catch her as she got on the train.

I almost wanted a second, early morning gin. There was a reason why I had not been here for all these years.

I walked straight back out of the first-class lounge. It was a horrible place, atmosphere-free and built for transience. Lara had, I knew, spent hours there before and after her journeys, but I would not be stalking her on that front.

In the café up the stairs, on the station concourse, I ordered something substantial, and took out a notebook to make a plan.

The station was massive. It was enormous compared with Truro station, at least. They should, I thought, make that its official motto: 'Bigger than Truro.' It could, in fact, be a slogan for the whole city.

I was able to position myself at a table that allowed me to see the people walking around. Most of them came from trains, walked directly to the Tube and vanished underground. I was more interested in the ones who milled and meandered around, killing time. Some of them queued for bagels and doughnuts. A man picked his nose, trying to be surreptitious about it. A woman stumbled, nearly fell over, then walked on, looking down, trying to pretend it hadn't happened.

The waitress brought me a plate of eggs and beans, defrosted hash browns and cooked tomatoes, and this was soon joined by a vast bucket full of milky coffee with froth on the top. I was not hungry, but I balanced some beans on the fork anyway.

My heart was pounding and I made an effort to calm myself down. I was here because Lara had vanished and had quite possibly taken my passport with her. This sounded stupid, but I knew it had been in that filing cabinet. I knew that I had never taken it out. I was certain that Laurie hadn't either, because he would have been shifty, and I would have known. She had been in the room, alone, when I went to answer a phone call that never was. I partly thought I was being ridiculous, but I was increasingly uneasy, too. I was going to apply for a new passport first, and then I would try to discover whether I had taken a flight anywhere lately.

Despite the fact that her face was all over the news, she could easily disguise herself and slip into a different life in the city. She would just need to change her hair, and no one would recognise her. London was big enough for that: even though everyone had been looking for her for ten days, she could be hiding here.

I tried hard to focus. When I had applied for my passport, I was going to find her sister, because Olivia Wilberforce was an intriguing character, and Sam hated her with a disconcerting vehemence. She was pregnant, I knew that much, and this had upset Lara. They had not been on speaking terms for a while, according to Sam, and I remembered Lara, on our trip to St Mawes and when she came over for mince pies, muttering unhappily about her sister.

I knew where Olivia lived, so finding her was going to be easy. I was not going to run into anyone from my previous life in London. That would be so unlikely as to be impossible. Like winning the lottery.

I had absent-mindedly eaten half my breakfast. Now I knocked back the coffee and went up to the counter to pay the bill. Olivia lived in Covent Garden, Sam had told me that, in Mercer Street, just off Long Acre. She had a job in PR, which presumably involved normal office hours, and I knew she was back at work, in spite of everything, because I had seen her in the paper. I would stake out her street at approximately the right time of day, and sooner or later she would come home. That was my scientific plan, at least. It involved my going nowhere near Putney, or Notting Hill.

By the time I was loitering near Olivia's flat, I was almost feeling comfortable. It was the anonymity that did it. It would be difficult not to be at ease in a city in which nothing you did, or wore, could cause anything more than a raised eyebrow.

I had not been to this city for five years, yet I was instantly back at home. I lived, now, in a world in which you generally said hello to people when you passed them out walking, in which you knew not just your neighbours, but the names and temperaments of their dogs. Here, I could have been anyone, could have done anything. Nobody had looked at me in my short skirt and biker boots, and no one was looking at me, now, in my brand-new skinny black trousers and a bright blue top that I had secretly bought because it was the kind of thing I felt Lara would have worn. I was going to get a serious haircut next, and lose the blond ends that had entertained me for a while. Then, if I could overcome my distaste for that sort of thing, I would go to a department store and get somebody to do my make-up so it suited me, and then I would buy everything they had used. Meanwhile, though, I had put on the tiny amount of make-up that I still possessed (black mascara, some clumsily applied eyeliner, and a dark pink lipstick that I felt certain made me look like a vampire with bad table manners). I was trying to be the most ordinary Londoner I could possibly be.

Going to the passport office had been a good way to start. It was all forms and queues and officialdom. There was nothing to do but follow the rules, tick the boxes, hand over the evidence and the money.

I felt sick with guilt, but I pushed that from my mind. All I could think about was the task at hand. The rest of it I would deal with later. I needed to phone Alex and talk to him about my lost passport, but I knew that making contact with him would be treacherous.

I paced outside a vintage clothes shop for a while, and then went in and lost myself in the racks of old dresses and wonderful shoes. I wandered across the road and into a courtyard that certainly hadn't been there last time I was in Covent Garden: it was new and moneyed, containing a Jamie Oliver restaurant, a shop that only sold expensive ballet pumps, an upmarket-yet-funky florist. However, being away from Olivia's street made me nervous in case I missed her.

At the bottom of the road there was an appealing-looking pub, a print shop, and, often, passers-by on their way to Pineapple Studios in the next street. Some of them were indisputable ballerinas. They held themselves gorgeously, heads poised upon swan-like necks. Others were much cooler than that: they were the kind of people who appeared in the background of music videos, casually performing the kind of moves I would not even be able to come close to naming.

I stamped my feet and walked back along the street, looking up, occasionally, into a sky that was leaden with clouds. It was freezing and I was bored.

I headed to the other end of the road, to see what was happening there. People were strolling along Long Acre. That was what was happening there. I walked to the middle. Nothing was happening there, either. Every time anyone came into the street, I would give them a good look, but for a long time none of them was Olivia Wilberforce; right up until, suddenly, one of them was.

She was walking and tapping on an iPhone at the same time, but although her head was bent and I could barely see her face, I knew it was her. She was visibly but not massively pregnant. My pulse quickened as she walked towards me. She had black hair, cut in a chic and geometric style, short at the back and longer at the front, with a fringe that would have looked ridiculously short on most people, but which worked for her. Her jeans were so tight they were probably leggings, and over them she wore a military-style coat that somehow looked wonderful.

I tugged at the velvet jacket I still had on over my new clothes. It was threadbare and stupid, clearly an item from a charity shop hundreds of miles from London.

'Hello,' I said, as she walked past me. She stopped and gave me a look of the most phenomenal disdain.

'No thanks.' She walked on. Her features were spookily even. She looked like a china doll, or a sexy assassin from a film. Somehow, in Olivia Wilberforce, those two looks were able to coexist. The bulge of her fertile stomach made her more unsettling still.

'I'm not from the press.' She kept walking, and I turned and trotted after her. 'I'm a friend of Lara's.'

That made her stop, but only for as long as it took her to say, 'Sure you are.'

'Well I am. I live outside Falmouth. I was with Sam straight after she went missing. I stayed with him until the police took him for an interview. I called his brother.'

She narrowed her eyes. 'What are his family like?'

'His brother was horrible and aggressive. I was surprised, actually. Sam's so . . . Well, he's so unaggressive, so gentle, that I hadn't expected that at all. His mum looked like a sweet old lady, but she was incredibly tough.'

She looked into my face for a moment, then suddenly relaxed. Her whole demeanour changed, though she was still guarded.

'Well, that's true enough. They were vile at the wedding. It was dysfunction city. What's your name?'

'Iris. Iris Roebuck. Lara and I met on a ferry to St Mawes one day and we got chatting, and after that we were friends.'

Olivia laughed a sudden and odd laugh that stopped as abruptly as it had started.

'If you wanted to speak to me, couldn't you have called? You know, you don't get to just show up and stop me in the street. The world may be fucked, but it doesn't mean no one needs manners any more.'

I liked that. It was what I would have said, in her place.

'Sorry, Olivia. You're completely right. Truly, I am sorry. I just – well, I happened to be in London. And I was thinking of Lara, obviously. I'm sure she didn't kill Guy. I know it looks as if she did, but . . .' She looked at me, not helping me out at all. 'Well. I knew that when she first came here she was living with you, and I knew where you lived, and . . .'

I was not used to this. No one made me beg for anything.

'I can go away again. I mean, the last thing I want is to upset you or disturb you.'

She was looking into my face. Her blue eyes were piercing.

'The thing is, Iris,' she said, 'she never mentioned you. You apparently know all about me. But I know nothing about you. And everyone knows all about my family, because the papers have been obsessed with us. I'm not exactly hard to research at the moment. Any old nutter can stop me in the street. Believe me, you're not the first.'

'Oh.' I struggled for credentials. 'Would she have mentioned me to you, though? She wouldn't, would she?'

'Well, not to me. No. She wouldn't have done to *me*. I'm sure she never mentioned you to Mum and Dad either, though. We were talking about her friends. You know. The world implodes and you go over every detail. We thought she didn't have any close friends in Cornwall.'

I shrugged.

'Ask Sam, if you like.'

'He did say there was someone with him that day. It could have been you.'

'You know, I wish I had done that tabloid interview I was offered a million times over. Then I could show you the evidence.'

'Oh, tell me about it.'

She took her keys out of her handbag, then visibly thought better of it. I was fiddling with my phone, glad I had upgraded it recently.

'I'll show you,' I said, and there was my name, in a newspaper report. I was mentioned as a friend of the family who had been waiting with the tragic husband. 'Look. That's my name. I can show you ID.'

She looked at the phone for a long time, then back at me, and nodded, and her face changed. She went from grey to a mournful pale green.

'Look. This is horrific. We all know that. Every time the phone rings . . . I can't believe she did what they're saying she did, but at the same time I can't see what else . . . Our dad's drinking, and Mum's up to the eyeballs on tranquillisers. If you know Lara, you'll know about my relationship with her. Do you know that stuff?'

'You didn't get on. At all. She lived here with you for a while and then moved out.'

'Let's go for a drink.'

'Sure.'

'A soft drink on my part. I would love a small glass of wine, but not in public, not when there's a chance of someone from the press lurking with a camera. And not at the pub down there. Everyone would be listening.'

She set off back up the street without waiting for an answer, and I had to do my fastest walking to catch her up.

The bar was big and clattery and completely anonymous. I could see why Olivia had chosen it. It was populated with a mixture of people in work clothes knocking back drinks with serious levels of concentration, and tourists being happier and more leisurely about it.

I bought her a freshly squeezed orange juice, and without intending to, added a glass of white wine for myself.

'Oh, you lucky sod,' she said with a small smile, eyeing up my drink. 'What is that?'

'Sauvignon Blanc. I don't often drink, actually, and when I do it's red wine, but there was a woman at the bar buying this and it looked nice, so I decided to have one too.'

'When Lara first turned up at my flat, she had a bottle of Sauvignon with her. I hadn't realised how nervous she was, but she knocked it back. It was being on my territory, I suppose. She normally drank red too. Look. Iris. Let's get straight to the point. What do you think's happened?'

A man pushed past my chair, so close that I could smell the meat he had just eaten. I leaned towards Olivia.

'Well.' I saw a woman holding herself together by a thread. 'I just don't think she killed him, like I said. I really don't.'

'Of course she didn't kill him.' Olivia was leaning forward too. 'The police interviewed me for hours and hours. It was awful, like you've suddenly stepped into a TV drama or something. You kind of think you know the script, except that it's all about your sister and whether or not she murdered her lover. Not in a million years. I kept saying that. Lara and I are not close, but I'll defend her to the death on this one. She didn't do it. Cheat on Sam, yes, of course – wouldn't you? Murder someone? Well – no. That's just ludicrous. Unthinkable.'

'I agree with you.'

'Someone's set her up.'

'What did the police say about that?'

She shrugged. 'That she wanted Guy to leave his wife and he wouldn't and she cracked up and stabbed him. She would never have carried a knife, so where did that come from? The trouble is, I know I'm right, but when I hear myself saying it, and look at their sceptical faces, I can see that, to them, I'm like one of those people who lives next door to a serial killer and says "but he was so quiet and polite". They feel sorry for me and they think I don't have a clue.' She sighed. 'Can I have a sip of your wine?'

I pushed it towards her. 'Thanks. Lara and I hated one another, and that's actually not too strong a word. Right from when we were children. She was perfect – I could never match up. We'd compete endlessly in everything and she'd always beat me. She was the good girl, so I had to be the bad one. All of that. It was complicated and I'm not proud of certain things. After university she went away travelling and she was in Asia for ages, and that was the only time I ever felt I had the space to be myself. But she came back and reinvented herself as the high-flying professional, and I was in second place again. She had the perfect wedding, while my love life was one long car crash. And then she didn't get pregnant and I did, without meaning to, and my own parents were insanely furious with me for upsetting her. Neither of them was remotely pleased about the baby, not even for half a second. It was just another bitchy thing I'd done, as far as they were concerned.

'I knew she was seeing Guy, because I ran into them in a bar that night – the night she vanished. They were having a beer round the corner. I could see at a glance that she adored him, and I knew her well enough to know that she'd want to leave Sam rather than have a long-term affair. We're sisters. No matter what baggage there is, we're still sisters. And she would never, ever have hurt that man, even though the press is going wild for the "good girl turned monster" thing.'

'So where do you think she is?'

Olivia leaned back in her chair and stroked the bump of her baby.

'I think,' she said. 'No one else wants to hear this. But I think something terrible has happened to her. Whoever killed Guy has done the same to her. Wherever she is, Iris, I'm absolutely certain that she's dead. But I have no idea who could have done it. A random lunatic is the only option, but that makes no sense. That doesn't really happen, or if it does they get caught straight away. So then I wonder, could it be someone she knows? I can't think of anyone.'

She paused.

'But look. I know for sure that something dramatic happened to her when she was in Thailand. She was up to something. She had a boyfriend, Jake, and then suddenly she was back home and subdued and in her room all the time. That's the only time Lara was ever different. Mysterious. I've been going through her boxes of stuff in the parents' attic, because you never know. I'm clutching at straws, but there could be something there, couldn't there? I can't think what else to do. Jake, with no surname, from, what, nearly fifteen years ago?'

I nodded. 'If you find anything,' I said. It seemed presumptuous to ask, so I didn't finish the sentence.

'It's nice that you believe in her,' she said. 'Makes me feel less alone. Sure. Let's swap numbers, and if I find anything I'll give you a call. You do the same.'

I opened my mouth to tell her about the passport, then stopped. It seemed too ridiculous, and I could not bear to get her hopes up and then dash them. I put a hand on hers and passed her my wine glass.

'Of course I will,' I told her.

chapter nineteen

Lara and Guy's hotel was a functional place for business people, opposite St Paul's Cathedral. I could see why she wanted to stay here: it was not outrageously expensive (in the central London hotel world, at least), you could check in by machine, and nobody bothered you. The little foyer was filled with men and women, mainly men, in work outfits, bustling around in bubbles of their own importance.

I looked at a few of them, but they seemed interchangeable. I wished I could let them know how easily their bubbles were popped. As well as the 'work trip to London' brigade, there were the obligatory tourists carting enormous suitcases in and out of lifts.

My room was number 253. It was a door on a corridor, the same as all the others. Lara and Guy might have used this room, but statistically, they probably hadn't.

I had not been in a hotel for years. The bland room, the rigorously smooth bed, the little kettle and the tiny plastic tubs of non-milk came together to create an environment that was nothing like the last hotel room I'd been in, yet it took my breath away all the same.

Superimposed on this one was a room with character, a room with bare floorboards and a colourful bedspread, huge open windows and a breeze blowing in from the sea.

I closed my eyes tightly. If I kept breathing, in and out, it would be all right. That other hotel room was miles from here. It was not in London. It was in Italy. It had no business intruding here.

Laurie was at home. The Laurie who had taken me to Italy was long gone.

My legs were wobbling, but I managed to manoeuvre myself to the bed. Even when I was lying curled up, my big boots transgressive on the covers, it took a few minutes before it all subsided. I did not like it; but I had known that this would happen. In London, little bits of that other world would seep in.

I concentrated hard and thought of Lara, and soon it was all gone and I was back in Lara's London life. She and her dead lover had lived in rooms like this, all through the week, for weeks and weeks. I imagined their suitcases side by side, their contents spilling out and mingling. Their work clothes would have hung in a wardrobe like this, on the same non-removable hangers. Then one day they caught the train together, and by the time it reached Cornwall, he was dead and she was gone.

I had expected to hide in my room that evening, sheltering from London and its barrage of reminders, but in fact the city was strangely welcoming. I could go anywhere and do anything, and I felt certain that nobody would notice me. I sat in a pub that was busy despite its being a January Monday. There I had a glass of orange juice and a plate of cheerily generic fish and chips, and tried to decide what on earth I should do next. Olivia had spoken to me, and, unexpectedly, I liked her. I was supposed to be investigating, but I had no idea how.

Someone had left a newspaper on the next table, and I grabbed it and flicked through the pages. There was nothing new in the news pages, just speculation and some weak sightings. I flicked past a cobbled-together feature about people working away from their spouses. While it said very little about Lara and Guy, the words 'they spent their evenings in the bars and clubs of central London, living openly as partners' jumped off the page. It went on to list a sparse set of unconvincing sightings of them that journalists had assembled.

'Eyewitnesses report seeing them in a seedy underground cabaret bar in a former toilet in central London, the day before the murder,' I read. 'Lara Finch might already have known what she was going to do the very next night.'

I knew about the underground bar, vaguely, but I had not given it much thought. In the absence of much else to go on, and before I worked out a way of talking to Lara's colleagues, I would retrace their steps. If I could go, alone, to a seedy bar in a converted toilet, I would be able to do anything.

With some relief, I reminded myself that there was no point going to a dodgy bar on a Monday. I would have to wait until the end of the week for that challenge: in fact, I would go on Thursday, as they had. For now, that meant I could put it out of my mind.

I realised slowly that someone was looking at me. People were leaving the pub, and everything felt as if it were winding down. There was only a handful of people left, all of a sudden, one of whom was standing across the room from me, looking at me without even trying to pretend he wasn't.

I looked up, looked away, and looked back again. For a fraction of a second I wanted to run. My heart struggled in my chest as if, given half a chance, it would escape my rib cage altogether and run away. My legs tensed up, ready to go.

Then it was over. He was just a man in a bar, staring at a woman because she was on her own. That was all. I had mistaken him for someone he could not possibly have been. This man had thick black hair, and he was about the right height, and his skin was the same caramel colour that spoke of a mixed heritage of a similar sort. He was the right kind of age. That was all.

He could not be Laurie, because I had left Laurie in Cornwall. Laurie would not have followed me here and ambushed me with accusations.

I looked back up at him quickly. The man smiled and started to walk towards me. I stood up, grabbed my bag and left, without looking back. I hoped he was not taking that as an invitation, and I started to run, in case he did.

The hotel's corridors were identical, inevitably. I could have gone straight to my room, but instead I started at the top floor and walked around and down. I passed door after door, many with 'do not disturb' signs on them, others with empty trays outside. I was passing every room in which Guy and Lara had ever stayed.

I wished I had known her better. I wished that she had confided in me, even though I had only met her four times. I longed to know whether she was in love with him, whether her time in this hotel was spent in a whirl-wind of non-stop talk and sex and obsession, or whether she was bored at home and miserable and seeking solace in destructive behaviour. I hoped it was the first one. I pictured the two of them ripping one another's clothes off the moment the hotel door clicked shut behind them.

It was bland here. Everything was uniform – it was a place to sleep and that was all – so the entire building became a surreal blank canvas for anything anyone wanted to do. Every few steps took me past another room, with another bed. Anything could have been going on behind those doors.

I walked quickly, trying not to think about the man in the bar. He had done nothing wrong, even though approaching a strange woman in a pub was completely out of character. It was not necessarily out of his character, not out of the real man's character. It would only have been odd behaviour for the man he looked like.

It would have been odd behaviour for Laurence. Laurie was at home in Cornwall. He was in our home, where we lived.

Finally, on floor four, I found a chambermaid's trolley. I stood beside it, shifting my weight from one foot to the other, fiddling with my hair, picking at a loose corner of wallpaper, until a woman appeared. She was small, her hair scraped back, and she was wearing a grey and white uniform.

'Good evening,' she said, her eyes cast down.

'Hello.' I tried to think what would make her talk to me. I needed to get this right. 'Hi. Um. Do you work here every day?'

She was suspicious. 'Mostly. Do you have a problem with your room?'

'No, no, not at all. My room's absolutely fine. Um. A

friend of mine used to stay here. Lara Finch. With her . . .' I struggled to find the right word, and failed. 'With her friend. Her boyfriend. You know? People have been looking for her.'

'Oh yes.' This woman was, I thought, Latin American. She did not look like someone who had time to stand around gossiping. She pushed her trolley a little way down the corridor and I walked with her. 'I know.'

'Did you ever see her, when she was here? Do you remember her?'

She shook her head. 'We see many people.'

'You might have cleaned her room.'

'Maybe. How would I know?' She took a key from her pocket and opened the door to room 413. 'When we clean the room, no people are there.'

And with that she went inside and closed the door.

The man on the reception desk was not helpful either.

'We see so many people,' he explained. 'I recognised them, sure. But I never paid them any attention. It's not my business if they're having an affair or what they're doing. I mean, this is a hotel. People do what they like. To be honest, I'm just glad she didn't kill him right here in the hotel.'

'Do you think there's anyone here who might have talked to them, or noticed anything about them?'

'No,' he said. 'Believe me, we've had the police here going over every room they ever stayed in. We've had journalists like you wouldn't believe, and we have nothing to say. If she's your friend then I'm sorry, but the reason people come to a hotel like this is so they won't be bothered. We don't notice the private lives of our guests.

We don't have time to wonder about them. It is not our business.'

He smiled a brightly white toothy smile, and I knew I was dismissed. My vague dreams of finding a member of staff at the hotel who would confide all sorts of inside information were shattered. I had no idea what I'd been expecting.

I called Alex, desperate to hear a friendly voice, to speak to someone who might not scoff at the fact that I was here, chasing ghosts. I had committed fraud that day, filling in the backs of my passport photos with the name and signature of a teacher I had once known. I was going to confess that, when I spoke to him.

However, he did not answer. I left him a stiff little message, feeling stupid. He had liked my skirt, and had drunk wine with me. We had chatted, and it felt as if I had known him for a long time. I was comfortable with him. That meant nothing.

I did not sleep well. I felt her ghost, and Guy's, all around me. I felt my old life, my London life, pressing in on me, and I did not want to think about it.

chapter twenty

My phone rang at nine the next morning. I was dozing, and I nearly didn't answer. The London noises outside the window made me wake in a state of unexpected excitement. Engines thrummed non-stop, buses chugged, horns sounded, and occasionally a voice was raised in sweary reproach. Before I came fully through the sleepy curtain into proper consciousness, I was pleased to be home.

Then I woke up properly and shrank away from that thought. The phone was still ringing, blasting away with the tune Laurie had set for me when I first got it: an obscure, lovely song by I Am Kloot, called 'To The Brink'. It was our special song. I decided to change it as soon as I could.

I answered mainly to stop it ringing, forgetting, in my confused haze, that voicemail would have had the same effect, had I left it a second or two longer. I didn't look at the screen because I wanted his voice to be a surprise.

'Hello?'

'Iris. Are you OK?'

I had wanted a surprise, and I got my wish.

'Hello.'

'Sorry. It's Alex. I didn't mean to startle you. Sorry.'

'Alex. That's OK. I called you last night. You're calling me back. That's nice of you. You don't have to say sorry for something nice.'

I was sitting up in bed, pulling my hair away from my face, remembering that I needed to get it cut. It was tangled and annoying. Maybe I would have it dramatically shorter.

'How are you, then?' His voice was warm. 'How's Budock?'

'Oh.' I got out of bed and unplugged the little kettle, the phone still held between shoulder and ear. 'I'm not in Budock. Highly unusually for me, I'm in London.'

'Seriously? I thought you rarely left your house.'

'I know! And look at me now.' I turned the bathroom tap on, and water crashed loudly into the kettle. It echoed around the immaculately tiled room, and I cringed because I knew it sounded as if I were weeing. 'Sorry about the noise,' I said quickly. 'That's me filling the kettle. I'm in a hotel.'

'Blimey, Iris.' I laughed. *Blimey* seemed an incongruous thing to say, but in a sweet way. 'Are you really? What are you doing?'

I tried to explain. It was not easy, because I could not properly explain it to myself.

'I'm staying in Lara and Guy's hotel,' I said, immediately realising it made me sound mad. 'I'm kind of going to places where they went. I'm so sure she didn't kill him. I know she didn't. Someone else did. I want to find out who.'

'Ah. And is your . . .' He hesitated. 'Is your boyfriend with you?'

'No,' I said quickly. 'No, he's stayed at home. He's not really keen on London.'

I could not believe I was talking about Laurie to a policeman. The kettle was making a big fuss of boiling, cranking itself up loudly, demonstrating the effort it was making just so I could have a cup of nasty, UHT-addled tea.

'And your family? Are they still in London?'

'Yes. Probably. As far as I know.'

'You don't get on with them?'

'No. But they're lovely. Long story. How are you?'

'Oh, you know. I'm fine. Supposed to be doing all sorts of other things, but I'm following the Lara investigation. Not that there's any change. Guy's funeral happened yesterday. You know that already, I'm sure. They're scaling back the search and assuming her body's somewhere inaccessible near the train track.'

'They can't scale it back! They haven't got a clue.'

'What do you mean? What don't they have a clue about?'

'Lara. She's . . .'

The silence hung in the air for the amount of time it would have taken me to tell him about my missing passport. I could feel Alex, too, nearly saying something, hesitating. I decided to tell him, a fraction of a second after he started to tell me.

'Iris,' he said suddenly. 'I'm on leave, starting tomorrow night. I was wondering about making a visit to London myself. I always feel I have to get away when I have a couple of weeks off work. You know? Otherwise it doesn't feel like a break. If you wouldn't mind, we could maybe grab a drink or a bite to eat or something. You could tell me about your researches. I'm as intrigued as you are, because in fact all the spots along the train track have been pretty well checked, and unless Lara flung herself out with great abandon, or did it at an odd time in the journey, they would have found her by now. It's just possible that she could have got off at Reading, as you know, but no one on the CCTV looks remotely like her. When the train stops between stations there's no CCTV, but if she got off in one of those places she must have gone somewhere. I can't come up with a theory. Can you?'

I pulled the lid off a little carton of milk. It spurted, inevitably, over my fingers, and I dumped it splashily into the teacup.

'It would be nice to see you if you're going to be here,' I said carefully. 'And Alex. Let me say this without you thinking I'm mad. Please?'

'Mais bien sur,' he said.

'One of the things I've done here is go to the passport office and apply for a new passport. I did the thing when you do it quickly, just in case. Bloody hell, it's expensive. But anyway. I had to apply for a new passport.' I paused, planning how I could say this to make it sound plausible to a policeman. 'I had a passport at home. It was in a filing cabinet. It still had three years before it was going to expire. But it vanished. And you remember I told you that Lara came to see me on Christmas Eve?'

I could hear the scepticism, even though he was trying to hide it. 'Yes?'

'Well. She asked if she could look around the house. Laurie was away. So I was giving her a tour of the place and she was saying what she'd do to it if we had the money to make it amazing. When we got to the second bedroom upstairs, which is the study, my landline rang. A rare event. I went off to answer it but there was no one there. Then I came back and we carried on as normal. And a couple of weeks later both my passport and Lara have vanished.'

He did not speak for several seconds. I felt intensely stupid, but I did not allow myself to backtrack or back down or qualify everything I had just said with 'of course it's probably nothing', because I was sure that it was, in fact, something.

'Really?' he said. 'Are you telling me this as a police officer, or as a friend?'

I shrank inwardly from that word.

'I'm telling you as Alex Zielowski. You're . . . well, I suppose you're both of those things. Whichever you would like it to be.'

'Yes. Well. Look, I'm at work today, and I do actually need to get on with it, and as you know, the whole Lara thing is not remotely within my remit because it's a Penzance investigation. But what I'll do is, I'll see if I can find a way to check out your details. It's not easy. I should fill in a Data Protection Form. But let's see. Do you know your passport number, by any chance?'

'I wish I did.'

'I'll do what I can. I have a meeting I should be in right now, but I'll call you later, if I may.'

'Of course. Any time.'

'Thank you. And Iris?'

'Yes?'

'Is your boyfriend all right? At home without you?'

'He's fine,' I said quickly. 'Don't worry about him.'

'Of course. Well, have a good day in London, and I'll speak to you later.' His voice suddenly went formal at the end, and I sensed someone in the room with him.

'Bye.'

I sat on the bed and stared at the phone and sipped my tea. I realised I was smiling. I had called Budock several times, but Laurie never picked up. Today I decided I would not even attempt it. He knew how to get hold of me.

I looked at the phone, knowing I could pick it up and do something radical. I could, for instance, call my mother. My hand stretched towards it. I would only have to say hello.

'Hello?' she would say, in that vague-yet-aggressive way of hers. 'Hello? Iris, darling, is it you? Oh, you ridiculous girl, where have you been?'

That was why I couldn't do it. They all thought I had overreacted to an absurd extent. Of course they did. The world was crammed with broken hearts, and the proper way of dealing with it was to be sad for a judicious amount of time, then move on. It was not to run away to Cornwall at the age of thirty-two and closet oneself and one's lover away indefinitely.

Alex's call made me get on the District Line, even though I didn't want to. There was something about him that made me want to do the right thing. I sat on the Tube with my mind blank, watching people. A man was asleep, his head leaning back against the window, jerking upright from time to time. An old woman frowned in concentration at the book she was reading, so absorbed that I wondered whether she would miss her stop. Perhaps she already had.

After Earls Court, it thinned out completely. The sleeping man and the reading woman were still on, as was a harried-looking man with a baby in a sling and a young woman with ill-advised patterned leggings and a top that was too short, who was doing something on her phone with furious concentration.

As we approached East Putney, now overground, with rain lashing tightly against the window, I stood up like an automaton and walked to the door.

It was the same as it had always been, and the familiar mundanity kept me going through the station hall, which was the same as every Tube station ticket hall with its stash of free newspapers and sparsely manned ticket office, yet different and particular to itself in its shape, its detail, its very essence.

All my journeys used to start here. I went to school from this station. I met my friends here. I bought my Travelcard and set out into the world from here.

My legs walked me along the road, still busy with cars, buses, vans and taxis, all belching out their fumey clouds, and across the High Street, which was smarter than it used to be, and then picked their way through the affluent streets close to the river. I stepped around the puddles, jumped over a little flood in the gutter.

The houses must have been worth millions by now. They were beautifully tended, with exteriors immaculately cleaned, the brickwork impeccable. Some of them were flats, of course. That had always been the case. Even the flats were magazine-smart these days.

The house on the corner had grass that was so lush and so beautifully tended that every fat blade was the same length. A child's tricycle, wooden of course, was parked neatly on a honey-stone patio, and a mosaic-topped table with four matching chairs stood stoically in the rain, waiting for spring and the sun.

That house used to belong to the Grimaldis. They were in their seventies, a gay couple, and they had lived there for ever. Bert and Jonno, those were their names. Jon had taken Bert's surname because, I recalled him saying, 'Why would you go through life being called Bottomley when you could become a Grimaldi?'

They had moved, or died, since I was last here. I wondered which it was.

Every house I passed assaulted me with memories. I walked on, tramping the street on which I had learned to ride a bike, the road to my nursery school. I remembered racing my sister, Lily, from the corner to our front door, both of us arriving red-cheeked and breathless, laughing, desperate to be the winner.

I was glad it was raining. My hair was bedraggled, down my back, and my clothes were clinging uncomfortably. That felt right.

I passed a woman pushing a huge buggy with two babies in it, side by side. She was probably younger than me, but she was exclusively a mother. Her exhaustion was covered with make-up and, I supposed, expensive creams, yet was impossible to erase. She had the chunky look of someone once slim who had given birth to twins within the past six months. Her clothes were expensive yet practical: jeans, Fly boots, a blue anorak zipped against the elements, and her hair was blond with dark roots, scraped back into something like a bun.

I smiled as we passed, and she smiled back, conspiratorial, assessing me, I felt, as someone who might have been through it myself.

I was almost surprised that she could see me. I felt I was walking this street like a ghost.

The house was still there, and my parents still lived in it. Their black Volvo was parked on the drive. The same curtains hung at the downstairs windows. I stood on the other side of the street and looked.

All I needed to do was take a few steps and ring the bell. They might not be there. I would not need to explain myself. They would, I knew, be unequivocally delighted to see me back. They loved me. They had lost me.

When I saw a figure at the window, however, I knew I could not do it. Perhaps one day I would, but for now I turned and fled, back along the claustrophobically familiar streets, down to the river, across the bridge and, randomly, into Fulham. At first I thought I heard someone calling my name, but then it stopped.

I called Olivia from a street corner. Happily, she did not bother asking how I was.

'I was thinking,' she said, instead. 'You should talk to Lara's godfather. Leon Campion. She was close to him. She is, I mean. I tried to talk to him about her when this happened, but he wasn't going for it. He doesn't like me. Never has. I'm the enemy, in his book. If there were T-shirts being made up, his would say "Team Lara" across his tits.'

'Oh. Right.' The opportunity to concentrate on something other than myself came as a glorious relief, and I forced myself to focus. 'Who is he? Her godfather? Her actual godfather?'

'Yes. An old mate of Dad's. He's a bit of a player, I think. He's into mysterious business deals and all that. Kind of smooth. He and Lara have always been close. I've never really worked it out. I thought they were shagging for a while, and I still think they might have been at some point. There's something between them, anyway. It might not be sex. But it's something.'

'Where do I find him?'

'I'll text you his number. He'll tell you to fuck off, but it's worth a try. He must be incredibly cut up about Lara, and I know he's been at Mum and Dad's house quite a bit. You should probably do to him what you did to me, if you can bear it. Go to see him face to face. Turn up at his office, not his home. Just in case there's anything he wouldn't want to say in front of his wife. Sally. She's nice.'

I memorised the address and remembered to ask about the baby.

Olivia hesitated.

'I think everything's OK. It can't have done it any good, having this kind of shock flung at it in the womb. I'm knackered and on my own, and my parents are obviously totally fixated on my sister, and I do utterly dread presenting them with a grandchild when Lara's missing and everyone – including, I think, my parents themselves – is assuming that she accidentally killed a man she was sleeping with. Bringing a new life into the world with a great flourish feels like such an out-of-step thing to do. You know. Typical Olivia. That kind of thing. Always awkward. And fuck knows how I'm going to pull it together to look after a baby.'

'Is the father . . . I mean, are the two of you together?'

She laughed, a quick, unamused laugh. 'No, that was never on the cards. It was a one-off. He doesn't even know, because I decided I could do without those sorts of complications. He'd either want to play happy families – perish the thought, frankly – or he'd start accusing me of doing it on purpose. Either way, no thanks. This is a one-woman show.'

'God, Olivia. You're strong.'

'Not really. You just do what you have to do.'

*

I sheltered in the doorway of an office building, and called Leon Campion the moment the number arrived. It was a mobile number, and he actually answered it. I assumed an imperious tone.

'Hi,' I said. 'Is that Leon Campion?'

'Who is this?' His voice was deep and cultured.

'Iris Roebuck. I'm a friend of Lara's. Sorry to disturb you, but Olivia gave me your number . . .'

He cut me off. 'Did she now? I have nothing to say.'

'I'm a friend. I just want to . . .'

'Nothing to say.'

'But surely you . . .'

'Oh, sorry – was I not being clear enough? Fuck off.'

And he hung up. I looked at the phone and laughed. When I called back, it went, inevitably, to voicemail. I left a long message anyway, despite the fact that he had not sounded like a man who would listen to it.

I was holding on by a thread. Although I thought I was walking randomly through London with no sense whatsoever of where I was going, my legs took me to the one place I had been avoiding.

They walked me directly to a set of traffic lights in central London. It was an ordinary, humdrum junction close to the Euston Road. Railings that had once been covered in flowers with heart-rending notes attached to them were bare, had been bare for five years.

A man cycled by. He was wearing Lycra and riding a racing bike. He was a professional, possibly a courier, and he did not stop for the red lights. I wanted to yell at him. I wanted to tell him.

I had stood here before. I turned and ran away, as fast

as I possibly could. I sprinted through London until I had left the place far behind.

When Alex called, I was sitting in a bar near the hotel drinking vodka and tonic and thinking hard. 'To the Brink' made me jump. I nearly didn't answer, but then I did, because I wanted to speak, and I had barely said a word since our conversation that morning.

'Hi,' I said.

'Are you OK?' His voice was immediately concerned. 'Iris, you don't sound like yourself.'

'Can you tell from one word? No, I'm all right. Just a bit . . . assaulted by memories, maybe. It's OK.'

'Yes, I bet. That must be . . .' He tailed off, and I was glad. 'Look. I got lucky. I thought I'd try Heathrow, under the circumstances, and I took a chance, called their local police at the end of the day and slightly implied I was my boss. And they did the flight check without paperwork. Now, I cannot quite believe this, but it does seem to be true. Iris, according to the records, you caught a flight some hours after Guy Thomas was killed. At least, someone of your name did. From Heathrow.'

I could not take this in. I still half thought Laurie had done something to my passport, even though I knew he had not.

'Where,' I managed to say, 'did I go?'

'Bangkok. You were issued with a tourist visa, and you haven't left Thailand yet. Look. I'm going to come to London, like I said.'

'Have you told – I mean, I know you are the police, but have you told the ones in Penzance?'

I wanted him to say no. I wanted him to be like a

policeman in a film who goes off piste and carries out his own, unofficial investigation. I wanted him to say that together he and I would track her down, under the radar. He did not.

'Yes, of course. It got a lukewarm reception as far as ideas go. In fact the general feeling was that you were to be filed in the nutters drawer. You're not, though. They'll look at it, but I don't hold out great hopes of anything much happening. I'll carry on looking at it with you. Because you're right. If I may.'

'You may,' I told him. As soon as I ended the call, I drained the glass and stood up. My sitting around drinking alone was not going to help with anything.

chapter twenty-one

I sat on a bench in St James's Park and stared at my phone. It was so cold that my fingers hardly worked, and I had never, ever imagined I might become the sort of person who sat in a beautiful park in a huge city, with pelicans nearby, a palace to my right, Whitehall off to my left, and people doing interesting things everywhere I looked, and tried to puzzle out Twitter.

Nonetheless, I was doing it. If Lara was in Thailand, she would have to be looking at the internet. If she was looking at the internet, she might open her Twitter account. I knew, because the media had unearthed it, that she had only ever posted one tweet, that read 'Trying to work out how to use Twitter'.

She did, however, have over 27,000 followers. All those people had sought her out and followed her, just in case it became one of those dramas that played out on social media. The world was strange.

This was one possible way of reaching her. Facebook was no good, because I was not one of her 'friends', and her privacy settings stopped me sending her a message.

My breath puffed out around me. The clouds were pale

and low, the air lethal with the promise of snow. Other people were hurrying through the park, stamping feet in expensive boots, shivering in cheap anoraks, each heading to a destination that had walls and a heater.

I had set up a Twitter account. My picture, like Lara's, was an egg, and I had named myself, randomly, after my poor cats: I was @desi_ophelia. This was a whole new world. It took me a while to realise, to my dismay, that I still could not send Lara a private message, even after I had followed her account, because she had to be following me for that to happen. I forced my freezing fingers to compose something that would stand up to scrutiny when viewed by any random member of the public.

Hi Lara, my first tweet said in the end. *It's Iris. I hope you're OK and I think you are. If you see this, can you message me? I know you didn't do it. xx*

I had wanted to mention Thailand, but since my tweet was technically public (though I could not imagine anyone looking at my account, and so reading it), I didn't. I would save it for when we were speaking in private, in the unlikely event that that ever happened.

I stood up and started walking. I was not going to leave the park, but sitting still was no good. My fingers were white and unresponsive. I strode to the middle of the bridge and looked out over the ice that was half formed across the water. I had a flash of Holden Caulfield wondering where the Central Park ducks went when their pond was frozen over. These ones were stoically using the unfrozen areas, carrying on as normal, but they must have been miserable. They were putting brave ducky faces on it.

The Catcher in the Rye was Laurie's favourite book, and this was his favourite park. He liked it because it was small but rich: 'distilled', he used to call it.

Sometimes we would stand on the bridge and feed the ducks. He would never let me bring bread. 'That is terrible for them,' he would say. 'Why the hell do people think that ducks want bread? What good is a diet of processed carbs going to be for creatures that live in water and eat waterweed? Why would you take something that lives off veg and live protein, and stuff it with sugar and salt and preservatives?' He would pack a careful picnic for the ducks, containing pieces of bacon, and bags of nutrient-rich grains that he would pick up from a pet shop near his office. It was one of the reasons why I loved him so much.

Those were our happy times. We lived in west London and everything was perfect, and I could never have imagined us as we had been for the past few years, cowering away from the world, a shadow of a shadow of the way we had once been.

I walked along the pathways and across the grass, stomping around the park without much purpose. I liked the children, running about with rosy cheeks and excited anticipation of potential snowmen to come. I liked looking at the Whitehall people too, in their suits. They hurried along, still wearing their work auras over their expensive overcoats. They had brought a little bubble of politics to the park and they clearly felt the park should be grateful.

'There you are,' he said, and I looked up and there he was, tall and geeky, towering above me, smiling with a hint of nerves.

'Here I am,' I agreed, taking a step away from him. Although I was here to meet him, I had somehow not expected him.

Neither of us said anything. It was still freezing. It was still not snowing.

'You made it then,' I said eventually, and started walking. He walked with me. He was looking more casual than I had ever seen him before: an off-duty policeman, it turned out, looked nothing like you would imagine. If I hadn't known Alex was a detective constable, I would have thought he was something far less straight. He was wearing jeans and a bright red jumper with a pattern on it, like someone's Christmas jumper but somehow just stylish enough. His coat was a downy mountaineering-style one that I would never have chosen for anyone, but that I instantly envied for its obvious warmth.

'Yes,' he said. 'That journey gets longer, I swear. But it was fine.'

'I like your boots,' I told him. 'They're like cowboy boots, aren't they? Like rock-star boots.'

That pleased him. 'I got them in a charity shop,' he admitted. 'I wasn't sure they were me, but I bought them anyway, and it turns out they're the most comfortable piece of footwear that has ever been crafted by human hands, so that was lucky.'

'That is lucky,' I agree. 'Shall we go somewhere warm?'

'I'm starving. Did you collect your passport?'

I started to undo my bag so I could show it to him, but my fingers wouldn't work the catch properly, so I just said yes.

As we reached Trafalgar Square and started to head past the lions, tiny snowflakes began to fall.

'So,' he said, leaning back in his chair. 'Here's what I've found out, and they are getting pretty pissed off with my meddling, I can tell you. This did come up in the investigation when Mrs Finch initially went missing.'

'Lara,' I told him, eating a piece of cucumber.

'Yes. Lara. Sorry. I forget I'm off duty. I've always tried not to think about cases when I'm on holiday. I normally spend my holidays walking on the beach and not reading the paper. Anyway. Lara. About twelve years ago, she charged into a police station, very upset, and confessed to something completely outlandish.'

He took a chip off his plate. We were in an upmarket burger restaurant on the Charing Cross Road, and I was appreciating how very much better you can eat when you're with someone. Sitting in a restaurant by yourself could be all right, I thought, if you had a book and were in the right mood. However, there was nothing to beat company.

I was chilled to realise that I had not had a friend, apart from Lara, for five years. That was bizarre. Something inside me was waking up, happy. It was pushing aside the things I needed to address, and enjoying the moment.

'What was it?'

'Right. Now, this is a really weird one. She turned up on her own, in a state of considerable distress, and announced that she had been smuggling drugs in Asia for a period of some months and that it was her fault some woman was in prison. No one quite knew what to do with her, as you can imagine. Anyway, nothing came of it. She ran out of the building, and went back the next day with a guy, her father, in tow and retracted it all. He explained that she was under lots of stress and didn't know what she was saying, and that she'd made it all up. But in between those two things happening, someone had vaguely looked into it, and discovered that she'd confessed the same thing in Singapore and had been treated as a time-waster and put on the next flight home with instructions not to come back.'

'She said she was a drug smuggler?' I frowned and sipped my wine. 'Lara?'

'I know. No one believed her. The question is, though, why did she say it? Was she protecting someone? Trying to flag something up? We don't have any details from Singapore, but I've asked for them.'

'And all this already came up? And you guys ignored it?'

He widened his eyes. 'Penzance ignored it. It's not my case. The trouble is, her affair with Guy Thomas overshadowed everything. There was no need to go into her deep past, when her more recent past – her present, really – seemed to offer all the answers.'

'Yeah. I can see.'

'Much as I'm not at work, if you're trying to figure it out, which you are, I'll help.'

I smiled at him and lifted my veggie burger. 'Thank you.'

We wandered through a tiny snow shower to the National Gallery, and I took him to my favourite painting, Titian's *Bacchus and Ariadne*.

'It's the blue,' I said. 'I used to come and stand in front of it, any time I needed calming down. And I like it that she's been abandoned by the person she thought was the great love of her life, and along comes Bacchus and not only offers to marry her, but also to give her some stars as a wedding present. Actually, I'm surprised I've been in London for this long without coming to say hello to it.'

In fact, I wasn't surprised. I had been trying to keep away from my old haunts, until today.

'I can see it would do the job,' Alex agreed. 'Did she take him up on the offer, out of interest?'

'I think so.' I was sure she had, in fact, but for some reason I did not want to tell Alex that.

He nodded. 'You know what used to do it for me?'

'Tell me.'

'Just wandering around a gallery, like this one, looking at all the Madonna-and-Child pictures. Often the babies look so weird that they make you laugh. They have little-old-men faces and strange creased necks. You can see the artist has tried to make him look more serious than a real baby. What with him being the son of God and all that. And it's an incredibly hard thing to pull off.'

I was staring at him. 'I used to do that too. Most of the babies look as if they're from horror films. And occasionally you'll come across one that is just so gorgeous and tender, it makes you forget about all the others.'

'Yes! Those are surprisingly rare, though.'

'Do you like the Leonardo cartoon they've got here? The one with St Anne and John the Baptist?'

He laughed. 'I hardly think I'm in a position not to like something by da Vinci. Shall we go and look at it? I love it, actually. It's one of my favourite babies.' He looked at me with a smile. 'Are you going to say the thing about it not being very funny for a cartoon, or am I?'

'I was waiting for you to do it.'

'And I was chivalrously going to leave it to you.'

'Well, let's just consider it said.'

I realised, as we walked around the gallery, that I knew almost nothing about Alex, and that I was, effectively, looking at paintings, speculating about school groups and gaggles of students, listening into parts of other people's lectures, with a stranger. Until today, we had talked only of Lara.

'What do you think of this jungle stuff?' he said, as we stood in front of a painting called *Surprised* by Henri

Rousseau. It was a jungle scene painted by someone who had never been to a jungle, with a tiger baring its teeth, and stylised greenery.

'I like it, but I wouldn't stand in front of it for hours,' I decided. 'Though it's funny that in a room that also contains Van Gogh's *Sunflowers* and a load of Cézannes, we both headed straight over here. It's kind of compelling. It's very much of its time, isn't it? Wasn't Rousseau a customs officer?'

'*Le douanier* – exactly.'

'But it's quite problematic these days, isn't it? I mean, there are layers to that: he's a customs officer, feted by the art world, treated as a darling little man accidentally producing these adorable primitive paintings. And his paintings are of jungle scenes, full of colonial undercurrents and steeped in orientalism and "the other". It says here that he copied the leaves from the botanical gardens in Paris.'

Alex was looking at me, smiling his little smile. 'Absolutely. It's a historic relic of its time, rather than a timeless masterpiece. It's fascinating, though, isn't it? The social strata. The hierarchy. The way everyone condescends to the layer below them.'

'It is,' I agreed. 'And you know this gallery as well as I do. I half thought I was going to be condescending myself, you know. Showing the Cornish policeman a bit of London culture. And yet that is not the case. I know nothing about you, Alex Zielowski. So you've lived in London?'

He looked down at me, amused. 'The Zielowski should have been a clue. I'm not Cornish through and through, though I did grow up there. But yes, I came to university in London. I lived here for years, then went back to Cornwall for the whole "lifestyle" thing, the way people do. Also, because it felt like home and I suppose I got a bit old and boring and fancied running into old school mates in the pub and all of that. Going for a Sunday surf. Walking the coast path to a pub.'

'Was there a girl involved? I bet there was.'

He laughed. 'Is it that obvious? Yes. Juliet. It didn't work out. Evidently. I thought about leaving Cornwall when we split up, but by then I found I didn't want to. She's still there. She's married now, with a baby. And weirdly, we're the best of friends. We get on far better now than we ever did when we were together.'

We were in the hall of the gallery now, walking towards the exit. I thought it was nice that he was friends with his ex. That said nothing but good things about him. Alex was lovely, and gentle; he was not fiery like Laurie. He was predictable, where Laurie was tempestuous.

I pushed the thought out of my head.

chapter twenty-two

The bar was indeed in an underground public toilet, the steps leading down to it on the corner of Aldwych, right in the middle of the West End.

'You're sure about this?' asked Alex, as we stood at the top of the staircase. 'We do seem, literally, to be heading down the pan.'

'This was the last thing Lara and Guy did together. Well, nearly. I know things have moved on, but we have to check it out.'

'We don't *have* to. But we will. It's a bit intriguing. I mean, why the hell, of all the places around here . . .'

The doorman was watching us from a couple of steps down.

'We booked,' I told him, realising that I had to take charge. 'Iris Roebuck. Two people.'

'Sure.' He had dimples in his cheeks when he smiled. 'You have a great evening, now.'

As soon as we reached the bottom of the staircase, I saw that it was going to be fine: this place was nowhere near as weird as I had expected it to be. It was a tiny bar, with mirrored walls disguising exactly how small it actually was. Six tables were crammed into the small space, three high ones with bar stools and three normal-sized ones. All of them were occupied by a clientele that looked like the least threatening crowd in the whole of central London. Two tables were taken up by a crowd of women with short skirts and heels and laughing red mouths. They were, I thought, in their thirties and forties, on a big night out. A couple in their fifties sat at the next table, resolutely dressed down and wearing the slightly baffled air of the new-to-London. There was a young Japanese couple; a couple who looked slightly awkward with each other as if this might be a first date; two women giggling and drinking Prosecco.

The bar itself was stocked with spirits.

'Hi there,' said a young man behind it. He was fair and relaxed, confident in his familiar role as dispenser of booze. 'You get a free glass of bubbly. Would you like it now?'

'We certainly would.' Alex was at least as relieved as I was. As all the tables were taken, we stood at the bar, shifting around. I was uncomfortable in my new shoes, even though they were flat. The ten pound booking fee did not guarantee us a table, clearly. It did, however, get us our first drink.

I shrugged my coat off, awkwardly.

'Oh my God,' said Alex, suddenly, fervently. I was startled, even scared. He said it so loudly, sounded so incredibly surprised.

'What?'

'You. You look sensational.'

We both looked down at my dress, which was red and velvety. I had bought it on my first day in London.

'And that is so incredibly astonishing?'

'Take the compliment,' the barman told me, to my mortification. 'And you know what? He's right.'

'Um,' I said. 'Thank you.'

He slid two glasses of pale bubbles across the counter. I took one.

'Thanks. Look. You know, you'll be sick of people asking you this, but a friend of mine was here a few weeks ago. I know you've had journalists and everything here, but I'm just wondering if you remember her. And her friend.'

I thought of Guy, suddenly ambushed by the fact that this man I had never met was dead. I wanted to meet him. I never would. He was gone: someone had stabbed him with a knife until he no longer existed. And the night before that happened, he had been right here, exactly where I was now.

He sighed heavily and started fiddling with something behind the bar.

'Here.' He passed it to me. It was, incongruously, a basket of popcorn. I gave it to Alex. 'Yeah. Your friend? Terrible business.'

'She didn't kill him, you know. She can't have done. It was someone else, and they've got away. With her.'

'People do weird things when they're obsessed with somebody.'

I tried a piece of popcorn and remembered that I didn't like it. Alex was quiet; I sensed disapproval.

'She can't have done it. I know she didn't. Do you remember them when they were here?'

'The police say she did. That's probably good enough for me.' I looked at Alex, who frowned his reluctance to be introduced by his job title. 'And yeah,' the barman continued. 'Actually. I do.'

'What were they like?'

A waitress with artfully tousled long hair and a pair of children's fairy wings on her back came to the bar and pushed a piece of paper at him.

'And two Proseccos,' she added.

'I'm on it.'

I watched him making three cocktails, pouring two glasses of Prosecco and taking the top off a bottle of beer. At last it was all done and the waitress returned to load it on to her tray. Alex did not say a word as we waited, and I did not look at him.

'Yeah, sorry. Have to concentrate. Um. So, your friend. They sat at that table over there.' He pointed to where the out-of-towners were sitting. The woman looked back at us with a startled face, wondering why we were talking about her. 'They knocked back cocktails. Talked to each other. Laughed a lot, as I recall. Listened to the singer. They didn't do anything weird or unusual. Weird to think that he was dead the next night.'

'Nothing unusual at all?'

'No. Nothing. Sorry. Hey, you should grab that table!'

Alex was already there, sitting down the moment the Japanese couple got up, clearly happy to be away from the conversation.

Hours later, the room was spinning. I was drinking what I thought was my fourth martini, eating popcorn in an attempt to soak up the alcohol and leaning on Alex, who had pulled his chair around so he was next to me. We were talking about Cornwall, and art, and what it was like to be a policeman. I was telling him random facts about myself.

'I don't have many friends,' I informed him. 'I used to.

But I don't now. It's nice that you're here. Why are you here anyway?'

'Because I like you,' he said.

'As a friend.'

'Yes.'

'That's good.' I nearly started to talk about Laurie, but decided not to. It was definitely a better idea not to mention him. I didn't want to cry. The singer was a tall, slender black woman, and she was giving the crowd exactly the right sort of undemanding singalong songs, and trying to engage everyone in banter.

'Who's going to get up for this one?' she demanded, surveying the extremely small amount of floor space optimistically. 'You all know it, so you can all help me out with the singing. It's called "Hey Jude".'

And somehow, after the first few bars, Alex and I were on our feet belting it out drunkenly. It was, of course, a song that went on and on, and by the end, the whole bar was singing along. I nearly tripped over while attempting to perform a little dance, and Alex grabbed me and stopped me from crashing into our table. He held me tightly around the waist until I pulled away.

We stumbled out into the night. I had no idea what time it was, but the city was still busy. Taxis and buses thundered by, and people were walking around, and the lights were on everywhere. I could feel my heart rate picking up. The evening had suddenly turned into more than I could handle.

Alex took my hand and held it, even when I tried to pull away.

'Iris,' he said. 'This is a weird thing for me. To come to London, to follow you here. I've been telling everyone for so long that I'm self-sufficient and I don't need to be in a relationship. I completely believed myself. I couldn't bear it when people tried to set me up. The idea of being somewhere on a "date" seemed so artificial. When I met a woman I half liked I'd run a mile. And then I meet you on a work day, and something about you, and being with you – just everything about you – turns my world on its head. Could you tell? Could you tell I was hiding it when I turned up at your house? I mean, I had no reason to do that, really. I should have called you into the station and got someone else to take your statement. But I wanted to see you. It was such an overpowering feeling that I went with it. And then . . .'

'Shh. Please stop! Please.'

I did not want him to be saying these things. He put a hand on my shoulder and I turned to look at him, to tell him again to shut up. He had been my friend, and now he was close to ruining it.

His face was close to mine, and then closer. He was so much taller than I was that he had to lean right down to reach me. I should have pulled away, but at the crucial moment, I didn't, and his mouth was on mine.

I had forgotten completely what it felt like. Kissing a new person was so strange, and assaulted me with so vicious a slap of newness that I joined in with it, suddenly curious. It was like being thrown into icy water when you are very hot. It was horrible and astonishing and wonderful, all at once. This was real. It was happening. I had left Laurie in Cornwall, and I was kissing the detective. I was kissing another man.

As soon as that thought solidified in my mind, I pushed him away, and ducked under his arm.

'I can't,' I said. 'I just can't, Alex. I have a boyfriend. You know that. I'm sorry, but I just really, really can't.'

He held me by the upper arm and turned me around, gently, to face him.

'Iris,' he said. 'Come back. Iris. Look. I'm not really sure how to say this, but . . . I know about Laurie. I know. It's OK.'

I tried to get away, but he tightened his grip.

'You don't,' I informed him. 'You don't understand a thing.'

It was freezing. I felt drunk and sick and I wanted to be away, alone again.

'I do. I'm so sorry, Iris. I really am, but I know. I looked him up when you told me his name, but I knew already, because after I met you at the Finches' house I went home and looked for everything I could find about you. And then I discovered that this friend of mine, Dave, an old colleague – he was in the Met at the time of the accident. He was at the scene. So I know what happened. I'm so sorry, but Iris, you are amazing. And I will of course back right off. But I want you to face the world, and that's what you're starting to do. I want to help you.'

'No.'

'Iris?'

'No.'

'Iris – Laurie Madaki is dead. You know that. I know it. He was knocked off his bike five years ago. And he was killed instantly, pronounced dead at the scene. I know you haven't felt able to let him go . . .'

The moment he loosened his grip, I ducked away while he was still speaking. He had spoken the unsayable words and I could never forgive him. I ran around

Aldwych to the bottom of Kingsway, and set off along Fleet Street heading for St Paul's, not caring about the people staring. I hoped he would not chase me, and after a while I managed to hail a taxi and get back to the hotel, where I fell, still sobbing, into a drunken, heart-broken sleep.

chapter twenty-three

The day I met him, I knew it would happen. I knew we had to be together for ever, and that I would do everything in my power to achieve that. I knew that if I ever had to be without him, my life would be in tatters. I knew there was nobody else for me. If I could not be with Laurie, I would never be with anyone. I had clung on to him far, far longer than I should have done, but I was going to have to let him go.

Everything Alex had said was true. The cracks had been getting wider for more than a year, and finally they were wide open. The house I had built from denial and delusion had crumbled around me.

I lay half asleep in my hotel bed, the morning light shining through the net curtains as I had forgotten to close the thick drapes, and forced myself to revisit the day I met him. Until that moment I had been perfectly independent, with a job at a publishing house, a rented flat, friends and family and a life that was contented by anyone's standards. I never had quite enough money, and I perpetually felt that I should have been making plans for the future, but I was fine.

Then, at a friend's birthday party in a bar, I saw him. We were both twenty-seven, and the last thing I was expecting was to meet the love of my life. I nearly didn't go: I'd had a long day at work and I just wanted to get back to my flat and run a bath. The only reason I forced myself to put some lipstick on and head into Covent Garden was because I had Alice's birthday present with me, a bottle of champagne in a box that I had just managed to squeeze into my biggest handbag, and I didn't want either to leave it at work or to cart it home with me.

I was at the bar buying a bottle of house wine when I realised he was standing next to me. Until that moment I had never believed in love at first sight.

'Hi,' he said. He was tall, dark, with soft brown eyes, and he was wearing a nice suit.

'Hello.' I could not think of anything else to say.

'Are you with the birthday party?'

We both turned and looked at the table. I did not know Alice well – we had been at university together and became friends again when we both found ourselves working in London – and her close friends had made a far bigger fuss of her birthday than I had been expecting. Helium balloons were moored on the backs of chairs, and pieces of wrapping paper and discarded envelopes littered the floor in our corner.

'I am,' I admitted. 'But I didn't realise it was going to be quite that full-on.'

'You're not the birthday girl, then?'

'No. That's Alice.' I pointed her out. She had long blond hair and was wearing a huge badge announcing her status.

'Oh yes. She'll be the one with "Birthday Girl" written on her.'

'It's a clue.'

261

I wanted to say something else, but I could not think of one single thing. I wanted to keep talking to him, but without letting him realise that I felt I already knew him, that I wanted to abandon the party and come and sit with him. I was being ridiculous. I knew I was. He was probably with his girlfriend, for a start.

'So,' I tried. 'You're not with a party, then?'

He smiled. 'No. I'm just here for a quiet drink. At least it was quiet until you lot turned up.'

'Yeah. Bars in the middle of London at six thirty p.m. being where you go if you're after a haven of solitude.'

'I know.'

I had to ask. I said it quickly. 'Are you here with your girlfriend?'

'No such person. What about you? Boyfriend?'

'Nope.'

'Fancy doing a runner and getting some food?'

'Yes.'

We didn't even know each other's names, but we stepped out on to Long Acre and wandered along together until we decided, randomly, to go to an Indian restaurant next to the Royal Opera House. I knew nothing about him at all, but I knew, without a doubt, that we belonged together. Astonishingly, he knew it too, and we were at one another's side from that moment onwards. Everything worked between us, the way I had known it would the moment our eyes first met.

Our last few years, though, had been a pale shadow of our real relationship. The Laurie of back then would not have wanted me to be living like this. He would have been horrified to see it. If things had happened the other way round he would have moved on, met someone else.

If he, the original Laurie, could have seen me with Alex

last night, I thought he would have been pleased. Sad, but pleased. Five years had passed since we were properly together. They had been five long, sad years of pretending. The spectral Laurie I had created had turned into a demanding, grouchy figure: he was not the man I had loved at all.

It was a crisp winter's morning outside. My phone needed charging but I did not do it: I knew Alex would have tried to contact me and I could not face him yet. I felt deservedly terrible, physically and mentally. Something was pounding inside my skull. I got up early and did what I always did when I woke up sad: I went out. I was on my own. I had been on my own for a long, long time.

The blast of cold air did me good, and I was pleased to find a café on the corner and to slump into a rattling metal chair next to a radiator. I ordered a double espresso, a freshly squeezed orange juice and a vegetarian breakfast, and tried to read a free newspaper instead of thinking.

The world looked different. I was weighted down with grief, but, in a small way, liberated. I was on my own, but that meant I could go and look for Lara. In fact, I would go to Bangkok and see what happened when I got there.

I had not been drunk for five years. For a week after the accident I was horrifically drunk every night. I never wanted to be sober, ever again.

I tried as hard as I possibly could to think of Laurie at home in Budock, waiting for me. It did not work. For the first time, that cottage was not our house. It was where I lived, with my cats. I lived alone, with cats. I did not have a boyfriend, because he was dead. I suddenly hoped the cats were all right: later I would call the neighbours and check. They had a cat flap. They would have been able, I hoped, to fend for themselves for the few days I had been away. I would get the neighbours to start feeding them.

I cast around, desperate to focus on something. The floor was black and white, chequered. It was a bit of a posh hotel transplanted to a little corner café. You could have played chess on it, with the right-sized pieces. You could even have done it with little pieces. They would have looked strange, on their enormous squares, but that would have made it an interesting game. It would have been like playing on a normal chessboard with tiny little pawns and a miniature queen.

My breakfast arrived and I forced a smile at the waitress and anchored my thoughts in the present. Today I was going to ambush Leon Campion. I started eating nervously, half hungry, half nauseous.

I never drank more than a small glass of red wine. It was a decision I had made for my own sanity (if sanity was a word that could be applied to a person like me), and I knew now that it was the right one. There were flashes of memory, jumping up and assaulting me again and again. Kissing Alex had been electric. I was not sure if I could ever bear to see him again. But he knew the truth, and had known it all along, and he had still wanted to spend time with me. He still wanted to kiss me.

'Do you mind if I plug my phone in?' I asked the waitress next time she passed.

'Sure,' she said. 'There's a socket over there.'

The texts arrived as soon as it started charging. There were several from Alex, which I did not read, and one from an unfamiliar number. I took that one first.

Hi Iris, it said. *This is Sam Finch. Just wondering how you're doing and if you'd maybe come over 2day. It would be gud to CU. Also there's something I want U2C.*

His phone rang five times, and just as I was composing the voicemail in my head, he picked it up.

'Iris. Hey.'

'Hi, Sam. How are you doing?'

There was a long pause.

'Crap. Fucking hell. You know what? I never used to swear. Now I do it all the time. Even when we failed at IVF and everything, I never needed to swear about it because I had my wife. Or so I thought.'

'Oh, Sam.' I tried to think of a good thing to say. The fact was, there was nothing. 'It's awful for you. I can't imagine.'

'I wish she'd killed me instead of him.'

'She didn't kill him! She didn't. You know Lara – she . . .'

His voice was harsh. 'That's the thing, though. I don't fucking know Lara. Nor do you. You can spend as much time as you like saying "but Lara was so lovely and she can't have killed anyone", but you didn't know her. You thought you did. I thought I did. I thought we were happy. More than happy – I thought we were absolutely rock solid. I thought we understood each other. I thought she was doing the London thing to pay off the cards so we'd be ready to start the adoption process, from abroad. I'd been looking into the logistics of Nepal, because she claimed she'd always had a yearning for the place, and the only time she'd been really up for the idea of adopting was when she thought about finding a baby up there, in the mountains. I was going to make it work for her. It literally never occurred to me that she was living with another bloke most of the week. I mean, what a mug. What a stupid fucking mug. And that's barely the start of it.'

It was impossible to say the right thing, because there wasn't one.

'I'm so sorry, Sam.'

'I know.'

'Had she been to Nepal before?'

'No, never. I was going to take her, to look at orphanages.'

'She'd been to Asia, though.'

'Yeah, Thailand and shit. That's what I wanted you to see.'

I frowned, not following. 'What did you want me to see?'

He paused. 'Oh, don't worry. Forget it. It was only if you were going to come over. Are you?'

'Can't. I'm in London. My family live here, you know.'

'You said you didn't see your family.'

'It's complicated. What is it?'

'Oh. Don't worry. I started going through her things. It was doing my head in, having it all there. My brother, Ben, he was on at me to chuck it all in a skip, and then him and Mum finally went back to Sussex, which meant I knew I had to deal with it somehow. So I went through all her stuff – I've been up all night, doing it. Piling it into bags and shit. She ain't coming back, after all. And I found this old book, that I never knew she had.'

'Old book? What sort of an old book?'

My phone was barely charged enough for this conversation. I shifted my chair close to the socket, and plugged it back in.

'It's a diary,' he said. 'An old diary of Lara's. From when she was in Thailand. I flicked through it. Couldn't really bear to read it. There's some weird shit in there. That's why I thought I'd show it to you. So you could have a read and then we could give it to the police or whatever. You're the only person I could think of, who would read it for me.'

'Sam. What sort of weird shit? Is it about drugs?'

'Did you know that about her? Yet another thing she never thought to mention to me.'

'Not at all. Sam – can I read it? Could you – well, would you send it to me? I know you should hand it over to the police, but I can take it to them here when I've read it.'

He said nothing for a while.

'Why not,' he agreed, in the end. 'What the fuck. You're more together than I am. If I post it, it'll get me out of the house. Going to the post office, I mean. A little errand to run. I'll walk through town and back again. See who stares at me. Give me an address.'

'Sure.' I took a piece of the hotel's paperwork out of my bag and read it to him.

'But Iris?'

'Yes?'

'When you're back, you have to come and see me. Right? Please?'

I squirmed with guilt. 'Of course. Promise.'

'Bring your boyfriend if you like. I mean, don't think I'm being creepy or anything.'

'Oh, that's OK. My boyfriend's . . .' I inhaled deeply and was surprised at how calmly my voice came out. 'My boyfriend's not really around any more.'

'Sorry to hear that,' he said dutifully, and as he was drawing breath to ask something else, I interrupted him.

'Look, Sam? You know Leon Campion?'

'Unfortunately.'

'Someone was talking about him the other day.'

'Lara's godfather. Hates me, always has done. He's all over her. If you see him, don't send him my regards. Tell him to fuck himself. In fact if anyone's done away with her, he'd be top of my list of candidates. Him and Olivia.'

'Oh.'

He hung up, promising to post the diary. I hoped he actually would: I was not holding my breath.

Lara's parents' house was large and ugly, a big block of property, and more intimidating than I had expected it to be. My head was still swimming in the toxic residue of martini and Prosecco, a drink I was certain I would never look in the face again.

Where there must once have been a garden, now there was tarmac, and two cars were parked on it. One (her father's, I presumed) was a huge Jeep, ostentatiously and unnecessarily equipped for all terrains and eventualities, and wholly ridiculous in so suburban an environment. The other looked like the run-around, the wife's little Peugeot.

It was odd to think that this was Lara's origin. As far as I knew, she had grown up here, though I was not completely sure. It was an unremarkable house, unstylish, moneyed and boring. I tried to picture a teenage Lara, blonde and gorgeous and bursting with potential, arriving home in school uniform. I imagined Olivia, sulking stroppily in her wake.

She was shifting in my mind, becoming elusive. Sam was right: I did not know this woman at all. I had only met her four times and I had considered her to be a lovely potential friend; I'd never so much as guessed at her dark side.

The doorbell played 'Twinkle, Twinkle, Little Star' audibly inside the house. I stood on the doorstep with no idea what I was going to say, and after a while, I heard the sounds of someone approaching. Whoever it was undid what sounded like many locks on the inside, and then the door was pulled open, and Lara was standing in front of me.

It was not her. Of course it was not Lara. But she was

so like her that for what felt like a very long time I could not say a word. It occurred to me, in slow motion, that this woman, with her blond hair, her green wrap dress, her strong bone structure, was Lara's mother. She, too, was not what I had expected. This woman looked so ethereal that she could not possibly have given birth once, let alone twice.

She was looking at me with narrowed eyes, questions on her face, but she said nothing.

'Um, hello,' I managed in the end. 'Mrs Wilberforce?'

She gave the wariest of nods.

'My name's Iris. I'm a friend of Lara's. From Cornwall. I just . . .'

Words deserted me. I had no idea why I was here.

'Hello.' Her voice was faint, quiet. She did not invite me in, or move at all. She was a pale ghost of a woman.

'I'm sorry. You look like Lara.'

She nodded. 'Yes.'

'I don't know if Olivia's mentioned me? We had a drink together the other day. I'm . . .' And then I found I couldn't say it. How ridiculous to announce that I had come from Cornwall to do some sleuthing and prove their missing daughter's innocence. I could not announce to this woman that her daughter might have stolen my passport and flown to Bangkok. The words, in my head, were beyond implausible. It would sound insulting, and she would think I was mad.

I drew in a deep breath. 'I'm in London and I was thinking of Lara and I just wanted to come and see you and say I don't believe what everyone's saying about her. I'm sorry. I should have called.'

'Oh,' she said. 'Maybe you should come in, dear, since you're here?'

She opened the door a little wider and I saw a man, Lara's father, approaching from across a wide, thickly carpeted hallway. He was enormously fat, balding, and he was sizing me up.

'What can we do for you?' he said. His demeanour was utterly, flatly hostile.

Lara's mother shrank away. He took her place, filling the doorway. I stuttered out my story again.

'You're what? Lara's friend? Well, I appreciate your coming by, but to be honest, we've had so many journos turning up making that claim that I'm not prepared to risk it.'

'But Olivia . . .' I started.

'I don't care what Olivia says,' he said, and as he closed the door in my face, I heard him shout: 'You were going to let her in! You were, I heard you! Fuck's sake, Victoria!'

I stood there for a while, hoping that Lara's downtrodden mother might reappear and talk to me in secret, but she didn't. In the end I walked away, back to the mainline station. I bought a Ginsters cheese pasty at a convenience store, had it microwaved to a state of scalding sogginess, and set off back to the city. On the way, I told myself, I would read Alex's messages, and I would hope that the right words might come to me, so that I could reply.

chapter twenty-four

Leon Campion's office was on the third floor of a grand building near Liverpool Street. The building was one of those huge white-fronted ones that in some parts of London would be broken up into mansion flats, but in the City housed office after office.

I had not planned anything. My head was still aching gently, and I could feel the alcohol throughout my system. I hoped I didn't smell boozy. My shoes clipped and clopped across the floor to the reception desk. I wanted to call Alex and apologise. I was nearly ready.

The thing about today was that I did not care at all. I didn't care if Leon Campion swore in my face. Lara's dad's dismissal of me would have left me humiliated and angry coming from anyone else, but I was utterly untouched by it.

'Hello?' asked a bored young woman. At least she didn't look me up and down in horror.

'Hi,' I said. 'I have a meeting with Leon Campion at Campion Associates.'

'Sure. If you sign in here.'

I wanted her to finish the sentence. What would happen,

were I to sign in here? The answer was not forthcoming, but at least she was not challenging me. I had not really expected to get past this point. My plan B was to hang around outside the building and hope he came out for lunch at some point.

I signed in, using my real name, got in a small mirrored lift, and pressed the button with the '5' on it, as instructed.

I stepped out into a large reception area and saw an intimidating woman behind a desk, on the phone, fiddling with paperwork, not looking at me.

She was groomed like a horse, her thick mane shiny and tamed. She was wearing so much make-up that it was impossible to imagine what she really looked like, and her gold earrings were pulling her ears down so hard that the hole in the ear that was not pressed against the phone was elongated and looked close to snapping point. I winced in sympathy. I had never managed to wear earrings.

There was a thick carpet on the floor, an expensive air of polish and luxury permeating the place, but this, I realised, was actually a small company. Only one door opened out of the reception area, and I could not imagine it leading to an enormous suite of offices or a huge space crammed with desks and activity. It felt more like a one-man enterprise.

The woman smiled at me and signalled that she would just be a moment.

'Yes,' she said, 'but we'll need more than that, I'm afraid, sir. We'll require detailed inventories of all of it before Mr Campion is able to commit himself even to a preliminary discussion . . . Yes. Those terms absolutely stand . . . I'll look forward to hearing from you then. Goodbye.'

She hung up without waiting for the reply to this.

'Hello?' She had attached a professional face with a

smile that did not come anywhere near her eyes. 'Can I help?'

This was the crucial part. I had to get it right. I had spoken to this woman on the phone, but she did not need to know that. I could not begin to guess whether she remembered every conversation she had or not.

'Good afternoon. I'm wondering whether I could have a word with Mr Campion,' I said as an opener.

She did not betray a thing.

'I'm afraid he's not available. Is he expecting you?'

'I'm a friend of Lara's. I'd really like to have a word with him. It's personal business.'

Again she did not react.

'Well, as I said, Mr Campion is unavailable. He's out of the country, in fact. If you'd like to leave a note or something, I can certainly make sure he gets it.'

'Thank you. I'll maybe write down my number and my email address.'

'As I said, it may be a while before you hear from him.'

'He's Lara's godfather, isn't he?'

'That would be his personal affair.'

She turned her attention to her keyboard, aggressively tapping away with fingers flat enough to preserve her long and immaculate nails. I took the hint, and went to sit on the little sofa in the corner, with the sheet of paper and the pen the woman had handed me. I used a glossy magazine to lean on – *Management Today* – and tried to decide what to write. It would have to be good enough to grab the attention of the person who seemed actually to care about Lara.

Leon, I began, attempting a self-assured tone. *I've been trying to reach you on the phone and in person. My name is Iris Roebuck and I'm a friend of Lara's from Cornwall. I'm . . .*

At this point I ground to a halt. How could I make it sound right? I scribbled out the 'I'm' and wrote: *Like her family, I am desperately concerned about Lara and convinced she did not do this horrible thing. I have a very good idea of what happened to her, and this is something I would like to talk to you about, because it's connected to her past, to Asia. Olivia . . .*

My flow was interrupted by the lift doors opening. I looked up and knew at once that it was him. I tried to sit as unobtrusively as I could in the corner in the hope that he would speak to the receptionist without noticing me, but he stared right at me, straight away.

I already knew what he looked like, with his longish grey hair and his long nose, but I had expected someone far more intimidating. This man looked friendly, and sad. I liked him at first sight, more than I had expected to.

He looked at me, half smiling, for a second, then turned to the woman.

'Anything I need to know?' he asked, and I was unsure whether he meant me or in general.

She reeled off a bland list of calls and messages, some of which were from journalists, and added, 'And this lady, Miss Roebuck, is a friend of Lara Finch's. I told her you were unavailable and she was just writing you a note.'

'Thanks, Annie.'

My heart pounded as he came closer, but his manner disarmed me.

'Miss Roebuck,' he said, smiling politely as he sized me up. I stood, hating the disadvantage of being on the sofa.

'Mr Campion,' I replied, and he offered a hand. His handshake was firm and warm.

He was reading my note. 'You've come from Cornwall?'

'Yes.'

'Was I terribly rude to you on the phone? I do apologise. Sincerely. It's been a difficult time. You know that.'

'It's fine.'

'No, it's not. You see, I look at you now, and I know that Lara had talked about you. You're the friend who rides a bicycle and has long hair. You were pictured climbing over the gate to see Guy Thomas's poor widow.'

'Yes. Yes, I was.'

'What were you doing there?'

'Conveying sympathies from Sam.'

'And I see,' he said, glancing back at my part-written note, 'that you know something of her past in Asia, which I agree may be key here. Come into the office, my dear. Though I'm afraid I am a little paranoid, and I'll have to check a couple of things. You understand?'

'Of course.'

'I've always felt responsible for Lara. And it's shattering that . . .' He looked at me, unable to finish the sentence. 'Annie,' he said instead. 'Some coffee?'

'I'll bring it through now.'

His office was huge, with massive windows on two sides that must once have offered panoramic views across London, and that now looked over a rooftop or two to the side of the nearest taller buildings. Nonetheless, the place was flooded with light. Buses ambled and taxis scrambled below, but there was no sound at all. The air in here was layered with upmarket smells, from expensive paper to wood polish; from coffee to Leon's cologne.

He ignored the huge wooden desk piled with paperwork, and led me to a couple of semi-comfortable chairs in the corner.

'Now,' he said, when we were both sitting down. 'Tell me about Lara. I don't mean to test you, because I do believe in you, but I can't risk not running through the basics. How do you know her?'

I was surprised by his businesslike tone. 'Right,' I said, taken aback. 'Well. I've lived in Cornwall, just outside Falmouth, for nearly five years.'

He took an iPhone out of his inside pocket.

'Just outside Falmouth? Where, specifically?'

'Near Budock. It's a village, but a big one, and you can walk to the edge of Falmouth easily from it. I'm outside the village, though. Pretty remote, but it doesn't take long to get to places.'

He was locating my house on Google Earth. I directed him to it, and then he passed the phone over.

'So you live here? Alone?'

There was our house. It was my house.

Laurie's ghost might still be around: he had been there so long that he could not evaporate, just like that. I wondered if, when I went back, I would feel his lingering presence, even for a fraction of a second. I hoped I would. I would cling to the last vestiges of him, if I could.

I missed my wood burner and my cats and my static life away from the world. I missed Laurie more than I had ever missed anything.

'Yes,' I managed to say. 'I live there. Alone.'

'OK. And you know Lara how?'

'We met on a ferry. I was going across to St Mawes for no particular reason, and she was doing the same thing.' I told him the story. 'We kept in touch. I went to her house for tea one afternoon. While I was there, she got a phone call which turned out to be someone offering her the job in London.'

He smiled a tiny smile. 'That would have been me.'

'She wanted to talk to Sam about it, I could see that, so I left. I saw her in town after she started working up here, but really her weekends were for Sam. She came to my house on Christmas Eve and we had mince pies. I had no idea she was having an affair or anything like that.' I carried on talking, setting out my credentials in an eager way that made me hate myself.

'So when she went missing . . .'

'I turned up at their house that Saturday morning, just because I wanted to see her. In fact, I . . .' I trailed off, not wanting to say too much about myself. He gave me a kind, questioning look, and I carried on, telling him about my lottery win and my increasing feeling that I needed to do something.

'I moved to Cornwall for a particular reason,' I said, hoping that my tone was firm enough. 'And I was thinking, actually it's time to move on.'

I paused for a moment. Breathe, I told myself. Go on. Breathe in and out. You need to be able to say this. The wave of grief engulfed me as it had five years ago, and this time I was not going to be able to hide from it.

Leon took a perfectly ironed handkerchief out of an inside pocket and handed it to me.

'Thank you.'

I made an enormous effort and spoke through my tears. 'I wanted to talk to Lara because she's the only person I know down there who'd have been able to advise me.' I got that far, and blew my nose messily into the handkerchief. 'Sorry,' I added.

'That's quite all right. And *I'm* sorry. For whatever your trouble was, and for making you relive it. Take your time.'

'Thanks. So I rang the bell, and Sam answered, and

. . .' I talked him through that day, and the police, the phone call about Guy being killed, the police taking Sam away for questioning. 'And I knew she hadn't done it,' I finished. 'I know she didn't.'

'Yes. So you've unearthed a little of the Asia fiasco?' His voice was unexpectedly warm. 'You've turned Miss Marple?'

'If you want to put it that way,' I said, wiping my face again, 'sure. If I was a bloke you wouldn't be so dismissive. Laugh at Miss Marple, fine. I decided to come back to London, which incidentally is an enormous and massively difficult thing for me, and to see if I could work out what might really have happened. But you can belittle that, if you want. Lara wouldn't.'

'Sherlock Holmes, then. A female Sherlock. You could use Sherlock as a female name. It would be quite enticing. Apologies if I was sexist. Sincerely, I didn't mean to belittle you. I'm impressed by you, Ms Roebuck. And when you got here, you went to see Olivia.'

'She was lovely.'

He raised an eyebrow. 'Olivia?'

'Yes, actually. I was prepared to hate her, but I don't. I like her. She and Lara had a terrible relationship, but I think Olivia's had a bit of a raw deal.'

'Interesting that you say that. OK. You tried the Wilberforces?'

'I didn't get very far. Lara's mum – Victoria? – she would have let me in. But her dad shut the door in my face. I don't blame him. Obviously.'

There was a tap at the door, and it swung open before Leon could respond. Annie put the coffee tray on the low table beside us and left without a word.

'Thanks, Annie. Look, Iris. I'm sorry. I really am. I know

why Bernie shut the door on you, and it's the same reason why I had to put you through your paces. I loathe the media and at first you seemed likely to be a journalist. I believe you, as I did from the moment I actually saw you, though I didn't when you called me. If you'd been a hack, you would have fallen apart when I was finding your so-called house on Google Earth. You wouldn't have been able to give a convincing cover story. I'm half tempted to call Sam and check who was with him that dreadful morning, but to be honest I can't face the ensuing conversation. In fact. Annie?'

He had barely raised his voice, but she was back in the room almost instantly.

'Annie, can you do me a favour? Could you bear to give Sam Finch a call and find out who was with him on the morning of Saturday the fifteenth?'

She didn't bat an eyelid. 'I'll do it now.'

He turned back to me. 'This has been horrific. A living nightmare. I'm trying to tell myself she'll turn up safe and well. Of course she didn't kill Guy Thomas. Of course. She wouldn't be capable of such a thing. And, as you say, she went through an enormous trauma in Thailand which she always thought would catch up with her. I used to tell her it wouldn't, that it was over, but she never could quite forget.

'I mentioned it to the police as an urgent line of inquiry, but they weren't interested, because as far as they were concerned the case was closed and all they need to do is to find her body. Which of course they haven't done, because she's still using it. Or so I very much hope.'

I thought of Alex. I thought of the diary, but decided not to mention it until I had read it.

'Yes. I've spoken to the police too, but they weren't

really into looking at Asia either. Look, I'm thinking I might go out there and find her myself.'

He sighed, suddenly looking older and weaker.

'But Iris. If I may call you Iris?'

'Of course.'

'Iris. If she'd flown anywhere, or left the country by any means, there would be a record. And there isn't. There just isn't. That's the one thing that makes me fear for her safety. Lara is a resourceful young lady – I've known her all her life. But even she cannot vanish without leaving a trace.'

'Leon,' I said. 'Right. Well, here's the thing.'

As I was about to tell him about the passport, Annie came back into the room with an apologetic smile.

'Sorry to interrupt again. I spoke to him. He was initially hostile, but in the end he said he spent that day with Mrs Finch's friend Iris, and he described Ms Roebuck,' she nodded to me with a little smile, 'exactly. She turned up on a bicycle, with two-tone hair. He was grateful for the support. He said he spoke to you this morning.'

'He did,' I agreed.

'Thank you, Annie. Right. Again, apologies, Iris, for the paranoia.'

'That's fine. Understandable. Good to be thorough.' And I told him about the passport, and about the flight to Bangkok.

'This is astonishing,' he said. He was on his feet, pacing the room. 'Then we must get out there and find her. You have brought me the only good news I've had in a very long time. I will help you at every stage. I'll do anything. Funding, whatever it takes.'

'You – at least I presume it was you – went to a police station with her and she retracted a statement she'd made about drug smuggling,' I told him. His eyes widened.

'My God, you are good. If you ever want a job, come to me, seriously. You know about it?'

'Yes, I do.'

'So you'll understand how sensitive this is.'

'Yes.' I was bluffing, but he was barely listening.

'She flew to Bangkok.'

'I want to go out there,' I heard myself say, again. 'And search for her.'

He was not looking at me. He was frowning, thinking.

'Would you? Would you do that? If we could do it ourselves, without involving the police, we might not scare her off. I can't imagine why she'd go back there. Unless she might not have gone of her own accord. If Jake were at large, if he'd somehow got her under his control. Then, perhaps, I can see why she'd be in Bangkok. When the user of your passport took that flight, do we know if she did it alone?'

'No idea.'

I was desperate to ask about Jake but I did not. I wanted Leon to think I knew more than I did, so that he would trust me properly.

He sighed.

'Iris. Come out for a drink with me. Let's get away from this office and do some proper planning.'

I smiled at him, sensing that, at last, things were moving.

'OK,' I agreed, 'but I'm only on soft drinks today. I overdid it a little last night.'

I woke the next morning stretched out across my hotel bed. I was going to fly to Bangkok: Leon and I had booked my flight last night. He had persuaded me to have one glass of velvety red wine with him, in a little bar in the City, and we had discussed everything.

I had an idea, now, of who Jake might be. Even if Sam had not managed to cross Falmouth to post me the diary (and I was sure, in fact, that he would have thought better of it and gone to the police), I would still be able to go to Bangkok and look for her. I yawned and stretched, luxuriating in the fact that I was not hung over any more. I needed to call Alex.

There was a knock on the door, and I staggered across the room to answer it. It was, I noticed from my phone, half past nine. I had not slept this well for years.

'Some post for you, madam,' said a young man, and he handed me a Jiffy Bag. I thanked him, wondering whether he wanted a tip, and put the kettle on before I ripped the envelope open. Sam had scrawled my name and the hotel's address with a thick marker pen.

The book was a battered hard-backed diary, black and thick, dirty along the edges of the pages. I sat down on the edge of the bed and began to read.

part three

Lara's diary

March 21st 1999
Sydney

Jake is back!! I can hardly bear it – it's so wonderful and so tinged with terror. I just want to touch him and look at him.

Nearly time to leave Australia. He arrived this afternoon, from wherever it is he goes in between things, and so this morning, to while away some time, I went and picked up my letters from the poste restante. I wasn't going to bother, and now I wish I hadn't. One from Mum, a nasty little postcard from Olivia, and a letter from Leon and Sally, written by Sally.

I dashed off a quick reply to Mum.

I'm in Sydney for a week or so, because I needed to renew my Thai visa, I wrote primly. *It is a lovely city and I look forward to coming back for longer one day, but for now I need to get back to Bangkok for my job.* That will keep everyone happy. That is the sort of thing golden Lara would have written.

The job I am claiming to have would come with its own

visa, but no one would bother to think about that, except perhaps Leon.

I can't wait to get away from here. Australia is too clean! I need to get back to Thailand. At least I have Jake with me now – it means things are moving.

I wish Dad would tell me whether Mum knows (his part of) the truth or not. Her letter has made me feel really down. I envy other people their motherly mothers. My life would be totally different if I'd had one who would talk to her children as if they were not little inconveniences she vaguely recognised. Imagine a mummy-ish mother who treated school plays etc. as something she actively wanted to go to! She is the person who could have made Olivia and me tolerate each other, but she never bothered to try. If Mum had been open to any sort of meaningful interaction, I would never have had to court Dad so much, and I would not be here now, doing this to bail him out.

So all this is her fault! If I told her that she'd just say 'Oh, is it? Sorry,' and drift away.

When we write our little letters, are we both leaving the huge thing unsaid, or is her innocence genuine? 'Things have been difficult with Dad's business,' she said in today's letter, 'but onwards and upwards!'

Yes – things have been so difficult with Dad's business that he asked me to pay him back for my private school, which of course I never asked to go to. And that is what I am doing. Mum can't know about it or she wouldn't have written that. Would she?

I ripped up Olivia's ironic postcard of Buckingham Palace. She didn't even apologise, just wrote something like 'I hope you're having a good time', which was her at her very friendliest. She's not going to be hearing from me any time soon, or indeed ever again.

Anyway. The family are on the other side of the world, which is the best place for them. Tomorrow is the day. The thrill of it makes me alive in a way nothing else has ever done.

Now I must go because Jake is waiting for us to go out for some low-key food and a couple of beers. I will force myself to eat even though I am not remotely hungry. I'm too excited to be hungry.

Tomorrow I will be in Thailand. Trip number four. Maybe I should have stopped after three. This seems to be pushing my luck a little, but I know I can do it. I am good at this. Fingers crossed . . .

March 22nd
Bangkok

It's hot. Muggy. Smelly. I love it.

I did it. My writing is terrible because my pen is trembling all over the place again. I actually did it.

This is the most incredible high. I want to sing and dance all the way down the Khao San Road. I want to climb on to a precarious corrugated-iron roof and throw my arms up and yell at the heavens. No one beats me. I beat the system.

I wish I could tell Olivia, just to shock her. She would never believe it.

I did nothing that was visible to the outside world. I just did the exact same thing that everyone around me was doing. Then I got a taxi to the Khao San Road to hide amongst the backpackers, and checked into an anonymous fleapit guest house. I was in the café reading a book and drinking my third Coke when Jake arrived, hugged me, told me I was wonderful, while Derek (looking worse than ever – he's taking that wild hair, wild beard backpacker disguise to its outer limit, I feel) picked up the jacket and vanished. Mission four successfully completed. I was completely calm throughout.

Every time, there's a part of me that wants it not to work. I couldn't do it otherwise. If I was desperate to hang on to my normal life and to go home and carry on being the golden bloody girl, I would not be able to keep my head and channel the icy cool. I would be living like every other dull backpacker does round here, treating the world as my playground and thinking I was being original or different.

I can't believe that, at last, I get to be bad. I remember how I would watch the scary crowd at school, the people who didn't go to lessons if they didn't fancy it, who didn't bother with homework, who fought and swore and shrugged at the consequences. And I knew that I could have been one of them. For some reason, I wasn't. It was there, deep inside me, and now it is out.

I break the rules on a scale none of those idiots at school could ever have dreamed of. And now I need to put this book away (Jake would go crazy if he knew there was a paper trail) and go out for some serious celebratory drinks.

Bangkok – I love you.

March 25th

I sent almost all the money home. I am, depressingly, the good girl after all.

It's strange just to be hanging out in Bangkok like every other traveller. In a sense it feels completely safe, but it's also a bit of a comedown. I haven't got the energy to do any more sightseeing. Today Jake and I stretched out a 'full English breakfast' in the best people-watching café, playing Scrabble and watching the passers-by. I like to look at the extremes: at one end, the teenagers who are away from home for the first time, wide-eyed and scared, still wholesome. You can almost see them filing away their first impressions for transmission home. When I see them, I want to get up and follow them around for a few weeks, to watch what happens as they settle in.

At the other extreme, there are the casualties. These are unnerving, and for different reasons than the obvious ones. All I see along here are the white people, the privileged travellers, and the ones who are the hopeless addicts make me flinch. With their wild beards (every casualty I have ever seen has been a man) and their crazed eyes and the clothes they've obviously been wearing for years, they are a little reminder of the fact that it can go wrong.

Anyway. I beat Jake at Scrabble and he pretended not to be annoyed. Then he told me our next trip is in three weeks' time.

'I've got stuff to take care of,' he said. 'So, babes, I'm going to have to leave you to it for a bit. Get yourself to a beach. I got you a mobile phone. I'll call you when we need you.'

I was a tiny bit annoyed, but I hid it. I can do a few weeks on a Thai beach – it's not really something to take umbrage at. In fact, I just love him calling me 'babes'. No one in London would ever have done that. I was never a babe type, back there. Head girl Lara has gone, for ever.

She is dead. In her place is a lawbreaking babe with a Thai mobile phone.

March 27th
On the bus out of Bangkok

Jake has gone away. I don't want to know any more than that. I know that I am brilliant at my role, and my job ends there. It is odd how it makes me glow inside when they tell me they've never met anyone who can carry it off like I can. What a strange thing to have a talent for.

My brand-new phone is tucked away in my bag. I will keep it charged and hidden, and I must check it several times a day. Other than that, I am on holiday. I miss Jake, but there are not many things in life that are better than being on a bus with a hefty crime novel, watching the Thai countryside fly by, being aloof whenever anyone looks like they want to talk to me.

This is a tourist coach (at the cheapest possible end of the tourist scale), and everyone on it is a backpacker like me.

This bus is heading for Krabi, and from there I'm going to get a boat to Koh Lanta, and go to a beach and read and chill out. I don't care if I don't speak to a single person.

My backpack, devoid, as far as I can tell, of all dodgy contents, is tied to the roof with everyone else's bags. As this is a cheap bus, it rattles along with its windows open and no air conditioning. It's hard writing on it.

I think I'd get away with it, if anyone found this book. I'd tell them it was fantasy, and they'd look at me and believe me. Plus I don't think I've actually said it.

A man across the aisle keeps trying to talk to me. I can't be bothered, so I'm going to pretend to be asleep.

March 31st, I think

I'm lying on the beach, thinking about Jake. We have no future, and that's one of the things I love about us. We barely have a thing to say to one another. It's brilliant!

When I first met him, all naïve and hurt by Olly, I thought differently. My mind instantly started to try to fit him into what was expected of me.

A handsome Australian: what a great souvenir, I thought, to bring home from my trip. A handsome Australian husband, perhaps. That would have shown them.

Then, when I realised what he was about, I had to make adjustments to the narrative. That was liberating. He is definitely and hilariously not husband material. This is an adventure we're having together, and soon, very soon, we'll both move on. That is the most exciting thing of all. We are only about sex and business, and only for as long as it suits us both.

We met on the Khao San Road. Where else? I was on my own, newly arrived from London and utterly shaken. Dad was apoplectically furious with me for leaving, and even more furious with Olivia for making me go. I was single and on terrible terms with everyone. I knew no one on this entire continent, and had not a clue how to navigate things. I'd bought some clothes from one of the stalls earlier that day so I might blend in a bit, and all I was planning to do was to sit in a café and read a book, perhaps with a beer. That would have been an achievement.

And then I looked up, and he was watching from across the street.

He walked straight over to me, and stood there and smiled.

'Hi,' he said. 'I'm Jake.'

I couldn't help myself. I smiled back. 'Lara,' I replied.

We walked along the road next to each other, and that was it. That night, that actual night, I discovered the joys of sex, and realised what I had been missing in my boring relationship. He is thirty-three, eleven years older than me. I adore his Australian accent, his curly hair that falls into his face all the time. I love the way he looks at me. I love the way he makes me want to break the rules, to be bad for him. We are not soulmates. It's the best thing that's ever happened to me.

April 2nd

I'm sitting in bed, under my mozzie net, writing this. Today I made a friend, Rachel. This makes me very happy.

I still haven't heard from Jake, even though I check my phone all the time. I didn't really expect to, because I don't want to know about the transactions etc. That is utterly not my department. My three weeks off come with the understanding that there's a big job on its way.

All the same, he's my boyfriend, and I wouldn't mind the occasional hello. I sent him a text to say I was here and he hasn't replied. I hope he's OK, because it occurred to me today that anything could have happened and I wouldn't know.

There's nothing I can do, though, but wait.

I know there's an internet place up on the main road, but I'm staying away from it. I don't want to read emails and send postcards or anything like that. I just want to lie on the sand and read.

Koh Lanta is a bigger island than I expected – there's one the boat passed on the way called Koh Jum which was smaller, and loads of very alternative-looking people got off there, so I might move on and see what that's like in a bit. I probably won't, though, because that would require momentum and packing, and I'm enjoying not doing those things.

I'm staying at the south of the island, eking out my budget as best I can.

I've sent home thousands and thousands of pounds now. Money that I earned by risking my life. Dirty, filthy junkie money. He must know that, really. Only Leon has thought to question my job at the 'American bank'. It's much easier for Dad if he takes it at face value.

He even said 'wherever you're getting it from' in his last letter. Bastard.

Anyway. Koh Lanta. I'm staying in a wooden bungalow, very shackish, that I reach by climbing hundreds of steps up the rocks above the sea. It looks out over the water, and across to the land at the other side of the bay. In the night you can see the lights of the boats, fishing boats out on the water. It's warm and still up here. When I switch the ceiling fan off it gets so hot, sometimes, that I wake up in the night slippery with sweat and hardly able to breathe. That is the only time the anxiety creeps in.

I love living like this more than I can ever say. Whatever happens in the rest of my life (and I have a pretty good idea now of the way I'd like it to go – more of that in a minute), I know that it will never get better than this. This has been my turning point. Talking to Rachel today was the first time I felt I just wanted to hang out with someone and relax. I felt the tension drift away.

I come with no baggage, here. Travellers all dress the

same, in the clothes you buy at the stalls. The baggy
trousers, Thai Coca-Cola T-shirts, flip-flops. I'm a million
miles away from the privately educated uptight London
girl who avoided trouble at all costs.

So, things could go two ways for the new improved
me. I might get caught this time. Then I would just see
what happened. It would be horrific, I know, but I almost
don't care. I'd rather that happened than that I went back
to the life I used to have. If I were caught, I'd be in the
papers and they'd pardon me because I'm young and
female. Everyone at home would be astonished. My dad
would feel terrible, and he would be mightily embarrassed
in front of all his 'contacts'.

Alternatively, I stop. And I stay in Asia, and I get a
sensible job, in Bangkok or Singapore or Kuala Lumpur.
I could live out here and travel around. The more I think
about it, the more I want to do that. For the first time, I
don't want to be caught crossing the border. That is slightly
worrying. It means there is too much at stake.

April 3rd

I'm sitting out on my little rotting balcony now, in the
early morning, and I can see Rachel bustling around her
own shack, checking if the sarong and bikini she hung up
last night are dry.

Rachel is my new friend. She's from New Zealand. A
couple of days ago we had a 'friendship at first sight'
moment, actually quite like Jake and me with our 'lust at
first sight'. Sometimes being a backpacker is like being a
four-year-old. When you're four, you go to a playground,
walk up to another child and say 'I'm four,' and they say
'So am I,' and you're friends. It's like that. I saw Rachel,

liked her, and we started talking, and so we became friends.

She's tall and slim and gorgeous. I'm looking across at her now, wishing I had her bone structure and her long hair. She looks like a French film star or something, and she's funny.

She's just turned round and smiled at me and asked why I'm staring. She even said, 'Are you writing about me?'

We met right here, when I was standing on my balcony early in the morning a couple of days ago, looking out at the sea. I woke earlier than this and went out to watch the fishing boats in the pinkish glow of the sunrise. I was standing there in just a baggy T-shirt and knickers, gazing and thinking, when she said, 'Morning!' and it shocked me so much that I screamed.

Then I laughed because I felt stupid, as she was just on the next balcony, a few metres away, doing exactly the same thing as me. Standing there looking out at the sea.

'I'm Lara,' I told her, though I am never that forward. Normally I keep the wall up for as long as I can.

'Rachel,' she said.

'Australian?'

'Kiwi.'

'Oh, sorry, is that a faux pas?'

'Yeah. It would have been if I was incredibly precious and chippy.' And just like that, we were friends. We went to breakfast together, lay on the beach together, and chatted when we felt like it, swapped novels, said nothing when we felt like saying nothing. She found an unlikely little Scrabble set on a shelf in a bar, and we've played over and over again. We're very evenly matched.

I've never had a friend like Rachel before. Which, I can now see, is because home life has been so constrained, so uptight, so miserable that I never managed a proper friendship. How pathetic.

She doesn't have an idyllic home situation either, though she hasn't said much about it. I haven't told her the tawdry story of my boring boyfriend either – the thing that brought me out here – but I will.

And now the sun is getting stronger and I need to put some cream on, and a hat, or I'll get burned. Rachel's setting off from her bungalow, heading down the steps towards mine. I might suggest we halve costs by moving into one of them together.

April 6th

I keep the phone on a splintery little shelf that I can only reach by standing on my rickety chair, and although I still switch it on and check it twice a day, more and more I don't actually want to hear from Jake.

I wish I could stay here for ever. No one can reach me. There are no letters, no cards, no emails, and only Jake has my phone number. Nobody from the wider world has the faintest idea where I am.

It is strange to live in a world in which my own parents, Bernard and Victoria Wilberforce, depend on filthy money procured for them by their corrupted favourite child. Just so they can keep up appearances in suburbia. They might not know where their money comes from, but they should ask. How could they let me be doing this on the other side of the world? How can they not care? It makes me wonder if they even like me at all.

I always pretended I wasn't their favourite, even though nothing could have been more obvious. Olivia told me they loved me better than her hundreds, probably thousands of times, and I always denied it because I was hardly going to say 'yes, of course they do'. Now I am far enough away. I have no idea why, but Dad always appeared to hate her. No wonder she turned out so vile.

I will never forgive Dad for that day. He took me aside, into his study, a room we were rarely allowed to go into. It smells of stale cigarettes in there, because he smokes with the window slightly open and thinks that means it's ventilated.

We sat at his stupid shiny desk, and I remember that it was so polished I could see my face in it, though I pretended I wasn't doing that.

'Lara,' he said. 'Look. I'm going to tell you something that I need you to keep to yourself.'

I assumed he was going to introduce me to some girl-friend. It flashed through my mind that she must be pregnant, if he was reduced to telling me about her.

But instead he said: 'My business. The wine trade. It's not doing quite as well as I've led people to believe. I've got plans in place and we can do fine with a few provisos that I won't go into. But for the moment it's lurching rather closer than I'd like towards, well . . . bankruptcy, I suppose. That's what I'm looking at. Your mother has an idea that things are difficult, but of course one goes through difficult times as a matter of course. This is not like that.'

I remember holding my fingertips on the polished table and watching them meet their reflections. That was because I could not think of anything to say.

'I know you're job-hunting, but you'll find one soon, won't you, darling? You're qualified in an excellent profession.'

'Yes. I'm sure.'

'You girls had expensive educations.'

'Right.'

And that was when he told me his backup plan. The thing he would do if I didn't, somehow, help to bail him out of his mess. He said that Leon had helped him so far but that he couldn't ask him for any more. He mentioned life insurance. I knew what he was implying.

I hated him. I had only ever hated Olivia before. A whole world opened up before me in that instant. He was vulnerable and needy and pathetic. I didn't have to court his approval any more. I could hate him. That meant I didn't have to behave like a terrified sheep, always anticipating what would please him and what wouldn't. New pathways appeared, shimmering in front of me.

I muttered something.

'You have no idea what it means to me,' he said. 'My Lara.'

I should have told him to go ahead and top himself. He wouldn't have done it. Businesses collapse all the time. People deal with it, without threatening their twenty-two-year-old daughter with suicide unless they magic up some cash.

I worked as a waitress in a chain French café near Victoria for as long as it took me to save a chunk of cash, and then, instead of giving it to him, I flew to Bangkok with a backpack.

He was apoplectic. I didn't care. He could have topped himself then, but he didn't. And then when Jake made his proposal, I realised I could solve everything.

April 8th

Rachel has moved into my hut. We are sharing a double bed, tucking our mosquito net into the mattress around us at night, creating our own little fortress.

We have plans. I need to stay around here, away from London. This is where I want to build a life.

Rachel needs some money. She was talking about going home to NZ because she's almost out of funds. I'm paying for things for us both while I try to convince her otherwise. And my desire to stay here, and her need for cash, have made me come up with a plan. I told it to her today, in the bar.

'We'll go to Singapore,' I said. 'It's not far from here. We can fly there from Krabi, I'm sure we can. Then you can get a teaching job. You can teach English, or work in an English school, or whatever. I'll find work too. We'll work hard and share a flat in Singapore, and save our money. Then we could go to Nepal and live in the mountains for a while.'

She agreed that that would be an excellent plan. We are both going to look into it.

She is the only person I've ever met who doesn't think the idea of living on a Nepalese mountain is silly and weird.

April 10th

Oh fuck.

Rachel came up to the hut earlier than me this afternoon. I was still on the beach, half dozing while wondering when I was going to hear from Jake. I was fantasising about throwing the phone into the sea. I had left this book out on the bed, without thinking, and she must have picked it up.

You should never read your friend's diary. It will never lead to good things. I can imagine her opening it out of curiosity, starting reading, then carrying on, and on, and on as she began to realise the truth.

By the time I got here she had read every word and packed her bags.

'Drugs?' she said, as soon as I was close enough. Her face was savage and she looked completely different. 'You're a drug smuggler?'

I tried to reason with her. I said, 'It's because . . .' but she didn't care.

'You send money back home, yeah, I know. I read it all, Lara. Your dad, blah blah. I knew there was something you weren't saying and in the end I just thought, well, I'll read that book you're always writing in, and then I'll know. You carry terrible things across borders, you stupid girl, and you send the money to your dad. That is more fucked up than anything I've ever heard in my life.'

Those were her exact words. I will never forget them. She was right.

I asked where she was going. She said she would get her brother to send her some money, and she was going home to NZ. Then she stopped speaking to me. She just walked past. I didn't move out of the way, so she stepped up on a rock beside the path to get past me.

April 15th

No sign of Rachel. I look for her all the time.

Jake called. Finally. With news.

We've got a 'project' on. For the amount he's paying, I can surmise that it must be something major. I have to meet him in Krabi in three days' time, which means I need to start thinking about leaving Kantiang Bay.

I'm not sure I've got the nerve to do it any more. I told him that. He scoffed and said there was no way I was backing out.

I could just run away. He would recruit someone else.

If I do it, it would be the last time, and it would set me up for a new life. I will find a job in Singapore on my own, and I will write to Dad and tell him there's no more cash coming from me. When I've saved up, I'll go and rent a house in Nepal, exactly as I planned with Rachel, and I'll write to her and tell her where I am, and perhaps one day she will turn up, walking around the mountainside.

Or I could start that process without doing this job. I could walk away right now. I could catch a plane from Krabi tomorrow, and go on from there, and Jake would never find me. He wouldn't even try. I wouldn't have any money, and I'd have to find a job quickly, but that wouldn't matter. I would manage, because people do.

The money he would pay would buy me a house in the Himalayas outright: I am sure it would. However, it is mad and wrong on so many levels that I cannot begin to imagine what I've been thinking of. Have I really done that four times already?

Got to go. Someone's coming up the steps.

Later

I was terrified when I saw her. I thought she'd come back to tell me off. I accused her of having gone to the police. I was waiting for them to come and arrest me.

In fact I must remember to keep this book properly hidden. I should actually drop it into the sea, and I will. I'm going to lob it off the balcony, straight out across the rocks and into the water.

She says she needed to go away and think about things. She's different with me – I keep finding her staring and not speaking. But she says she missed me and she couldn't walk away leaving things like that. We had to talk.

There's a bonfire on the beach tonight, and as ever when that happens, people have appeared with guitars that they have magicked out of somewhere. Right now some local boys (I think) are playing and singing 'American Pie'. Rachel and I are about to go down and join them. I could completely manage a load of drinks and a drunken singalong.

Later still (a bit drunk)

We sat down by the water's edge in the hot night air and we talked. If anyone came close we stopped, but mainly I've just spent four hours drinking and talking to Rach. I told her everything, every single bit of it. Dad's business, Olivia/Olly, the lot.

She wanted to know how I do it. I told her about the trance, the way I am completely confident, acting like the head girl. I told her how I spend the flights reading or writing or watching a film, absolutely in control and perfectly calm. I told her about the icy cool that descends when I see the right bag on the conveyor belt. I described how I wheel the trolley, or carry the bag on my back, right through Customs in the absolute certainty that I look conventional beyond question, without feeling the tiniest bit afraid.

And then I described the high, the amazing, all-encompassing joy of having got away with it.

I started to say that I was considering not doing this last one. At the same time, she started to say that I should, that I should do it one last time since I was so good at it. She asked if she could fly with me, just so she could watch what I do. Then we would be in Singapore together, and we could start our new lives as long as I promised my smuggling money would be mine, not Dad's. We talked about Nepal. She loves that idea as much as I do. I can see the two of us living on a mountainside. It's something I've always dreamed of, and we could actually make it happen. The money I've made out here could have set me up for life, but instead I've given it all to my dad so his friends don't have to know his business went wrong. Rachel says it's my turn to get something out of it.

I'm going to do it.

April 16th

I'll miss Jake. I'm unbelievably excited at the prospect of seeing him. I want to rip all my clothes off in preparation, and it amazes me that Rachel can't see that in me. Perhaps she can. She's had a boyfriend, but I can't quite work out if it was a boring Olly-boyfriend (I'm laughing now at how much O is completely welcome to him!) or a Jake one. From the way she talks (bitterly), I think her heart must have been in it.

Anyway, I'll miss him when Rach and I start our new law-abiding lives in Singapore, working towards the mountains, but I'll find someone else. I don't want to be a part of his world in the long term. He's been amazing, and now I know never, ever to settle for someone safe and dull. I'll always thank Jake for teaching me that. I'm going to hold out for the next person who makes me tingle from head to foot, who makes me unable to think about anything but sex.

I'm looking forward to this job, and even more so to the moment it's over: the first moment of my new life.

Of course I have to start my life on a different continent from the one where my family live.

I told Rachel all about what happened with Olivia, too, when I read that one-word email – 'Sorry' – that must have cost her so much. When I read it, I smiled at how much I don't care any more, and so I described the scene and made myself (and Rachel) laugh. As I'm lying on the beach and Rachel is off swimming in the sea, I'm going to write it down now, to prove that it has no power over me at all.

I'd been going out with Olly for nearly two years, since the end of my first year at university. He was Mr Sensible. A public school boy with impeccable manners. He liked me because I was eminently suitable for him – a privately educated girl with no apparent wild side. We made the world's blandest couple. He was, of course, taller than me, broader than me, and a rugby player, with a florid complexion and a fogeyish manner that will mean he'll really feel at peace with the world on the day he turns forty-six.

So we were heading inexorably towards a dull future. We would get engaged (he would have asked Dad's permission, I know it), and then have a church wedding, and I'd wear white and be given away, and my sister would glower in the unflattering bridesmaid's dress I would force her to wear, for my own amusement. Then we'd have two children, a boy and a girl, and Olly would have a career in the City while I'd work part time and coordinate the nanny.

At some point I would have had a breakdown and done something crazy, that much is for fucking certain.

Anyway. I thought we were trundling along happily, having duty sex a couple of times a week and going to bars in Fulham that were full of people like us. We were middle-aged before our time, but this, we thought, was great. We felt quite the grown-ups.

And then, one day, I was in Bloomsbury, walking through Tavistock Square, and I decided, on a magnanimous whim, to go to Olivia's student hovel and say hello. She was living in a flat in the basement of one of those crumbling town houses. The flat had six tiny bedrooms over two floors, with a minuscule bathroom on each floor, a kitchen in the corridor by the stairs, and a concrete patch of 'garden'. All the same, its location, in a row of cheap hotels in Tavistock Place, was amazing. Olivia insists she'll always live in central London. It's one of her rebellions against growing up in suburbia.

One of her flatmates answered the door. It was the blonde fat girl with the glasses, who always puts her hair in a bun that falls out, strand by strand, hair grip by hair grip, over the course of the day. As soon as I saw the stricken look on Fat Girl's face, I knew Olivia was up to something.

'Hi,' I said. 'Is Olivia home?'

I could see her brain ticking over. 'Um,' she said. 'No! She's not. Sorry. I can get her to call you?'

I was intrigued, so I edged past her into the grimy hallway, and through the front door of their flat. It smelt of curry and stale alcohol and uncleaned bathrooms. The fat girl tried to stop me, so I sped up, passed the bathroom (a man wearing just a towel came out and widened his eyes at the sight of me), tried not to look at the state of the little table at the top of the stairs or the dishes piled in the sink, and rushed down the stairs to the basement level.

Her room was the last one, right under the stairs and

beside the door that led out to the courtyard. Fat Girl, in her desperation, yelled out, 'Olivia! Lara's here!'

There was a scuffle. Whispers. Panicky shufflings and mutterings. Even then, though, it did not occur to me for half a second. If I hadn't seen the evidence, I still wouldn't believe it.

I rushed forward and opened the door, still believing that this was none of my business, even though, it transpired, it was. And there was my sister, quickly doing up a dressing gown cord, and my boyfriend, wearing just a pair of pants, halfway out of the window that led into the courtyard.

The two of them had been shagging for quite some time, it turned out. Olly tried to explain, to talk to me about how things weren't 'quite right' with us, otherwise this wouldn't have happened, but I couldn't be bothered with a word of it.

'I'm going travelling,' I told Olivia, 'and you are welcome to him.' To Olly I said nothing at all, not one word, not ever. The only thing I wanted to do was go away, and the most appealing idea was Thailand. I did it without a backward glance. Oliver and Olivia: the perfect couple.

Dad had just asked me for money to bail out his sinking business. He was incensed that I was going travelling instead, but I told him I'd find a way to help, and I have.

I have ignored every letter and email from my sister, and I will continue to do so. I have no sister.

Olly hasn't come to find me, and he won't, thank God. I know that he is logical enough to have factored the possible fallout into his decision to sleep with my sister, and to have accepted that if I found out about it, we would be irrevocably over. He's stupid, yes, but not that stupid. I won't be seeing him again.

How refreshing to revisit that scene and find that, in fact, I'm grateful to the two of them for their treachery. They're the ones that have to live with themselves. Not me. I don't have to have anything to do with either of them ever again. And that is the most liberating thing in the world. I don't have to marry a crashing bore who's crap in bed. I don't have to marry anyone. I don't have to have a sister. I'm on my own. Rachel's my sister, and we're heading down to the beach again.

April 18th
Krabi

Krabi is full of 'falangs', i.e. foreigners. While I'm all too well aware that I am one myself, I still don't like to see this many others. There's something annoying about the way all of them – all of us, I should say – think that we're special. It only takes a quick glance around to see that this is not at all the case. Everyone's dressed the same, acting the same, treating Thailand as a theme park. I'd like it if the Thai people could go to a different part of the world and swan around there thinking they're slumming it.

Anyway. Rachel and I left Koh Lanta – lovely Koh Lanta – this morning. We sat on the deck of the boat for hours as it took us towards the mainland (pausing for the alternative crowd at Koh Jum), and I spent a long time trying to quell my nerves.

I held this book and considered throwing it into the water. I knew it was what I ought to do.

I couldn't quite bear to. Perhaps before we get on the plane I'll destroy it in Krabi.

Jake's always brushed aside my objections. One thing

he said which has stayed with me is this: 'Every country has people addicted to drugs. Very few of them are home-grown products. How much smuggling do you think happens? It's a thriving industry, Lara, and the number of people who are caught is minimal. You'd only get caught if Customs were tipped off, or if something about you made them suspicious. Which is never going to happen because you're such a fucking genius. Our operation isn't like that. It's a tiny little operation working below the official radar. No one's tipping anyone off because we're not treading on anyone's toes and we're not screwing each other over. It's safer than crossing the road.'

I laughed at that part, because it was clearly rubbish. Half an hour later I stepped into the path of a rickshaw and got a cut leg and a bruised arm, so in fact, as far as I'm concerned, he was right.

All the same, I am having an attack of conscience.

We got to Krabi at lunchtime, took a cab to a cheap guest house on one of the main roads, and checked in to two little rooms with fans but no A/C, next to each other around a courtyard. You reach the rooms by walking through the back of the check-in, directly through the middle of the kitchen (battered aluminium pots and smells which are half enticing, half gross), and through the family's sitting area. Then you emerge into the court-yard with its six huts and three loo/showers round the corner.

Everything feels straightforward, living like this. Who needs TVs or carpets or any of the rubbish I grew up insulated by? The sun is shining on my diary, I'm sitting at a plastic table, and I'm feeling I can do anything. Rachel's reading *The Beach* next to me. We're meeting Jake in a bar later. I feel excited and sick.

April 19th

Bit hung-over today. We had beers while we were eating, but afterwards Jake produced a bottle of Sang Thip, and when that comes out I know it's the beginning of the end.

I was nervous introducing him and Rachel in case they hated each other. They are not only my two best friends, but they're actually my two only friends. Rachel knows that, but Jake doesn't. Anyway, it turned out that they got on perfectly well. Straight away they were all 'I've heard so much about you' to each other (Jake was exaggerating as he and I have barely spoken, but he was extremely charming to her), and then it felt as if the three of us had been friends for ever. We all ignored the weird reality of what we were up to.

I'd forgotten how much I love to be beside him.

I'd like to visit myself a year ago, when I was going out with Olly and heading to see the parents for Sunday lunch every week, and tell that boring bland idiot (me) that I'd soon be hanging out in Thailand with an Australian drug-smuggling boyfriend. I'd like to see her face.

I've got up early: Jake's still sleeping in our bed, and there's no sign of Rachel yet. I don't know what time it is, but the cockerel is crowing so loudly that I'm amazed no one else is awake. I want to go for a walk, but Krabi is a staging post, not a scenic destination in its own right. I'll just sit here in the cool morning sun for a bit.

When we were all drunk, Rachel asked Jake if she could travel with me.

As far as I can recall (and that's unreliable, as my head hurts), he laughed and said yes, she could, as long as she didn't do or say anything that might risk fucking it up.

I need some water. A German man just came out of the bungalow opposite, wearing a pair of baggy Y-fronts and carrying a towel and a paisley-print sponge bag, heading towards the shower. He smiled and said good morning very politely. People are beginning to get up. I'm going to the shop to buy a bottle of water. Then we can go for the biggest hangover breakfast Krabi can provide. If anywhere will come up with the goods, it's Krabi. An unpretty town that's like a Wild West frontier town, a gateway to other places. It's a place to eat and drink and wait for a bus or a boat or a plane.

April 20th

The flight is tomorrow. It takes forty-five minutes, and then everything will change.

When we get to Singapore, I'm going to ditch Jake.

Any time he's passing through Singapore, however, I will welcome him with open arms, in a no-strings way.

Rachel and I sat at neighbouring computer terminals yesterday, and looked up websites of potential employers in Singapore. There are opportunities for both of us. She phoned all the international schools, and has made appointments to go and chat to two of them next week. I've found two jobs advertised that would suit me. I've printed out the (lengthy, bureaucratic) application forms and started to work out how to apply for a working visa.

Derek's going to meet us at Changi airport when we arrive. We'll put my backpack in the boot of his car, and he'll drop us at a hotel with enough cash to do whatever we want.

I must overcome my misgivings about Rachel coming along. She won't freak out. She will be fine.

April 21st

Excited. Nervous. Unable to string a sentence together.

We're going to go for cocktails at Raffles hotel tonight. That's what people do in Singapore. All we have to do now is get there.

I'm sitting on the plane. Rachel is not sitting next to me, because Jake said she couldn't. I'm just on the plane, summoning my cool. I must get through this. I can't wait. No alcohol on the plane for me. Cocktails at Raffles later.

Later

This cannot be happening. It cannot. Cannot cannot cannot.

April 23rd

Singapore

I can't bear to write it down.

So instead I'll say I'm lying on a bug-infested mattress in a disgusting hostel on Orchard Road in Singapore.

And I can't even cry. The world has ended.

I'm on my own. It's just me.

Later

Try to write it. Try to write what happened, step by step. Then I can show it to people who don't believe me, as proof. Nobody believes me. WHY DOES NOBODY BELIEVE ME?

We caught the plane, Rachel and me. I had the khaki backpack Jake gave me. Rachel had her normal one, her blue one, with a load of my stuff crammed into it. The rest of my stuff had gone with Jake, as usual.

Krabi airport is small. I was busy getting myself in the zone. I almost ignored Rachel. We queued for check-in for ages.

Rachel was quiet, but she looked all right. Every now and then she'd look me in the eyes and force a smile, but we weren't really speaking. I didn't want to be distracted.

Jake queued a long way behind us. He wasn't sitting with us. It's always like that. Men are much more likely to be pulled over than women. Women aren't pulled over at all, unless there's a tip-off.

We checked in just fine. I did all the talking, and we both gave a wide-eyed 'no' to the 'Could anyone have interfered . . .?' question. Our backpacks vanished, with airline labels bearing our names.

We didn't acknowledge Jake in the departures lounge. I tried to cheer Rach up. We had coffee, then lunch, and we meandered around the shops. She was terrified for me – I could see it in her eyes – but it was too late.

Neither of us had a fucking clue.

Of course it wasn't too late. We could have faked an emergency and got ourselves let back into Krabi. It was only a walk of a few metres. Who cares about the bureaucracy? We could have flown here and walked straight out without bags. But it all seemed inevitable and compulsory.

By the time we got on the plane, she was struggling to hold herself together. I tried to ignore her, but she was sitting five rows in front of me, and she kept getting up and going to the loo. I tried to smile when she walked past, but her face was like a mask, and I had to ignore her because I needed to stay in my zone.

Then we landed. I waited for her, so we could get off the plane together. That was not the plan, but she needed a talking-to.

'We'll split up,' I said. She looked too scared; I couldn't walk through with her. She was like a beacon. I needed to go on my own to do my usual trance. If she was pulled over for looking suspicious, I thought, it wouldn't matter because she had nothing to hide. If I were pulled over with her, it would, I thought, have been disastrous.

The backpacks, both a bit battered, one blue and one khaki, appeared on the carousel fairly early. That was good. I took mine (the khaki one), put it on a trolley and set off. 'See you in a second,' I whispered. 'Nearly there.'

I became the head girl, strolled through Customs with my head held high, and grinned as I got to the other side and the relief started to course through me. Cocktails at Raffles, that's what I was thinking. My first step on Singaporean soil was, I thought, the moment my new life began.

Derek was waiting. He kissed me on the cheek as if he were meeting a friend, picked up my bag and swung it on to his shoulder. While he set off for a taxi, I hung back, waiting for Rachel.

I didn't realise for ages. It wasn't surprising that she took a while to come through. If I were a Customs officer, I would have pulled her over. I was glad my bag was gone, so that if she tried to tell them everything there wouldn't be any evidence.

She still didn't come.

I couldn't see Jake, but I knew he would be watching, from a distance. I watched and waited, but from the concourse it's impossible to know anything. I thought Derek would come back, but he didn't.

Jake was suddenly there. He walked straight over to me, took me by the arm and marched me towards the exit.

'What's happening?' I said. 'Where's Rachel? Jake? Where's Rachel?'

I pulled away from him. He shook his head.

'Don't, Lara. Don't make a scene here, of all places.'

'But she hasn't done anything. Nothing can have happened.'

'I'll tell you,' he said. 'I'll tell you, but not here.'

He dragged me out of the air-conditioned building into the muggy outside world, towards a taxi.

I wasn't getting into it. I couldn't leave her behind. We argued furiously in low, polite voices, both of us desperate not to attract attention.

'OK,' he said in the end. 'Get in this cab, or I'm leaving you here without any of your money and without any way of ever finding out what just happened, and you'll never see your friend again.'

I hated him, but I went. He got the cab to take us to Chinatown, and we went to an outside table at a bar and he ordered beer. I wasn't going to drink it, but then I did, quickly. I didn't taste it or want it, but the alcohol immediately did something. It made me slightly braver.

'Go on,' I said. 'Where is she?'

And then he told me. And when he'd told me, he got up and left, and I know I will never see him again.

April 25th

I have begged people to arrest me. They refused and said they're going to deport me.

The khaki backpack contained nothing but heroin. It was by far the biggest consignment I'd ever taken, and by bringing it safely into Singapore, the world's scariest place, I'd done something brilliant and exceptional. Said Jake.

He had (and I had worked this out by now) also hidden a kilo in Rachel's bag. He wouldn't say why. Either he couldn't help himself, or he deliberately used her as a distraction, knowing that she would look uncomfortable and guilty no matter what. He set her up and now he doesn't give a shit.

He told me that everything about this trip had been a huge gamble to start off with. He and Derek knew that the Thai authorities were looking at them and their movements. This, he said breezily, was the last time they'd been planning to use me anyway.

I screamed at him. 'This was MY last time! I was dumping YOU!'

I'd strolled through Customs carrying so much heroin that a death sentence would have been inevitable. Rachel was carrying enough for that and didn't even know it, and she was stopped and her life is over.

When he finished telling me, he grabbed me by the wrist. 'Don't do anything stupid, Lara,' he said. I couldn't pull away.

I started crying because I knew there was absolutely nothing I could do. I would try, and I did try, and I am trying and I will never stop trying, but it is pointless. I raged at him, told him I hated him, all of that. He didn't give a shit. He never loved me, or even particularly liked me. He's just a businessman, and he's moving his business on somewhere else.

He told me that he too had been carrying. As if that would somehow make me like him again. He never usually actually carries it: a couple of times he's had Derek tip the authorities off against him, so that he would walk through just before me and they'd pull him over, leaving me to stroll through an unguarded Customs area. But this time he did. This time we pulled off something massive, and all it took was the ruthless sacrifice of my best and only friend.

Before I left, he gave me a much smaller backpack and said I had to take it. 'You're checked into a private room at the YMCA, and all your stuff is there,' he said.

I couldn't look at him. I gave the small bag back, but he made me take it.

'Seriously, Lara,' he said. 'You've earned it. Don't be stupid.'

It was my clothes, a room key and a tiny amount of cash, plus a piece of paper with the hotel room number and a safe combination on it. We have done it that way before, but only once. Normally we just get in a taxi together.

So I took it, and left. I didn't even look at Jake.

I got a taxi back to the airport and ran into the arrivals hall. When I tried to go backwards through Customs, hoping she'd be somewhere around there, unsmiling men in suits stepped out and stopped me. They were small and slight, but very uncompromising. There were no smiles, and the eye contact was stony.

I broke down completely. I just couldn't hold it together. I wailed and screamed and cried. It destroyed any chance there had ever been of their taking me seriously.

'My friend,' I kept saying. 'She's here.'

First they ejected me from the Customs area, and then from the entire airport. I kept confessing, again and again. The first time I told them I'd carried drugs, they asked to look through my bag. They took it away for a bit, but there was nothing interesting about it.

After that, with no evidence and nothing but increasingly wild ranting to go on, they picked me up and threw me right out.

I sat on the concrete outside Changi airport (a tidy place where no one sits on the concrete), and I knew I was at the lowest point of my life.

A policewoman came and told me to move. She was quite nice, but when I started ranting, she changed. That gave me an idea, and I tried to act madder and madder in the hope of being arrested and finding my way into the judicial system.

In the end she took my bag, found that I had money and a YMCA key, and put me in a taxi there.

The money was in a portable safe, blocks and blocks of it. I tried to make a plan, but it was hard. I had to get Rachel out of wherever she was, all on my own. Last time I was properly on my own, I was walking down the Khao San Road in Bangkok, about to meet Jake. I would give anything to be able to go back and walk straight past.

I went to the police and told everything to a terrifying man who had an air of such authority that I quailed as I spoke. I almost wet myself when I told him all about our smuggling thing, but I was so relieved to be confessing that I managed to carry on.

The sole point I was trying to get across was that Rachel was a tiny player, unwittingly involved, and she should be released. I could feel, though, that my 'why don't you let her off this once' line was not going to go down well.

He did write it all down, though. He was only interested in Jake and Derek, so I told him absolutely everything I knew about both of them. I know nothing will happen to them. I realised as I spoke that those aren't even their real names.

And when I kept talking about Rachel, he wouldn't even confirm that she'd been arrested. He wouldn't tell me anything about her whatsoever. Then, since I hadn't got any drugs or any proof of anything I was saying, he told me to go.

'I believe your tale, Miss Wilberforce,' he said. 'Even without evidence. And for this reason I am instructing you to leave Singapore as soon as you can, and not come back.'

He took my passport and put something in there, and later I realised I had been politely deported, in my own time.

That was two days ago. I haven't left. I need to go and visit Rachel before I do.

She's been in the papers here a bit, but because she's from NZ, I doubt there'll be anything in the British papers. I moved out of the YMCA, and into this horrible hostel. Partly because this feels like a good place for keeping a low profile, and also because I like the squalor in a strange sort of way.

She was arrested with a kilo of heroin in her bag. That comes with an automatic death penalty.

April 29th
On the plane

They didn't like me at passport control. I didn't care. I hoped they'd arrest me, but of course if they want you to leave a country and they only find out you haven't when you're on the way out anyway, they're hardly going to detain you.

I screamed as they put me on the plane. I hated them. I swore at them. It was perverse: I wanted to be arrested and they wouldn't take me. They just sent me home. Once the plane doors were locked and we were in the air, I stopped. I couldn't give a fuck what anyone thinks. I can't do anything. I will never do anything but try to get Rachel out.

Jake is such a fucking bastard. I hate him beyond anything, and if I can ever get even with him, I will.

May 15th
Mum and Dad's house

I'm going to choke on the horrible stale air if I stay here a moment longer. I cannot bear it. They are so preoccupied with trivialities. Who cares? Who cares when the bins go out or what the neighbours are doing?

I managed to find news about Rachel on a New Zealand website. I am never going to see her again, because there's every chance she's going to be executed.

My friend is going to die, because of me. She's likely to be hanged, as far as I can discover. My very best friend, the only real friend I've ever had, is going to be suspended by a noose around her neck until she is dead.

It's my fault. If she hadn't met me, she would be going back to New Zealand and carrying on with her life. I have killed her by being a drug smuggler. Whichever way you look at it, I'm evil.

And I know I'm powerless to stop it. I'm writing letters every day. I'm keeping copies of them all because I do so many of them I'd forget otherwise.

I can't give up on her. Mum and Dad are worried about me. Because I'm not being the good girl any more.

They have no idea.

September 21st

I saw something in the paper.

I'd kept this book hidden so tightly away, wrapped in a cloth, at the very top of the back shelf of my wardrobe. This is the only place I can write it down. I don't want this in my home any more.

I was reading the Saturday paper today, sitting in my flat on my own, fighting off the urge to revisit all this stuff. My place is just a studio in north London, and not in one of the parts that people consider 'nice'. In an area, in fact, that is best known for its women's prison, which sometimes feels like the universe taunting me and making sure I never forget.

The flat itself is nice enough. All mine (rented), though I've just made an offer on a little terraced house in Battersea. But I'm not very good at being on my own yet. I actually need a boyfriend or something, I think, to stop my mind attempting to swerve into bad places.

I was reading the paper, trying not to think about R. Every moment of every day I try not to think about her. And there it was, suddenly: a blurry photograph of him. Jake. 'Mastermind of drug ring arrested in Thailand', it said. His name wasn't Jake; it was actually Donald, and it seems that his 'tiny little operation working below the official radar' was nothing of the sort. He was arrested in Bangkok: not at the airport, not for smuggling, but after police trapped him. It didn't say much, but I think he recruited a young woman, an undercover officer.

I should be happy. I should not be hysterical, crying and shaking and throwing things around the flat. I know this stops him doing it to anyone else, and I know that he, unlike R, deserves it. But it brought everything back. I can't control myself.

So Jake is in prison. So is Rachel, caught in the crossfire. I'm sure they've got Derek by now too, or that they're about to. Jake would hardly protect him.

I sat in a tiny room in Singapore and told the police everything about Jake. I took them to him, I am certain of it. Rachel and I did it. They listened to me a little after all.

Out of everyone I knew who was involved in this business, I'm the only one who got away.

I'm the one who ruined everyone else's lives.

I looked Rachel up. She's still alive. I wrote to her again, but I know the best I'm going to get is another stiff, furious letter from her brother telling me to leave her alone.

January 24th

One more entry. Then I'm going to hide this book somewhere. I can't throw it away, and I can't ever open it again.

Today I met a man. After turning down people asking me out for drinks, ignoring people approaching me in the street, everything, I finally met one. I knew I would know him when I met him, and I have.

He's not Jake, and that is why I have chosen him. He doesn't make me feel wild and impulsive. I didn't want to fling my clothes off when he looked at me. But he feels safe. He would never ask me to risk my life to make him rich.

Saturday afternoon, and I was in Soho on my own. I have friends from work but I can't really be bothered with them. R was the only friend I had, and look what I ended up doing to her. I killed her.

She wrote me one letter, months ago. I burned it in the sink because I couldn't bear it, and now I wish I had it. She said she had known what she was doing.

It's not actually your fault as much as you think, she wrote. *I asked Jake if I could do what you were doing. He told me not to tell you because he didn't want you worrying about me. So it's not quite what you thought.*

It explained why she had been so terrified on the plane. But I was not thinking about it, and that was taking all my energy.

The plan was to stroll around and enjoy London, and perhaps end up at the cinema or an art gallery. In my head I was in Changi jail, the exact place where I should have been. I was with Rachel, Rachel who hated me so much she would not let me visit her, would not speak to me, just got her brother to tell me to go away. I pictured her crammed into a cell with other prisoners, unable to understand them, stripped of all dignity.

I pictured her dead. I tried to shut it out, but I knew that today was the day she was scheduled to be hanged.

And I suddenly couldn't take it. I went into a bar and bought a bottle of beer and sat by the window on my own. All I was going to do was get drunk. It was raining.

There was condensation on the inside of the window. I drew a prison on it. Just a square building, but one with bars on the window. I drew a stick Rachel outside it.

Just before I could put the noose around her neck, someone interrupted me. An 'Is this seat taken?' interruption.

I said no. I thought he wanted to take the chair away to join his friends, but he sat on it, at my tiny table, instead.

And then I looked at him. He was nice-looking. I need

someone. He felt safe. He, I thought, would do. He could save me.

I ordered a coffee, to pretend I hadn't been drinking on my own in the afternoon. If he'd asked about the empty beer bottle, I would have told him. He didn't, and so I won't.

We talked a bit. He was fine. Then, somehow, we went to the cinema. It was gloriously ordinary. He was normal. He was not going to recruit me for anything. He was smitten with me, and I knew I was safe.

His name is Sam.

part four

Thailand

chapter twenty-five

Iris

Everything almost made sense.

The sun was hot and high, but it was a hazy, choking warmth, not the blazing heat I had imagined. This city was too much for me to take in, and all I could do was cling on to the edge of my seat and squeeze my eyes tightly closed whenever it got too much.

That did not, of course, block out the smell, which was a mixture of dust and dirt, food cooking, rubbish rotting, dizzying heat and toxic waste. I had never thought of air as anything other than a pure and negligible thing, but now it was assaulting me. It was hot in my nose, in my throat, in my lungs, and it made me cough.

I was in the back of a tuk-tuk, which was vibrating violently underneath me as its engine strove to compete with the proper vehicles, and there was far too little between me and a potential grisly end under the wheels of a lorry. I barely cared. It had happened to Laurie, and it would almost be fitting if it happened to me. I had hidden away for all those years exactly to escape things like this.

The tuk-tuk was open to the world on both sides, and it was only the fact that it was moving, blasting my face with fiery hot wind, that was stopping me collapsing in the face of the hostile climate. I was not built for this.

When I opened my eyes, I noticed that we were weaving in and out of cars, lorries and taxis, all of them a million times better armed for the roads than we were. The buildings were higgledy-piggledy, some of them crumbling concrete, some modern glass and steel. There were stalls selling street food, people shouting, people everywhere.

I was propelled right off the seat by a sudden application of the brakes, and my driver turned and grinned.

'We're here?' I asked.

'We here,' he agreed, and I paid him gratefully and watched him rattling away. As I stood on the pavement and felt my body still tingling with the remembered vibrations, I wanted to cry.

It had seemed such a clever idea, flying to Thailand to find Lara, either hiding from the terrifying Jake/Donald or under his control (or, possibly, dead at his hands). Now that I was here, I could see instantly how ridiculous it was. I had come nowhere close to finding out what had become of her in London, and that was a city I knew, home to her family and the people who loved her and were desperate to trace her. Now I was on a continent in which I knew not a single person (except, if she were still alive, Lara), on the trail of a convicted drug smuggler who had, as far as I could tell from the internet, been transferred to an Australian jail four years ago, and released two years after that; at which point, ominously, he seemed to have vanished without trace. He could have been anywhere.

I had texted Alex my apologies, and before I left I posted him the diary. I had not been able to bear, so far, to talk to him. When he had read Lara's story, he would know why I was here.

Lara had sent Jake to prison. He would have come to get her. I could imagine him getting on the night train and killing Guy to set Lara up. She had known something was coming; she must have done, or she would not have taken the precaution of stealing my passport.

What, I asked myself, was I planning to do? Wander around Bangkok with an old photo of him printed off a computer, and ask anyone who looked a little dodgy if they had seen him lately? Amiably stalk a psychotic druggy killer, all on my own? Walk up and down the fabled Khao San Road staring at everyone in case they were Lara? I had not thought this plan through and it was stupid.

Coming here had been a grand and futile gesture, and it was solely serving to remind me that I was not up to this kind of thing. I never had been one for adventures, not even back when Laurie was alive and I was happy. This was beyond me.

I had booked a random guest house. It was quite expensive, so I thought it ought to be nice enough. The outside was painted pale green, and as soon as I walked through the plastic front door, the air conditioning attacked me with the force of a cold shower. The hairs on my arms instantly stood up on end, and I shivered.

This place, this city, this continent: it was not for me. I thought of Lara's description of strolling along, making eye contact with a handsome Australian and becoming an excellent drug smuggler. It was so unimaginable that it was almost funny. Lara had been so much better than me at everything. She had effortlessly hooked up with a gorgeous, unattainable man on the train. She had stolen my passport in the coolest possible manner. She had loved

Asia so much she wanted to make money in one part of it and then retreat to the mountains in another. I would never actually have been interesting enough to be friends with her. I was built for a small life.

The room was small and basic, but it had a tiny bathroom attached, and its door locked, and there were both an air-conditioning unit and a ceiling fan. It was a good place for waiting around in; this was a hiding place. I sat down on the bed, which had a thin, hard mattress that was probably good for backs, and tried to tell myself to be brave.

This was ridiculous. I was paralysed. All I could do was blank it out, by reading the book I'd bought at the airport. It was a literary thriller and I did not take in a word of it. Every muscle in my body was tense.

In the end I called Leon. He answered after half a ring: 'Iris!'

'Hi, Leon.'

I could hear how expectant he was, across the world, and I hated the fact that I was going to disappoint him. I said nothing.

'You've arrived safely?' he checked, in the end.

'Yes, thanks. It's quite a . . .'

'A culture shock?'

'A huge one. Oh God, I'm not sure I'm up to this.'

'No, you can do it. Try her email and all her social networking accounts again. Tell her you're here. Don't mention anyone else or you'll scare her. Make sure you say it's just you. No Olivia, no Sam, no policeman, no me. Don't write Jake's name down in case that scares her. Keep it simple. Make it just about you and her.'

I nodded, then remembered he couldn't see me.

'OK,' I managed to say.

'And Iris? Have you seen half the idiots who go to Thailand from round here? If they can manage it, then believe me, my dear, you can. All right? Get out there. Go to that Khao San Road place and walk around. Or look at a temple or something. You'll acclimatise.'

I took a deep breath. 'You're right. OK, I'll give it a go.'

'Keep in touch. You're doing a great job. I'm at the end of the phone any time at all. Day or night.'

I would never get used to the heat: I knew that for certain. I was made for London clouds and Cornish drizzle. All the same, once I had changed into a loose skirt and a T-shirt, regretting not thinking about footwear when I'd packed, I felt a little more ready for it. I pulled my hair back into a ponytail, instantly making myself feel like a style-free twelve-year-old, and cursed myself for still not getting around to having that long-overdue haircut.

Then, with my biker boots incongruously on my feet, I set off in search of sandals. It was good to have something to aim for.

The pavements were uneven, the air as solid a wall of heat and unfamiliar scent as it was before, and there was not even the shadow of the gentlest of breezes. My feet were sticky and sweaty. I knew the area I wanted: the famous Khao San Road that Lara had written about in her diary, that even I had heard of as the backpacker centre of South East Asia, was a few blocks away. I knew I would get there and find some shoes to buy. I did not know anything else.

It was the afternoon. The evening, and the next day, and days beyond that stretched ahead of me. When I lived in Budock with just my cats and a ghost for company, I had been a lot less lonely than this. And yet I was in Thailand, and everyone knew that was heaven.

I was getting closer to the backpacker nirvana. I could tell because there were a lot more white people about. They were alien to me, and I wanted to hide from every one of them. When I saw a shoe shop with its door wide open, I decided to be brave.

It was staffed by a chubby man who smiled broadly at my approach. He must have been baking in his formal shirt and woollen tank top, but he didn't look it.

'You'd like some shoes,' he surmised, then looked at my feet. 'Oh, my word! You *need* some shoes.'

'Yes,' I agreed. 'I forgot about shoes.'

'We'll find you some sandals. When you wear them you will find them so marvellous that you will never buy shoes from any other shop again.'

I imagined myself flying all the way over here every time I needed some shoes.

'Maybe,' I agreed.

'You tell your friends: the best shoes are at the top of Khao San.'

'I'll tell my friends,' I echoed, wondering what this man would say if I told him how few friends I had: a woman widely suspected of murder, who had stolen my identity; a policeman who'd kissed me despite being aware of my alarming delusions; a dead boyfriend who had now evaporated; and a City trader in his sixties who was the only person I was speaking to. 'Yes,' I added. 'I'll tell them all.'

I left the shop wearing a pair of comfortable sandals that let the air, which suddenly felt fresh and clean, soothe my hot and smelly feet with every step I took. I decided to go and buy a cup of coffee. I would set myself one goal at a time. Once I was sitting down with a drink, I would switch my phone back on, and do things with it.

The infamous Khao San Road, the place in which Lara had met Jake, and where, perhaps, either one of them might be hiding out right now, was not at all the way I had pictured it. In my head it was grubby and intimidating, packed with terrifying drugs casualties and smugglers, with the insane and the cool and the confident looming out of the gloom at me. I had pictured a place in which I would stand out as naïve and foreign and a target for all sorts of sinister characters.

This, however, was just another street. There were food stalls at the top, and I bought a bag of pineapple slices on an impulse, and walked along letting the juice drip down my chin. The street was lined with shops, many of them clothes stalls, and with cafés and guest houses and proper shops with doors on them. There was the tiniest of warm breezes, and I turned my face into it, in gratitude.

A middle-aged couple nodded at me as they passed. They both had grey hair cut sensibly short, and long shorts and Aertex T-shirts, and they looked like people who would go on sturdy walking holidays in the Swiss Alps, rather than backpackers slumming their way around Thailand. Two women of about my age were sitting at a table nearby, poring over a guidebook and making notes. They were dressed in vest tops and short skirts, and they could have been in Italy. I scanned the place for the freaks and the dropouts, but the best I could manage was a man with a long grey beard and darting eyes, and I had seen odder than him on the Tube. He was not Jake; at least, I assumed not. I did not have a clear photograph to go on. The chances of his being Jake were remote.

I chose a café with a strange thatched roof, and sat at a table beside the road.

Alex had emailed me five times. For the first time since I had run away from him, I forced myself to open one.

Iris, his most recent said. *I went to your hotel. Not in a stalkerish way, but because I am so intensely worried about you. They said you'd checked out a few days ago. I called your house in Cornwall but of course there was no reply. I'm not sure what else to do. Have you dashed to Asia to look for Lara? Or are you hiding away from me in London? You don't have to see me ever again, but could you please, I beg you, tell me that you're safe. Otherwise I'm going to have to reach for my policeman's hat and start to look for you properly.*

I apologise again for everything that happened between us. I came on too strong. I recognise that. I was crass. I have no idea what I was thinking.

That's all. Please look after yourself, and please, please tell me that you're fine. Then you'll never have to have anything to do with me again.

Your friend, Alex

I swallowed hard. This was an email that needed a reply, and I forced myself to write it, typing out a stiff little response on my phone and sending it without reading it through.

I'm in Bangkok, not doing very well but I'll be OK. Sorry for dashing off like that. It was mad of me. Anyway don't worry. I'll call you when I'm home. I'm perfectly safe. And Alex – I posted you something that will explain what I'm here for. I didn't know where to send it so it's gone to the Falmouth police station. You need to get it and read it. Thanks.

I regretted it the moment it was gone: none of the huge affection I was feeling for him came across in that reply. All the same, at least he knew I was safe, and he knew to check the post in Falmouth. I wrote another tweet to Lara's account, though I knew she would be unlikely to respond. I told her I had money: unless she had gone back to her old ways, she could well be struggling for cash. Then I emailed her old email address, which I knew was futile because Alex had told me it was being monitored, and if she logged into it something would beep somewhere in a police station. Lara would not be that rash.

I left a pile of baht on the table and set off back towards my hotel, my unwanted boots in a carrier bag that cut into my wrist. I made a phone call as I went, booking myself on a flight back home. It was easily done, with my bank card.

I was on the corner, turning towards the guest house, when my new sandal flapped into a little hole in the tarmac and I tripped. Someone materialised in front of me and put out both hands to steady me. I stumbled, but regained my balance all on my own.

I looked up, embarrassed, and when I saw him, I closed my eyes.

'No,' I said. 'No. Absolutely not.'

'Hey, Iris,' he said in his own, unmistakable voice. 'Steady, OK?'

I shook my head.

'No,' I told him. 'You're not here. This is over.'

'It's nearly over.'

I turned away.

'You're in my head. You look better, though. I'm sorry I made you so pathetic by the end of it.'

'Hey,' he said. 'That's OK.'

I looked quickly at him, then away. He was different from the Laurie who had hung around the house in

Budock. This one was like the real Laurie; this was how my partner had actually been. He was tall and strong, with glinting eyes and smooth soft skin, and he was dressed for Thailand in shorts that were exactly right, and a loose T-shirt, and flip-flops. I reached for him, then pulled my hand back. I wanted to keep the illusion, just for a little while.

'You would have loved it here,' I told him.

'Of course I would! It's Thailand! You'd be loving it too if you'd let yourself. And Iris?'

Something in his tone was scaring me.

'Yes?' I looked at him. His eyes were shining, and he was blinking hard.

'Iris. You're an idiot. You met someone. He's a good guy. You'll be happy with him. Tell him you're sorry for being a twat and you'd love to see him again. Because you and me, we were great, but that barrier is insurmountable. You did your best to overcome the logistics, but even the great Ms Roebuck couldn't keep it up, and you know what – I'm glad you couldn't. It was no good for you at all, you idiot. I want you to be happy. You'll find her, you know. She's here. Look out for him.'

'Laurie.' There was so much I wanted to ask him about everything he had just said, but he was gone.

I sat on the pavement and cried until a tuk-tuk driver stopped to check on me. Then I went into the hotel and lay on my bed, staring at the ceiling, planning.

chapter twenty-six

Lara

My finger hovers over the keyboard. Both my hands, held up and ready to type, are trembling. I have no idea what to do.

At first, I followed the plan: everything depended on my getting it right. At least I knew what to do. I made the plan for different circumstances. Never for a moment did I think Guy would be dead.

It hits me again. Guy is dead. The love of my life, the man I adored, is gone. His children have lost their father, his parents their son, his wife her husband. I have lost my future. And it happened because of me.

When I got here, I pictured myself as someone else, a puppet, skulking in the only city I thought I might be able to disappear into, escaping from the bad guy. That stopped working quickly. Now I have no idea. I'm on borrowed time. Something is going to have to change.

I scratch at my hairline. This thing is so hot. I hate it more every day but I don't dare take it off. Even at night

I have it on the pillow like a shredded octopus, ready for emergencies. It stops me going in the sea to cool off.

And now I have run out of money.

I would like to ignore her. She should not be a part of this: it has nothing to do with her at all. But I have to let her find me. I have no money, no peace, nothing at all. I have lost literally everything I had, everything I was. I am half feral.

I left the city because it was sucking me in and I was going to do something terrible. She says she has money. That is all that matters. She has money and she is the only one to have come this close. I can trust her. I have to trust her.

I take a deep breath and tap the screen.

So, I type. *You found me. Tell no one else. No one!*

I do not write his name. I cannot begin to think of him. But it is Iris who has found me, not him. She must know, by now, that it was him.

I write down a plan. It takes many private Twitter messages. I end by saying, *Backup: if things go wrong, go to Food Street.*

It is a gamble. But I have no choice: I have enough money left, if I barely eat, for five days. She will be here in three.

chapter twenty-seven

Iris

She had been right about Koh Lanta. I shivered as I stood
on the bungalow's balcony, trying to shake my terror. This
was where Lara had met Rachel, and Rachel had died
because of that. Kantiang Bay was a place I had read about
days earlier in Lara's diary; and now I was here.

It was as idyllic as she had said. The long beach curved
around the bay, with rocks at either end, and palm trees,
and restaurants and guest houses at intervals. At the end
where I was standing things were relatively built up, with
café leading to café and guest bungalows in every available space. Further along I could see a luxurious resort,
where people were carried around on little buggies and
the villas were distant from each other, with manicured
gardens.

Rachel was dead. I had checked and double-checked
that. I had even sent an email to a man I thought was her
brother, and received a coldly annoyed reply very soon
afterwards.

Who is this? Please leave my family alone. My sister

took her life three years ago. Kindly do not email again.
Philip Atkins.

It could be fake, of course, but I thought it was not. Rachel had not been executed, but pardoned and sent back to a New Zealand jail, where she had killed herself. There was plenty online about it, if you accessed the New Zealand press. Jake, however, was not mentioned anywhere, after the briefest note of his pardon. He, like Lara, had disappeared into thin air.

He would have wanted revenge. He must have come to her and got it. Yet she (I presumed) had written to me on Twitter, terrified. She was hiding out, and she was scared, and she was imploring me not to tell anyone. She was in danger, and I knew I had to protect her; though as far as I could see there was no chance of Jake following me anywhere, because he could have no idea who I was.

Though he could, of course. I realised that he would know my name, because of my stolen passport. There were two Iris Roebucks in Thailand, and I was one of them. That made me conspicuous.

The person who had tweeted me from her account might not, of course, have been Lara at all. It could have been Jake, monitoring her communications. It could have been Rachel: anyone could have written that email from her brother. Words on a screen were not in the least bit trustworthy. I had no idea whatsoever what I was walking into, and I could not tell Alex what I was doing because I knew he would tell me not to.

Lara, or whoever I was meeting, had picked a difficult spot, a place that would involve a hike over rocks across inhospitable shoreline, to the south of the main beach. If it was a trap, there would be no way out; but I was going anyway. I was feeling rash.

There were people lying on the sand, basting themselves. A perfect-looking family, blond and tall, were playing with a frisbee, the little children running to retrieve it whenever it went wide, apologising cutely to sunbathers. A man was out in the water, doggedly swimming across the bay. The place was busy with holidaying Westerners.

I had never been very good at climbing, and I kept stubbing my toes as I made my way over the rocks. It was horrible terrain, particularly in this heat. My phone was tucked inelegantly into my bikini bottoms, and I wished, as soon as I had gone too far to be able to go back, that I had worn a T-shirt, because although it was glorious compared with the sleety February I had left behind, I was now beginning to feel too hot.

I splashed through a little pool between the rocks. The water was so hot that it almost scalded my feet and I jumped out quickly. My toenails were still lilac: I remembered painting them beside the fire, conducting an agonised conversation with Laurie in my head. It seemed a lifetime away. The varnish was chipped now, disappearing.

I rounded the headland, and the rocks flattened out into a very narrow stretch of stony beach. This place was perfectly secluded and almost unreachable. My heart was pounding, and I knew that this was it: I had come here and I, like Lara, was absolutely vulnerable.

There was a figure sitting on a rock, her face turned in my direction, unsmiling. And it was me.

I was waiting for myself. This woman was my height, though skinnier than me, and she was wearing my sort of clothes. I had never got around to sorting out my two-tone hair, and neither had my double. Her hair was a little longer than mine, and it was dark at the top and blonde at the ends. I had done that on impulse, months ago, and semi-regretted it ever since.

For a moment we stood at opposite ends of the tiny beach and stared at one another.

When I spoke, my voice came out quietly.

'Lara?'

She stood up. I saw her face properly. It was actually her.

'Iris.'

I could not help myself. I wanted to stay cool and collected, but instead I dissolved into hysterical tears. It was Lara's face, under my hair, on a scrawny, underfed body. This was Lara Finch, my friend. It was Lara Wilberforce, terrifyingly competent young drug smuggler. It was Rachel's friend and nemesis, Jake's girlfriend, Leon's goddaughter, Guy Thomas's illicit lover, Sam's faithless wife.

She was at my side.

'Iris,' she said. 'Oh my God. It really is you. I can't believe it. It was the passport, wasn't it? I'm so sorry about the passport. Did anyone follow you?'

'No. Everyone thinks you're dead. Everyone.'

'I know. I lost my mind reading the coverage.' Her voice was wobbling. 'They think I killed Guy. How could I . . .'

'I don't. I never thought you did for a moment. I worked it out, Lara. Sam found your old diary and he didn't know what to do with it, so he gave it to me. And as soon as I read it, I knew it was Jake. What happened? He found you on the train and set you up? How did you get away?'

She frowned slightly. 'What?'

The sun was burning the top of my head, radiating off

my hair, carving, I felt, a pink strip where my parting was. And then I heard somebody behind me.

'Hello, girls,' he said, warmly. 'Fancy seeing you two here!'

I turned, recognising the voice, not able to place it. Before I could even make the connection, which made no sense, he was right there, pressing something to my face, and although I kicked and struggled, belatedly beginning to piece things together, it was no good. I felt my senses deserting me, flying away into the air, everything that made me cogent dissipating until it was gone.

chapter twenty-eight

Lara

I pulled off an escape. I tricked everyone, when the only person I wanted to trick was him. And he found me. He killed my lover, the person I adored, in front of me, telling me it was for my own good. And now he has found me again.

And I am back on the train, living again through those most terrible minutes of my life.

I pushed open the narrow door of the sleeper compartment, expecting to see Guy, woozily wanting to kiss him, ready to spend the rest of the night squashed into his arms. He was lying on the bed in a pool of dark red blood. There was a knife. I ran to him, held him, tried to shake him awake. I pulled the knife out of his neck. I didn't realise there was someone else in the cabin until he spoke.

He puts Iris down carefully, lying her on the sand as if he actually cared about her. I suppose he owes her something: she brought him directly to me. I should have been more specific about my instructions not to trust anyone, but I did not even want to type his name, out of some kind of paranoia that he would have an alarm that would sound if I did. I thought someone would have seen him on the train, that when she said she had worked it out, she really had pieced it together.

But she thought it was Jake. Jake was long ago, and he has nothing to do with any of this. I always thought it was Jake who would come to get me one day, too. I have imaginary Jake to thank for the fact that I was constantly prepared for an escape. It never occurred to me, though, that Iris would think that, because it never occurred to me that she would, somehow, read my old diary.

'Right,' he says, with a smile, and though I have thought of little else for weeks, I cannot reconcile the man I thought he was with the man I now know him to be. 'Here we are then. That's her taken care of for now. Back where we left off. How are you, gorgeous girl? How have you been? You've done so well. I told you to get away, and you did. I'm proud of you.'

I cannot look him in the eye.

'What are you doing here?'

'I found you. Like I told you on the train, I'm in love with you. That means I'll do anything for you, Lara. Anything.' He laughs. 'I think I've proved that by now.'

I knelt beside Guy, turned the knife over in my hands and stared at it. I stroked his face. I needed to call for help but I felt I was still dreaming. Then someone touched the top of my head, standing behind me, and I looked around.

'You weren't meant to see this,' said Leon. 'I just couldn't bear the fact that he had his dirty great hands all over you. Sorry, sweetheart. Don't hate me. I always knew I'd have to tell you some day, and soon, but I didn't quite mean it to happen like this.'

I stood there, unable to compute what he was saying, as he told me that he'd always loved me, right from when I was a little child. 'I didn't mind when you were with Finch,' he said, with distaste, 'because you didn't love him, not really. You were still my Lara. We were special. But this one. He was going to steal you. I'm sorry, but I just couldn't let it happen.'

'I thought it would be Jake,' I remember saying, stupidly.

'You were wrong,' he said.

I had always been prepared for an ambush, though not that one, and I sprang, shocked and numb, into action. I had known I might have to run away quickly from someone who wanted to hurt me, and I had everything I needed. I just hadn't expected it to be Leon.

He watched me and smiled.

'Probably best you get out of here,' he agreed. 'I'll come and find you when I can.'

I thought I was assembling my emergency kit out of nit-picking paranoia. In fact it transpired that I had done exactly what I needed to do, though I was not fleeing from someone who hated me but from someone who loved me dementedly.

As the train pulled into Reading, I stepped down from a door in cattle class, with a little group of other people, wearing the wig I'd had made in Hendon to look exactly like Iris's hair. I swished it over my face and scurried through the open ticket gates in a clutch of strangers, and then I was on a coach to Heathrow.

I chose Bangkok because it was the only place where I knew someone like me would be able to disappear, where I could live on next to no money. I moved farther and farther from the places where the Westerners were, sleeping in the cheapest places I could find that still let me feel halfway safe, eating from street stalls, regularly getting alarmingly ill. Logging on to computers and watching in horror as the fact that I was a murderer swept across the globe, and scanning the reported sightings of me with terror. None of them was here, or anywhere near. I wanted to tell the world that it was Leon, not me. I wanted to talk to Sam, to my parents, to Olivia, who, I could see from the world's press, was standing up for me. I wished we had not wasted so much time hating each other, when the real bad guy was simmering away unnoticed in our midst.

In the end, Bangkok was too much. I lost all sense of everything, and I fled to the only other place I could imagine: Koh Lanta.

Iris, who brought Leon right to me without meaning to, is knocked out cold, and my godfather, the man I loved and trusted for thirty-five years, is grinning at me conspiratorially, as if now I am going to agree with him that all obstacles are out of our way and we will be together for ever.

Guy has died because of me. Now Iris is going the same way. I cannot escape from this place because it is surrounded on all sides by rocks.

There is only one thing I can possibly do. I swallow hard and attempt to play for time.

'Well, you really seem to want me, Leon,' I say, with grotesque coquetry. The words stick in my throat, but I force them out. 'You found me here. Well done. You win.'

He steps closer to me. He looks ridiculous, in a white T-shirt that is too tight over his horrible nipples, and a pair of long shorts, and flip-flops. Heat does not suit Leon Campion.

'You mean it?' he says. 'You'll give it a go? Me and you? I'm like one of those princes from the old stories. I've been through all sorts of trials for you. Do I win the hand of the fair maiden?'

I walk up to him and kiss his cheek. 'Of course you do.' I push the words up through my throat. 'Now. What are you going to do with Iris? Please don't hurt her. Please, Leon. She's my friend. She's done you no harm. She's helped you. Don't kill her.'

I smile at him and wish I could work out what is behind his eyes. He considers my request.

'All right,' he agrees with a sigh. 'For you, Lara, I won't. Don't say I never do anything for you, my love. I will take her away, but I will not kill her. You have my word.'

chapter twenty-nine

Iris

I woke bleary and hot. The air was stifling and I was gulping down scalding air, taking shallow, panicky breaths. As soon as I realised that, I made an effort to slow them down, to slow my heartbeat, to take stock of whatever was going on.

I had no idea where I was, but I could hear water. It was half dark, but that was because I was inside a structure of some sort. I was surprised to be alive, and then I wondered whether I might be dead.

I struggled to make my eyes focus. I was inside something wooden, I thought. It was a hut or a shack, a shed. Water was lapping near it. I was in Thailand, almost certainly, on Koh Lanta, near the sea.

It was Leon. Leon! I had trusted him implicitly. I had gone to him, jumped through his hoops to prove myself, then told him everything. I remembered him standing there, smiling the gentle smile I had liked so much. I had trusted him, and he had used me to take him to Lara. I could not focus on the details, but I knew I had done a terrible, horrible thing.

All along I knew someone had set Lara up. I had never imagined that it was him. He was her kindly godfather, her greatest supporter and champion.

He was a monster. I had known she was in danger, and I had as good as killed her by coming out here.

I could not move, and it took me several long minutes to work out that this was not just because of whatever he had put over my face, but because he had tied my hands behind my back, and my legs together. My face was all right, though. I tried to speak, and it worked.

'Laurie,' I said, and then I remembered about Laurie. 'Alex,' I added. Alex was a more realistic source of help, but he was thousands of miles away, and he had no idea. I rolled over to try to work out if my phone was still tucked into my bikini, but it wasn't. Of course it wasn't. A man who would put drugs over your face and tie you up and hide you in a shed was hardly going to leave your phone sticking out of your knickers.

I could not begin to address what this was all about, but I knew I had done the most terrible thing of my life. My absolute joy at finding Lara had lasted seconds before irreversibly changing into its ugly inverse.

He had left me alive. I hoped that Lara was all right. I hoped she had another plan. I was impotent. I lay on the floor and let myself drift off, back into darkness.

I woke up when the water touched my foot. At first, as I drifted into consciousness, I was pleased. It felt lovely. I was sweating and it was getting harder and harder to breathe, and it was not at all like Cornwall or London. I told myself that I would appreciate European weather when I got back. And the water felt lovely, and it was soothing and wonderful.

Then I remembered that I was tied up in something like a little hut in Thailand, and that the water had not been there last time I was awake. That meant that the tide was coming in.

Yet no one would build a hut that would be submerged by high tide. Buildings were not on beaches and rocks. It made no sense, so it could not be happening.

I was more lucid this time, so I wriggled around and tried to investigate. My shoulders were aching, the muscles stretched and sore, and as soon as I noticed that, it became unbearable. He had tied my wrists with orange string, the sort that separates itself out into waxy strands. I imagined it being easy to find it lying around on a Thai beach, and that thought made me suddenly hopeful that I could break it. I was surprised that he had not used something better.

My legs were tied with the same stuff, with lots and lots of it, all the way up and down their length.

The water was getting higher. It could not be the tide. Yet before it had been on my toes, and now it was on my ankles. All the same, I had wriggled around since then, so perhaps I had moved down the hut without noticing. I shifted as far away from the water, lovely as it was, as I could. That was when I discovered that I was also tied to a post on the inside of the shack.

After twenty minutes, I had to admit that the water really was rising. Leon Campion had, somehow, located a hut that would be covered by the high tide. I knew that Alex would be worrying when I hadn't checked in with him after my meeting with Lara, but I also knew that it would take a long time for that worry to translate into someone actually finding me. It would take far too long. I was on my own.

I cowered as far as I could from the water, but I could not stop it lapping at my legs. Soon it reached my thighs, a warm bath that carried grotesque overtones of spa treatments and paradise beaches. There was no chance that the tide was going to turn and recede before it covered me completely. A man like Leon Campion would not leave something like that to chance. I was going to be submerged in glorious warm seawater until I could no longer breathe.

It was at my waist. It was creeping up my midriff. I rubbed the orange twine furiously against the walls of the hut, but there was nothing that had any chance at all of breaking it. The man knew what he was doing.

I was incensed with my mind. For nearly five years it had kept Laurie alive because I could not bear to lose him. Now, just when I could really have done with hallucinating him next to me, holding my hand, kissing me as the water covered my neck, my chin, my mouth, there was nothing.

There was nothing, and there was nobody.

chapter thirty

Lara

'Promise you didn't kill her,' I murmur.

He strokes my hair.

'I promise, darling. I'm not a monster! You asked me not to kill her, and so I didn't.'

'Really?'

'Yes. Really, honestly and truly. I did not kill her.'

'Thank you.'

'For you, my darling. Anything. She's your friend and that means something. She brought you back to me, and that means even more. I owe Iris Roebuck. We both do.'

We are in an outrageously smart villa. Guy is still dead. My darling Guy is dead, and there is nothing I can do about that and there never will be. I have shelved the grief for the past few weeks and I am forcing myself to continue to shelve it now. I will deal with it when I can. Not now. Now I have to focus.

Being with his murderer, and going along with what he wants, and knowing that if I had never met Guy he would still be alive – all of that is making my horrible play-acting almost impossible. Yet I force myself to do it because I have no choice.

The furniture here is tropical hardwood, and there are vases of exotic blooms everywhere. In Bangkok I lived on a pittance, knowing that every baht I saved kept me hidden for longer. I wished for a source of money back then: now I would give anything to go back to skulking poverty, to a world in which Iris was safely in Britain and Leon had no idea where I was.

I could so easily have told him about my contingency plans, the stolen passport and the Hendon wig. If I'd told anyone in the world, it would have been Leon. Now, it turns out, I might as well have done.

The walls are wood-panelled. The air conditioning keeps everything slightly colder than is comfortable. The king-sized bed is massive, and my next challenge is going to be to get Leon to let me sleep in the second bedroom. There is a lock on its door; I have checked. If I could get in there, at least I would be able to breathe.

Leon is watching me from across the room. He is standing up, walking around, looking down at me with satisfaction.

'Do you remember,' he says, 'a day when you were about twelve? I took you out shopping in Marylebone. Do you recall? Just the two of us. That, I think, was when I decided that one day I would be more than a godfather to you. I knew then that you were going to grow up into a beautiful woman. And here you are.'

I do recall that, much as I no longer want to.

'You bought me a yellow dress.'

'And some shoes.'

'They were lovely. I wore them until they were much too small.'

'You *do* remember.'

'But Leon – you're married. You and Sally . . .'

'That's nothing. Sally and I haven't been together for years. Don't worry about that. She's glad to see the back of me.'

'Does she know . . . I mean, where does she think you are?'

'Oh, away. She doesn't give a fuck.'

'Oh.'

I have been longing to stop wearing that wig, but now that I no longer have to keep it on, I want it back. It was hot and itchy, but it was a spectacular disguise. No one – not immigration officers, not random police officers, not sleazy men on the Khao San Road – looks beyond hair like that. It defines its wearer completely.

I knew all along that Iris was the weak link in my escape. I knew she might notice her missing passport and connect me with it at some point. I never imagined, however, that she would rush out here and find me, nor that she would confide in Leon, a man she had never met, never seemed likely to meet, before she came.

Despite his promises, I am sure she has paid a horrific price for it. Like Guy, like Rachel, if Iris had never met me she would be alive and living a perfectly happy life, and all of this would have been entirely unimaginable for her. I could have changed this simply by warning her explicitly about him. By being scared to type his name, I have condemned her to . . . whatever he has done to her. Death.

'And now,' muses Leon. 'Now, what, I wonder, shall we do?'

I stretch and yawn. The back-up plan was Food Street, Singapore. I need to try to get him to take me to

Singapore, just in case she has escaped him, or in case she told the police or anyone else where she was going and why.

'Let's go to Bangkok.' I tuck my legs up under myself. 'I mean, we can't stay here, can we?'

'No indeed. We cannot possibly, enticing as it is in many ways.'

He walks over to me as I lie, pretending to relax, on the sofa. When he crouches in front of me, I try not to shrink away. I can smell his breath. I have loved this man, in a paternal way and as, I thought, the sole person in the world who had my best interests at heart, for my whole life. Leon was the person I went to when I sent Rachel to prison. Leon got me back on my feet: I remember him taking me to lunch, writing me emails, calling me at my parents' house when I was spending days and nights staring at the wall and stewing in a rich broth of self-hatred. When I ran into a police station and demanded to be arrested, Leon was the one who made me retract everything. When, on his advice, I applied for jobs, he wrote me references and told me what to say in interviews.

Now I see that he was only doing it because he wanted to own me.

'Here's the thing,' he is saying, inches from my face. I hope he cannot see how much I don't want him to kiss me, because if he knew that, I am sure he would do it. 'I'm not so sure about Bangkok. You've just come from there, you see. You know the place inside out. Lying low. I fear I might be at a disadvantage, were you to try to give me the runaround. It's not a city I have ever visited, you see.'

The skin on my arm is standing up. I can see every little hair.

'Oh.' I bite my lip. 'If I promise to be good?'

'Lara, my dear. You are going to be good. I'm just covering all the bases.'

'Don't make me go to Singapore,' I say suddenly, then close my eyes tight shut. 'Please don't.'

'Open your eyes. Look at me.'

I do. How had I never been afraid of him for even half a second? I knew he was different from other people. I knew he was ruthless with his enemies, and I suspected that his business methods could be nasty, but I never cared because he was kind to me.

'It is because of Rachel? The Singapore phobia? The last time you flew there your friend was thrown into a stinking prison?' I nod. 'So, I think you need to overcome that, darling girl. It's something you have to face. You're with me now. Those things are from the past.'

'I'm not even allowed into Singapore. They sent me away and wrote something in my passport.'

'No. They did that to Lara Finch. Lara Wilberforce, should I say. Not to Iris Roebuck. You're the only Iris Roebuck who's going to be walking through Singapore immigration any time soon, believe me. And our silly friend, the original Iris, has never been banned from anywhere, that is for sure, because the stupid bitch has never done a single thing in her tiny little life.'

'Oh.'

'I'm going to book some tickets. You've never spent any time there. You don't know the place. I know it fairly well. It's where we're going.'

'Oh.'

He leans right up close to me. 'Don't worry, my Lara. It's a wonderful place.'

As he taps at his laptop, looking up at me from time

to time, I realise that I am too calm. I should be jumping through a window, yelling Iris's name, calling the police and trying to save her. Yet I am just lying here. He has done something to me, and until it wears off, I am entirely under his control.

chapter thirty-one

Iris

I fought it until the last moment, struggling at my bonds, trying to break the twine. I felt I should have been able to, but, with all my strength, I could not do it. I was as far as I could possibly get from the water, but it was chasing me, inching its way up my body.

I pictured my parents, ostracised by me for five grief-stricken years, answering the door to a police officer. I imagined them rejecting the news at first. Iris? Tied up in some bizarre shed on a beach on a Thai island? No, that cannot possibly be true. And then, gradually, having to accept that, inexplicably, it was.

No one would know why I was here and what I was doing. Leon had caught Lara; for all I knew, he would hide out with her for ever, though (I made myself focus) he would be more likely to make her go along with what he wanted by holding the threat of the police over her head at every stage. Would he take her back to England and make her live with him as his plaything? Had he done this because he loved her or because he hated her?

The idea of him keeping her hidden and at his bidding for ever made me retch, and then I was sick, vomiting noisily into the water that was nearly at my neck. It was disgusting: with few currents, it floated, stagnant, around me until the fish started to notice it, and within a minute they were all around me, even quite big ones, feasting on the floating contents of my stomach. I saw the hole in the wooden wall that they were using as a door, and that made me try to push at the underwater parts of the walls near me. This was not a shack that was in good condition. It might have been rotten, and I might have been able to punch a hole in it.

I did. I kicked away and made a little hole in it. I bent around, my head just above water, and made the hole bigger with my hands. I pulled a whole section away. It made no difference whatsoever to anything, because I was tied on to a strong beam, and that was definitely not going to break. In any case, I was going to die from thirst before long. The heat was so stifling that there was almost no air to breathe.

I tried shouting again. I had done that before, but nothing had happened, and I had decided to conserve my strength for breaking the bonds. That had not worked. Now I yelled.

'Help!' I screamed. 'Help!'

If I were going to die, I needed Laurie to come and help me. He knew what it was like, to feel the life force leaving your body. He had been through this, differently but the same, and I needed him. I yelled his name, screamed it over and over again. He did not come. I had said goodbye to him, to the real Laurie, in Bangkok, and I knew that his ghostly manifestation was over.

'Laurie!' I shouted, all the same. 'Help me! Help me! Come and get me!'

I tried hard to believe in an afterlife. I told myself that when the water, which was at my mouth, reached my nose, I would walk through a long tunnel towards a light, and there at the end of it would be Laurie, and my grand-parents; and my old dead pets, hamsters and cats and three rabbits, would be skitting and lolloping and running around at my feet, and everything would be gorgeous and magical and that would last for ever.

Even in my desperation, I could not make it happen. I could not believe in anything apart from annihilation. I was about to be wiped out for ever.

The warm water filled my mouth. I could not spit it out, so I swallowed it. For a horrible second I thought it was going to make me sick again. That would not work well: I pondered for a while what the logistics would be. Could you be sick straight into water without being able to gasp air in through your mouth? It would not be pleasant, and I used all my willpower to keep it down. I could no longer shout. If I tipped my head back, I would be able to breathe for a little while longer.

Then it started to come in little waves, dancing up and filling my nose, and retreating, and doing it again, and retreating again. This was annoying. I wanted to succumb to it now, but something, some instinct to cling to life for as long as possible, made me keep my head tipped back, my nostrils above the water, for as long as I possibly could.

Then it was there, lapping at my nose. I filled my lungs with as much air as I possibly could, and just as I took what was, surely, my last breath, I thought I heard the sound of an engine, somewhere in the distance, and then a voice, and then a motor coming closer and closer.

chapter thirty-two

Lara

He is feeding me tranquillisers: as soon as I worked that out, everything made sense. A day ago I could focus and hold a conversation, of sorts. Now to move an arm or a leg demands a concentrated effort, a determined focusing of mental resources. To speak is a triumph, particularly if the words are to end up anywhere near distinct. All I do is sleep and lie around. I prefer sleeping: at least everything is blocked out. Whatever these tranquillisers are, they stop me thinking. They keep me here, turn me almost into a willing captive. My whole existence feels lazy, and I live within a rosy glow of there being no bigger issues to worry about.

Guy is dead, but that is all right, because everyone is heading in that direction, and it doesn't matter whether it happens now or in thirty years. To the universe, those times are the same. Iris is gone too. That is also all right. Whatever he does to me, it doesn't matter, because he is Leon, my godfather, and I will be all right with him.

He has bought me lovely clothes, and brushes my hair. He makes me put on make-up, which I do with a careful, heavy hand. I eat and drink what he puts in front of me, knowing that he will be judging it all just right, to keep me healthy and drugged, to keep me slim despite my life of lounging.

As far as I remember, he has not touched me. I am glad, because it would be unbearable. Yet it terrifies me, because it means he has a longer-term plan. If he had nowhere to go from here and was waiting for the police to show up, he would be leaping on me. He could do anything to me now – we both know that – and the fact that he is keeping me in a state of constant dread, that he is waiting, is almost worse than its alternative.

It is only when the effect starts to wear off, like now, that my heart rate increases, my mind suddenly sharpens and the horror starts rushing back. Now I try not to let him see that my powers are returning, and I desperately start to plot. I need to find my phone and call for help. Or his phone: that would do. I could call home, call my parents, and get them to raise the alarm.

That is ridiculous. The alarm is already raised, for me, and set to its highest possible alert level, yet only Iris found me. I could try to call her, but he took her phone and threw it into the sea. I saw him. And anyway, in spite of what he says, I am sure he has killed her. He probably just didn't do it outright, so he could swear to me that he had left her alive. She will be dead by now, because she is the only one who knows it was him.

I could climb out of a window, but this villa is air-conditioned, and its owners are so confident of the system's efficacy that the windows don't even have the capacity to open. I found that out last time I was lucid, and he caught me trying to smash one, and gently sat me down and made me drink a cocktail that was full of alcohol and whatever those drugs are, and I accepted oblivion again. This time I will be more careful.

I can hear him in the bedroom on his laptop. I sit up on the sofa and look around. There is no phone within reach, naturally. He has his iPhone with him. He put my Thai phone into the safe; I have a fuzzy memory of having watched him do it. It is a smart phone I bought in Bangkok, one I top up with pay-as-you-go to make it untraceable (I have seen *The Wire*; I have a vague idea of how these things work), but I have no idea of the combination for the safe.

All the same, I know where it is.

I stand up as quietly as I can and tiptoe across the polished wooden floor. Leon's typing stops. I freeze, wondering whether to fling myself back on to the sofa. He starts typing again. Then his voice barks out, and for a second I am terrified, and then relieved.

'Annie!' he says. ''Tis I. Just checking in. How are things? . . . Oh yes, fine, thanks. But I just want to know whether the paperwork's through from that Hitchens thing. I've got my eye on them and you can tell them that. No sob stories will be accepted.'

I pull the cupboard door open. It squeaks a tiny bit, but Leon's bluster continues. The safe is right in front of me. It is one of those little ones you get in hotel rooms, and its door is smugly closed.

I press a number. It beeps loudly. Leon pauses for a second, and I run back to the sofa and lie down with my eyes closed.

'Excuse me a second, Annie,' he says, and then he is there. I feel him looming over me, but I do not open my eyes.

Some time later, my senses start to return again. I know there is no way I will ever escape like this. My lucid periods are so short, because he watches me constantly, and he knows my senses will sharpen between pills. I will never get away in those times.

I have tried pretending to eat, but he forces me. When I tried to shout and raise the alarm, he threatened to inject me instead.

'I don't want to,' he said mildly. 'But if it comes to it, I will. Don't worry, darling. You'll understand when you're ready.'

'I will not,' I shouted. I lost control. It was a mistake, and I won't be doing it again, because he slapped me across the face, hard, and then cried at what I had made him do until I apologised.

The only time he is not with me is when I go to the loo. The window in the bathroom is small, high up and frosted. He sometimes stands outside the door, possibly to make sure I'm not killing myself. Often, though, he doesn't. I think he likes to be a gentleman and give me privacy in the bathroom.

I have no idea how long I have been here, or what day it is. It might not have been very long. I know I have been to sleep, and that he tucked me into the king-sized bed and took the single one in the corner of the huge master bedroom. He drugged me heavily before bed so that there was no chance of my escaping while he slept.

If I concentrate very hard, I might be able to try something out. However, it involves the lucid me making a plan that the drugged me will need to carry out. If I think about it now, very, very hard, then I might be able to implant it in my brain. I wish I could write myself a note, but I know that is impossible.

There is a knock on the villa's front door. I try not to respond. Leon is there in a second.

'Stay right where you are, sweetheart,' he says, and I nod. He opens the door, hands some money over, and says, 'That's quite all right – I've got it from here.' Then he takes a tray, kicks the door shut, and carries it into the second bedroom, the one he's been using as an office.

He brings it back and puts it in front of me, doctored with drugs.

'Darling,' he says, sitting next to me and smiling. 'It's time for your lunch.'

So it's lunchtime. I file that knowledge away.

'Come. Sit at the table with me.'

My lunch is a bowl of tom yum pak, vegetable soup, a plate of chopped fruit and two drinks. He has a plate of pad thai, a beer and a bottle of water. We sit opposite each other at the shiny table, and he watches me carefully.

'Now, we're going to be leaving here tomorrow, darling,' he says, checking my face for a reaction. 'I don't want any silly business. Is that understood? I'm doing this for you. You'll realise it one day. You can't go back home ever, not without far too many stupid questions being raised and ridiculous police officers popping up at every stage. I'm not letting them take you to one of their prisons. Not you. So I've organised something wonderful. Are you listening? Are you concentrating?'

I nod that I am.

'Where have you always wanted to live?'

'Um.' I want to say the right thing, but I have no idea what the answer is. I've wanted to live in different places at different times. 'Er. London?'

'Oh, Lara.' He smiles, and I can see his approval of the fact that I have said something ridiculous, because it means his drugs are working. 'No, no. Don't worry. I can see you're finding it hard to focus. But don't you remember how we used to talk about Nepal? You used to tell me that one day you would buy a house in the mountains, in the Himalayas, and you would just leave everything behind and live there. No Sam Finch, no silly dalliances with married men, nothing. You would breathe fresh mountain air, and walk every day, maybe have a few goats and chickens, or whatever people do up there.'

I nod again.

'I've bought it, sweetheart. We have a house, three hours' drive from Kathmandu. It's far away from the treks the tourists do. There's no other house near it. It cost me a fucking pittance! So we're going to live there, you and me, for ever. Your dream come true; my dream come true.'

I try to imagine it. It could never work. People will come along and they will find me.

'But,' I say carefully, because I can feel the drugs doing their work, shutting down the horror so I experience the most enormous surge of terror, followed almost instantly by calm. 'Your business. It's in London. And Sally. People will look for you.'

'That's the thing, my dear. They won't.' He pauses for a mouthful of noodles. 'I've left Sally. That has been on the cards for a long time. She's looked after financially. As far as she's concerned, I'm cut up by the split and I've gone away somewhere hot to get over it. She probably thinks I'm holed up with a bevy of Asian girls. That's fine by me. Annie knows not to ask anything, as long as I'm on the line and on top of the work side of things. No one else gives a shit. I can just say I'm living abroad for a while and that's that. I'm a free agent.'

'Oh.'

I cannot compute everything he has just said, but I know it was bad. I put my spoon down.

'Just finish that up for me, sweetheart. Come on, quickly, and then you can lie down.'

I pick up the spoon and do as he says. He makes me drink the water and the other drink, which is an alcoholic cocktail that, I am sure, is laced with all kinds of things. I want to leave it but I am not allowed.

Then I rise, shakily, to my feet. He smiles his approval.

'Good girl,' he says.

'Go to the loo,' I manage to say.

'Of course. Will you be all right?'

'Yes.'

'Quick as you can. We can't have you keeling over.'

He is still eating his lunch, sipping his beer. I lock the bathroom door and fuzzily remember. The chemicals have not quite taken effect properly yet. I was exaggerating. Quickly, while I still can, I turn the tap and the extractor fan on for cover, kneel in front of the loo and stick my fingers into the back of my throat.

I used to do this a bit when I was a teenager. I am sure that most teenage girls do it. It turns out that once you've got the technique, making yourself sick is like riding a bike. I find the right spot and push my fingers back, and my lunch reappears. It takes four vomits before there is nothing left to come up.

I flush the loo three times to get rid of the scum on the surface, and brush my teeth. Then, when I am sure I look all right, I compose myself into someone about to keel over, and stagger to the sofa.

'Everything all right?' Leon asks from across the open-plan living area.

'Mmm?' I reply, collapsing into my usual position.

'Nothing. Don't worry.'

I close my eyes. This is more like it.

chapter thirty-three

Iris

'Excuse me.'

The woman was on the phone, behind her wide desk that was cluttered with a spread-out map, two old-fashioned accounts books, a pair of binoculars and many pieces of paperwork. She smiled at me and put her hand over the receiver.

'Just one moment,' she said.

I looked at the board behind her, with its keys on hooks. My hut was number 36. There was a key up there, even though I had lost mine en route. I smiled and pointed and nipped behind the desk, behind the woman, and unhooked it. She did nothing to stop me.

The sun was hot in my eyes, shining off the stone path. I was desperate for food, but more desperate to get back to my things, to check whether that psychopath had thrown everything I owned into the sea and burned down my hut, just to cover his bases. He could have booby-trapped the bedroom, or paid a gang of mercenaries to dispatch me from nearby rooftops if I went close.

If he had left me to die like that, I did not want to think about what he was doing to Lara. I could not piece it all together, not yet, because I had no idea what had actually happened on the train. I did know, however, that she had been hiding from him, and I had found her for him. I knew that if I had not vomited into the sea, attracting all the local fish, the fishing boat would not have discovered the submerged hut, and the fishermen would not have cut me free and brought me to land.

My hut was intact. He did not seem to have bothered with it. I grabbed my money and ran back to the woman, who was now off the phone.

'I need to make a call,' I said. 'It's really urgent. Please?'

'International?' She was not really listening. She was taking pieces of paper, guest registration forms, out of a filing cabinet.

'Yes please.'

'You can use this phone. Then pay me after.'

'Thank you!'

'Dial 1 and then country code.'

I realised I did not know Alex's number. I cast around wildly for anyone else I could call. I had not seen Alex since I ran away from his kiss, a million years ago, on a planet away from here. I had last contacted him from Bangkok. He could have no idea of what had happened.

I could not call my parents. There was so much else to go through before I could begin to explain to them where I was, and why. The only people who knew anything about this were Alex and Leon.

In the end, I alighted on Sam Finch's landline number, which had been stuck on their fridge that day when Lara had failed to appear from the train. Calling him was the only thing I could think of to do. I recalled reading it out to people on the phone when we were trying to find her. It was, I thought, 551299.

He answered after six rings.

'Hello?'

I took a deep breath and closed my eyes.

'Sam,' I said. 'It's Iris.'

'Iris. Hi. Are you OK?'

'I didn't wake you up, did I?'

'It's five in the morning. I'm always awake. Are you still in London?'

I hesitated. 'Kind of. I won't be back in Cornwall for a while. Look, Sam. I need something really urgent from you. Do you have DC Zielowski's mobile number?'

He grumbled and fumbled for a while and then found it.

'Why do you want him? He's not even part of the investigation, not really. He was just doing the legwork. None of them are interested in me any more anyway. Back to kittens up trees for our boys.'

'It's urgent. I'll call you back when I can and tell you everything, OK?'

I hung up and called Alex, without checking with the woman that I could make another call. She was talking to some people who had just arrived. I was looking very carefully at everyone who passed by: for the moment, I was visible to anyone, and there was nothing I could do about it.

Alex answered his phone with a sleep-befuddled 'Iris?' and I was so relieved I nearly lost control.

'Look,' I said. 'Don't say anything until I've told you all of this. We have to get moving and there's something you have to do for me.'

I waited for him to catch up, knowing I had propelled

him out of sleep and into the middle of something utterly surreal.

'. . . He might have killed her by now,' I finished by saying, 'but our backup plan was a place called Food Street in Singapore, and so I'm going to head there and see if anything happens.'

'Iris. No. Let me call the Operation Aquarius guys. They'll get the police over there to pick him up. Leave this with me.'

It was logical.

'Sure,' I agreed. 'Have the Thai police look for them. Of course. That would be great.'

'And you come back. OK? Your involvement stops here. I've been desperately worried – with good reason, it turns out. I can't believe you're all right. Don't push it. Come home. You've done more than enough, and you don't want to mess any more with that man. God knows what else he's done.'

'I know. Look, I'll go to Singapore, just in case Lara gets to Food Street, and then I'll book a flight home. OK? Compromise.'

He paused. 'OK. Keep me informed. Be in touch. Get a Thai mobile and let me have the number. I'll . . . well, I'll get things happening. I can do this, Iris. You're not alone.'

'Thanks.'

'Promise to keep in touch.'

'Promise.'

When the fishing boat rescued me, and I realised I was actually alive, I begged the men to say I was dead. It would have been a great plan, had they understood. They were lovely: one of them was big and strong, the other smaller, younger. Both looked after me: they held me as I vomited my watery stomach contents over the side of the little wooden boat, gave me their bottles of water, and tried to ask me what on earth I was doing tied inside an underwater shack.

I coughed and spluttered and was grateful that we could not understand each other. I would not have had a clue where to start.

When I saw it from the outside, I could see that the hut had once been on stilts, and that was why it had been so easily moved. There were others like it, abandoned, nearby, rotting away. Leon had pulled it down the beach to below the tide line, and left it there. He was insane.

The men had wanted to call the police. I said no, and got them to drop me at the beach below the huts. They were incredibly concerned for my well-being, and the older one hopped out of the boat with me, with the intention of taking me to someone in authority – to the woman at the guest house reception at the very least – and handing me over, explaining my ordeal, but I shook him off. In the end I had to shout and cry at them to go away, and they did, with the greatest reluctance.

I would be much safer if they would pretend they had found a body, and if it could somehow reach the media. The chances of their actually doing that were nil. I was going to have to be careful.

The island flashed by outside the taxi window. I did not speak to the driver, and after a few attempts he gave up trying. I looked at the boards advertising interminable 'full moon parties', at the strings of roadside cafés and guest houses. In places, signs announced a 'tsunami zone'. The sun was relentless today, and I had the window open, tropical hot air blasting into my face. There were some people about: locals, travellers, people with backpacks. I had expected this place to be heaving with backpackers, after reading Lara's old diary, but it was not. In fact, I wasn't sure people went backpacking any more; not, at least, in the way in which they used to.

Everything looked technicoloured and unreal out there. I did not want to think about the bigger picture. All I could do, right now, was get off the island.

I sat with my face in the hot air, and tried to think of nothing. I was useless, and this was beyond me. Alex was right: all I could do now was leave it to the professionals, get myself to Singapore, check out Food Street just in case, and fly home. Having found her once, I might never do it again.

The taxi pulled up at the ferry terminal on the north of the island, and the driver opened my door, then unloaded my bag from the boot. I stood in the heat, instantly sweating, my head feeling it was about to crack open. When I paid the driver, who was wearing a burgundy Aertex shirt, and he drove away with a smile, I realised I needed to get moving. I could not stand in the mid-afternoon heat, visible to anyone, and expect things to be all right.

Immediately, a wiry man strode over and asked what I wanted.

'Taxi? Hotel? Restaurant? Boat?'

I exhaled in gratitude. 'Boat,' I told him. 'Thank you.'

'Ferry to Krabi? Tomorrow morning. Now? You want a private boat?'

I had plenty of cash, so I nodded. Wherever Leon was, and wherever he was heading, he would have to pass through this port. He might already have done so, but I needed to get away as soon as I possibly could.

'How much?'

Twenty minutes later I was on a speedboat, with a bottle of cold water, paying what I thought was about a hundred pounds to be taken to the pier at the centre of Krabi. It was, as far as I was concerned, money extremely well spent.

I had barely paused in Krabi on my way over. Now I rushed off the boat, thanking the driver, tipping him frenziedly, running into the travel office on the other side of the road. I could hear a dog barking somewhere nearby, and normally that would have scared me, but today I didn't care. If it rushed at me with its teeth bared, I would kick them all out of its head.

A large woman with her hair in a bun grinned as she saw me coming.

'Hello, yes?' She gestured to me to sit down. Two children in formal school uniforms were sitting at the other desk in the room, their heads bent over something, giggling. A faded poster of a smiling young woman was beginning to come off the wall.

'Hi,' I said. 'Can you sell me a plane ticket to Singapore?'

She pulled a keyboard closer to her. 'Most certainly I can,' she agreed. 'When would you like to go?'

'Today?'

She shook her head and sucked her teeth. 'Not today. I am sorry. Too late. Tomorrow. Wednesday.'

I inhaled deeply. 'Yes. Tomorrow. Thank you.'

'It will be nineteen hundred baht.'

'No problem.' I nearly asked her for a ticket to London, but thought better of it. I would source that online, or when I got to Singapore. Buying it here would not feel secure.

'Great.' She grinned at me. 'Your passport, please? I can book you a taxi to the airport too. You come back here when you want to go.'

I happily acceded to that, and then I was walking through Krabi, the sun too hot, wondering where to go. Krabi had dusty pavements with potholes in them, and the laissez-faire air of a frontier town. Foreigners were meandering around, many of them sweating under the weight of huge bags. It was hot, and one particular fly kept settling on my forehead. I imagined it feasting on my delicious sweat.

I did not even try to summon Laurie. He was gone, and I was all right with it. This was reality: me, on my own, without much of a plan.

I needed to lie extremely low. It was only when I caught sight of myself reflected in the window of a tatty-looking shop, however, that I remembered the other thing I needed to do.

The shop seemed to sell a bit of everything: there were containers of nails, padlocks, pens and hammers. You could buy binoculars here, or, if you preferred, inform yourself thoroughly about the Thai and British royal families. Dust hung in the air.

'Do you have scissors?' I asked the man sitting on a high stool reading the paper.

'Scissors? Yes, I do!' he said delightedly. 'Over here. Which sort of scissors?'

I looked at them. His array of offerings ranged from the blunt ones you fail to cut paper with as a child to chunky kitchen scissors with plastic handles.

'For cutting hair.'

He picked up a pair. 'This one.'

I looked at him. He was a nice man. He wore a pair of blue work-style trousers with a crease ironed into the front, and a crisp white shirt, with flip-flops on his feet. His aura would be warm and gentle, maybe yellow and amber.

'Could I use your mirror?'

'Of course.'

He watched me cut my hair off, just above my shoulders, and then he laughed and held out a hand. I put the rope of two-tone locks into it, and he turned it over, staring at it in wonder, before lowering it carefully into his rubbish bin. Then he was behind me, taking the scissors, evening up my ragged bob as best he could.

He gave me a conspiratorial look that said 'I'm not even going to ask' more clearly than any words could have done, and I handed back the scissors even though I had paid for them. I watched the man wipe them carefully with a cloth and replace them on his display.

I found a room in a nearby guest house, one that I was sure would hold no appeal whatsoever for Leon Campion. Its rooms were huts built around a courtyard that was accessed through the kitchen. There were shared loos and showers, and the bedroom was entirely basic. There was a bed with an iron frame, a thin mattress covered with a pale blue sheet, a folded white top sheet, and absolutely nothing else beyond a padlock for the door. The bathrooms were across the courtyard. I could smell serious spices being fried, and could hear two conversations, one in Thai from the kitchen, the other in German from right outside my door.

I wondered, suddenly, if this could be the same guest-house at which Lara had stayed, aeons ago, when she was with Rachel and Jake and Derek. The night before her life collapsed for the first time. Did Rachel spend the last free night of her life exactly here? I shivered at the thought.

Leon would never find me here. I sat on the bed, then stood up again. It was not yet time for me to relax. I needed to go out and find the right shop.

Two hours later I was sitting on a wobbly plastic chair outside my hut, fiddling with my new phone. It had baffled me – I had been too long out of the modern world to have a clue how to set up a Thai phone – but the guest house staff had gathered around and set it up for me. It was odd, I thought. For years I had hidden myself away from everything and everyone, terrified of social interaction and shunning it all. Now I was finding kindness at every turn; or rather, at every turn save the one that had taken me to Leon Campion.

I had called Alex, but had got through to his voicemail, where I had left him several messages. Now I was wondering whether to call Sam again and get Olivia's number. She needed to know the truth about Leon; and in fact she would be a formidable person to have on my side. I would trust her instincts and advice implicitly.

Not only that, but the Wilberforce family needed to know that Lara was (or had been, until very recently) alive. And that she was in Asia. They needed to know the truth about the man they had picked as her godfather. That information needed disseminating as widely as possible, just in case.

I called Sam. There was no reply.

Then it was evening, and I decided not to go anywhere. I bought a vegetable curry and rice from the kitchen, and added a beer, and sat on my wobbly chair next to a wobbly table I'd pulled across the courtyard, since no one else seemed to be using it. It had got dark quickly, and the air was thick with heat and swarming with mosquitoes.

I ate everything in my bowl. Until I arrived in Bangkok, I'd had no idea how much I liked Thai food. I had vaguely remembered it from my London life as an option in the 'where shall we go for dinner' conversations Laurie and I used to have, but now I decided it was my favourite food in the world. The beer was cold. This was exactly what I needed.

I wished Alex would call me back. I tried Sam again, and after a difficult conversation he gave me Olivia's number.

'Look,' he said, 'I'm not your personal directory enquiries service. I don't sit by the phone thumbing through my numbers wondering which of the people I despise you're going to want to speak to next. You're busy because of the diary I sent you, aren't you? You could at least tell me.'

'I'm sorry,' I told him. 'I really am. I owe you. I'll tell you everything as soon as I'm back.'

He exhaled. 'Oh, who gives a shit? It's actually nice to get a call from someone who wants something I've got. No one else bloody bothers any more. No one knows what to say to me, and now all the excitement's over, I'm kind of on my own.'

'Oh Sam.' I wondered whether to tell him what was happening, that he had been right about Leon Campion, and I had been wrong. 'Look, I'll come and see you, I really will.'

'Sure.'

*

Olivia took on board everything I was saying instantly.

'Oh my *God*,' she said. 'Leon. The fucker. I cannot believe it. He's doted on her all her life. She trusted him more than anyone. My parents trusted him. He's in the inner circle. The absolute fucker. I'd kill him right now with my bare hands. The bastard. And you know, even as you were *saying* that, I realised I wasn't surprised. Maybe I already knew it in a fucked-up way. Right. So you're in Thailand, and you saw her? You've actually seen her?'

'Oh, Olivia,' I said. 'Yes, I did. I saw her, but suddenly Leon was there. I saw her for less than a minute. Alex, from Cornwall. The police detective who was briefly involved in the investigation. He's getting the police here on to them. I don't want to talk to them. I don't want to get caught up in red tape and statements. Leon's gone, with her, and all I can do is head to Singapore and find a place called Food Street, which was our meeting place if things went wrong. I'll be there late tomorrow night. My flight from Krabi's at six. I'll go straight there and wait, and I'll leave messages, and if there's a Food Street hotel I'll stay in it.'

'I can't really believe you're in a place called Crabby. It doesn't sound pretty.'

'It's not pretty,' I allowed, 'but it's good. I like it. I won't see any of it apart from the courtyard of my guest house, but there was a woman who sold me a plane ticket and a man who helped me cut my hair and the hotel people set my phone up. So it's good.'

'Fair enough. So we have no idea where that absolute fucker has taken my sister?'

'No, except that she's travelling as me, so if his name and mine appear on any flight lists, that'll be them.'

'And if it's just his name, it'll mean we'll never see her

again. Even though it turns out she was alive all along, she might not be now.'

'Yes.'

'And the police here already know, so there's no point in my going to them right now. I'm not going to tell the parents, either. Not until there's something to report. I'll tell you what I am doing, though – I'm going to see Sally, his wife.'

'Oh God. Really? Be careful.'

'*You* be careful. You nearly died. You saw Lara.'

'I thought it was Jake. When I realised there was someone behind me. Right up until I placed his voice, which must have been just before I blacked out.'

'Jake?'

'Her boyfriend from years ago. It's a long story. I never imagined Leon. I mean, I helpfully showed up at his office and told him she'd flown to Bangkok on my passport. When I told him I thought it was Jake, he leapt on it, you know. He made me feel I was definitely right.'

'Suited him perfectly. Well, keep me informed. Please, Iris, I beg you. Every step of the way. If I wasn't so pregnant I'd be out there, at your side, in a fucking flash. But call me. Will you? Will you call me every day?'

She sounded so strained and sad, so uncharacteristically vulnerable, that I wanted to rush to her side and hug her.

'Of course I will,' I promised. 'Of course. Look after your baby and I'll do the rest. I'll do whatever I possibly can.'

I hung up feeling desperate and impotent. All I could do was fly to Singapore, go to our meeting place and wait. I was sure nothing would happen. She could have been anywhere. He could have taken her to Bangkok or Kuala

Lumpur, both of which were closer than Singapore, and on from there to any place in the world.

If only Alex would answer his phone. I would know if the police had managed to do anything. I stared at my mobile, willing it to ring. Nothing happened.

I picked up my bag and started walking towards the taxi office.

chapter thirty-four

Lara

The long wig makes my head so hot and itchy that all I want to do is take it off. Every time I try, reaching up reflexively, he pushes my hand away. Then he takes my hand and holds it. I try to pull away because his big dry hand is making mine sweaty and slippery, but he just holds tighter.

We are in the back of a car, and we're heading into Krabi, from the airport. We went to the airport first so Leon could buy our tickets to Singapore. From there, he has told me, we have tickets booked to Delhi, and in Delhi we will change on to a flight to Kathmandu, where our new life will begin.

I am managing to keep making myself sick, but I am still feeling wrong. The wooziness of the drugs is almost gone, but the fact that I throw up almost everything I eat means I'm still at a huge disadvantage. I struggle to focus. My stomach rumbles often, but he doesn't seem to have realised, yet, what that means.

I miss food.

I close my eyes. I sleep whenever I can, because it is the only place I can go to escape him. He saw me crying on the boat across from Koh Lanta.

'What's the matter?' he asked.

The man who murdered my lover and the friend who came to rescue me. The man who let the world think I'd killed the man I adored, the man who came out to Thailand and trapped me, who was taking me to the mountains so he could keep me like a pet. He wanted to know what the matter was.

'Nothing,' I told him.

We are sitting in a restaurant on the main road out of Krabi. It is an odd place for Leon to have chosen, a completely normal tourist restaurant, open to the world on three sides. There is no polished and varnished hardwood, no artfully arranged tropical stems, no air conditioning.

I see him wincing at the clientele, with their backpacks and their sweaty hair. Leon is doing his best to dress down and be inconspicuous, and is wearing grey shorts and a white T-shirt. He doesn't stand out at all; he is extremely good at this.

He picks a table at the edge of the restaurant, beyond a row of wooden pillars and away from the road. We are next to a wire fence and a house, with a row of pastel-coloured garments drying on a frame outside. I look as surreptitiously as I can at the window. There is a vase with plastic flowers in it on the windowsill and no sign of anybody inside.

I look back at Leon.

I am wearing the travelling clothes he bought for me: a plain green T-shirt and a pair of slim-fitting capri pants. There is a green flower clip in my wig, and strappy green sandals on my feet. I always liked Leon's sense of style. Now it makes my skin crawl. I am trying not to think about a future in a little house in a remote area of Nepal, just Leon and me, for ever. He will dress me up, his doll, in clothes he will buy from the internet, and no one will ever bother to question why. He will never trust me enough to let me go anywhere or do anything on my own. I will be his toy, his pet, his object, and we will stay there until one of us dies.

I picture the tiny house on the mountainside with the spectacular view of dramatic landscape, deep blue sky, snowy peaks. When we get there I will start letting him drug me again, just to block it out. I will beg him to tranquillise me.

He is looking at me with the same warmth in his eyes that he always had.

'Are you all right, darling?' he says, leaning forward and looking at me with the gentle concern I am used to seeing on his face.

'Yes,' I say, speaking slowly, as I always do, to feign druggedness. 'Leon?'

'Lara?'

'Why . . .' I unfocus my eyes, frown in concentration. 'Why did you kill Guy? You never even told me how you felt about me. You should have told me first.'

He nods and signals for a waitress.

'One green chicken curry, one green vegetable curry, one boiled rice and two beers, please,' he says crisply, and she writes on her little pad, reads it back to him and leaves. I wonder whether I could pass her a note, but if he caught me, the consequences would be intense. All the same, I am going to have to take a risk at some point. I have no pen and no paper, but I could go to the loo and ask the staff to call the police as I passed them.

I can only do it if it has a high chance of working, but I have to try something, because my time is running out.

'You won't follow this, but I'm going to explain it to you anyway, before you have your medication,' he says, tipping all the rice on to his plate. I am not allowed carbs because I have to stay slim.

'OK,' I say, in my dreamy voice.

'As you now know, I've loved you for a long, long time. Not in a creepy way, because I would never have touched you as a child or a teenager. I mean, I haven't even touched you in that way now, have I? Not yet. I'm waiting for it to be perfect. I adored you. My marriage to Sally was happy enough, most of the time. But my heart has belonged to you, Lara, for the past twenty years.

'You really didn't know? I thought you did. I thought we had a connection that even you would have noticed. We were both in our dull little marriages to people who didn't get us, not at all, not properly. We had each other. We were special, and I was patient, because I knew that one day we'd be together. I always knew that. Always.

'Then you came to me for a job, wanting to come to London, where I was, and wanting to escape Sam Finch and everything he stood for.

'I knew our time had come. I would wait until you and Sam cracked apart, and then I would step in and save you. I'd give you everything. The first thing I was going to do was bring you to the Himalayas on the holiday of a lifetime. After that, we'd do whatever you wanted. I had so many plans and ideas, Lara. I was going to live out my twilight years in absolute happiness. Me and Lara Wilberforce. It was the only thing I ever wanted.'

'And here we are.'

He looks at me sharply.

'As soon as Guy Thomas appeared on the scene, I knew I had a serious problem. You may remember I told you to steer clear of him? In the pub that night when Olivia had announced her happy news? I did hope it was a flash in the pan, a catalyst that would expedite your exit from your marriage. But then you were both leaving your partners. You were wild about him. You were going to have a new life together. I had to step in then and there. Immediately. I knew I could look after you, if you were grieving. Darling, I never meant for anyone to think *you'd* killed him. That was why I got something into your drink, so you'd crash out and be out of the way. But when I saw that it did look that way, and when you took off into darkest Reading, I wondered if that might not work for us after all.'

Staying calm while he says all this costs me almost everything. I blink back the tears. The only thing I want to do is run into the nearest police station. I hate him. I hate him, and I hate my parents for pushing me into his sights when I was a baby – for making him stand in a church and promise to look after me – and I hate myself for spending my entire fucking life thinking he was a kindly, concerned godfather, thinking that the person who was after me was Jake.

Most of all, however, there is a ragged, gaping hole in my being where Guy ought to be. If Leon gets me to that mountain, I will throw myself off a precipice the first chance I get.

Suddenly he is brisk.

'You hate me now, and that's just the price I have to pay for a while. You can't go to the police because you're wanted for murder, so don't even think about that. You

won't always hate me, you know. You'll come round to
my way of thinking. I haven't touched you, have I? I don't
want you to have to force yourself to go through with
anything. I want you to come to me willingly, and offer
yourself.'

He genuinely appears to believe this might happen.

'Though when we get to the mountains, perhaps a little
seduction might be in order on my part. We'll celebrate
our new life. But we'll have all the time in the world. I'll
have to keep you inside for a few years. You'll understand
that. No jumping off mountain paths or bridges. No passing
notes to villagers. Nothing like that. Until I can see in your
eyes that you're ready, I'm going to carry on taking precau-
tions.'

'But you won't even want me,' I tell him. 'Now you've
got me. Hasn't the whole point been that you *couldn't*
have me?'

I am feeling much stronger for eating this food. Even
Leon wouldn't sprinkle ground-up tranquillisers over food
in a restaurant. The beer is going right to my head.

'You need your medication,' he observes. 'That was
sharp. You're right: in some ways, the reality of being
with you day and night is not what I'd hoped. That will
change. Your skin was always perfect, and now it's – well,
I won't be cruel. And your figure. Scrawny. And we can
mould your behaviour until it's right. I expected more
grace from you, my darling, I have to say. A little more
poise.'

He looks at me as if I ought to apologise. I do not, and
this, I suspect, proves his point.

'In any case,' he continues, passing me two pills, 'you'd
better take these. If you knock them back with the beer,
they should keep you beautifully calm until we've been

into Singapore and out again. I realise that flying into Singapore is a difficult thing for you, but those days are far behind you. Rachel's long departed this life, and everyone has moved on.'

I wish he was not the only person who knows about my drug-smuggling past. Every time he mentions it, I feel he is holding it over me. I wish he had not given me genuinely good advice at that time. I wish it were not the case that he single-handedly got me back on my feet and showed me that I had to carry on with my life in spite of everything. I hate it that I will always owe him for that.

My wig is itching unbearably. I want to take it off. I know I can't. I take the two pills and put them in my mouth, stash them in my cheek and pretend to swallow with a slug of beer.

'Show me.'

I open my mouth wide. Leon stands up and walks over to me. I quickly swallow the pills, which is agonising without liquid, a second before he gets to me. He puts a finger into my mouth and I let him. I do not even bite him. I must be getting 'moulded', as he said.

'Good,' he says. 'Though I do believe you utilised the last minute. Now. We'll give them a few minutes to start to work, and then I'm going to have to make a fairly urgent visit to the gents'. You stay with our things. I'm trusting you. This is a test.'

I nod, and take several gulps of water to soothe my throat, which feels as if those two pills gouged out a bloody trail as they descended.

'Right.' He looks pained. 'Trusting you.'

'OK.'

He makes a quick exit. The moment he is out of sight, I reach for his leather man-bag and grab his phone. I have never been alone like this before, not with his stuff, and I cannot use the precious time to run to the loo and throw up.

I can't make a call because he would see it in his history immediately, and before anyone turned up we would be long gone.

I go into settings and switch Safari to 'private browsing'. Then I open it up and go to my Twitter account, ready to post a message to my tens of thousands of followers. I will give details and trust that enough of them are journalists for people to take it seriously and send someone along.

However, I click on the message icon, and find a series of private messages from Iris. That makes my heart stop. I read quickly, then reply.

In Krabi too. Right now – café on road out of town towards airport. rooftop bar, backpack accommodation, next to coffee shop. Flying to SG tonight. Help.

Then I post a general tweet saying *Help! I am alive and hostage. Lara.* I panic as I write that. Leon could see it very easily. I quickly delete it.

I change Safari back to its normal settings and replace the phone in Leon's bag. I am still on my feet when he reappears, so I stroll over to the fence and pretend to be looking at the washing. My legs are starting to tingle and I can feel my brain beginning to shut down.

I slump into my seat, my focus blurred, and I feel myself passing the point at which I can be bothered to go and throw up. It would do no good now anyway. I want to sleep. Leon is talking to me.

'Scrabble,' he is saying. 'Once you have your faculties back.'

'Mm,' I agree, and I put my head on my table. I should never have let this happen. By the time I come back to full consciousness, I realise, I will be on the flight to Delhi.

I will be lost for ever. This is the biggest mistake I could possibly have made. I should have vomited right over the fence, rather than tweeted.

I make a supreme effort, clutch my stomach and say, 'Loo.'

'Of course,' says Leon. 'I know the feeling. Go ahead. Want me to walk you there?'

My head is swimming. I try to say no, but he takes my arm and stands me up anyway, and, holding tightly to the top of my arm, he walks me to the toilet.

It is around the corner, off an echoing hallway, at the foot of a flight of stairs.

'I'll be back at the table,' he says, 'because I can see you're not going anywhere.'

I lock the door and stand for a moment, holding the white wall.

Must focus. Cannot let this happen.

I take my wig off, kneel and throw up everything from my stomach, even though I know it is in my bloodstream now. Throwing up will not help the way I feel, but it might lessen things a little. I am not used to having so much in my stomach, and it is sad to see that curry go, its mushrooms and mangetout floating on the surface of the water. I have to flush it five times before it all goes.

I am washing my hands when a voice says, 'Lara?'

Because I am so spaced out, it doesn't even startle me. I look round, and eventually locate the window at the top of the wall. It is barred, with no glass. She is outside, and she must be standing on something, because the window in here is high up in the wall. She is staring in at me, with short hair. We no longer look the same.

'Hey,' I tell her. 'Oh. Hello.'

'My God, Lara. You're here. As soon as I read your

Twitter message I got in a cab and described this place, and he knew exactly where I meant. It's the rooftop bar, apparently. Everyone knows it. I can't believe you're OK. Are you OK?'

'He gives me pills. I try to throw them up. Too late with these ones.'

'Right. Well, look. Go out of here, and through the back, and there's an exit. I'll see you there.'

I think about that. My head is swimming.

'He'll catch me. I won't get anywhere, and he'll catch me and it'll be worse.'

It takes all the strength I have to say these words. Seeing Iris, knowing that she has found me, lets me be the most together I can possibly be with the drugs coursing around my system.

'You have to run. Now, Lara. Come on. We'll get into a taxi and go all the way to Bangkok.'

'Seriously. Can't. He'll find me. Police will believe him. Everyone thinks I killed . . .' I cannot say his name, not now. 'We have to do it properly. I know how to do it. I've thought for days. About it. I tell you what to do. You'll do it?'

I tell her my plan, making a superhuman effort to get the message across. She looks terrified. I leave without waiting for an answer, and stagger back to my table, to my jailer.

'I was about to come and check up on you,' he says. 'I'm glad you're back.'

I nod and close my eyes.

chapter thirty-five

Iris

I did not want to do this. I had spotted her tweet about being held hostage, and although she had deleted it instantly, I had seen it being retweeted as a screen grab. It would make the news. That meant that Leon would, at some point, see it too. Now that I was aware of the state he was keeping her in, I could see why it was so vague a cry for help.

She was skeletally thin. Her skin was dull and pitted, her eyes lifeless, and I could see that being halfway coherent as she spoke to me had cost her all her strength. As soon as she had the wig on, nobody – not her parents, not Sam, not even poor departed Guy – would have recognised her as Lara Finch or Wilberforce. He had disguised her by destroying her.

I remembered the Lara who had come to my house at Christmas. She had been full of life and sparkle. I remembered us talking about mince pies and the way we would use our skills in a post-Apocalyptic world. Now she had lost it all, lost her verve, herself, everything.

And that was in spite of her efforts to throw up as many of the pills as she possibly could. The man had caught her, and he was killing her. He would destroy her as surely as he had murdered Guy Thomas.

Her idea was crazy, but I was tempted by it. It would give the man exactly what he deserved.

I called Alex. He still did not pick up. There was no sign of the local police anywhere. I did not have time to stop and worry about it. Olivia answered straight away. I knew it was early morning for her.

'Hey,' she said. 'Lara tweeted something. Was it her?'

'Yes. She sent me a Twitter message saying where she was and I found her. I saw her. I managed to speak to her while she was throwing up in the loo.'

'You saw her again! And?'

I wondered how to answer that.

'She's alive. Not in a good state. Not at all. But look, Olivia. She asked me to do something that is completely insane. I need a second opinion before I do it.'

I explained the plan. Olivia thought about it. When she spoke, she sounded stronger than I had ever heard her.

'If you don't mind taking the risk,' she said, 'then I think you should do it. Give the bastard exactly what he deserves. If it goes wrong, we'll rally round for you. You won't be going into it alone. I promise you that. We'll make sure you're OK, no matter what.'

I found the area Lara had sent me to, eventually. It was surprisingly close to the tourist streets, but I supposed that made sense.

I tried not to be self-conscious as I loitered around, doing my rubbish best to look like the kind of person who did this sort of thing. The street was dingy and narrow, a place to hide in even in bright baking sunlight.

A skinny cat came and rubbed itself hard, viciously in fact, on my legs. A bird screamed somewhere above me. There were potholes in the road, and a pavement only down one side of it. I could feel eyes on me, and I wanted to turn and run. Instead, I walked slowly, stopped for a moment, walked slowly again, stopped again.

I had as much cash as three cashpoints were prepared to give me. I hoped it would be enough.

I walked around that street for twenty minutes, and I was about to give up when the man approached me.

'You want to buy something?' he said.

I nodded, afraid of sounding too English if I declared 'Yes! I do!'

'What you want?'

I bit my lip, and when I spoke, my words accidentally came out in the voice of a Radio 4 newsreader.

'Do you happen,' I asked him, 'to have any heroin?'

chapter thirty-six

Lara

The airport is small. I lean on Leon's arm, acting even more idiotic than I actually am, exaggerating my drugged-ness to try to get him complacent.

I know I have made a stupid plan with Iris. She might have been arrested by now. I could have sent her, like poor, poor dead Rachel, into the black hole of Asian prison. Of all the things to do, I have sent the woman who has shown herself to be my best friend in the world to buy drugs in Thailand.

I wish I'd put the word Krabi on that tweet. I wish I hadn't written it. I hope no one saw it. But if I'd said where I was, then somebody might be here at the airport to look out for me, just in case. I look around, focusing on people in uniform. There are a lot of them here, but they're probably airport security. Airports always have people in uniform.

My legs buckle beneath me. That was genuine. The beer and the pills have not reacted well. I am getting worse and worse.

We stand in a check-in queue. Leon looks at me a lot but we do not speak. I am not sure I would be able to say a single word. He puts his suitcase flat on a luggage trolley and sits me down on it. I pull my legs up, like a child.

'Something she ate,' I hear him saying to someone. That is a lie. I have eaten nothing, for ages.

Then we are in the departures lounge. It is small, with lots of chairs in rows, and I am leaning on him and forcing my legs to walk. There is a shop and I know what I need to do, and I try to practise the words in my head. I need to say them. I have to go into that shop and buy something. Anything. I need to be carrying an airport shopping bag because that is an essential part of the plan. I cannot quite formulate the words, but I will do it. I will do it before we leave this lounge.

Leon leads me to an area where hardly anyone is sitting, and pushes me down into a chair. He is next to me. I lean my head on his shoulder and close my eyes.

'Lara! Sweetie! You just need to walk on to the plane, darling, and then you can get back to sleep.'

I let him pull me to my feet. I lean heavily on him, and force my legs to walk. We go to the front of the departure hall, and through a door. Leon shows someone our boarding passes, explaining: 'My wife's had a bit of food poisoning, I'm afraid,' and we follow the crowd down stairs, around corners, and out into the hot sun, which immediately makes my head hurt.

On the plane, I slump against the window and close my eyes. I know I have messed this up, but I can no longer remember why, or what I was supposed to do. I was meant to say something, and then I fell asleep and didn't do it.

'That's right,' he says. 'You sleep it off.'

*

I wake with a jolt when the wheels touch the tarmac. I cannot focus on the tannoy announcement, but I know it will be saying we have arrived.

A small part of my brain recognises that I am in Singapore, the place I never, ever wanted to revisit. Last time I was here . . . In this state I cannot even articulate it. Rachel was with me, and then she went for ever. Her life was gone.

Slowly I remember my half-baked plan. I twist in my seat, wondering whether Iris is on the aeroplane, but all this does is make Leon look away from his paper and notice that I am awake.

'Singapore,' he says gently, and he pats my knee with his hand. I am too dopey even to wince. 'But only in transit, OK? Nothing bad is going to happen here. We'll be out before we're even in.'

'Not going out of the airport?'

'Almost. As good as. Sadly this shitty little airline takes us to some dump called "the budget terminal". We can't transfer from there: we have to go through immigration, transfer to the airport proper and check in there. It's irritating, sure, but *c'est la vie*.'

I find myself nodding blankly. 'OK.'

'That's my girl.'

I know that he is right. I am his girl. I haven't seen Iris. I don't think she is here. I hope she didn't do her part of the plan, because I certainly haven't done mine.

It flashes into my mind: I could still do it. After that sleep I am slightly more alert. I have to try. I must make one last-ditch attempt.

I hang back, and Leon waits for me with infinite patience. He likes me being slow and useless. Eventually we are off the plane, walking down the steps in stifling humidity, Leon's hand, as ever, above my elbow. He supports me as I feel my way to the next step, again and again, with my foot in its impeccably tasteful shoe.

The sky in Singapore is grey and low. I am prickling with the heat. It is tangible in my lungs. I hate this place.

In the building, I see a shop.

'Can I have perfume?' I ask, tugging pathetically at his arm. 'Please, Leon? I want perfume. Will you . . .?'

He hesitates. 'You want perfume? Really?'

'Want to smell nice.'

He laughs. 'By all means. How can I argue with that? Come on then. We have hours to kill, after all. But sweetie? You are going to have to walk through security at some point. This is the only stalling I'm going to allow you to do. It's going to be all right.'

Leon picks me a perfume, carefully sniffing until he laughs and takes a white box to the counter.

'If in doubt,' he says, and hands a woman in a white lab coat the Chanel No. 5 box. I pass him a scarf that I have picked up randomly, and he swaps it for a different one, rosy pink, and buys that.

'Thank you, sir,' says the woman behind the counter, and I take the bag from him and look into it.

'Thanks,' I say. He nods and strokes my wig.

'We'll get you back to yourself,' he says, fingering a strand of it, and I am not sure whether it is a threat or a promise. 'My Lara.'

I walk along swinging the bag. I have done too little, too late, but this is an attempt at following the plan. I try to tell myself that at least I have some perfume and a scarf, and wonder if I could escape in Delhi. At some point I might be able to get his phone again.

It won't work. None of it will work. The only way I will get away is by leaping off a mountainside to my death. That will do. That is my next plan. I can't wait.

We are approaching the queues for immigration when a woman with short hair walks into me, brushes me, and, before I realise what is happening, gently takes my bag out of my unresisting hand and replaces it with another. I look down. The new bag also says Duty Free on it. It looks the same as the old one. I look around. Was it her? I am not even sure that it happened. I could have imagined the whole thing.

All the same, I know what to do.

'Leon?'

He looks at me, his grey eyes serious. 'Yes?'

'Could you take this? Bit . . . wobbly.'

He smiles and takes the bag without a word, without looking at it. We queue up and present our passports. Nobody stops us. The man who stamps them looks at me hard, but lets us in.

We have the bags, and Leon piles everything on to a trolley.

'Right,' he says. 'Here we go.'

I clutch my stomach.

'The loo!' I say. 'See you in a second. Sorry.'

I walk away from him, carrying nothing but my handbag. I have done this before. I hold my head high, and I walk casually, as elegantly as I can in this state, through the Customs area and out into the airport concourse, pretending that I am hurrying towards a bathroom.

Last time I did this, Rachel never followed.

This time, Leon doesn't follow. I hardly dare to hope that he will not be along in a moment, taking my arm, steering me to the next check-in.

I wonder what to do. I am on my own. I don't know where to go. I have no phone and no money, and I might not have time to get anywhere. He is going to come along at any time. But he isn't here yet.

I try to concentrate. Need to get away. I cannot think what to do, but I need to do it quickly.

Focus.

I turn to look back. Leon is still not there. I cannot go anywhere without money. Leon took everything I had, such as it was. He took my mind and my memory and my lover and my life. I walk in an aimless line, heading approximately for the exit.

I stand still, letting the people pass me. The air conditioning is strong here. The little hairs on my arms are standing on end. He will be here in a moment, and I cannot order my thoughts for long enough to get away.

I stand and watch. People are coming through the door, but not one of them is Leon. He doesn't come.

And then he still doesn't come.

I will sit here for a bit. I lower myself to the floor and cross my legs and wait.

A moment later, a hand is on my arm.

'Get up. Come on. Get up and come with me.'

But it is not his voice. The person taking my hand and helping me to my feet is not Leon.

'Come on, lovely. Come on. Your insane plan, you nutter. It seems to have worked. Up you get. You're all right, Lara. He's gone.' She puts a hand on each of my shoulders and turns me around so her face is right in front of mine. I stare at her. 'Lara. You're going to be OK. We're going to look after you.'

I look around. Who, I wonder, does 'we' include?

There are five police officers nearby, looking at us. That scares me.

'Don't worry,' she says. 'You're not in trouble. Not at all. You're *out* of trouble. Don't tell them what we did to Leon, though, OK? That's a secret. Not something the police need to know about. I made the call and they stopped him. It's done. Look, this is Alex. Don't tell him either. He's from Falmouth. I was trying to call him for ages but he didn't answer because he was flying out here, to meet me. To find you.'

A tall white man walks over to us. He looks at Iris, who nods.

'Hello, Lara,' he says. 'Alex Zielowski. You don't know me, but I must say it is a privilege and a delight to meet you at last.'

I look at Iris. We don't look the same any more, not now that she has cut her hair. That reminds me of the wig. I reach up and pull it off. She takes it from me and puts it into her bag.

'There you go,' she says. 'Lara Wilberforce. Lara Finch. Welcome back. We're going to take you home.'

epilogue

Iris
September

I am standing in a cemetery in west London, talking, as ever, to a man who isn't there. I am talking aloud, because there is no one nearby, and I do not feel ridiculous. I have spent years talking to this particular dead man: it is, it transpires, a hard habit to break.

The autumn sunlight is slanted straight into my eyes, and I am squinting, dazzled yet cold. I'm stamping as I speak, trying to keep my optimistically clad feet warm. I cannot bear to stop wearing the sandals I bought in Bangkok, even though it is definitely too cold for them now. In fact I am still dressed for summer. It has been an emotional year so far, but largely, strangely, a happy one.

There is a headstone with his name on it: Laurence Jonathan Madaki. There are the dates of his birth and, thirty-two years on, his death. I have brought him some flowers, and it is strangely comforting to see them here. Remembering him in the conventional way gives me a huge feeling of solidarity with the unseen visitors who tend to the other graves, who remember all these other people.

'And so,' I tell him, 'I'm going away. You don't mind, do you? I know you don't. You'd want me to do this.' I politely leave a space for him to talk. 'It's all fixed up. Well, it's kind of fixed up. Actually, I'm terrified. But it's going to be incredible. Why do you buy a lottery ticket if you're not going to do something life-changing with your prize? I know that. I need to do it. I'll always miss you, Laurie. Always. You'll always be the love of my life. But since you're not here, and since it's all short and definitely unpredictable, I think I'd better carry on living it.'

I sense his approval. Even if it's not really emanating from his grave, I know that the Laurie I loved would have wanted me to do this.

I have moved out of the house in Budock, and the furious Shakespearean cats have moved in, grudgingly, with Sam Finch, who is just beginning to discover how desirable a single, childless man in his thirties really is. Last time I spoke to him he said, 'Can you believe it, Iris? I've got dates lined up for the next three Fridays and Saturdays. Different women each time! Amazing ones! What the hell do they see in a boring twat like me, hey?'

'Oh, women like a boring twat,' I assured him.

'Cheers.'

'Broody women who've been done over by boyfriends in the past. They love a . . . well, a stable man who's not going to turn on them. That sounds better, doesn't it, than a boring twat. It's the same thing, though. I mean that affectionately.'

He laughed. 'Thanks. If at some point I do settle down with one of them, I'll get you to vet her first.'

'Thanks,' I said. 'I will do my best to be utterly terrifying.'

Lara is living back in London: she and Sam spoke awkwardly and unhappily a couple of times when she got home. They will never speak again unless they have to to finalise the divorce. Some relationships will never have a happy-ever-after.

I have spent much of the summer with Lara, talking to her, wandering around London with her, looking at paintings, going to the cinema, walking by the river. She is wobbly, and she will be for a long time to come: she is only just beginning to contemplate the idea that one day she might get over Guy. She is eaten up with guilt and horror, and the renewed media frenzy when she was discovered was as much of an ordeal for her as anything that had gone before it. People still point her out on the street, even ask for her autograph. She is living in a studio apartment and taking things one day at a time; yet there are green shoots that I don't think she can see yet. She has distanced herself from her parents, which she needed to do, and as a result she has become oddly close to Olivia, particularly in the months since baby Isaac was born on the first of May. He is an adorable baby: he makes me yearn for one of my own, and that has never happened before, not even when Laurie was alive.

Motherhood has changed Olivia. She is softer and gentler, but still one of the most formidable women I know. She and Isaac fill her Covent Garden flat perfectly, and she goes everywhere with him strapped into a sling on her stomach, gazing up at her with adoring eyes. 'He's the best thing I've ever done,' she said the other day, watching him lying on the rug on her sitting room floor, cooing and gurgling for attention. 'Whoever would have thought that? Isaac, would you like Auntie Iris to change your nappy? Or Auntie Lara?'

Lara did it. She still feels she owes the world everything, that she will be atoning for what happened to Guy and Rachel and Sam for the rest of her life. I hope she will move past that one day.

I walk out of the cemetery and into the busy London street. I have said goodbye to Laurie, and now I am free.

I call my mum. 'I'll be there in half an hour,' I tell her, and she says happily that she will put the kettle on. It has been odd coming back into my family's lives, and I, like Lara but differently, am forever trying not to be obsessed with my own feelings of horror at what I inflicted on them. They loved Laurie too; and when he died, they lost me as well. Now I am back, and although things are weird, they are good. We are nervous around each other, and my sister Lily is resentful of my strolling back in like the prodigal daughter when she has held my parents together for five long years, but things are better like this, at least, than they were before.

Lara and I never told anyone that we planted the heroin on Leon. Her addled plan to do to him what Jake had done to Rachel had actually worked. He was arrested for smuggling, and then, when everything else came to light, he was extradited to Britain and charged with murder too. One way and another, he will not be out of prison for a long time. Lara is dreading having to give evidence at his trial, but I know she will do it: she will look him in the eye and tell the world everything. Then, perhaps, she will move on.

As I approach the bus stop, I decide to make a phone call. Alex answers at once.

'Iris! Are you OK? Been to the grave?'

'Yes,' I tell him. 'And yes, of course I'm OK. That was good to do. I told him we're going away. I said we'd be gone a year or so, at least. I know he can't hear me, but I'm glad I did it.'

I step on to the bus and pass my Oyster card over the reader. It beeps, and I walk up the narrow staircase, still talking. I sit beside a window, turning to the view so the other passengers won't have to listen to me.

'No qualms, then?' he is asking. I picture him, on his way to London, in his red jumper, his face newly shaven and eager.

I laugh. 'Are you joking? A trip across the USA, and that's just for starters? Of course no qualms at all. You?'

'Oh my God. I can't wait. I'll see you at your parents' place in a few hours. OK?'

'I can't wait either,' I tell him, and I put the phone in my pocket and watch a flock of birds far away in the distance, heading south for the winter.

Now you can buy any of these other bestselling
books by **Emily Barr** from your bookshop
or *direct from her publisher*.

FREE P&P AND UK DELIVERY
(Overseas and Ireland £3.50 per book)

The First Wife	£7.99
The Perfect Lie	£6.99
The Life You Want	£6.99
The Sisterhood	£8.99
Out of my Depth	£8.99
Plan B	£6.99
Atlantic Shift	£8.99
Cuban Heels	£7.99
Baggage	£8.99
Backpack	£8.99

TO ORDER SIMPLY CALL THIS NUMBER

01235 400 414

or visit our website: www.headline.co.uk

Prices and availability subject to change without notice.